LONE STAR
HOLIDAY PROPOSAL

BY
YVONNE LINDSAY

MILLS &
BOON

Published in Great Britain 2015
by Mills & Boon, an imprint of Harlequin (UK) Limited,
Eton House, 18-24 Paradise Road, Richmond, Surrey, TW9 1SR

© 2015 Harlequin Books S.A.

Special thanks and acknowledgement are given to Yvonne Lindsay for her contribution to the Texas Cattleman's Club: Lies and Lullabies series.

ISBN: 978-0-263-25289-7

51-1215

Harlequin (UK) Limited's policy is to use papers that are natural, renewable and recyclable products and made from wood grown in sustainable forests. The logging and manufacturing processes conform to the legal environmental regulations of the country of origin.

Printed and bound in Great Britain
by CPI, Barcelona

A typical Piscean, *USA TODAY* bestselling author **Yvonne Lindsay** has always preferred her imagination to the real world. Married to her blind date hero and with two adult children, she spends her days crafting the stories of her heart, and in her spare time she can be found with her nose in a book reliving the power of love, or knitting socks and daydreaming. Contact her via her website www.yvonnelindsay.com.

As always, I'm strengthened by the support of my fellow authors when working on a project like this, whether they are directly involved in the continuity or not. In particular I would like to dedicate this book to Soraya Lane to thank her for her constant cheerleading and encouragement, and for challenging me to bigger, better word counts than I ever dreamed I could achieve in a single day. Deadlines become so much easier when you're haranguing me from the sideline! Thank you.

One

Nolan rolled to a stop in the parking area at the Court-yard and looked around. The four-mile drive out of Royal had been pleasant, quite a difference from the Southern California freeway traffic that was a part of his daily grind back home.

Home. He grunted. Royal, Texas, was really his home, not the sparsely furnished luxury apartment he slept and occasionally ate in back in LA. But he hadn't lived here in Royal, or even been back, in coming up on seven years. Even now he'd chosen to check into a hotel rather than stay with his parents. The reminders of his old life and old hopes were still too fresh, too raw. He gave his head a slight shake, as if to jog his mind back on track, and pushed open the door to the brand-new SUV he'd hired for his visit. He alighted from the vehicle, grabbed his suit jacket from the backseat and pulled it on before taking a moment to adjust pristine white shirt cuffs.

The wind cut right through the finely woven wool of his

suit. It seemed even Armani couldn't protect you from a frigid Texan winter breeze. Nor were highly polished hand-made shoes immune to the dust of the unsealed parking lot, he noted with a slight grimace of distaste. But when had he gotten so prissy? There'd been a time when even baby spit hadn't bothered him.

A shaft of pain lanced through him. It still hurt as if it was yesterday. Nolan buttoned his jacket and straightened his shoulders. He'd known coming back would be hard, that it might rip the scabs off wounds he'd thought already healed. But what he hadn't expected were these blindsiding moments when those old hurts threatened to drive him back down on his knees.

Pull it together, he willed silently, clenching his jaw tight. He'd lived through far worse than these random memories that were all that was left of his old life. He could live through this. It was time to harden back up and get to work.

As private attorney for Rafiq Bin Saleed, Nolan was here to do a job for one of Rafiq's companies, Samson Oil. He loved his work—particularly loved the cut and parry of entering into property negotiations on behalf of his boss and friend. The fact that doing so now brought him back to the scene of his deepest sorrow was tempered only by the fact that he also got to spend some time with his parents on their home turf. They weren't getting any younger and his dad was already making noises about retiring. From personal experience working there, Nolan knew that his dad's family law practice was demanding, but he couldn't quite reconcile himself to the fact that his dad was getting ready to scale down, or even walk away, from the practice he'd started only a few years out of law school.

Again Nolan reminded himself to get back on track. Obviously he'd have to work harder. Being back home after a long absence had a way of derailing a man when he least expected it—but that wouldn't earn him any bonuses when it came to crunch time with his boss. He looked around the area that had been christened the Courtyard. The name fit, he decided as he took in the assembly of renovated ranch buildings that housed a variety of stores and craftsmen. His research had already told him that the tenants specialized in arts and crafts with artisanal breads and cheeses also on sale, while the central area was converted into a farmer's market most Saturday mornings.

To Nolan's way of thinking, it was an innovative way to use an old run-down and unprofitable piece of land. So what the hell did Rafiq want with it? He knew for a fact that there was no oil to be found in the surrounding area. Hell, everyone who grew up in and around Royal knew that—which kind of raised questions as to what Samson Oil wanted the land for. So far, Rafiq's quest to buy up property in Royal failed to make economic sense to Nolan.

Sure, he was giving owners who were still battered and struggling to pull their lives together after the tornado a chance to get away and start a new life, but what did Rafe plan to do with all the land he'd acquired?

Nolan reminded himself it wasn't his place to ask questions but merely to carry out the brief, no matter how much of a waste of money it looked like to him. Rafiq had his reasons but he wasn't sharing them, and it had been made clear to Nolan that it was his place to see to the acquisition of specific parcels of land—whether they were for sale or not. And that's exactly what he was going to do.

Regrettably, however, it appeared that Winslow Properties, despite their shaky financial footing, were not open to selling this particular parcel of land. It was up to him to persuade them otherwise. He'd hoped some of the tenants would be more forthcoming about their landlord but so far, on his visits to the stores, he'd found them to be a closemouthed bunch. Maybe they were all just scared, he thought. Royal had been through a lot. No one wanted to rock the boat now.

There was one tenant he'd yet to have the opportunity to talk to. He recalled her name from his memory—Raina Patterson. From what he understood she might be closer to Mellie Winslow than some of the other tenants. Maybe Ms. Patterson could give him the angle he needed to pry this property from the Winslow family's grip.

He began to walk toward a large red barn at the bottom of the U-shape created by the buildings. The iron roof had been proudly painted with the Texas flag. The sight of that flag never failed to tug at him; as much as he'd assimilated to his California lifestyle, he'd always be Texan.

Looking around, Nolan understood why the Winslow family had, after initial interest in Samson Oil's offer, grown cagey at the idea of selling this little community and the land it was on. For a town that was still rebuilding, this was an area of optimism and growth. Selling out from underneath everyone was bound to create unrest and instability all over again. Not everyone here could just pick up and create a new life in a new town or state like he had.

Damn, and there he was again. Thinking of the past and of what he'd lost. His wife, his son. He should probably have sent someone else on the legal team to do this job but Rafiq had been adamant he handle it himself. He mentally shrugged. It was the price he paid for the obscenely high salary he earned—he could live with that as long as he didn't ever have to live here again, with his memories.

Raina made a final tweak of the pine boughs and tartan ribbons she'd used to decorate the antique mantelpiece and looked around her store with a sense of pride and wonder. *Her* store. Priceless by name and by nature. She'd been here in the renovated red barn a month now. She still couldn't quite believe that a year after the tornado that had leveled her original business and much of the town of Royal, she'd managed to rebuild her inventory and relocate her business rather than just fold up altogether.

It certainly hadn't been easy, she thought as she moved through the store and let her hand drift over the highly polished oak sewing table she'd picked up at an estate sale last week—but it had been worth it.

Now all she had to do was hold on to it. A ripple of disquiet trickled down her spine. Her landlord, Mellie Winslow, had been subdued yesterday when she'd visited Raina but had said she was doing everything she could to ensure that her father's company, Winslow Properties, didn't sell the Courtyard.

Raina needed to know this wasn't all going to be ripped away from her a second time. She didn't know if she had it in her to start over again. Losing her store on Main Street, and most of her underinsured inventory of antiques, had just about sent her packing from the town she'd adopted as her own four years ago. She had to make this work, for herself and for her little boy.

No matter which way she looked at it, though, she still couldn't understand why anyone would be interested in buying the dried-up and overused land, let alone an oil company. If only Samson Oil—who'd been buying land left, right and center around Royal—would go away and let her have the peace and security she'd been searching for her whole life. Heck, it wasn't even as if they seemed to be doing anything with the properties they'd bought up. At the rate Samson Oil was going, Royal would become a ghost town.

"Mommy! Look!"

Raina turned and smiled at her son, Justin, or JJ as he was known, as he proudly showed off the ice cream cone her dad—his namesake—had just bought him. JJ was three going on thirteen most of the time, but today he was home from day care because he'd been miserable with a persistent cold. He was back to being the little boy who wanted his mommy and his "G'anddad" most of all. The theory had been that he'd rest on the small cot she had in her office out back, but theory had been thrown to the wind when JJ had heard his beloved granddad arrive to help Raina move some of the heavier items in the store.

Looking at JJ now, she began to wonder if she'd been conned by the little rascal all along. The little boy had protested his granddad's departure most miserably, but he was all smiles now with an ice cream cone and the promise of a sleepover on the weekend.

"Lucky you," she answered squatting down to JJ's eye level. "Can I have some?"

JJ pulled the cone closer to him, distrust in his eyes. "No, Mommy. G'anddad said it mine."

Raina pouted. "Not even one little lick?"

She saw the indecision on his face for just a moment before he proffered the dripping cone in her direction. "One," he said very solemnly.

Raina licked off the drips before they hit the floor and theatrically sighed in pleasure. "That's so yummy. Can I have more?" she teased, reaching for JJ's wrist.

"No more, Mommy! Mine!" JJ squealed and turned and ran, laughing hysterically as Raina growled and lumbered playfully behind him.

Through her son's shrieks of delight, Raina heard the bell tinkle over the main door, signaling a potential customer.

"Justin Junior, you stop right there! No running through the store," she called out, but it was futile. JJ was barreling away from her at top speed.

She rounded the corner just in time to hear a muffled "oof!" as JJ ran straight into the man who'd just entered the store. The man was wearing a very expensive looking suit, which, she groaned inwardly, now wore a fair portion of JJ's ice cream cone, right at the level of the man's groin. JJ rapidly backed away. The stranger looked up, a startled expression on his face as his eyes met hers. A frisson of something she couldn't quite put her finger on ran between them like a live current. It unnerved her and made her voice sharp.

"JJ! Apologize to the gentleman, right now."

She couldn't help it—even though it was her fault for chasing him, she couldn't prevent the note of censure that filled her voice. And she still felt unsettled by that look she'd just exchanged with a total stranger. A look that left her feeling things she had no right to feel. Raina dragged her attention back to the disaster at hand and searched around for something to offer the man to help him clean up.

The only pieces of fabric she had close by were a set of handmade lace doilies from the early twentieth century. She certainly couldn't afford to lose inventory, but then again, nor could she afford to lose a potential customer either.

JJ turned his little face up to hers. His blue eyes, so like her own, filled with tears that began to spill down his still-chubby cheeks. His lower lip began to quiver. He dropped what was left of his cone on the floor and ran to her, burying his face in her maxi skirt as if he could make himself invisible.

"Hey, no harm done," the man said, his voice slightly gruff and at odds with his words.

Raina definitely noticed a hint of Texas drawl as she glanced from her son to the customer, who, despite that initial look of shock, now appeared unfazed by the incident. He reached into his suit pocket and pulled out an honest-to-God white handkerchief. Was that a monogram in the corner? Raina didn't think they had such things anymore.

"I'm so sorry, sir. Here, let me," she started, reaching for the cotton square.

"Might be best if I handle this myself," the man replied.

Oh, heavens, she was such an idiot. Of course he'd have to handle it himself. It was *his* groin, after all. She had no business touching any man's trousers, let alone there. She gently set JJ to one side and got busy picking up the cone that he'd dropped on the floor, gathering the sticky mess in her left hand.

"JJ, can you go fetch me the tea towel that's hanging up in the kitchen?" she asked her son. "And no running!"

It was too late. JJ raced away as if he couldn't wait to put distance between himself and the mess he'd created.

"Kids, huh?"

The stranger finally smiled and Raina looked up at him—really looked this time—and felt a punch of attraction all the way to the tips of her toes. Before she could answer, JJ was back and, ridiculously glad of the distraction, Raina used the cloth to wipe up the residue from the floor and then wrapped up the cone in the towel to deal with later. Her customer had likewise dealt with the mess on his trousers.

"See, all cleaned up," he said, rolling up the handkerchief and shoving it in his pocket again.

Raina cringed at the cost of getting all that fine tailoring back into pristine condition again. "But the stain. Please, let me get your suit dry cleaned for you."

"No, seriously, it's no bother. Is this your boy? JJ is it?"

She nodded and watched as the man squatted down so he was at eye level with JJ, who had cautiously turned his head around when he'd heard his name. She couldn't help but notice how the fabric of the stranger's trousers caught snugly across his thighs and, despite hastily averting her gaze, she also couldn't stop the disconcerting rush of acute feminine awareness that welled inside her.

"Hey, JJ, no harm done, except to your ice cream. I'm sorry about that, champ." When Raina started to protest that he had nothing to be sorry for, he merely put up one hand and kept his attention on her little boy. "Are you okay?"

JJ nodded.

"But you lost your ice cream. Maybe I can talk to your mommy about buying you another one. Would you like that?"

Again Raina went to protest but the man shot her a glance and a smile that made her hush. As embarrassed as she was by what had happened, she found herself prepared to follow his lead.

JJ nodded again and the man put out one hand. "Good," he said with another smile. "Sounds like we have a deal. You want to shake on that?"

Raina felt a tug of pride as her son extended his grubby little hand to be engulfed in the stranger's much larger one. But pride was soon overtaken by something else as she noticed the man's hands. They were tanned and broad, with long fingers and neatly kept nails. Definitely an office worker, she surmised, and not from around here, but—oh boy—there was that swell of attraction again. What on earth was wrong with her? After Jeb, she'd sworn off men. She couldn't trust her own judgment anymore.

The man rose to his full height, which dwarfed Raina's own five foot seven by a good several inches. He held out his hand toward her.

"Nolan Dane, pleased to meet you."

Automatically Raina took his hand but realized her mistake the moment she did so. A sharp tingle of electricity sizzled up her arm the second their palms met.

"I… I'm R-Raina. Raina Patterson."

She groaned inwardly. Great, now she sounded like a complete idiot. Her heart skittered in her chest as she no-

ticed he was still holding her hand. She gently pulled free
and fought the urge to rub her palm on the fabric of her
skirt. "Welcome to my store, Priceless. Were you looking
for something in particular? Perhaps I can help you," she
asked, forcing herself to put her business voice on.

His first reaction to her had been instant, visceral and
totally unexpected. Now Nolan could barely tear his eyes
from her. She looked so much like his dead wife, Carole, it
was uncanny. Her shoulder-length hair was the same shade
of glossy brown that hovered between dark chocolate and
rich espresso. She had the same shape of chin and brows.
But it was only once he looked more closely at her that he
saw the differences that set them apart.

The woman before him now wore only a bare minimum
of makeup, letting her natural beauty shine, whereas Carole had been so caught up in projecting the right appearance that even he had rarely seen her without makeup on.
Even at breakfast. Carole's argument had been that while
he'd comfortably slipped into a law practice with his father,
she'd had a harder road to travel, proving herself against
the good ol' boys in one of Maverick County's corporate
law firms. She'd needed all the armor she could get.

But there was something in the way that Ms. Patterson carried herself, too, and the sweetly serene smile she
wore, that continued to remind him of his late wife. Raina
presented a strong and untroubled facade to the world. A
facade that he already knew hid a vulnerability that had
been evident in her hesitant introduction and which had
appealed to the protector in him with surprising force.

Hell no, he reminded himself forcibly. No matter how
much she fascinated him, he absolutely couldn't go there.
Women like Raina Patterson were completely out of
bounds. Even if she wasn't married—which she probably
was—she had a kid, and he had strict rules about not com-

plicating his life any further. He'd already had his heart torn out and shredded to pieces once and he would bear those scars for the rest of his life. Dating was strictly for brief respites—and this woman did not look like the type for a quick roll in the sheets followed by an even quicker farewell.

"Thank you," he said, finally pulling himself together. "I just came to look around, to be honest. The Courtyard hasn't been operating long, has it?"

"No, not terribly long. It stopped being a working ranch a few years ago. The ongoing drought forced the original owners to sell and the new owners, the Winslows, came up with the idea to convert it to shops and studios. It's helped a lot of us get back on our feet after the tornado."

Nolan nodded as he processed the information and matched it up with what he knew already. "And you're selling antiques here?"

"Yes, and running craft classes out back. My first one is tonight. Would you be interested in signing on for a lesson in candle making? They're going to be a hot gift item for Christmas this year in Royal."

She laughed softly and, unexpectedly, he delighted in the sound. It was refreshing. Genuine amusement wasn't often heard in the circles in which he moved, at least not without some malice in it somewhere.

"I'll take a rain check," he said with a wink, and he was delighted to see a faint blush color her ivory cheeks.

"A shame," she said averting her head slightly. "I'm sure all the ladies would have been thrilled to have you."

And then he felt the heat of a blush on his cheeks, as well. Ridiculous, he thought. He hadn't blushed since the day he'd asked Carole out in high school and yet here he was with cheeks aflame. The memory was just the cold dose of reality he needed. It was time to get out of here before he made a complete fool of himself and broke his own rules about dating and asked the enticing Ms. Patterson out. He made a show of looking at his watch and made a sound of surprise.

"I need to get on my way, but first I should remedy the demise of JJ's ice cream."

"Oh, please don't worry. He'll be fine and, besides, the homemade ice cream store will be closed now."

"And I'm holding you up from closing, too, I see," he said, gesturing to the face of his watch. "I'll head off."

"Please, don't rush away. Look around—you never know—something might grab your attention. We'll be a little while closing up anyway."

Despite his determination to put some distance between them, Nolan found himself agreeing to prolong his visit.

"Okay, thanks. Let me know when you want me out of your way."

She nodded and gave him another of those serene smiles that delivered a solid whack to his solar plexus.

As he moved among the pieces she had on display, he reexamined his options. He was here to do a job. Part of that job was gathering information. He hadn't missed the spark of interest in her eyes. Perhaps he could use that interest to his advantage. Ms. Patterson, whether she knew it or not, had just become his best opportunity to get an angle on Winslow Properties and hopefully the leverage he'd need to pull off this purchase. Somehow, he needed to get past his emotional barriers and see her purely as a means to an end. If he didn't, all bets were likely off, and he'd have to deliver Rafiq his first failure in this acquisitions venture. Nolan's need to succeed pushed through. He could do this. And he would.

Nolan could hear Raina moving around toward the back of the store. He flicked a look her way and saw her laying out egg cartons and wicks and precut blocks of what he assumed was wax. JJ was doing his best to help. Raina moved quietly behind him and straightened up the things he laid out for her, and every now and then she paused to wipe his little nose.

She did everything with grace and an effortless elegance that mesmerized Nolan, and he had to force himself to look away and remind himself he was here to gather intel about the Courtyard, not spend his time mooning over one of the proprietors. He was on the verge of leaving the store when he overheard Raina talking to JJ.

"Well, how about that?" she said, putting her hands on her hips and looking around the workroom. "We're all done, JJ. I couldn't have done it all so fast without your help."

Nolan fought back a smile. He had no doubt she'd have had it done in half the time, but it tugged at his heart to see how she took the time to make JJ feel special and his efforts valued. Then came a fresh debilitating wave of sorrow as he remembered all he'd lost. Even so, he still couldn't tear himself away from the tableau in front of him.

"I'm a good boy, aren't I, Mommy?" JJ said, his little chest puffed out with pride.

"Yes you are. The very best. And you're all mine!" She reached out to tickle him and he giggled and squirmed out of reach. "How about, as a reward, I take you to the diner for dinner before your sitter comes tonight."

The little boy nodded vigorously. An idea occurred to Nolan. This was an opening he could use. He still owed JJ an ice cream. What better opportunity to fulfill his promise to the kid and to *accidentally* bump into his mother again and draw her back into conversation.

She'd mentioned a sitter. Did that mean there was no Mr. Patterson around? He gave himself another mental shake. Whether there was or not, it made no difference.

This would merely be another opportunity to ask her more questions about the Courtyard and Winslow Properties.

At least that's what he told himself.

Two

Raina heard her cell phone ring in her handbag as she was securing JJ in his car seat. Whoever it was would just have to leave a message, she thought as she did up his harness and checked to make sure he was snug. Finally satisfied, she got in the driver's seat and turned on the ignition.

"Seat belt, Mommy!"

She smiled at JJ in the rearview mirror. "Yes, sir!"

He giggled in response, the way he always did, and it made her heart glad. She thanked God every day for the gift of her son. Jeb Pickering might have been a useless no good son-of-a-bitch but he'd left her with a gift beyond price. While it would have been her ideal wish to have provided JJ with both a mommy and a daddy who loved him, she was happy to parent alone. In fact, given Jeb's reliability, or lack of it, and his predilection for gambling and drink, JJ was better off not knowing the man even existed. Of course, being a single mom running a business brought its own issues, including relying on sitters when her dad wasn't free to help out. Which reminded her—the phone call. Maybe it had been her sitter calling.

"I'm just going to check my phone, JJ, then we'll head to the diner, okay?"

"C'n I have nuggets 'n' fries?"

"You sure can."

"Yum!"

Satisfied that he could have his favorite meal, JJ hummed quietly to himself, kicking a beat on the back of the front passenger seat while he waited. Raina stifled the admonition that sprang to her lips when he started to kick. She didn't want to enter into an argument with him now. Instead, she reached into her bag and dragged out her phone. One missed call, unknown number. A sick feeling of dread crept into her gut. Quelling the sensation, she listened to the message.

"Hey Rai, it's Jeb. I hear you got your little shop up and running again. That's good, 'cause I'm in a bit of a bind. I really need some money, honey." He sniggered and Raina cringed. He sounded drunk, again. "Anyway, I owe some guys... I, uh, well, I'll tell you when I see you. Soon, babe. By the way, how's that kid of ours? Later!"

Raina deleted the message instantly, her skin crawling. She felt as if she needed a long hot shower. Hadn't it been enough that he'd emptied out her bank account and skipped town when she'd been at the hospital in labor with JJ? And what about the extra five grand she'd given him early last year for what she'd told him was absolutely and totally the last time ever?

"Mommy, I'm hungry!" JJ demanded from the back, his kicks picking up in tempo.

Raina reached across to still his little legs. "JJ, what's the rule about kicking in the car?"

His little mouth firmed in a stubborn line. *Pick your battles*, Raina reminded herself, morphing into distraction mode instead. "Are you having ketchup with your chicken nuggets?"

"Yay! Ketchup!"

"Let's go then," she said with a smile as she put the car into gear.

It was a short drive into Royal but traffic was heavy. Raina was lucky to get a parking spot on the road about a block away from the diner. JJ skipped and jumped, holding her hand, as they walked along the pavement. Judging by his energy levels, she hoped he'd be okay to go back to day care tomorrow.

When they entered the Royal Diner, JJ hopscotched along the black-and-white checkerboard linoleum floor. They took a booth near the back and settled in on the red faux-leather seats.

"Be with you soon, hon," a waitress said with a smile as she poured glasses of water and left them with the sheet menus that everyone knew by heart but still pretended to study anyway.

Raina's appetite was gone, but she decided on a green salad with ranch dressing because she knew if she didn't eat, she'd be running on empty by the time her craft class started in a couple of hours. Shoving all thoughts of her ex to the back of her mind, she focused instead on her son and the evening ahead.

All going well, JJ would eat his dinner and she'd take him home to shower before the sitter arrived. Once the sitter was there, she'd be able to head back to Priceless to open up for her first class. Bookings had initially been slow but they'd picked up in the past day or so, and she hoped the simple candle-making class would be well received and that word of mouth would bring more students. With more students would come more overhead but she'd done her homework. After the initial outlay was met, the classes would bring in more sorely needed income, as well.

A movement across the booth made her look up from the menu she was staring at but had stopped actually seeing several minutes earlier. JJ was waving at someone. Thinking it might be their waitress returning for their order, Raina looked up with a smile, only to feel it freeze on her face and the hairs at her nape prickle to attention as she recognized the man walking toward them. Nolan Dane. What was he doing here? Surely he was more likely to be dining out at the Texas Cattleman's Club, or at the hotel in town?

It took only a few seconds to notice that he'd changed. His jeans were new and fit him perfectly, and the black Henley he wore under a worn leather jacket seemed to stretch across his chest as if it caressed him. Her cheeks flamed at the thought.

"Mommy! Man!" JJ said from his booster seat, and he waved again.

"Hey there," Nolan said as he drew next to the table.

"I'm having nuggets 'n' fries," JJ informed him importantly. "You wanna eat with me?"

"Oh, no, JJ. I'm sure Mr. Dane has other plans," Raina said quickly, feeling her blush deepen on her cheeks.

"Please, call me Nolan and, actually, no, I don't. But I don't want to intrude. I can eat at another table."

Raina felt terrible. She'd all but told him he wasn't welcome to sit with them. JJ's face fell. How bad could it be? she asked herself.

"Oh, please sit down. Seriously, it's okay. We haven't ordered yet, anyway. Join us."

"Well, if you're sure."

She nodded and gestured to the empty space next to JJ's booster seat. Nolan slid into the booth and stretched his long legs out under the table. She shifted slightly as his leg brushed hers.

"Do you guys eat here often?" Nolan asked.

"No, this is a treat for JJ. Aside from the mess with your suit, he's been a really good boy for me today, haven't you, JJ?"

JJ nodded emphatically and reached for his water glass. Nolan helped him steady the large glass as he drank and then put it back on the table for him.

"You're good at that," Raina commented. "Do you have kids of your own?"

A bleak emptiness appeared in his eyes, its presence so brief she wondered if she'd imagined it, but it was enough to make her realize she'd been prying where she had no right to.

"Oh, I'm sorry. I shouldn't be so rude. I didn't mean to pry."

"No, it's okay," Nolan brushed off her concern. "Maybe we should just put it down to self-preservation. I've seen how lethal he is with an ice cream cone."

Nolan watched Raina from across the table and silently congratulated himself on managing to keep his past locked firmly where it belonged. The waitress came by and took their orders, distracting Raina from asking any further questions. She was less relaxed than she'd been when he'd left the store. Was it his presence at the table that did that to her, he wondered, or was it something else? The waitress returned promptly with JJ's order, and while the little boy dug in, Nolan thought it time to ease conversation back to the Courtyard.

"So tell me a little more about the Courtyard," he started.

"The idea for it really only took off a few months after the tornado. A lot of us lost our stores and several of Royal's local artisans lost workshops and homes. The Courtyard gave us all a fresh start—gave us a new community to be proud of." Her eyes grew worried and a frown marred the smoothness of her forehead. "There's talk that some oil company is looking to buy the land. It worries me."

"Why's that? What difference would a new landlord make?" Nolan probed.

Raina looked away, her face thoughtful, before directing her blue gaze straight back at him. "The Courtyard actually became a symbol of hope for a lot of us. A chance to get our feet back firmly on the ground and get us back to normal in a world that got turned upside down in one awful day. You can't put a price on that. We need stability now. We need to be able to know from one day to the next that after all our hard work, we aren't simply going to be turned out.

"An oil company isn't going to want to keep us as tenants, you can be sure of that. They'll want the land for testing, although why they think there's oil there, I don't know. I haven't lived in Royal all that long and even I know the land is barely suitable for grazing, although with the drought that's questionable, too."

She fiddled with the salt and pepper shakers in front of her. "No, the Winslows did the right thing turning the ranch buildings into the Courtyard. Mellie assures me they're not selling. I only hope nothing happens to change her mind. None of us there can afford to have our businesses fold or see our rents increase. What with the cost of increased insurance premiums and setting up all over again, it wouldn't take much to destroy us."

A pang of guilt pulled at him. If he was successful in changing the Winslows' minds, and Rafe got hold of the Courtyard, Nolan knew there were no guarantees that his boss would keep the tenants. And it was true. Raina had a point—while the greater Maverick County area had yielded some successful oil fields, none had been in this general area. Nolan shifted uncomfortably. For the first time he was seeing the personal face of his assignment:

someone who'd be directly and negatively impacted by his boss's plan. And he didn't like it. Not one bit.

He took a sip of his water and decided a change of subject might be in order.

"So, the tornado. That must have been terrifying. People are pretty resilient here, though," he commented.

Raina smiled and once again he was struck by how natural and effortless her beauty was.

"Sometimes I think Royal is the epitome of the 'get down and get on with it' ethic. Some people have moved on, which is completely understandable, but most have just licked their wounds and carried on. And of course there are also the lucky ones who are benefiting from the damage. Tradesmen have been at a premium in the district and we've seen an influx of out-of-towners coming in to fill demand. Bit by bit Royal has found its way back to a new normal. Is that what brings you here? The rebuild?"

Nolan was saved from immediately answering as their waitress dropped their meals in front of them with a smile. "Good to see you back, Nolan," she said before racing off to her next customer.

Raina looked taken aback. "You're local?"

"No, not anymore. I'm here to see family."

"You grew up here, then?"

He nodded. "Yeah, but I've been living in California for several years. I'm only here for a visit."

"Then I'm sure you would have heard all about the tornado from them." Raina's voice held a note of reserve that had been missing before.

"From their point of view, yeah. Dad's in family law, and he said he's seen an unfortunate upswing in business in the wake of the tornado. Families breaking up under the strain of trying to put their lives back together—more domestic abuse."

Raina nodded. "Yeah, it's sad. So often these events

pull people closer together, but if they don't they seem to have the complete opposite effect. I guess I'm lucky I didn't have to factor that in. It's just me and JJ, and my dad. Dad's retired and usually travels around the country, but he came to stay in the trailer park just out of town so he could be on hand to help me reestablish Priceless and get me and JJ back on our feet again."

Nolan couldn't help it: a swell of relief that there was no partner in Raina's life bloomed from deep inside. He pushed the sensation away. She was still out of bounds. She was the kind of woman who had long-term written all over her, while he was only planning to be here long enough to complete the land purchases to Rafiq's satisfaction.

And then there was the kid. He certainly didn't want to take on a package deal of mother and child, no matter how much his libido sizzled like a drop of water on a hot skillet whenever he was anywhere near Raina. He needed to keep his eye on the main goal. He was here to do business, not dally with the locals or become emotionally involved in the town he grew up in. He'd made his choice to walk away from Royal and all the pain it represented seven years ago. He had no plans to stick around. Even so, he perversely wanted to know more about the woman sitting opposite him.

"So, what brought *you* to Royal?" he asked.

She laughed, the sound self-deprecating. "I followed a man. He left and I stayed. It's as simple as that."

Somehow Nolan doubted that it was quite as straightforward as she said.

"Mommy, my hands dirty." JJ spoke up from beside him.

"Use your napkin, JJ."

"But it dirty," he grumbled.

"Here, use mine," Nolan offered.

JJ held his hands up for Nolan to wipe them. "P'ease?" he implored.

Nolan automatically enveloped JJ's hands with the large paper napkin and made a game out of cleaning the little boy's fingers. When he was done, he wiped a bit of sauce from JJ's chin, as well.

"Hey, you're good at that," Raina said with a smile. "Are you sure you don't have kids?"

Nolan swallowed. This would be the perfect opportunity to segue into the past, to admit he'd had a wife and child, but he couldn't bring himself to say the words. It just opened up the floor for too many questions—questions that had no answers and only evoked pity, which he hated.

"Maybe I'm just a clean freak," he joked, scrunching up the used napkin and tossing it on the table.

"Can we go now, Mommy?" JJ asked.

"No, son. Mr. Dane and I haven't finished our meals."

For a second it looked as though JJ would object, but then Nolan remembered his earlier promise.

"What about some ice cream? You never got to finish the one you had before, right?"

"Oh, but I said you didn't need—" Raina began to protest.

"Need doesn't enter into it when ice cream is concerned," Nolan interrupted her smoothly. "What do you say, JJ? Do you want a junior sundae?"

"Wif sprinkles?"

"Sure, my treat." He looked across at Raina. "How about you? Do you want a sundae with sprinkles, too?"

JJ laughed next to him. "Mommy doesn't have treats, she's a mommy!"

Nolan read the subtext in JJ's words. It didn't take a rocket scientist to figure out that Raina went without so that her son could have little treats every now and then. How much had she foregone to ensure her son could still enjoy special things while she rebuilt her business and kept a roof over their heads? Again that urge to protect swirled at the back of his mind.

"Even mommies like treats sometimes, don't they?" he asked, looking straight across the table at Raina.

"Not tonight, thank you. I need to get back to Priceless. My first class starts this evening and I can't be late, not even for a treat."

"Another time then," Nolan promised, and as he called the waitress to order JJ's sundae, he found himself wondering just how soon that might be.

Three

Another time? Did he mean to ask her out on a date? Raina wasn't quite sure how she felt about that. She hadn't dated since Jeb—hadn't even been interested in dating as she came to grips with his betrayal, single parenthood and running a business. It had been a painful irony that she'd been duped by the person she'd thought would stand by her, exactly as her father had been.

She had never known her mother and pictures of her had been few and of poor quality. Raina's enduring memory of the woman who'd borne her was the story of how she'd come home from the hospital with Raina, put her in her bassinet and gone out to buy some milk and never returned. Growing up, Raina had always had more questions about the whole situation than answers and, in retrospect, she could understand why she'd been drawn to the losers.

Despite all the security and love her father had poured into her, Raina's sense of self-worth had been low. She'd found herself desperate to be accepted by others, only to be walked all over again and again. Jeb had been the last in a string of disastrous relationships, and when he'd cleaned out her bank account while she was in labor with his son, she'd finally learned her lesson—and with it, who she was and where she belonged in her world. Now, she was at peace with her decision to focus her energies on JJ and provide a home for them. She finally, at the sage old age of thirty, felt grown up.

Her friends still teased her about her dating moratorium but she'd avoided all potential setups they'd thrown her way. And in the aftermath of the tornado, it had made far better sense not to get involved with anyone. Life had become incredibly precious and despite her need to nurture and to try to "fix" broken souls, aka the losers she'd dated previously, she'd had to draw a line somewhere.

But a date with Nolan Dane? He was nothing like the guys she'd been out with before. He owned a suit, for a start, and showed the kind of manners her father had always told her to expect from a man.

She looked across the table and noticed that JJ had made short work of his sundae and was now rubbing his eyes and fidgeting in his booster seat. She glanced at her watch— a 1920s timepiece she hadn't been able to bring herself to sell after she'd discovered it in a boxed lot she'd bought at an estate sale a couple of years ago. If she didn't get on her way soon, she'd be running late for the sitter and for her class.

"This has been lovely," she said, gathering her bag and searching for her wallet. "But JJ and I really must get going. Thank you for joining us."

"No, thank *you* for *your* company. Please, let me get this. It's the least I can do for crashing your dinner together."

"Oh, but—"

"Please, I appreciated having someone to talk to over my meal."

Before she could say anything, Nolan left several bills on the tabletop, including a generous tip, and helped JJ from the booth.

"Are you parked far away?" he asked as they walked toward the exit.

"No, not far. A block."

"Let me walk you," Nolan said, falling into step beside her on the sidewalk outside the diner.

"Mommy, up," JJ interrupted, and he lifted his little arms in the air.

"Sure, sweetie," she said, bending to lift him into her arms.

She wouldn't be able to keep this up for too much longer. JJ was getting so big and most of the time she had trouble keeping up with her energetic wee man. The fact that he wanted her to carry him spoke volumes about how tired he was. She reminded herself to cherish these moments while they lasted.

They were halfway down the block when she had to readjust JJ's weight in her arms.

"He looks heavy," Nolan commented. "Can I carry him for you?"

"No, it's fine, I can manage," Raina insisted, even though her back was starting to ache a little.

"Man carry me, Mommy."

JJ squirmed in her arms, almost sending her off balance.

"Are you sure you don't mind?" she asked Nolan.

In response, Nolan effortlessly hefted her son from her and propped JJ on one hip. "Of course not."

At the car, Nolan waited on the sidewalk while she strapped JJ into his seat.

"Thank you for dinner, and for your help with JJ. You didn't have to," Raina said as she straightened from the car and held her hand out to Nolan.

He took it and again she was surprised by the sizzling jolt of sensation that struck her as his hand clasped hers.

"Honestly, the pleasure was all mine," he replied, his eyes locked on hers.

She found herself strangely reluctant to let his hand go and Nolan seemed to feel the same way, but then a group of people coming along the sidewalk forced them apart. Thankful she could disengage before things got awkward, Raina gave him a small wave and settled herself in the car.

Her hand still tingled as she reached forward to put the key in the ignition. It had been a long time since she'd felt anything like this at a man's touch. As she drove away, Raina made herself keep her eyes on the road in front of her. She wouldn't look back. Looking back only invited trouble, she told herself, and she'd had bushels of that already in her life. No, she'd promised herself to keep moving forward the right way, and that didn't involve complicating her life with a relationship or fling with someone who was passing through.

Nolan watched from the sidewalk until he couldn't see Raina's taillights any longer. Why had he done this to himself? he wondered as he hunched deeper into his jacket and began to walk back to his hotel. Carrying JJ had brought back a wealth of hurt and repressed memories of his own son, Bennett.

Holding another small body in his arms…it had been a more bitter than sweet experience. He reminded himself very firmly that using her for information about the Winslows was one thing, but he was in no way embarking on any kind of friendship with Raina. It would be too easy, he knew that. He was already attracted to her, already felt that surge of physical awareness every time she smiled or her gaze met his. From the moment he'd laid eyes on her he'd been drawn to her and he'd been unable to get her out of his thoughts.

Being there in the Royal Diner with Raina and JJ had felt too much like his old life. The life he'd vowed he would never turn back to. No, his home was Los Angeles now. Royal held no allure for him anymore even though everything here still felt so achingly familiar.

He acknowledged the doorman at the hotel with a smile and went straight to his room. It was early. Any other time he'd have stopped in the bar and had a drink. Maybe enjoyed a bit of casual female interest before heading to his room—or hers. The mobile nature of his role as Rafiq's personal attorney gave him leeway in his life that he'd never allowed himself before and while casual hookups had never been his style, a man had needs—and clearly the women he'd met had needs, as well. But while those encounters may have left him physically sated, there always remained an emptiness deep inside him.

His thoughts flickered back to Raina Patterson. She was definitely not the type for a casual hookup. She exuded stability and comfort. A man could fool himself that he belonged in the softness of her arms, but only until he broke her heart by leaving again. Nolan promised himself he would not be that man.

He threw himself on the bed and reached for the TV remote. Maybe he'd be able to numb his mind and his awakened libido by watching some mindless sitcoms or movies until he was ready to sleep. But distraction was a long time coming that night, and he couldn't stop his mind wandering back toward the woman who'd so captured him.

Raina was glad she'd taken the time to prepare the workroom before she'd left Priceless earlier that day. JJ had been surprisingly clingy when she'd left him at home with the sitter, making her wonder if their company over dinner had unsettled him. It had certainly unsettled her.

Her students began to arrive, right on time, and once everyone was there and introductions were complete, Raina started the lesson. She'd decided to keep it simple for the first session, changing the style of the candles each week as they carried on. She smiled as she made eye contact with one of JJ's previous babysitters. Hadley Stratton was only a couple of years younger than Raina and had a delightful way with children.

"Okay, ladies, thank you all for coming along tonight. I see you all received my email with the instructions for preparing for this evening's lesson. Does anyone have any questions so far?"

Hadley spoke up. "You said we could dye the egg shells, but what if we could only get brown eggs?"

"No problem," Raina assured her. "You can choose to keep your candles in the shell and decorate the shells, or you can break the shell away after the candles have set and simply burn them in a container—like an eggcup or something like that. It's entirely up to you."

"I'm so brain dead after nannying all day and studying all night that I think I can only go as far as filling a shell. Is that okay?" Hadley laughed. "Maybe I can leave decorating to another lesson."

Several other women joined in with Hadley's laughter, obviously empathizing with her. Raina nodded in acknowledgment.

"How many of you would prefer to decorate or color?"

About half the women in the room put their hands up.

"Okay," Raina said. "How about we split into two groups for tonight? Decorators this side of the workroom, and plain beeswax candles on the other."

The women good-naturedly shifted around and, after showing the group doing plain candles how to start the process of melting their beeswax, Raina discussed with the group of decorators how to dye their egg shells or hand paint them with freestyle or stenciled designs. As everyone set to work, Raina began to feel a sense of excitement. The lesson was really going well and the atmosphere was both lighthearted and creative at the same time.

She stopped by Hadley's table for a minute, while making the rounds of the class to check that everyone was on track.

"It's good to see you, Hadley. We miss you."

"I miss you guys, too. But you know what it's like balancing everything."

"You always make everything look so effortless when you're with kids. You should really have some of your own one day," Raina teased with a friendly smile.

Hadley laughed out loud, drawing attention and several smiles from the people around her. "I've got so much on my plate right now I'm quite happy to put that off for a while longer. Besides, there's the important prerequisite of finding the right man for the job, y'know?"

Raina felt her smile slip a little, but she knew Hadley hadn't meant anything by her comment, that she hadn't been referring to Raina's poor choice of partner in Jeb.

"You make sure he's the right one, then," Raina said, with a light touch on Hadley's arm.

"Don't you worry, I will. When the time is right. In the meantime, at least I have your classes to look forward to on Tuesday evenings. This is about as far as my social life extends. Getting to spend time with other adults and relax and unwind is like gold to me right now, plus I get to make some cute Christmas gifts at the same time. What more could a woman want?"

With a murmur of agreement, Raina moved on to her next student. Hadley was right. What more could a woman want than to be surrounded by people she enjoyed being with and doing something creative? Even so, Raina felt an unexpected yearning that pulled from deep inside. She wanted that "right one" in her life one day. The man who would be her partner in everything and help her to guide JJ on his path in life. Right now, while JJ was small and so dependent on her, it was easy to imagine that she'd be able to cope forever. But sometimes she wished for more. For herself, as well.

Nolan Dane popped immediately to mind and Raina quashed a startling swell of desire as adequately as she was able. This was ridiculous. She'd only met the man today and she was already spinning a tale of happy ever after in her mind? Clearly she wasn't busy enough with her life already. Pushing all thoughts of men to the back of her mind, she went to assist one of her students with the placement of her candle wicks.

By the time the class finished, everyone was proud of their results—Raina most of all. Not only had she successfully pulled off tutoring her first official craft lesson, but everyone had commented how much they were looking forward to returning the following week when they'd be making mason jar candles filled with oil. Some were even talking about classes in the New Year and how they'd like to bring other friends along.

When everyone had cleaned up and gone, and Raina had locked up, she drove herself home. After paying the sitter and checking on JJ, she decided to run herself a luxurious deep bath. She'd earned the hot soak, she decided as she stripped and pulled on a robe while waiting for the bath to fill. In fact, she'd earned a celebratory glass of wine to go along with it. After a quick trip to the kitchen she was soon back with a glass of merlot. She disrobed and lowered herself into the soothing water.

Everything was going to be okay, she told herself. While the antiques business was a little slow in getting off the ground again, she knew it wouldn't take too long before her old customers would discover her new location. A bit of careful advertising across the county would help, and now, with the popularity of the craft classes, as well, she could afford to place those advertisements. She took a sip of her wine and allowed the mellow flavors to roll across her tongue before she swallowed.

Yes, everything would be fine from now on. She and JJ wouldn't want for anything. Or anyone.

Later, as she readied for bed, she checked her phone for messages. She'd turned it off during her class and hadn't gotten around to turning it back on yet. A bit of the shine of happiness from the evening's success dulled when she saw she had another missed call from Jeb and that he'd left another message. Her finger hovered over the button to simply delete the message, but she couldn't bring herself to do it. Instead, she listened and felt her happiness dull a little more.

"Rai, c'mon, babe. Call me back. I really need some money fast. I know you're good for it. Look, this is pretty urgent. Call me."

Raina closed her eyes in frustration. When would she ever be rid of the man? She'd taken all the legal steps she could to have sole custody of JJ, so she knew the little guy was safe from his father. But what would it take for Jeb to leave her alone?

Stop giving him money. The words echoed in her head as clearly as the last time her father had uttered them to her. Not for the first time she wondered why she continued to help her ex. It wasn't because she still bore any love for him. That had died long ago. Was it because she felt beholden to him because of JJ? No. She'd made the decision to go ahead with raising him, knowing it was unlikely that Jeb would provide any support. Maybe it was just because, despite herself, she couldn't help but reach out when she knew a man was down. Her father had often teased her about her need to make everyone happy and feel safe. The thing was, if she kept helping Jeb, when would he ever learn to stand on his own feet and accept some responsibility for everything that happened in his life?

She came to a decision. This ended here and now. She'd no longer be Jeb's cash cow or his go-to person. She deleted the message and shoved her phone in her purse and climbed into bed. Let that be an end to it, she thought as she closed her eyes and drifted off to sleep.

Four

Nolan strolled around the Courtyard the next afternoon, telling himself he wasn't there to see Raina Patterson at all, he was merely doing his job and finding out a bit more about the other tenants. If he could present the acquisition of this parcel of land to Rafiq as an ongoing business concern rather than merely as a land purchase, maybe he could preserve the jobs and incomes of these hardworking people.

He was taken by the work in the silversmith's shop. The delicacy of the silversmith's designs was exquisite and Nolan knew his mother would love the pendant designed to look like a peacock tail with tiny cabochon amethysts and peridots inset at the ends of the feathers. He eyed the price tag and decided that the cost didn't matter. His mother's pleasure on opening the gift would bring its own reward. She'd had little enough joy from him in the past few years as he'd avoided returning to Royal. Maybe this would help show her that despite his withdrawal from home, she was still very much in his thoughts.

The shop assistant was effusive about his choice, almost talking him into purchasing a matching set of earrings, but he knew that less was very definitely more when it came to his mother's tastes and that she preferred a few well-chosen pieces to a cacophony of color and design.

"Is this a Christmas gift?" the woman asked.

"No, just something my mom will enjoy," he answered.

"Ah, that's lovely. Would you still like me to gift wrap it for you?"

"Please."

"Are you new to the area?" the assistant asked as she deftly wrapped the pendant in tissue and wrapping paper.

"I grew up here but I've been away for a while. Just here to see my family."

"Oh, that's lovely," the woman said with a friendly smile. She tied off a length of organza ribbon around the little packet and popped it in a gift bag. "Well, thank you for supporting the Courtyard with your purchase. I hope we see you back before you head home."

Murmuring a note of assent, Nolan took the gift and left the store. It was only midweek but the parking lot was almost full of vehicles and people were bustling around, their arms filled with bags emblazoned with the local artisans' logos. This place really was a gold mine. Yesterday he hadn't spent enough time wandering about, getting a real feel for the place—it was something he was determined to remedy today.

A flash of color caught his eye and he turned his head to see Raina Patterson outside her store, assisting a customer putting a small side table in the back of their car. He felt a now-familiar wallop of awareness as he took in the way her bright red sweater dress clung to her feminine curves and skimmed her hips like a lover's caress.

His body heated and sprang to life, arousal beating a low thrumming pulse that reminded him all too much of the dreams he'd endured last night.

Dreams where he'd begun to make love to his late wife, but when she'd turned toward him it had been Raina's face before him instead.

Nolan swiftly veered into the nearest store, determined to bring his body back under control and rid himself of the desire to walk those few yards toward the big red barn and spend time again with its proprietor. He wasn't here to embark on an affair, he reminded himself. He was here to work.

Raina looked up, surprised to see Nolan Dane on the other side of the Courtyard. She raised a hand to wave, but it appeared that he hadn't seen her as he abruptly turned and headed into the cheese maker's store. She told herself it didn't matter, that she hadn't hoped to see him again anyway. Even so, she felt a tiny twinge of disappointment that she forced herself to rapidly shove aside. She had enough on her plate for today as it was. The class she had lined up for tonight was mosaic work, and she had yet to check the inventory of stock she'd ordered for her students to buy and use for their lessons. The simple mirror frame kits would hopefully be a quick and easy project for her students to tackle, all of them first-timers to mosaic work, and she was looking forward to the class.

A prickle of uneasiness ran down her spine—the sense of disquiet making her look around before heading back into the store. She must be imagining things, she thought, pushing the feeling away and delving into the boxes of stock she'd left on the workroom tables. Last night's message from Jeb was making her paranoid and goodness knew she had little enough time for that.

* * *

The week went quickly and her classes were going from strength to strength. As a side bonus, several of her students were also avid collectors of a variety of antique items including some of the delicate English china she had on display. She was excited to have sold several pieces already and had requests to look out for more. Things were going better than she'd anticipated.

By the time Friday night rolled around, she was really beginning to feel the strain of carrying the responsibility of the store and the classes on her own, and she wanted nothing more than to sit at home with JJ, tucked up in front of the fire and reading a few of his favorite storybooks. But she'd already promised him that they'd go downtown to the Christmas tree lighting ceremony organized by the Texas Cattleman's Club. It was her goal to one day be sponsored to join the club. Of course, she'd need to make a better than average income before she could afford to do that.

While the club had been a solely male domain when it was founded, in recent years women had become members and the club had become more family-oriented in general. And they did such good work in the community, too. Something she hoped to be able to participate in when the time was right. It was important to give back.

The evening air was cold and Raina made sure JJ was bundled up snug and warm in a jacket and hand-knitted wool beanie that one of her customers had made for him. He looked as cute as a button with a few dark tufts of hair poking out from beneath the beanie.

She helped him from the car when they got to downtown Royal, and for a second she felt a pang of regret that Jeb couldn't be a part of JJ's life. But JJ deserved a father he could rely on. Not one who drank and gambled and drifted from one town to the next, looking for work to support his habits.

She'd been blind to Jeb's faults for a long time and for-given him time and again, believing his well-spun lies, right up until the day he wasn't there when she needed him most. JJ's birth had been a roller coaster of emotions: intense joy to finally hold her child in her arms and meet him face-to-face that was tempered by the realization that the only people Raina could honestly rely upon were her-self and her dad. She'd grown up a heck of a lot that day. She'd thought herself so mature at twenty-seven, so ready to be a mother.

"Will there be gifts under the tree, Mommy?" JJ asked as he skipped along beside her on the sidewalk, holding her hand.

"Not real ones, my boy."

"Not even one for me?"

Raina laughed and tugged his beanie more securely over his little ears. "Not even for me either! But don't worry. I'm sure that Santa will remember exactly where we live and will bring you your gifts in time for Christmas."

Satisfied with her answer, JJ turned his attention to the growing crowd. In the distance, Raina caught sight of Clare Connelly. The chief pediatric nurse at Royal Memorial Hospital had been a wonderful support when JJ had been severely jaundiced after his birth and Raina had worried herself sick over him. Newly abandoned by her partner and with her father still on his way to Royal, Raina had had a severe dose of the baby blues as she began to doubt her ability to look after her newborn son. It had been Clare's confident and capable manner with the babies in her care, not to mention the gentle support she'd offered to the new mothers, that had made Raina begin to believe she could do this parenting thing all on her own.

Raina caught Clare's eye and waved a hello. Clare was involved in what appeared to be a very intense conversa-tion with one of the pediatricians who'd also attended JJ at the hospital, Dr. Parker Reese. Raina raised her eyebrows in surprise. Was there something going on between the petite blonde nurse and the sometimes prickly pediatrician? The thought brought a smile to her lips. It had been a joke among the mothers in the hospital that Dr. Reese would make a great husband for someone one day—if he could ever let go of his work and develop a social life. The man was dedicated to his career but everyone needed some balance in their life.

The reminder of balance prodded at Raina's thoughts. Lately everything had been JJ and work for her. There'd been no time for herself, but she was okay with that. One day, maybe, when JJ was a bit older and when her business was on a stronger footing, then yeah, she might think about dating. Until then, she had to stay focused on keeping her financial footing and being the best mother she could be for her little boy.

"Mommy, I can't see," JJ complained, tugging at her arm. "Up?"

"Sure, baby."

Raina bent and lifted JJ into her arms, settling him on one hip. It probably didn't make a world of difference to his line of sight but it was all she could manage.

"Still can't see," he fretted, twisting in her arms and making her clutch his jacket to stop him from falling.

"JJ, settle down. Trust me, when the lights go on, you'll see everything."

"Here" came a familiar male voice. "Maybe I can help?"

"Man!"

JJ flung his arms toward the newcomer with an exuberance that dismayed Raina and almost sent her off balance. Nolan Dane loomed up beside her. She should refuse his offer of help, but JJ was already transferring himself into Nolan's arms and was soon deposited high on Nolan's shoulders.

"Better now?" Nolan asked, looking up at JJ who was holding on tight to Nolan's head.

JJ nodded.

"What do you say, JJ?" Raina prompted.

"T'ank you."

"You're welcome." Nolan turned his smile to Raina. "I hope you don't mind. You look tired and I could see he was getting heavy."

Raina's lips twisted into a smile. "It's okay, thank you."

So, he thought she looked tired, huh? Wow, way to build a girl up, she thought, then immediately chastised herself for being so churlish. She did look tired. The three late nights this week with the classes, on top of everything else, had taken a toll. She made a mental note to try to get to bed earlier on the nights she wasn't working.

The crowd around them thickened as the local singers and dance groups performed on the makeshift stage that had been set up for the evening. Raina's gratitude to Nolan for taking JJ increased. There was no way JJ would have seen the show, or enjoyed it, from her arms; nor would she have been able to hold him for this long.

The night sky was fully dark and the atmosphere quickly became one of excitement as, over the loudspeakers, the master of ceremonies and the newest Texas Cattleman's Club president, Case Baxter, led the countdown to the lighting of the tree. Everyone in the crowd counted with him.

"… Three, two, one!" Raina shouted along with the rest of the crowd, then she joined them in the oohs and ahhs of delight as the switch was thrown to bring a multitude of colored lights to life in the massive tree that now dominated downtown Royal. Tearing her eyes from the tree, Raina looked up at her son, whose face was a picture of enchantment. A deep sense of contentment filled her.

She might not own the world, but it sure felt like it when she could still put a look like that on her little boy's face.

A choir began to sing "Joy to the World," and bit by bit the crowd joined them. Nolan had a surprisingly pleasant tenor, Raina discovered as he unselfconsciously added his voice to the singing. As the song wound to its end, the mayor of Royal took the microphone and thanked Case Baxter and the Texas Cattleman's Club committee for sponsoring the tree lighting ceremony, and he concluded by wishing everyone the very best for the season and inviting them to support the retailers who'd set up stalls around the square.

Raina turned to Nolan. "Thank you. I really mean it. I'm sure he'll remember tonight for a long time to come and that's because you helped us out."

"Only too happy to oblige y'all," Nolan answered. "Say, do you have to race home right away? How about a churro and some hot chocolate from one of the stalls over there?"

"Yummy, churro!" JJ crowed from on top of Nolan's shoulders.

"Manners, JJ!" Raina admonished. "What have I told you?"

"T'ank you, man," JJ dutifully responded.

Nolan laughed and Raina felt her heart skip a happy beat at the sound.

"His name is Mr. Dane, not man, JJ," Raina gently admonished.

"I think you should let him call me Nolan. Mr. Dane sounds so stuffy."

Raina nodded her head. "I'll try but I can't guarantee it. He can be pretty stubborn when he decides on a word."

Through the crowd, she spied Liam Wade. The rancher was clearly in demand with the ladies and looking none too thrilled about the prospect. A group of very determined looking mommas with single daughters in tow had circled him like a wagon train, ensuring he had no easy way out. A chuckle escaped her lips, prompting a question from Nolan.

"What's so funny?"

"Oh, just poor Liam. He's one of Royal's most eligible bachelors," she said, pointing him out in the crowd, "and one of Royal's most reluctant at the same time. I think he'd be happy if he never had to leave his ranch."

Nolan chuckled in sympathy. "Yeah, I guess when you have an operation like the Wade Ranch you're pretty self-contained. I can see why he wouldn't want to leave, especially if he gets mobbed whenever he sets foot outside his property line."

"Sure, but everybody needs somebody, don't they?" Raina countered without thinking.

Raina caught Nolan looking at her—a strange expression on his face as if he was weighing her words. Did he need somebody? His eyes lingered on her mouth and she fought not to lick her lips in nervous reaction. But it made her wonder: What would his lips feel like on her own? She immediately shoved the thought away. Here he was with her son on his shoulders and she was thinking about him kissing her? What was wrong with her?

Nolan shifted his gaze. "And what about you? Don't you need somebody, as well?" he asked.

She felt color flood her cheeks. "I have JJ," she said, her voice staunch. "He's all I need."

Nolan made an indeterminate sound and guided Raina toward one of the stalls off to the side. He swung JJ down to the ground and rolled his shoulders a few times before marching up to the counter and placing an order. Had she upset him by saying that JJ was all she needed? It was hard to tell. And besides, she reminded herself, it shouldn't bother her if it had upset him. She wasn't in the market for a relationship. Even so, it didn't stop her watching him as he picked up the tray with their hot chocolate and churros and led them over to a seating area that had been set up to one side.

"Don't let it all get cold," he warned gently as he set the tray down on the table in front of them.

"Thank you so much for this," Raina said, transferring some of JJ's hot chocolate to a sippy cup she'd pulled from her bag. "Sorry, I just like to be on the safe side with drinks when we're out. I know he's probably old enough to do without—"

"Hey, no need to apologize," Nolan interrupted. "You're his mom, you know what's best for him. I'm hardly in a position to judge."

By the time they'd finished their treats, JJ was getting cranky and tired. There was no way he'd make the trek back to where Raina had parked so when Nolan offered to carry him for her again, she didn't object. Weariness pulled at her, too, but the thought of curling up in her bed was tempered by the need to get up early the next morning. Saturdays she opened late, because they were her yard- and estate-sale mornings when she rose before dawn to try to pick up the occasional treasure to resell at Priceless. Her dad always came over super early to take care of JJ for the day so she could go straight to the store after doing her rounds of the sales.

At the car, Nolan stood to one side while she settled JJ into his car seat. Poor kid, he was almost asleep already, she noticed. Straightening from the car, she closed JJ's door gently and turned to Nolan.

"Thank you so much for your help tonight. I really do appreciate it."

"I enjoyed it. It's always fun seeing the lights through a child's eyes. Kids make everything so simple, so basic and enjoyable, don't they?"

Raina smiled at him, then struggled to stifle a yawn. "Oh, my. I'm sorry. Please excuse me. It's been a heck of a week. I'd better head off and get JJ into bed."

Nolan nodded and then stepped a little closer. "Raina, I'd really like to see you again. To take you out to dinner or the movies?"

Raina's breath caught in her throat. He was asking her for a date? For the briefest of moments she cherished the idea but then her practical nature set in. She shook her head gently.

"Nolan, I'm flattered. Truly I am. But I don't date. My life is too busy as it is. It's really not a good time for me to be thinking about stretching myself any thinner. I'm sorry."

"No, it's okay," Nolan said, his brown eyes gleaming under the streetlamp. He reached into his back pocket and pulled out a card holder. "I'm disappointed but I understand. If you ever change your mind, make sure you let me know, okay? My private number is on the back."

He slid one pristine white business card from the holder and pressed it into her hand. The instant he touched her, that familiar tingle came back, except this time it quivered through her veins along with something else. Something that felt curiously like desire.

She held on to the feeling for the briefest moment, wondering when had been the last time anyone had made her feel like a desirable woman, before ruthlessly quelling it again. She couldn't—no, shouldn't—entertain the idea. It was best that she didn't see Nolan again. Every relationship she'd ever had had extracted a price whereby she'd lost a little bit of herself in the process. She daren't do that to herself, or to JJ, again. Not now. Not ever. And yet she still found herself wishing she could say yes.

"How long are you prepared to wait?" Raina joked with a nervous laugh, unable to stop herself from asking the question even though she had no intention of taking Nolan up on it.

"As long as it takes," Nolan said with a slow smile that sent curls of delight all the way to her extremities.

Oh, yes. She was well-advised to steer completely clear of Nolan Dane. She'd only met him four days ago and he was already heating her blood.

Unable to think of a suitable response, Raina muttered a swift good-night and got into the car. She gave Nolan a small wave as she pulled away from the curb and drove away. A red light at the intersection halted her retreat and she glanced in the rearview mirror. Nolan still stood there on the sidewalk, his hands shoved in his jacket pockets, watching them go.

She couldn't stop thinking of him during the journey home to their little rented house and, even after she'd put JJ to bed and found refuge between her own sheets, Nolan Dane remained front and center in her thoughts. The way he looked at her made her feel like a woman. Not just a mom, not just a retailer or a tutor, but a warm, desirable and wanted woman. She'd pushed the idea away so hard and so vehemently after Jeb that it had become a concept she'd almost forgotten. Seeing that attraction reflected in Nolan's face empowered her. It was a sensation she liked.

She twisted in her sheets, her body aching with unexpected longing. Nolan Dane affected her in ways she hadn't wanted to acknowledge but now that she'd opened the door on those feelings, they'd all come rushing out. She liked everything about him so far—his manners, his careful way of speaking, even the tone of his voice. And his eye-catching looks didn't hurt either. He carried his height with confidence, with his broad shoulders set straight, and he met a person's gaze square on with no subterfuge—no lies. Having been on the receiving end of those looks Raina had come to realize that a woman could get happily lost in those deep brown eyes of his.

And then there was his manner with JJ. Even at the store, on the first day she'd met him, he'd been so good with her little boy—so understanding after the disaster with the ice cream. Nolan was an out-and-out gentleman, there was no denying it. And he treated her like a lady. Going out on a date with him would be something special. Suddenly Raina was swamped with regret that she'd said no to his invitation. She shifted in the bed again and thumped her pillow into shape. If only she could as easily reshape her life, she thought as she settled back down.

Nolan was the last thing on her mind as she drifted off to sleep. Nolan, and the knowledge that the next time he asked her out, *if* he asked her out again, she might even say yes. After all, what harm could it do?

Five

Nolan walked back to his hotel rather than grab a cab. He was filled with an energy that demanded release—although walking wasn't the first activity that sprang to his mind. No, his mind was filled with the image of a certain dark-haired, blue-eyed storekeeper who had somehow inveigled her way into his thoughts and lodged there like a burr under a saddle.

He could still see the flare of awareness that had dilated her pupils when they'd touched only a short while ago. Hell, he could still feel it within himself. The only other person he'd ever felt that way about had been Carole. The reminder was a daunting one, and it should serve as a reminder that Raina Patterson was not the kind of woman he needed in his life. He'd been there and done that. He'd lived and loved within a perfect marriage with his perfect woman and they'd had the perfect little family—until it all fell apart.

Nolan went to step off the curb and was jolted into awareness by the blast of a car horn. Damn, he needed to keep his wits about him and Raina had managed to scatter said wits to the four corners of the earth. She was definitely not what he was looking for. He didn't even know why he'd asked her out, except that, for all his mental flagellation, deep down he still wanted her.

He nodded to the doorman as he entered the hotel and headed for the elevators. The sounds of music, conversation and laughter echoed across the marble-floored lobby from inside the hotel bar, catching his interest. He looked at his watch. It certainly wasn't too early to return to his suite but he was sick of his own company right now. Perhaps a distraction could be found elsewhere—one that would hopefully erase or at least dull the throb of desire Raina had left him with.

At the bar he ordered a brandy. It wasn't long before he had company. A blonde woman took the stool next to his and cast him a smile. He reacted in kind automatically and waited for the flicker of heat that usually signified an initial burst of interest. As they embarked on conversation there was no mistaking her interest in him, and yet he couldn't seem to kindle an answering response in himself.

Instead, before he'd even finished his brandy, Nolan excused himself and went up to his suite. And as he lay staring at the dark sky through his open bedroom windows over an hour later, he wondered if sleep was as distant for Raina as it was for him. He forced his eyes closed, but even then all he could see were still shots of her beautiful face—sometimes smiling, sometimes pensive.

Nolan reached into his memory for the sense of loss he'd carried with him since losing Bennett and Carole, but it was further away than it had been before. Instead, he found his thoughts drawn to another woman, one whose gentle personality and sensual warmth somehow had begun to fill a hole inside him he didn't even want to acknowledge that he had.

It was late when Nolan finally rose the next morning. As he shaved, he considered his next step. He'd always prided himself on being a man of action. It was what had gotten him through the bleak empty horror of the death of his son soon followed by that of his beloved wife. And if something was worth doing, it was worth doing well. He also had never been one to take no for an answer.

As soon as he'd finished getting ready and had enjoyed a late breakfast in the coffee shop next door to the hotel, he was in his rental and heading out to the Courtyard. He didn't even bother trying to mentally dress this visit up as being in the course of his work.

Fact-finding mission be damned. He'd had a niggling feeling that Raina was merely going through the motions when she'd turned down his invitation to a date yesterday. The words had fallen all too easily from those sexy lips of hers. As if she'd trotted the phrases out often enough for them to become automatic. That left him with two options. The first was to find out if she really meant what she said and the second, to discover what it was that she'd left unsaid.

As he drove out to the Courtyard, he considered his strategy for getting the truth out of Raina. Sure, he could go in and ask her straight out but he had a feeling that the shield she'd built around her was pretty darn strong and could withstand anything he could metaphorically throw at her. No, he'd go gently, softly. Try to understand where she was coming from and why she was so adamant about not dating.

He shook his head. Why was he even bothering? It wasn't as if he planned on hanging around after he'd finished his job for Rafiq. There'd be more dragons to slay back in Los Angeles, or maybe even somewhere else.

A smoldering ember of desire sparked deep inside him. That's why he was bothering. He wanted Raina. It was as impure and as complicated as that. He smiled a little at his twist on the old saying of things being pure and simple. Given that what his boss planned for Royal could mean eviction for Raina's store, Nolan should stay well back. But he couldn't.

He had to at least try with her, didn't he? Maybe it was a just physical thing, something he needed to get out of his system. But maybe it was something more.

As soon as he gave the thought a moment in his mind, its tendrils secured themselves as tightly as a stubbornly clinging vine. The analytical side of him demanded that he define what that "something more" could be, especially when he'd spent the past seven years telling himself he wasn't interested in long-term ever again. He'd lived the life he'd always dreamed of right up until the day it had turned into a nightmare his family had never recovered from. He owed it to them, to their memory, to keep what they'd had sacred. To keep it in the forefront of his thoughts so that he never let down another person or another family like that again.

He totally understood the pain that had driven Carole to take her own life. After all, didn't he choose to live with it every day and face it like the demon it was?

All of which brought him back to why he was so persistent about seeing the delightfully warm and sensual Ms. Patterson. Even he knew this attraction was more than a simple itch to be scratched. One look at Raina and he'd seen complicated all the way.

Before he realized it, Nolan was parked in front of Priceless. Through the windows he could see Raina moving about inside. His gut clenched on a swell of need that took him completely unawares.

He wasn't a man who'd ever taken rejection well, and that was probably what made him so good at his job. If one method failed, then there was always another, and another. Strategy, for him, was all about finding the weak points, then mercilessly exploiting them. His lips pulled into a wry grin. Wow, like that sounded sexy and irresistible. What woman could refuse an approach like that?

He was still smiling as he pushed open the door to the store and heard the chime of the bell above announcing his arrival. Raina lifted her head with a smile on her face to welcome him. Her smile froze for a moment, her blue eyes wide and vulnerable, before she composed herself and straightened from her task to greet him.

"Good morning. What brings you here today?" she asked, setting down the cloth she'd been using to polish the top of a box she was cradling in her other arm.

In pristine condition, the box housed a fountain pen with nibs and a crystal inkwell with an engraved silver lid. It was a beautiful set and, by the look of it, had barely been used. She left the lid open to better display its contents and set the case down on a nearby table.

"Christmas shopping," he improvised, moving closer to take another look at the writing set. "For my mother. I was hoping you'd be able to help me. Say, that looks interesting."

Was it his imagination or did her pupils dilate a little as he stepped closer? Raina had her hair pulled back into a ponytail today. The style exposed the delicate curve of her neck and the soft line of her jaw. What he wouldn't do to be able to take his time and lay a line of sweet kisses along those very contours, and more.

She took a half step back. "It's a writing set, from the

1920s, I think, judging from the art deco design on the pen."

"It's beautiful," he said, tracing the engraved pattern on the silver with a fingertip. He wondered what sort of price tag she had on the set.

"I recognize that look in your eye," Raina said on a short laugh.

"Look?"

"Of longing. I feel that way with pretty much everything in my store. Regrettably, I can't keep it all. Are you looking for something like this for your mom? It's a bit masculine. Or does your mother collect anything in particular?"

"Egg cups," he said abruptly after racking his brain and coming up with the first thing he could remember. "She loves English china egg cups."

Raina's smile returned. "Oh, then you're in luck. I have a few you can choose from."

She gestured for him to follow her across the broad plank flooring of the store toward a glass-fronted display cabinet. Selecting a key from the chain she kept hooked at the waistband of her jeans, she opened the cabinet and pointed out the exquisite pieces.

"These two are English. One Staffordshire, which as you can see comes with a salt pot and pepper shaker in the stand, and the other is Royal Winton, hazel pattern, with the toast rack, as well. This one here, though, is French."

She pointed to a delicately patterned gold-edged porcelain tray with six matching egg cups arrayed around a carry handle in the shape of a porcelain chick.

"Good grief," Nolan exclaimed. "And people use these?"

"Well, given their age it's safe to say people more likely used these in the past, while they collect and display them now. Would you like me to lift them out so you can take a closer look?"

Nolan nodded and bent to peer at them when Raina put

them on top of a nearby sideboard. As he studied them, Raina gave him a little commentary.

"The Staffordshire piece certainly looks the more sturdy, doesn't it?" she asked. "This one is from the nineteenth century."

"So old?"

She laughed. "Well, this is an antiques store."

He found himself smiling back at her and this time there was no mistaking the dilation of her pupils or the slight blush of pink on her cheeks as they made eye contact. She was attracted to him, he knew it as well as he knew the face that greeted him in the mirror every time he shaved.

"Good point," he conceded as she briskly looked away. "Which one is your favorite?"

She hesitated a moment before speaking. "While the Staffordshire is an exceptional example, with no chips or cracks, and the Royal Winton is also, I prefer the whimsy of the French pieces. Yes, they're a little more worn, but that comes with use and for me, use brings character to a piece. I like to imagine the family who might have enjoyed these egg cups, the children who might have touched the chick coming out of its china eggshell as they enjoyed their breakfast."

She gave an embarrassed laugh. "But then, that's me. And you said your mom collects English china, didn't you?

He nodded. "Maybe it's time she diversified across the channel to France, as well."

He studied the pieces again and then gave a decisive nod. "The French one it is."

"Nolan, you didn't even ask me how much it is!"

He shrugged. "Does it matter? It's for my mom. She'll love it, and probably for the exact same reasons you do."

Raina nodded in acceptance and then carefully put the other two breakfast sets back in the cabinet.

"Would you like me to gift wrap it for you?" she asked, carrying the tray to the counter.

"Please. And double the bubble wrap for me, would you? I'm terrified that I'll break it before I give it to her."

Raina eyed him teasingly. "You don't strike me as a careless man."

"Accidents happen," he said without thinking, his voice sharper than he intended. He knew that for a truth…all too well.

"Bubble wrap it is then. Plus I think I have a box out back that would be perfect. Would that suit you?" she said, picking up on his change in mood and making her tone more businesslike than before.

"Thank you," he replied, determined to inject more warmth into his voice. "I really appreciate it. Mom will be thrilled, I'm sure."

"I'm glad. It's always nice to know things will continue to be appreciated when they leave here. I kind of feel like a custodian for them, you know. Like I have a responsibility to the original craftsmen and -women to see that their hard work continues to be loved as it changes hands."

Her words summed her up perfectly, he thought. She cared about things and about people. So why then did she keep herself so aloof? It was time to find out.

"I imagine that you don't get a lot of time to yourself," he said leaning against the scarred countertop that looked as if it had seen many years of service somewhere in its life. "What with the store and JJ and all."

She kept her head bent and her attention on her task but he saw the slight change in her posture. As if she was shoring up her defenses.

"I get enough. In fact I get most Saturday evenings to myself when my dad is in Royal and takes JJ for a sleepover. That is plenty for me. I wouldn't change anything in my life for something as ephemeral as time alone and definitely not at the expense of my son."

"You sound like a woman who knows her own mind."

"I like to think so. Now, at least. I wasn't always this certain, but I guess when you've learned the hard way, you tend to take things a little more seriously."

"The hard way?"

Raina finished wrapping his mother's gift and swiftly tied a cheerful Christmas bow around the wrapping paper. "There you are. All done. Now, will that be cash or credit?"

She was avoiding answering him. That much was clear. He slid his platinum card from his card holder and passed it to her before placing both hands on the countertop and leaning toward her.

"Raina, I meant what I said last night. I really would like to see you, to get to know you better."

She looked up at him, a little flustered and a lot startled. He realized how much he was encroaching on her space and straightened up from the counter again.

"I… I told you last night, Nolan. I don't date. I just don't have time."

"What are you afraid of, hmm?" he coaxed.

Her eyes shone with what he suspected—hell, *hoped*—was yearning. He pressed forward with what he saw as his advantage.

"At least tell me why. You can't let me go away with a complex. Just think of what that could do to a man like me."

His deliberate foolishness earned its own reward when she laughed, openly and honestly and from the heart.

"Oh, I think your ego is completely safe from me," she said, passing back his card. "But if you really must know, I haven't exactly had the best taste in men. Take JJ's father for example. I met him near where we lived, over in the next county. He swept me off my feet and dazzled me with his grand plans. We moved to Royal when he got work here as a ranch hand, but he never quite seemed to be able to hold down a job for more than a few months at a time. Then he left me broke after cleaning out my bank account. I promised myself, there and then, that no man would ever leave me that vulnerable again."

Nolan sensed there was a great deal more behind her words than she was letting on.

"You never pressed charges?"

"He's JJ's father. Of course I didn't. I just hoped that he'd taken enough money that he'd never need to come back. But—" she cut herself off abruptly and seemed to gather her thoughts back together "—but that's all in the past," she said with false brightness.

Nolan could read between the lines and he knew there was much more to her story than the potted history she'd just given him. But it could wait. Instead, he latched on to something she'd said a few minutes ago. "You mentioned your dad has JJ on Saturdays?"

She nodded slowly.

"Today?"

She nodded again. Nolan felt a glow of excitement light up in his chest.

"So, if I asked you if you could break your no-dating rule and have dinner with me tonight, could I persuade you to consider it?"

Raina pursed her lips and crossed her arms but even though her body language was all about the "no," the yearning he'd seen in her eyes before was still very much in evidence. He held his breath while she took her time making her decision.

"Okay," she said on what sounded like a long held sigh. "Yes, I'd like that. But just dinner."

He smiled and fought the urge to fist pump the air in delight.

"Just dinner," he agreed. "Where and when can I pick you up?"

Raina gave him her address and they agreed on the time he would pick her up. He knew the area. Not the worst in town, but not the best either. Still, after what she, and the rest of Royal, had been through just over a year ago, at least she and JJ had a secure roof over their heads.

He could do so much better for her. The thought hit him from nowhere and left him reeling. He pushed it back. Looking after Raina Patterson wasn't his business; she'd made that abundantly clear. She was a strong and independent woman.

Which only made her all the more appealing.

Six

Nolan pulled up outside the address Raina had given him. The area was worse than Nolan remembered and he hit the automatic lock on his car key as he got out and walked up the path toward the house. Raina answered the door before he'd so much as lifted his finger to the doorbell. As excited to see him as he was to see her, perhaps? He certainly hoped so.

He let his gaze roam her body. She looked beautiful. Her silky dark brown hair shone loose and long as it fell about her shoulders, and she'd done some incredible magic with eye makeup that made her blue eyes even brighter and more intense than he'd ever seen them. There was a faint hint of blush on her cheeks and her lips had a delicious watermelon-colored sheen. He ached to lean forward and see if those lips tasted as good as they looked.

She wore a long sheer burgundy blouse, with a matching camisole beneath it, over slim-fitting black pants and high heels. A fine gold chain graced her neck and small pear shaped gold drops hung from her ears.

"I'm so sorry," she started, and for a second he thought she was going to pull out of their date. But then she said, "Dad dropped JJ back home earlier. He has a leak in the trailer right where JJ's bed is and since he had JJ with him all day he didn't get a chance to repair it. When I told him I'd planned to go out he said he'd be back to sit for me, but he's not here yet."

Nolan felt himself relax. Waiting for her father to return was no problem.

"That's okay. We have plenty of time," he assured her.

"Man!" JJ slid to a halt on the polished wooden floor in front of him.

"JJ!" Raina admonished. "His name is Nolan, not man."

"No'an." JJ tried the name out for size, then reached for Nolan's hand. "Come see Spider-Man."

Nolan looked to Raina for approval. She shrugged. "If you don't mind?" she said helplessly. "He's certainly fixated on you. Dad said all he talked about today was 'man' and the Christmas tree."

"I don't mind," Nolan assured her before looking down at JJ's eager face. "C'mon then, JJ. Show me Spider-Man."

The sensation of the little boy's fingers so trustingly wrapped within his own somewhat soothed the ache Nolan felt in his heart. Bennett had been only eighteen months old when he'd died. Less than half JJ's age. Would he, too, have been a fan of comic-book heroes? Nolan would never know.

JJ's excited chatter yanked him back into the present and Nolan fell into an easy banter with the garrulous child. Sure, JJ still struggled with some syllables but his overall command of language made him easy to understand as he bounced around his room in excitement—dragging one thing and then another from his shelves and drawers to show Nolan.

Down the hallway, Nolan heard sounds of another person arriving. A man with a deep voice. When he got to JJ's room, Nolan took him for Raina's dad immediately. He had the same piercing blue eyes and that determined set of the jaw. Raina stood behind him, looking a little uncomfortable.

Nolan rapidly got to his feet and extended a hand to the newcomer.

"Nolan Dane, pleased to meet you."

"Justin Patterson. Can I have a word with you before you leave with my daughter?"

The man's eyebrows pulled into a straight line and the no-nonsense look in his eyes set Nolan back a bit. He hadn't seen a look like that in a father's eyes since he dated back in high school—and he hadn't missed the proprietary use of the word *my* when referring to Raina either.

"Sure," he answered smoothly. "Just let me help JJ put his things back."

"I can do that," Raina said, stepping into the room. "You go talk with Dad, then we can leave for the restaurant."

"I'll only need a minute," her father said dourly from the doorway.

Justin Patterson didn't take long to get to the point. The moment they were out of earshot of JJ's bedroom, he bluntly told Nolan exactly what he expected.

"Treat my daughter with respect."

"You have no worries on that score, sir. Raina is a wonderful woman."

"I don't know what your intentions are toward her, but I will tell you this. If you break her heart, or if you hurt her in any way, I will come after you."

Raina's dad was Nolan's equal in height and had at least twenty pounds on him. He had the look of a man used to hard work and Nolan had no doubt that he meant every word.

"Thank you for being honest with me. Now let me be honest with you. I know Raina doesn't normally date, and we haven't even known each other very long, but I have no plans to hurt her. We're going out for dinner tonight, and that's all."

"Humph." The older man crossed his arms over his chest. "Make sure that *is* all you do."

Nolan understood where Justin Patterson was coming from, especially based on what Raina had said to him earlier. "I'm not in town for long and I respect your daughter too much to try to take advantage of her—although you misjudge her if you think she'd let me. So far, I think it's safe to say that we like each other and I enjoy her company. JJ's, too. Raina is safe with me."

Justin narrowed his eyes at Nolan. "Dane, you said. Your father is Howard Dane?"

Nolan nodded. His father was well known in Royal and his family law practice was well respected.

"He's a good man. Let's hope the acorn didn't fall far from the tree."

With that, Justin turned and went into the kitchen where Nolan could hear him bustling around and putting the teakettle on. Raina came into the room with JJ trailing behind.

"Go see what Grandpa is up to, JJ," she urged. "Maybe he's making hot chocolate for bedtime."

As the little boy scampered toward the kitchen, she looked at Nolan with an apologetic expression on her face.

"I'm sorry about that. He's kind of protective."

Nolan put up a hand. "No problem. He's your dad. He's entitled to be protective of you. So, are we okay? Shall we go?"

She nodded and called out, "We're on our way, Dad. Call me if you need me!"

Judging by Justin's grunt they were free to go.

Nolan helped Raina into her coat and held the front door for her as they went outside. Streetlamps shone like golden orbs in the air, casting light onto the road beneath them. He guided her to his SUV and closed the passenger door for her once she was settled.

As he climbed into his seat, Nolan saw a furtive movement near a bush a few yards away. His eyes strained to see what it was but it appeared there was nothing there. He shrugged it off as something he'd either imagined or perhaps an animal that was now long gone. But as he began to drive down the street, he caught a glimpse of a man briskly walking down the sidewalk.

There was something about the way the man carried himself and how he kept to the shadows that made Nolan's instincts go on alert. As they cruised by in the SUV, the man furtively kept his face averted and hunched his shoulders. Sure, it was cold tonight—certainly too cold to be out casually walking anyway—which could explain the man's posture, but even if he was out for a constitutional stroll, why was he doing his best not to be recognized? In his work Nolan had seen a lot of characters and to him it was clear that this guy didn't want to be noticed.

Nolan didn't want to alert Raina to his concerns. She was busy looking out the window at the other side of the road and therefore oblivious to what he had seen, but he remained uneasy. Had the guy been watching Raina?

The idea plagued him during the drive to the restaurant, even while Raina kept up a patter of general conversation, asking him about growing up in Royal. By the time they were seated and perusing their menus, Nolan had decided to put thoughts of the walker, whoever he was, from his mind. He was here to enjoy Raina's company and he didn't want anything to detract from that.

Later, when they were about to make their selections

for dessert, his cell phone began buzzing persistently in his pocket.

"I'm sorry," he said, sliding the device out to see who the caller was. Rafiq. Damn. His boss was hardly the kind of person he could hold a conversation with in front of Raina. "Will you excuse me a moment? I really need to take this call."

"No problem." She waved him on with a smile. "I need some time to decide on dessert anyway."

He excused himself and, lifting the phone to his ear, he answered the call.

"Rafe, what can I do for you?"

"You can tell me how things are going with the Courtyard acquisition for a start," his boss said without preamble.

"The Winslow woman is very resistant to selling."

"The Winslow woman? What happened to Homer Winslow?"

"He has been removed by his board for mismanagement," Nolan said, summarizing how Melanie Winslow had wrested control. He strongly suspected the proposed buyout of the Courtyard had been the catalyst for that. "Ms. Winslow now heads Winslow Properties."

"But she's a maid, isn't she?"

Nolan fought back a smile. Rafiq was very modern and forward thinking in many ways, but in others he was still a throwback to his family's roots in ancient Al Qunfudhah, on the coast of the Red Sea.

"Ms. Winslow has a very successful business providing house-cleaning and house-sitting services. She is quite a bit more than a maid, and she is proving to be adamantly opposed to the sale of the Courtyard."

"Offer her more."

"Are you sure you want to do that? When word gets around, and it will in a place like Royal, any other owners of property you're interested in will simply increase their asking prices accordingly."

Rafe made a sound of annoyance and Nolan could just imagine the expression on his boss's face.

"They still owe money on that land, don't they? Can we get any leverage through their lenders?"

"It's an avenue I'm looking into now. Rest assured. If we can buy the Courtyard, it will most certainly be yours."

"There is no 'if,' Nolan. I want that land."

Not for the first time, Nolan started to bite his tongue against the question of why Rafiq was so adamant about his acquisitions around Royal. To hell with it, he decided. He wanted to know and, as Rafe's agent in all of this, he damn well deserved to know.

"Why, Rafe? What's so important about that or any other piece of land you're buying?"

"My reasons are my own. Do not overstep the bounds of our friendship, Nolan. I'll be in Holloway next weekend. We will meet Saturday at 10:00 a.m. at the Holloway Inn."

It was just like Rafiq to make a demand rather than a suggestion. But Nolan was well used to his boss's manner.

"I'll be there."

"Good. I expect to hear more progress has been made on the situation then."

With that closing statement, his boss ended the call. Rafiq hadn't said as much but the implication was clear in his tone. Friendship or no, if Nolan wasn't happy to continue to act for him, there were plenty of other lawyers who would. He slid his phone back into his pocket and returned to the table.

Raina looked up as Nolan approached.

"Everything okay?" she asked, as he settled back down into his chair. "Was that work?"

"What makes you ask?" he said, evading her question.

"Probably that frown you've got right now."

He forced himself to relax and smile. "Better?"

"Much. Seriously though, is everything okay?"

"Sure, nothing that can't wait until tomorrow anyway."

He picked up his dessert menu and briefly scanned the contents without even really seeing them. Rafe's unwavering determination to purchase the Courtyard and the barren acreage it sat on didn't sit comfortably with him at all. In fact the whole business was beginning to leave a bad taste in his mouth. Sure, Royal had changed a lot since the tornado. It certainly wasn't the town he'd grown up in anymore, nor was it the one he'd left seven years ago. But deep down, the values and the lifestyles remained the same. What kind of impact would Rafe's plan have on all of that?

And what of the traders, like Raina, who'd picked their lives back up after total devastation and who needed the stability and continuity the Courtyard provided? Did Rafe plan to continue to run it as it currently operated, or did he plan to scuttle everything? There were just so many questions buzzing around like angry bees in Nolan's brain right now. It made it hard to recapture the pleasure he'd felt in Raina's company only a few minutes ago.

It was clear her trust in him was growing and he appreciated that far more than he'd believed possible. But by acting for Rafe, he was betraying that trust and he didn't like it.

"What have you decided on?" Raina prompted from the other side of the table.

"What are you having?" he countered.

"It was a tough decision to make," she said with a short laugh. "But I think I'll go for the white chocolate cheesecake."

He closed his menu card and laid it back on the table. "Same for me."

By unspoken mutual consent, they lingered over their coffees and dessert. Nolan didn't want to break the fragile spell that had rewoven itself around their evening by drawing things to a close, but when he caught Raina stifling another yawn, he knew it was time to take her home. Despite Rafiq's interruption, Nolan had thoroughly enjoyed the evening. And he knew without a doubt that he wanted to get to know Raina better.

Their drive back to her house was done in a companionable silence and, once they got there, Nolan walked Raina up the path to her front door. Haloed by the porch light, she looked like a beautiful angel but his thoughts and intentions toward her were anything but angelic.

"Thank you for this evening," Raina said. "I'd forgotten how much I enjoy adult conversation and company that's not related to kids or work."

There was a smile on her face that was wistful and it sent a pang to Nolan's chest. He could imagine she had little enough time to herself, let alone to share with another person.

"It was absolutely my pleasure."

Afterward he couldn't be certain who had made the first move. But it didn't matter one bit. His senses filled with her—her scent, her taste, the feel of her in his arms and, above all else, the beauty of her kiss. A sense of rightness filled him as their lips met, as his hand lifted to thread through her hair and to cup the back of her head. Inside him a knot began to unravel and he knew, in that moment, that he wanted Raina in his life. That he could finally begin to let go of the pain of the past that had kept him in emotional isolation.

He traced the softness of her lips with his tongue as they parted beneath him. Desire unfurled through his body, doubling on itself until it consumed his thoughts. When Raina's hands pushed through his hair and held him to her, he knew she felt the same. She pressed her body against his and heat flared between them.

Nolan deepened their kiss. His tongue probed her mouth and she responded in kind. A shudder of need pummeled him and he felt an echoing tremor from her.

Overhead the light flicked off and then on again.

He felt Raina pull away. Her lips were swollen and curved into a grin.

"I can't believe this. My father is obviously letting me know it's time for me to come inside." She gave a half-embarrassed giggle before leaning forward to kiss Nolan sweetly, and all too swiftly, on his lips. "I'm sorry. I'd better go in before he comes out with a shotgun."

"You're kidding about the shotgun, right?"

"Of course I am, but he's very protective. Thank you again, Nolan. For everything."

"We'll see each other again," he stated firmly.

"Yes, I'd like that."

"Soon."

She nodded and laughed, her breath leaving a misty cloud in the air between them. "Yes, soon. How about Monday night? Dinner here, with JJ and me."

"I'd really like that," Nolan said. Even though every minute he'd spent with JJ so far reminded him all too much of all the things he'd missed out on with his own son, he enjoyed the little guy's company and his simple enthusiasm for life. It was a poignant reminder that he needed to inject some of that enthusiasm back into his own. And maybe, just maybe, he needed to consider telling Raina about the wife and son he'd lost, too. "Monday, then."

"Is six o'clock okay with you?"

"Perfect. I'll be there. Can I bring anything?"

"Just yourself is fine. See you then."

She turned, put her key in the lock and opened the front door. Then, with a small wave, she was gone from sight. Nolan shoved his hands in his pockets and jogged down the path to his car. He drove back to the hotel, his mind only half on what he was doing while the other half raced ahead and churned over a million different thoughts.

Sleep would be a long time coming tonight. He hadn't expected anything like this when he'd returned to Royal. Hadn't wanted it. He'd been meticulous about his relationships in the past and particularly about avoiding any emotional entanglements. But somehow this attraction had found him and lodged itself within the gaping hole of loneliness he had come to accept as being as much a part of him as every breath he took.

And it felt good. In fact, it felt better than good—it had brought back to life something he hadn't experienced in far too long—hope, which left him between a rock and a hard place when it came to the job he was really here to do. Did he compromise his professional integrity for this fledgling relationship or should he focus on the role he was here to complete and then walk away at the end of his time here in Royal, knowing he could be walking away from the best thing that had happened to him in a very long time?

Seven

Raina woke the next morning still locked firmly inside the bubble of joy that had enveloped her last night. Her father had taken one look at her face as she'd come into the sitting room and had shaken his head.

"I don't suppose there's any point in telling you to be careful," he'd growled from behind his beard.

She'd merely smiled and thanked her father for taking care of JJ. To his credit, he hadn't given her a lecture. Something he was inclined to do even though she was thirty years old and a mom herself. Instead he'd merely hugged her, pressed a kiss on the top of her head and, after telling her he loved her, made his way home to the trailer park.

Now Raina felt her heart skip with happiness as she made pancakes and bacon for breakfast. They needed to get some groceries this morning, her one day off, and she didn't want to waste any more time on the humdrum chore than was absolutely necessary. Today was a precious day with her boy and she wanted to make the most of it. Coaxing JJ out of his Spider-Man pajamas and into clothing suitable for the outdoors took a bit of doing but a promise to buy a new movie to add to his growing collection seemed to give him the impetus he needed.

She was in the process of buckling him into his car seat when she caught a dark movement from the corner of her eye. Raina quickly straightened up from what she was doing to see who it was who'd come up beside her. The second she did, her happy bubble burst.

Jeb.

"What are you doing here?" she demanded. "You promised you'd stay away."

"Where's my money, Raina?"

Raina quickly shoved the car door closed in an attempt to prevent JJ from hearing anything more from the man who'd done no more for him than provide a few strands of DNA.

"I don't owe you anything, Jeb Pickering. Now, please, get off my property and leave me alone."

"The boy's looking good. Growing fast. Does he ever ask about his daddy?"

"No, he doesn't," she responded flatly. God help her when JJ started asking those kinds of questions. How did you explain to your child that his father was no more than a lying no-good drifter plagued by gambling debts?

"I think it's time we met then."

"Are you threatening me?" Raina asked, her hands now clenched in tight fists of impotent rage.

Jeb had signed all the papers relinquishing his rights to any form of visitation with JJ two years ago but she should have known he'd renege on their agreement. His eyes narrowed speculatively as he looked at her car and then toward the house.

"You're doing pretty well these days, girl. I've been out

to that store of yours, too. Seems to me you could afford to help out the father of your only child, don't it?"

"You helped yourself plenty in the past. I'm done giving you money, Jeb."

Jeb's arm snaked out and his hand closed tight around Raina's wrist. She tugged against his grip, trying to free herself, but his fingers closed in a painful vice.

"Stop it. Let me go. You're hurting me," she said, pitching her voice low so there was no chance JJ could hear her. She didn't want to alarm him and from over Jeb's shoulder she could see his eyes were fixed on his mommy and the strange man talking to her.

"I need that money, honey." He gave her a crooked grin. "I'm in a bit of trouble. I need to get away. Maybe for good."

Did he mean it? She didn't dare believe him. If she showed one sign of weakness, just one, he'd exploit it. He turned back to the car and waved with his free hand toward JJ, who weakly waved back. Through the car window she could see JJ was getting upset and his muffled "Mommy?" tore at her heart.

"For good?" she pressed.

"Maybe."

"Maybe's not good enough for me, Jeb," Raina insisted, yanking her arm free. Her wrist throbbed with pain but she wouldn't look to see what damage he'd wrought. He'd done enough to her already without adding a few bruises to the list. "I don't want to ever see you again."

"Then give me my money."

His money? She stifled the urge to shove her hands hard at his chest and push him away. Give him a taste of his own medicine for a change. When had he ever had any money by honest means? She certainly couldn't remember.

"I'm mortgaged to my eyeballs with the house and I have rent to meet on my business. Pretty much everything else I have is tied up in inventory now. I don't have a lot to spare, Jeb."

"Whatever you can give me, then. And it had better be soon."

There was an urgency to his voice. An underlying thread of something he wasn't telling her, not to mention a significant threat in his tone.

"Jeb, what have you gotten yourself into now?" she sighed.

"Look, I owe a guy some cash is all. I want to clear my debts and make a fresh start."

How many times had she heard him say that? So many that she'd stopped believing him a long time ago. And look at him now. He was jittery and unkempt. Even at his worst he'd never looked this bad before. Was it really just owing money or had he gotten involved in something worse? Whatever it was, she needed to get him away from JJ as quickly as she could.

"I'll see what I can do," Raina said in defeat.

She knew it was just pandering to his dependence on her, but right now she didn't see any other way of getting rid of him. She knew she didn't have the kind of money he expected but he'd just have to make do with the couple of thousand dollars she'd put aside for emergencies when she had a chance to withdraw it from the bank. Just the thought of leaving her account empty again made her stomach burn with anxiety. All she'd ever wanted was to be able to provide her son with the same security her father had provided her—love, combined with a roof over his head, food in his belly and a warm bed at night. Was that too much to ask?

"Thanks, Rai."

"How will I be able to reach you?" The number on the mobile phone he'd been using was blocked.

"I'll be in touch."

And with that, he flipped up the collar of his jacket and began to walk away. Was it her imagination, or was he darting furtive glances left and right as he walked up the street—almost as if he expected someone to jump out of the bushes at him at any moment. She shook her head. What on earth had he got himself into, now?

She hurried to the car and, after giving JJ a shaky smile through the window, got into the driver's seat.

"Bad man, Mommy," JJ pronounced from the back-seat with all the solemnity of a frightened three-year-old.

She didn't know what to say. Jeb wasn't all bad, just misguided and selfish. She settled for an indistinct murmur as she fastened her seat belt and put her key in the ignition.

"I don' like bad man. I like No'an," JJ continued.

Raina smiled at her little boy in the rearview mirror. "I like Nolan, too, honey bun. C'mon, let's go get our groceries and then the rest of the day is just for you and me."

"Yay," he crowed in happiness, his fear already forgotten.

The next morning Raina was putting out her signs at Priceless and trying to quell her excitement about the night ahead. She'd woken earlier than usual, and with an energy she could only put down to looking forward to seeing Nolan again. Even the shadow of Jeb's visit yesterday and his demands, coupled with the bruises he'd left on her wrist as a reminder, couldn't overshadow her joy in planning their dinner tonight. She'd serve lasagna with garlic bread and salad. Simple fare, and filling and, best of all, easy to prepare ahead of time so she didn't have to get herself all flustered before Nolan arrived.

As she straightened and surveyed the parking lot, she spied Mellie Winslow walking toward her. She gave the other woman a wave.

"Good morning!" she called as Mellie drew closer. "It's a lovely clear day, isn't it?"

"It is," Mellie agreed.

Her landlady looked cute today in a forest-green coat that emphasized her clear green eyes and gorgeous soft red hair. Raina envied Melanie her curls.

"Would you like to stop in for a cup of coffee?" Raina asked. "I've just put a pot on."

"I'd love that, thank you."

Mellie pulled off her gloves and shrugged out of her coat as they entered Raina's tiny lunch room. She shoved the gloves inside her coat pocket and hung the garment on one of the ornately curved brass hooks on the rack by the door.

"I love this," she said, gesturing to the rack. "And I especially love that it has an umbrella stand, as well. Is it yours or is it for sale?"

"Everything here is for sale, except me," Raina laughed in response.

"What kind of wood is it?"

"Oak. You see a lot of replicas these days, but this is the real deal."

"Hmm, maybe I should get it for Case for Christmas."

"Things are that serious?" Raina asked.

In response, Mellie thrust out her left hand, exposing a beautiful ring on her engagement finger. The large square-cut emerald gleamed under the light and Raina gasped in surprise.

"Oh, I'd say that looks very serious. Congratulations!"

"Thanks, it was all rather complicated, what with everything that went on last month, but I'm so happy."

And she looked happy, too. There was a glow about her that Raina hadn't seen before. She tried to ignore the tug of envy that plucked at her along with a wish that her own life could have followed a more traditional path. But she quickly shoved it away. Traditional or not, her life was what it was and without the choices she'd made—both good and bad—she wouldn't have JJ or be where she was now, doing something she loved.

Mellie sat down at the small table in the center of the room. "I'm glad I have a chance to talk to you today. I just wanted to let you know that I'm definitely not letting the Courtyard go. It's not for sale. Not now, not ever."

Raina felt a swell of relief flood through her. "You're serious? Everything's going to be okay?"

She'd heard, along with everyone else in town, about Homer Winslow's financial issues and how he'd put Winslow Properties into financial jeopardy. It had only served to increase her anxiety about her position here.

Mellie nodded. "Definitely. Even if Winslow Properties' resources won't stretch far enough, and I believe that with some restructuring they should, Case has assured me that he will back us financially if need be."

Raina didn't quite know what to say. She filled two coffee mugs, put them on the table with shaking hands and sank into her chair. This was incredible news.

"I'm sure you know how much this means to me, Mellie. Thank you for telling me now. It's the best Christmas present I could have imagined."

"I thought it best to give you peace of mind as soon as I knew, and I wanted to do it myself. I know how much it means to you to be here and how hard you've worked."

"But what about Samson Oil? Are they going to back off now? Seems they've been busy buying up everything that's for sale around Royal and some of what's not."

Mellie nodded her head. "Yeah, I know. It certainly looks that way, doesn't it?"

"And why? Everyone here knows the land isn't worth squat for oil, and with the drought even ranching isn't so viable. What are they thinking? Do you know who is behind it all?"

"No, all I know is that their attorney, Nolan Dane, is one stubborn guy. Every time we say no to selling, he bounces straight back with another offer. Honestly, if I hadn't taken over from Dad, Winslow Properties' portfolio would be looking very slim indeed."

Raina gasped out loud and reeled at the name that had come from Mellie's mouth. *Nolan Dane?* A giant fist clutched at her chest and squeezed tight, making it nearly impossible to draw breath.

"Raina? Are you okay?"

"I'm fine," she replied, feeling anything but. She forced herself to take a breath, drawing it all the way in before letting it out again. "A-are you sure Nolan Dane is their attorney?"

"He's certainly the person we've been dealing with. And I've heard from a few of the stall holders and retailers here that he's been sniffing around, asking all sorts of questions about the operation and about Winslow Properties. He won't have any excuse to come out here now though. Our lawyers sent him a message today categorically stating that the Courtyard is not, and never will be, for sale. At least not as long as I'm running things," Mellie confirmed before taking a long sip of her coffee. "Ah, this is good—just what I needed. I have a meeting with our board in—" she glanced at her watch "—oh, heck, twenty minutes. I'd better fly! Thanks for the coffee. I'll see myself out."

Raina remained glued to her chair in shock as Mellie put her mug in the sink, grabbed her coat and headed out of the store. Nolan was acting for Samson Oil? Did that mean that everything he'd done had been in the pursuit of getting an edge on Winslow Properties and buying the Courtyard?

She felt sick as she remembered how open she'd been about her situation. About how much all this meant to her here, to be able to start up her business again after the hellish year she'd had. And all the time he'd been planning to rip it all out from under her. Pressure built up inside her chest, growing bigger and more painful until a sob broke free. She clapped a hand over her mouth in a futile attempt to hold back the grief she felt at Nolan's betrayal.

She'd really thought he liked her—and JJ. And all along he'd simply been using them both. This hurt far worse than anything Jeb had done. He'd made empty promises, sure, but never anything like this.

Raina tipped her head back and stared at the ceiling of the old barn, willing the burning in her eyes to stop before the tears that already blinded her began to fall. Man, she could pick 'em, couldn't she? Did she have some sign over her head, visible only to losers and liars that said, "Soft touch and fool"?

After Jeb she'd sworn never again. She wouldn't make the same mistakes—not when she had JJ to consider. She'd guarded herself and her privacy, spurning male attention on the occasions it had been offered, making it clear that her son and her business were her sole priorities. Until Nolan.

He'd managed to charm his way past her barriers, slowly and gently peeling them away and exposing her vulnerability. It had been more than just the physical attraction she'd felt toward him; there'd been an emotional connection there, too. It had been so tangible that she would have sworn he felt the same way. Man, had he ever taken her for a ride.

Just went to show what an appalling judge of character she was after all. Raina dashed away an errant tear from her cheek. No. There'd be no more tears over men whose sole purpose in life was to break her heart—or worse, her hope for the future. She was better than that and she deserved better than that, too.

Raina pushed herself up onto her feet and put her mug

in the sink alongside Mellie's. She was grateful the woman had come to see her today to tell her the news. What if it had been tomorrow, or even next week? Heck, she had invited Nolan to her house for dinner with her and JJ, and who knows where that might have led given the heat of their kiss on Saturday night?

She pressed trembling fingers to her lips. It took very little stretch of her imagination to relive the pressure of his lips on hers. To remember the taste of him, the strength of his arms around her and how safe and protected he had made her feel. And that hadn't been all. He'd wanted her, she'd felt it in the hard lines of his body, and to her shame she'd wanted him back with all the heat and hunger she'd ignored for too long.

Damn him for doing this to her. For sliding under her skin and for making her want things she had no right wanting.

With a sound of disgust, Raina reached for her bag and snatched her cell phone. She pulled up Nolan's number and viciously tapped the call button on the screen. He wasn't welcome at her house anymore, let alone anywhere near her son. She had to tell him tonight was off. Tonight and every other night in the future.

Eight

Nolan pulled up outside Raina's house and sighed. Today had been tough. They'd closed on several private deals today. While on the one hand he'd known that, under the guise of Samson Oil, Rafiq was offering many people a way out of a situation that had become untenable since the tornado—people who'd been underinsured and overmortgaged and living hand-to-mouth since the disaster—he also knew he was taking them from a way of life that had been in their families for generations.

It had taken a toll—seeing relief tempered with failure, hope for a new start tempered with sorrow at leaving behind the past. These were families and people whose kids had gone to school alongside him here in Royal. And now they were scattering to the winds, some leaving Royal altogether and others settling for a life they'd never believed they'd live in one of the new suburbs. Sure, there were those who'd ecstatically accepted Rafiq's money and were eager to move forward with new lives. But the majority were people whose pride had been beaten down by so much loss that they had no fight left in them. It had been there in every hollow-eyed stare, every line of strain on their faces.

The shining light in his day today had been the knowledge that he'd see Raina again. His body had been buzzing with suppressed energy ever since Saturday night, and he'd realized that for the first time since Carole's and Bennett's deaths, he'd begun to be able to think about them without the sharp stab of pain that always accompanied the memories. Instead, he saw two new faces. Faces that he knew were fast becoming equally special to him.

Nolan got out of the SUV, hit the autolock and reached into his jacket pocket for his mobile phone before remembering he'd forgotten to charge it last night and that he'd heard the warning beeps before it shut down earlier today. It had been a blessing in disguise, he'd thought at the time, that he hadn't had to deal with the text messages and emails while he'd dotted all the *i*'s and crossed all the *t*'s on each individual contract that signaled the end of life as many people had known it. He strode up the front path—eager now to rid himself of the clinging mental residue of the day.

He'd no sooner knocked when the door was flung open. He was assailed by two things. JJ's effusive greeting, as the little boy almost knocked him off his feet with a powerful hug around his legs, and the sound of Raina's stern admonition to let her get the door. Nolan reached down and tousled JJ's mop of dark hair. An unexpected surge of tenderness swelled inside him as JJ lifted his happy little face.

"Hi, No'an."

This was what a man's life should be filled with. Moments like this that were precious and memorable for their simplicity and purity. This was what he'd been missing for far too long.

"Hey, JJ. How're you doing?"

"Good!" The little boy disengaged from Nolan's legs and began hopping from one foot to the other. "We're having lasagna for dinner. Yum!"

"JJ, let me talk to Mr. Dane," Raina interrupted, coming up behind JJ and putting a hand on his shoulder to restrain him.

Nolan's senses went on full alert. He was back to being Mr. Dane? Something was very wrong. The chill that surrounded Raina cut through JJ's excitement and the boy stilled as he looked from his mommy to Nolan in confusion.

"Do you want money from my mommy, too?" JJ asked.

Raina's eyes flared wide at her son's words, and Nolan saw the shock that streaked across her face.

"Hush, JJ. Mr. Dane doesn't want anything from me."

Oh, she was very wrong there, he thought, but he didn't miss the silent message in her words or her tone. Nolan squatted down to JJ's level and gave the little guy a reassuring smile.

"No, I don't want money from your mommy."

"You sure?"

Nolan nodded. "Of course I'm sure."

"Bad man hurt mommy."

Nolan heard Raina's gasp of shock. "JJ, don't be telling stories."

"But it true," the little boy protested.

Nolan thought it a good time to interrupt before the atmosphere got any more difficult than it was already. "Hey, JJ, look at me. I would never hurt your mommy. I promise. Okay, champ?"

JJ nodded slowly and Nolan rose to his full height again. As he did, he caught a glimpse of Raina's arm. She'd pushed the sleeves of her long-sleeved T-shirt halfway up her forearm and there was no mistaking the livid bruising around her wrist. The second she was aware he'd noticed, she pulled the sleeves down but it was too late now. He couldn't unsee what was there and he wasn't a fool. He knew fingermarks when he saw them. He'd seen marks like that, and worse, often enough when he was working alongside his father at his family law practice.

"You okay?"

Nolan chose his words carefully, even though he wished he had the right to demand who the hell had dared to lay a hand on her—and then hunt them down for some payback. Before she could answer him, though, JJ jumped up and down and started to speak.

"No'an! No'an! I'm gonna be Spider-Man at the C'istmas show!"

"Settle down, JJ," Raina admonished her son. "What he means is he's been chosen to play one of the shepherds at his day care's Christmas pageant this year."

"Yeah!" JJ interrupted again, unable to contain his excitement. "Can you come, No'an?"

"I'm sure Mr. Dane will be far too busy to attend the pageant, JJ."

Raina gave Nolan a fierce look, warning him not to contradict her. In response he squatted back down to JJ's level and put one hand on the little boy's shoulder.

"I'm sorry, JJ. Your mom is right. I'm working that night."

"I hate work!" JJ shouted, before turning tail and running down the hall toward his room.

"You mind telling me what that was about?" Nolan asked as he rose again to his full height and met Raina's chilling blue gaze full-on.

From the second he'd arrived, he'd felt a cold vibe coming from Raina that was at complete odds with the way they'd parted last time they'd been together. What the hell had gone wrong between then and now? He could have sworn that they were both heading in the same direction and now it seemed that she was slamming on the brakes. Did it have something to do with those marks on her wrist?

Again Nolan felt the slow burn of anger flicker inside at the fact that anyone had dared to lay a hand on Raina. But it was nothing compared to the irritation he felt at being manipulated into letting JJ down just now.

Raina lifted her chin and crossed her arms in front of her. Her body language was clear. She was shutting him out in more ways than one.

"Sure," she said abruptly. "I don't mind telling you. I *know* why you're here."

For a split second he was confused and then it dawned on him. She'd found out about his connection to Samson Oil. "I'm guessing it's not because of your invitation to dinner, right?"

"Don't you dare try to make a joke of it. You used me."

Nolan couldn't refute her accusation. "I'm sorry about that. Believe me, I—"

"Believe you?" she interrupted with an incredulous expression on her face. "No way. Not ever. You may have missed this in Lawyer 101, Mr. Dane, but where I come from belief comes along with trust, and I don't trust you anymore. Not now. Not after what you've been doing."

"Raina! Please? Listen to me."

"No way. Do you even understand what you were doing to me? You were working to take away my sole security. If I can't run my business at the Courtyard, JJ and I will lose everything I've worked to provide for us—we're barely making ends meet now as it is. My son deserves a bright future, one that only I can give him because God knows there's no one else there for him. By doing what you were doing, attempting to buy out that land, you threatened everything I hold dear. So, no, I won't listen to you. Not now and not ever again. Get out of my house. I don't want to ever see you here again."

Her voice broke and there were tears in her eyes as she finished her impassioned speech.

"Look, Raina, you have to let me explain—"

"The time for explanations was when you met me. Before you started pumping me for information about the Courtyard and about Royal. Not now."

The fact that she was totally right made her scorn no less galling or painful.

"Can I at least say bye to JJ?"

"No, you may not."

Raina stepped toward the front door and hauled it open. The chill air outside rushed in, enveloping them both in its icy swirl. He stared at Raina's face for a moment, but her expression remained implacable. He knew he had to pick his battles. This was definitely not the time to press her.

Silent, he passed her and went out the door. Before his feet had even struck the paved path to the road, he heard the door slam resoundingly behind him. He didn't look back, not even when he climbed into the SUV and pulled away from the curb.

On the drive back to his hotel and during a lonely dinner, he couldn't stop thinking about those bruises Raina had so swiftly hidden and who might have been responsible for them. The very idea that someone had felt they had the right to harm her like that made his blood boil and roused every protective instinct in him. Who was the bad man JJ had referred to and what was he to Raina? Was it the ex she'd said so little about? Nolan was suddenly reminded of the shadowy figure he'd seen the other night. Was it him? The thought left a sour taste in his mouth and made him determined to get to the root of what had happened to her, one way or another.

Nine

Raina was still bristling mad about Nolan's lies two days later. It had been tough breaking it to JJ that Nolan wouldn't be staying for dinner. He'd gone to bed that night grumpy and woken yesterday morning in the same state. It seemed her little guy could hold a grudge, and he laid the blame for his new idol not being around very firmly at her feet. She could only hope that the rehearsals for the pageant would distract him from his disappointment.

She thanked her lucky stars that she hadn't had time to let things go any further with Nolan than they already had. One kiss, that's all it had been—*but what a kiss*, her subconscious reminded her uncomfortably. She shoved the thought to the back of her mind and tried to focus on her preparations for the mosaic class she had scheduled tonight. Her group had enjoyed getting started on their mirror frames last week and she had no doubt that a few of them would finish gluing their pieces tonight and be ready to grout them.

She felt another flush of anger at Nolan as she remembered how his actions, if successful, would have taken all of this away from her. She hadn't been kidding when she'd told him on that first night that the Courtyard had become a symbol of hope for so many people. But then hope was obviously a cheap commodity for a man like him, along with belief and trust.

No matter how angry she was, though, she couldn't help but feel a numbing sense of loss. Her attraction to him had come out of the blue, startling her with its intensity. "Hormones, just hormones," she growled under her breath as she did her final checks around the room. Obviously she'd never learned her lesson about the kind of guy she should be attracted to. In the future, if there was any spark at all, she'd take it as a warning and then run a mile in the opposite direction. Fast.

"Hi, Raina!"

She looked up and greeted her students as they came in through the workroom's exterior door. In no time the workbenches were full. She'd had to restrict numbers on this class, as well as her Thursday night stained-glass classes purely because people needed to be able to spread their tools and supplies out while working. It was something she needed to consider when she came up with costing out her next cycle of classes in the New Year. While this first cycle had been a short one, geared mainly toward making gifts in time for Christmas, for her to maximize earnings and rebuild that little nest egg she'd had to withdraw for Jeb, she might need to have two evenings with large classes focused on smaller crafts and only one evening devoted to the larger projects.

"Okay, ladies," she said once everyone was there. "You all know where your projects are stored. I've already set out all your tools and the pots of glue and scrapers, so let's get to it!"

The noise in the workroom steadily built and conversation began to flow between the women. As Raina did her rounds, checking to make sure that everyone had what she needed and offering advice where necessary, she was startled to overhear Nolan's name being mentioned. She hated eavesdroppers but in this case she couldn't help it; she hovered near the women talking about him.

"I have to say it was a surprise to see him back in town," one of the older women said. "Apparently even his own mother didn't know he was coming back."

"Do you know why he's here? I know he's not staying with his parents. They're neighbors of mine and I've barely even seen Nolan there," replied another.

Raina interrupted them both. "He's with Samson Oil. He's the legal counsel for their land grabbing."

Her words were laced with bitterness and more than one pair of eyes swiveled to watch her as she spoke.

"Really? Oh, that's a pity. He was such a nice boy and he grew up into a fine young man."

Raina was hard pressed not to snort at the woman's remark. Fine? Sure, physically maybe. Certainly not as far as his integrity went.

The woman continued. "It was such a shame about his wife and son. A thing like that is bound to change a man. Makes him harder."

A general murmur of assent rose around her and, as if by silent mutual agreement, the women turned their conversation in a different direction. Numbing shock overwhelmed Raina, holding her paralyzed in its grip. Buzzing filled her ears. She felt herself sway a little, as if she was losing her balance, and she put out a hand to a chair to steady herself. Breathe, she told herself. Breathe. After a few seconds, she felt as if she was regaining control. Had anyone noticed how she'd completely zoned out?

She looked around the workroom. Apparently not. Her

students seemed intent on their tasks and were happily chatting among themselves while they worked. Raina drew in another breath and walked slowly to the back of the workroom where she leaned against the wall. The buzzing in her ears began to subside, but as it did, questions began circling in her mind.

A wife and son?

Nolan had never so much as mentioned his parents, let alone anyone else. Sure, he'd made vague reference to visiting family in town, but that had been it. So who was she, this wife of his? Could she have been a customer of hers, or maybe Raina had passed her in the street somewhere? And his son—how old was he?

Suddenly it all became very clear to her why Nolan was so good with her little boy. Why he hadn't been grossed out by JJ's snotty nose on the day they'd met. Why he'd so competently cleaned JJ's hands at the dinner table that night. Why he'd so easily fallen into conversation with JJ about his Spider-Man obsession.

So, were he and his wife amicably separated or bitterly estranged? Which one was it? The latter would certainly explain him staying away from Royal for so long and probably would also explain him not bringing them up in conversation. Raina clenched her hands into tight fists of frustration, digging, her fingernails into her palms. She welcomed the pain. It was a distraction from the pain of the betrayal she'd felt on learning he was working for Samson Oil—and realizing she'd let herself begin to fall for him. Hard. Physical pain she could deal with. It healed. It was the emotional pain and the toll it took that were harder to recover from.

A new thought bloomed in Raina's mind. Maybe his wife had cheated on him. Would that have been the catalyst that sent Nolan to another state? Had he sought to escape the pain of a relationship breakdown by moving away? Was that why he'd never said anything to her about a wife and child?

Whatever his circumstances, no matter whether they were justified or not, nothing excused the way he'd sought her out under false pretenses. He'd deceived her about the Courtyard. Why wouldn't he do the same about a wife and child, too? It wasn't her problem. Not anymore. She'd sent him on his way and it was highly unlikely their paths would cross again.

Nolan was glad of the excuse to quit Royal, even if it was for only one day to meet with his boss in Holloway. He'd known coming back to Royal would be tough, would force him to face a lot of his personal demons, but he hadn't expected, or wanted, to find someone to whom he was so strongly attracted.

He struck the steering wheel with the heel of his palm and cursed aloud in the cabin of the SUV. How could he have handled things differently with Raina? No matter how many times he examined everything they'd said and done since he'd met her, he still couldn't see anywhere he could have prevented what happened. Short of telling her exactly why he was in Royal on the day he'd introduced himself at the Courtyard, of course. And he'd just bet how well that would have gone down.

Besides, the confidentiality clause in his contract with Rafiq prevented him from disclosing Samson Oil's business with anyone other than the party with whom he was negotiating. His hands had been tied.

Even though he'd rationalized everything, he still couldn't erase the look on Raina's face when she'd told him to get out of her house. He'd dealt with a lot of angry people in his time, but never before had there been such a palpable level of anguish beneath the anger. It had tortured him to know he'd put that look on her face.

He knew he should have stepped away the moment he'd recognized the fierce attraction he'd felt toward her. How often had he told himself that she was everything he *wasn't* looking for?

A speed limit sign shot by his window and Nolan realized that he'd been so lost in his thoughts that he'd lost track of what he was doing. He eased off the accelerator and focused on his surroundings. He was almost there. As much as he wasn't looking forward to imparting the news to Rafe that the Courtyard was completely off the table, it would at least some respite from constantly thinking about Raina.

The entrance to the Holloway Inn wasn't what Nolan had expected. From the moment he pulled up outside, he wondered if somewhere along the line he hadn't somehow traveled thousands of miles to England. The white stucco walls, with dark wooden battens, reminded him very much of a Tudor inn he and Carole had stayed in outside London during their honeymoon, although, he noted as he entered the lobby, that's where the similarities ended. There'd be no ducking to clear doorways here. He walked up to the reception desk and smiled at the receptionist.

"Good morning. Nolan Dane to see Mr. Ben Samson," he said, using the name Rafe had assumed while the property negotiations were ongoing.

"Welcome to the Holloway Inn, Mr. Dane. Mr. Samson is waiting for you in his suite."

The young woman smiled and gave him concise directions to the suite, and Nolan located the rooms without any trouble. His knock was quickly answered by Rafe himself. The fact his boss was alone was unusual but not entirely unexpected given how secretive he'd been about his involvement with Samson Oil from the outset.

"Good morning," Rafe said, shaking Nolan's hand and gesturing for him to enter. "Knowing how punctual you always are, I took the liberty of ordering coffee already. Help yourself."

"Thank you."

Nolan stepped inside, his feet sinking into the plush carpeting. He looked around the suite. It was no more and no less than he'd come to expect. The main living room was spacious and well lit. A fifty-inch flat-screen television took pride of place on one wall and a number of oversize leather sofas and chairs were grouped around it. Across the room, a dining table, large enough to comfortably seat twelve, was covered in what looked like a map of Royal and several stacks of papers.

He gave Rafe a look. His boss was as immaculately turned out as ever but there were shadows under his eyes.

"Hard night?" he asked, as he poured himself a coffee and helped himself to a Danish pastry from the white-linen-draped room-service cart.

"I met someone."

Rafe's terse response was characteristic of the man himself, but the second he reached for the cuff of his sleeve and gave it a tug, Nolan knew there was a great deal of meaning behind those three words. Rafe was a controlled man and generally very reserved. In fact, the first time Nolan had met him he'd been a little unnerved by the guy's intensity until he learned to appreciate the keen intelligence and mind for business that lay behind it. But he had his familiar mannerisms, as well, and Nolan knew this one—something had made Rafiq uncomfortable. Something… or someone.

"A woman?" Nolan pressed before taking a sip of his coffee.

"Of course a woman," Rafe laughed. "An intriguing and beautiful one at that."

"Have I met her before?"

"I only met her myself last night."

For a second Rafe's eyes got a faraway look, as if he was remembering something intensely personal.

In all the time Nolan had worked for his boss, he'd never known the man to indulge in anything as impulsive as a one-night stand. He wouldn't mind meeting the woman who'd managed to put that look in his boss's eye.

"She must have been something else, huh?" he probed.

"Yes, she certainly was." Rafe appeared to shake off whatever memory had gripped him and gathered himself together. "But that's in the past. We're not here to discuss my after-hours activities. Come, sit at the table. Bring me up to date. What's happening with Winslow Properties?"

Shaking his head, Nolan settled into a chair while Rafiq took one opposite. "No movement there at all. We don't stand a chance under the new management. It's like arguing with a wooden Indian."

Rafe raised one dark brow and Nolan waved a hand in response.

"Local terminology," he explained. "Basically, pressing forward with Winslow Properties is a waste of time. They're not selling."

Rafe didn't look pleased. "You're certain?"

"Absolutely."

To his credit Rafe accepted the news with better grace than Nolan had anticipated. Perhaps he realized that sometimes it was better to step away. Rafe pushed a folder toward Nolan.

"Let's move on these, then."

Nolan lifted the folder from the table and opened it. He ran his eye down the list on the first sheet. Not entirely surprising, he thought, and from what he'd seen and heard in Royal already, he had no doubt they'd manage to acquire these properties without too much hassle. His eye stopped on the name of one ranch, though, and a frisson of disquiet tickled at the back of his mind.

"All of these?" Nolan asked, looking up from the documents.

Not a man to waste words, Rafe merely nodded.

"This one—the Wild Aces ranch—what do you want with that?"

Again Rafe raised one brow. "I don't pay you to ask questions."

Nolan's sense of unease increased. He'd done plenty of research both before he returned to Royal and since he'd been there. He knew who was vulnerable and he knew who'd had enough hardship to be coaxed off their land and sent to newer pastures. And he knew, without a doubt, that with the right amount of coercion, the owners of the Wild Aces would in all likelihood accept a reasonable offer for their land.

"That's true," Nolan conceded. "But if I'm to perform my role properly, I need to know the background."

Rafe met Nolan's gaze full-on, not giving an inch and continuing to say nothing. Eventually Rafe made a sound of annoyance and leaned forward, placing his elbows on the table between them and steepling his fingers.

"Why is it so important to you all of a sudden to know why? It hasn't been an issue for you up until now."

"I'm your boots-on-the-ground man. As such, I'm a lot closer to the people of Royal."

"Which is exactly why I appointed you to this role. You grew up there. You know how best to attain my goals."

"But I don't know why you're doing this. People are already asking questions. Questions I can't answer."

"And you don't have to."

"No, that's true. But my parents still live there. My father still practices there. I would hate there to be any fallout for them."

"There will be no fallout. Are we not helping people by relieving them of useless assets? Offering them good money and a fresh start before they're forced to move on when their banks foreclose?"

"We are. But if the assets are so useless, why do you want them so badly?"

Rafe said nothing.

"If I'm to continue to act on your behalf I need to know."

Rafe leaned back in his chair again. "A threat, Nolan?"

"No, a statement of fact. Take Wild Aces for example. Most of that land is leased out to another operation, the McCallums', because their stored water supply was compromised after the tornado and with the drought they haven't been able to replenish their water stock. To keep their herds at optimum levels, they're leasing this land here." He stabbed a finger at the map on the table. "If your offer to purchase the land is accepted by the owners, do you intend to continue with the lease already in place?"

"My plans are mine alone. I don't disclose my reasons." Rafe paused before adding, "To anyone."

Nolan carefully closed the folder in his hands and, equally carefully, placed it on the table. "Then I cannot continue to work for you."

"You're serious?"

"Never more so. I will not represent Samson Oil unless I have a better understanding of what your aims are in relation to the land acquisitions. Like I said, people are beginning to ask questions and I have a few of my own."

"It is no one's business but mine."

There were times when Rafe's privileged background shone through—times like this when he held himself above others and believed his will was law. That might be the case back in Al Qunfudhah, his homeland, but the last time Nolan checked it certainly wasn't that way in Texas.

"Then I'm sorry, but I'm forced to resign. Effective immediately."

"We have a contract, Nolan," Rafe reminded him. "You are bound to honor that, are you not?"

"A contract I drew up," Nolan said on a sigh. "And under the terms of the exit clause, I believe you'll discover that I'm within my rights to do this. I'm sorry, Rafe. I've always liked you and admired your business acumen, but I can no longer continue to work for you. Not under these circumstances. I hope we can still be friends."

He rose and extended his hand. Rafe hesitated a moment before also getting to his feet and clasping Nolan's hand in return.

"I, too, am sorry it has come to this. Can I ask you one thing?"

"What's that?"

"Why? You were happy to continue working under my instructions before. What changed?"

Nolan gave Rafe a bitter smile. "I met someone."

Ten

Nolan drove away from Holloway with a sense of lightness he hadn't felt in a very long time. It was as if walking away from his contract with Rafiq had freed him from an invisible cell. It wasn't that he hadn't enjoyed his work, because he had. He'd always loved the cut and thrust of law, and property law had brought its own challenges to keep him sharp. But he'd never truly stopped to consider the peripheral effect of what he was doing. Not until he'd met Raina.

Would she allow him back into her life? He wanted to tell her he was no longer acting for Samson Oil, but after the way they'd parted, he seriously doubted that he could just pull up to her front door and expect her to see him.

He activated the hands-free calling in his car and spoke her name. Through the speaker he heard the phone at the other end begin to ring.

Pick up, he silently willed her. *Pick up*. But after a few short rings, the call was diverted to voice mail. He was disappointed but not surprised. In fact, he wouldn't have put it past her to have blocked his number altogether.

Nolan left a message anyway, asking her to please call him when she had a chance. As he ended the call he wondered whether she would call him back. Maybe she'd simply delete his message without listening to it. Well, he'd call her back again. Not too soon, of course. Even he respected that he'd done a serious amount of damage when it came to her trust in him. He had a lot of work to do before he won it back.

At a bit of a loose end, Nolan decided to drop in on his parents. Maybe his dad needed some wood chopped. He sure hoped so, because he suddenly had a burning urge to work off some energy and wood chopping felt like just the chore for it.

When he got to his parents' house, he sat in the car a moment and stared at the home where he'd grown up. He had so many memories from when he was a kid and more from when he'd reached his teens. He still remembered, clear as day, the first time he'd brought Carole over to meet his mom and dad. He and Carole had been in their last year of high school, each with the same goal for their future. Even then they'd hoped to build that future together.

Would he have changed anything if he could? He'd known Carole for what felt like forever, but he still remembered the day when he'd seen her and everything had changed. It was as if a switch had been thrown in his mind and from that moment forward he'd known she was the one for him. It turned out that he'd been a little slow on the uptake. She'd decided long before that she wanted him, too, and she'd waited patiently, biding her time until he woke up to the fact that they'd been made for one another.

Strange how he could think about her now without it hurting. Yes, he still missed her and he probably always would, but he could also remember the good times—the fun times before life got so frenetic and busy and pressured and everything fell apart. Before their son had died and she'd taken her own life in a cruel combination of guilt and grief and hopelessness.

A movement on the front porch of his parents' house dragged Nolan from his reveries. His dad—standing there in the cold, quite happy to wait until his son was ready to get out of the car in which he'd been sitting for, he now realized, upward of twenty minutes while his thoughts wandered.

Nolan finally got out of the SUV and walked up the front path. His dad greeted him with a hug. Although Nolan was a grown man, he still took succor from his father's grasp, from the warmth and unconditional love.

"Everything okay, son?" Howard Dane asked him.

Nolan met his father's brown eyes, so like his own, and smiled. "Yeah, Dad. Everything's okay."

His father gave him a nod. "Your mother was worried when she saw you parked out front. You know what she's like."

"I was thinking. About Carole and Bennett."

His father's eyes dulled with unspoken pain. "Thought as much. It's why we left you to it."

"So," Nolan said, clapping his father on the back as they turned and walked toward the front door. "Got any wood that needs chopping?"

His father laughed. "In that suit? I don't think so."

"Maybe you can loan me something to wear."

Howard Dane eyed him up and down. "Maybe I can. You look like a stuffed shirt, son."

"Not anymore, Dad. Not anymore."

Nolan's back and shoulders ached like he couldn't remember and the blisters on the palms of his hands reminded him he'd grown soft during his time in California.

It had been good to do some manual labor. It gave him plenty of time for thinking. His mom had brought out some lunch for him and his dad, who was busy stacking the firewood as Nolan split the logs. Once they were done and came inside, Nolan looked across the sitting room and saw the new gas fireplace installed where the old open fire had once been. He turned and looked at his father.

"You didn't tell me you'd gotten rid of the old fireplace."

His father shrugged. "Sometimes a man just has to chop wood."

Nolan gave his father a look. "Why'd you have it removed?"

"Debris from the tornado damaged the old chimney. We decided to remove the whole thing, fireplace and all."

"You might have told me." Nolan laughed.

His dad shrugged again. "It's no bother. Besides, the wood should come in handy come summer. Your mother made me buy one of those fancy brazier things for the back patio. We'll use it for that."

Nolan laughed again. This was what he'd missed living so far away. His father's quiet acceptance and solid support. It didn't mean he was a pushover. No sirree. In fact, Howard Dane was known through several counties as a tough lawyer who could be relied on to stand up for his clients.

Nolan's mother came through from the kitchen.

"Are you staying for dinner?" she asked, wiping her hands dry on a tea towel.

"I'd like that if you have room for me," he said with a wink that he knew would earn an eye roll in response. He wasn't disappointed.

"Go get cleaned up and I'll see if we can squeeze you in at the table," his mother teased, flicking the tea towel in his direction.

Over dinner, Nolan told his parents about his decision to quit Samson Oil.

"So what are you going to do now?" his mom asked with a worried frown on her still-pretty face.

"I haven't given it a lot of thought yet, Mom. I just made the decision today."

"But it's not like you not to have a plan beforehand. What on earth prompted you to do such a thing?"

Nolan eyed both his parents before answering. "I didn't feel comfortable with it anymore. Yes, I know we were doing a lot of good, giving people a way out they didn't have before. But somewhere along the line, others would get hurt and I figure Royal's seen enough hurt already. I just couldn't do it anymore."

His father narrowed his eyes at him and Nolan shifted in his seat. Howard was a man of few words but when he chose them, you generally listened.

"What changed?"

Not, why did *you* change, Nolan observed of his father's question. It made him think carefully about his response.

"I guess it mattered to me more."

His father continued to look at him in much the same way he had back when Nolan was a kid and had done something wrong. Howard knew that silence was a very effective weapon.

"I met someone. Someone who reminded me of what it's like to feel." Nolan heard his mother's gasp of surprise, but he kept going. "Someone who potentially was going to be put at a major disadvantage both financially and emotionally if things had continued the way they were. Regrettably, I withheld information from her. I abused her trust. I don't like the man who did that and I don't want to be that person anymore."

"Good to hear, son. So who do you want to be now?" Howard said quietly.

"The man who makes things right again."

Nolan watched his father take a sip of his wine and set the glass carefully back down on his mother's crisp white linen tablecloth.

His father sighed and looked up at him again. "And if you can't?"

Nolan shook his head. Failure wasn't an option. He wouldn't be his father's son if it was. "I will succeed. It won't be easy, but I'll get there."

"Does she know about your old life here?"

"No, and I need to address that. She deserves to hear it from me. It's just…not easy talking about them."

"You'll find the right time, son, and the right words," his father said encouragingly.

"Does this mean you're moving back to Royal for good?" his mom asked while she gathered up the plates from the table.

"I hope so," Nolan answered. "No, I know so. LA isn't the right place for me. Not anymore. It was a good place to run to. It let me grieve at my own pace and in private. But I'm back now."

Howard shifted in his seat. "You planning to set up a property law practice here?"

Nolan shook his head. "No. In fact, I think I'm ready to go back to my roots, to family law." He gave his father a half smile. "Do you know anyone looking for a lawyer?"

His father's smile was slow to come but when it did, it shone with a world of approval and joy. "I think I might know of a space. You'd have to brush up a bit, jump through a few hoops, untie some red tape."

"Oh, Howard, stop teasing the boy," Nolan's mom protested. "You know you need him back at the practice. It hasn't been the same since he left."

Nolan met his dad's gaze and stood as Howard rose to his feet. The older man extended his hand across the table and Nolan grasped it firmly, exactly the way his father had taught him more years ago than he could even remember.

"Then, welcome back aboard, son. We've missed you."

"It's good to be back, Dad. Thank you."

And Nolan knew the words were more than just that. Inside he felt as if everything had clicked back into place. Almost everything, he corrected himself. There was still some rebuilding to do, if that was even possible. But, like he'd reminded himself before, failure wasn't an option.

Number withheld. Raina stared at her cell phone screen and debated taking the call. It was quiet in the store; she had no reason not to take it, and yet there was a knot in her stomach that made her hesitate. She knew it wasn't Nolan. He'd been leaving messages every day since Saturday asking her to call him. She wished she had the courage to call him back and tell him to stop calling her, or even had the courage to block his number, but something always held her back. That same perverse something that gave her a quiet thrill of attraction every time she heard his voice.

Her phone went silent in her hand and a few seconds later the icon popped up telling her she had a voice message. With a sigh of frustration, Raina checked it. And there it was, she thought as she listened. Yet another call from Jeb. She'd already told him how much money she could give him but he insisted on more. Telling her his life depended on it. When she'd pressed him for details, he'd explained about the gambling debts he'd incurred in New Mexico. The loans he'd taken out with some guy who was now impatient to be repaid. The sum had staggered her. Surely Jeb couldn't have gambled it all away?

She had the impression that for all the things he'd told her, he was still holding something back. She decided it was time to get to the root of it and dialed the number he'd given her in his message.

"Rai, about time," he growled in her ear.

"What aren't you telling me?" Raina demanded, not wasting any time on pleasantries.

"Babe, I've told you everything you need to know."

Need to know? She looked to the ceiling of the old barn and prayed for strength. "Look, I might be able to borrow some money from my dad. But you have to tell me the truth, Jeb. Why so much?"

He laughed, a grating sound that was devoid of even an ounce of mirth. "I've gotta get out, Rai. Disappear and never come back. That costs."

Disappear? Never come back? Heck, if she believed— even for one minute—that he'd never be back it would be worth paying him what he was asking. To think that she wouldn't have to be wondering and waiting when the next call or visit would come. The next demand for more money. But what on earth had he done that was so bad?

"Forever?" she asked, the word slipping from her mouth before she even realized she'd said it.

"Aw, Rai, don't tell me you're gonna miss me. Or is it maybe that you really don't want to see me ever again?"

Raina shuddered. He was back to playing his word games, twisting everything around, including her, until she didn't know which way was up anymore.

"How much? Tell me, Jeb. Exactly how much do you need?"

He named a sum that had her rocking back on her heels. "I can't do that."

"That's what it's gonna take, Rai baby. And I need it by tomorrow."

"Tomorrow?" She couldn't get that kind of cash together by tomorrow and she doubted that even if her dad was prepared to lend her the money he could either. Besides, tomorrow was JJ's pageant. She didn't want Jeb anywhere near her or her son on what was a very important day for her little boy. "That's far too soon! Give me a few days."

"I don't have a few days." Jeb's tone became more urgent and a shiver of fear trickled down Raina's spine. "I'll see you tomorrow. Look out for me."

With that he hung up, leaving Raina staring at her phone and shaking. How on earth had she ever let things get to this? She should have drawn the line on being his cash cow years ago, but somehow it had always been easier just to pay him and send him on his way.

Raina stared at her phone and knew she had to do this. She dialed her father's number. He answered on the second ring.

"Dad, I need your help."

Eleven

Raina had been on tenterhooks all day. Her father, bless him, had come to see her at the store earlier in the day with a wad of bills. That he'd done such a thing, even knowing that the money was for Jeb, filled her heart with gratitude. No matter what happened in her life, she had him as her rock. When her mother had abandoned her, he'd been there. When Jeb had abandoned her, he'd been there. Every minute of every day that she needed him. But he wasn't getting any younger and it was time she was that rock for him, not the other way around. She needed to be able to stand on her own two feet.

And then there was the anxiety of carrying several thousand dollars in cash on her person for the rest of the day. Every time someone had come into the store and set the bell above the door ringing, she'd virtually jumped out of her skin. By the time she'd closed up shop and headed home, her nerves had been stretched so taut she felt as if the slightest thing would see her fracture into a million pieces.

"Mommy! Mommy! Look, I'm Spider-Man!" JJ zoomed around the house in his costume, looking like no shepherd any children's pageant had ever seen.

"JJ, we've talked about this. You can't be Spider-Man in the pageant," she said wearily and with an edge to her voice that JJ didn't miss.

"I am, Mommy. I am!"

His face took on a petulant look that reminded her all too much of his father, and Raina was hard pressed to remind herself not to visit her frustrations over Jeb's sins upon JJ. She had to pick her battles.

"How about you be Spider-Man in the car and then a shepherd when we get to the hall?"

"Spider-Man!" JJ shouted and hopped on one foot.

"C'mon," Raina said, fighting to hold on to her temper. "Let's get your coat on. If we don't go soon we'll be late."

By the time she had them both bundled up and in the car her hands were shaking. She took in several steadying breaths before putting the car in Reverse and backing out of the drive, all the time keeping an eye out for Jeb. But he was nowhere to be seen. She didn't know whether to be relieved or sorry.

Luck was finally with her when they got to the hall where the pageant was being staged and she parked her car in the last vacant space in the lot. Uttering a silent prayer of thanks, Raina helped JJ from the car and grabbed his shepherd's costume before heading toward the foyer. Inside was a cluster of angels on one side, shepherds on the other and all other variety of pageant costumes in between. And Spider-Man, Raina told herself. Don't forget him.

A tingle of awareness spread through her body as she sensed a movement to her right-hand side. Jeb?

"No'an!" JJ cried.

Raina felt her body sag. Was it in relief or in shock that he'd come? Right now he was definitely the lesser of two evils.

"Raina, I hope you don't mind me being here, but I didn't want to let JJ down."

"The pageant is open to everyone," she replied. "Just a small donation is requested for the local food bank."

"I know, I've already donated," Nolan said.

Just then, someone jostled her from behind, making her lose her balance, and Nolan immediately steadied her, his large warm hands at her shoulders. He let go of her just as soon as she was steady on her feet and for some stupid reason, tears sprang to her eyes. Raina blinked furiously to rid herself of them. She'd weathered tough days before and this one wasn't any different, she reminded herself.

A call went out for the shepherds to assemble and to go with one of the day care teachers.

"C'mon, JJ," Raina said, shaking out his costume. "Let's get you changed."

"No. I'm Spider-Man, Mommy."

JJ's voice was raised and Raina saw several faces turn toward them. Her cheeks flushed with embarrassment.

"Maybe we should just go home," she muttered to herself but JJ overhead her and pitched his voice so that everyone in the foyer could hear him.

"No! Not going home!"

JJ was normally an even-tempered child but when he threw a tantrum it had force equal to the tornado that had leveled so much of Royal more than a year ago. On top of everything she'd dealt with in the situation with Jeb, this was one thing too many for Raina. She reached for JJ's hand, determined to take him back out to the car, drag him if she had to, but Nolan put a hand on her arm.

"Maybe I can help," he offered, taking the shepherd

costume from her and squatting down in front of JJ. "Hey, champ, you've blown your cover."

JJ eyed Nolan with a wary but intrigued expression.

Nolan gave JJ a serious look. "No one knows who Spider-Man really is, right? He hides his suit until his special powers are needed, doesn't he?"

JJ nodded slowly, his eyes growing wide.

"Quick," Nolan suggested. "Before anyone notices. Let's cover you up."

To Raina's stunned surprise, JJ let Nolan dress him in the rough cotton overshirt, complete with rope belt, and secured the tea towel she'd brought for his head with another length of twine.

"Great work," Nolan whispered to the little boy. "I think your secret is safe."

"Raina, is JJ ready?" one of the day care teachers asked, clipboard in hand and a harried expression on her face. "Oh, great, I see he is. That's everyone accounted for. I'll bring him out back so you can go and take your seat."

Before she knew it, JJ was amiably holding hands with his teacher and walking away. But all of a sudden he broke free and ran back to Nolan and beckoned for him to lean down. Her little boy whispered something in Nolan's ear and gave him a massive hug around his neck.

This time Raina couldn't hold back the tear that spilled over and traced a line down her cheek. She brushed it away but not before Nolan noticed it.

"Thank you," she said to him, her voice shaking just a little.

Nolan didn't say anything right away, just pushed his hands in his trouser pockets and looked at her. Raina self-consciously looked away. She wasn't at her best tonight. A sleepless night followed by the tension of today, capped off by JJ's behavior, had left her feeling more raw and vulnerable than she had in a long time.

"Raina, we need to talk."

"No." She shook her head. "No we don't. Thank you for settling JJ for me, but we've said all we need to say to one another. And, to be honest, the time for you to *talk* to me was when we met. Not now."

She turned to go but Nolan caught the sleeve of her coat.

"Please, Raina. Just give me five minutes. You won't answer or return my calls—what else was I supposed to do but turn up to see you?"

"So you didn't come here for JJ then?" She challenged him with an angry glare.

"Of course I came for JJ. But I'd have been stupid not to want to see you, too."

Raina crossed her arms over her chest. "Fine. Say what you've come to say."

Nolan looked around the busy foyer full of parents and family members of the performers all milling about. "Can we step outside for a bit of privacy?"

He held his breath, waiting for Raina's reply, and felt a surge of relief when she gave him a brief nod and headed toward the main doors. They found a spot outside under the portico where they wouldn't be in the way of people coming into the hall. She still had her arms crossed and her eyes kept flicking this way and that, as if she was on the lookout for someone.

"Thank you," he said. "I appreciate it."

"Just get to the point, Nolan. What is it that you're so determined to tell me?"

While she still sounded as if she was madder at him than a wet hen, he could see she was barely holding herself together. Lines of strain pulled around her mouth and eyes and she looked exhausted.

"I've quit Samson Oil," he started, thinking he may as well get to the point from the beginning. She definitely wasn't in a mood to mess around. "I thought a lot about what you said and you were right. It made me look at myself with fresh eyes and I didn't like what I saw anymore."

Raina didn't respond, so he continued.

"I've decided to move back to Royal, to rejoin my father's practice. I know I can do good there and while I feel that I did a lot of good with Samson Oil, I also hurt a lot of people, too. Especially you. I'm sorry for that, Raina. It was never my intention to cause you any harm either directly or indirectly. Nor could I just stand aside and let my boss potentially harm people like you anymore."

Raina shifted from one foot to the other and rubbed her upper arms with her hands. It was clear she'd heard about all she was prepared to listen to.

"Why is this any of my business, Nolan? What makes you think I care where you live or what you do?"

The hurt was there, loud and clear in every word she spoke even though she'd kept her tone even.

"I'd like to think it's your business because before I messed everything up, you started to have feelings for me." At her sound of protest he continued. "The way I have feelings for you. Hear me out, please. Raina, I think I'm falling in love with you. Yes, I know it's sudden and that we barely know one another but from the first moment I laid eyes on you I knew you were someone special. Someone who had been missing in my life. Please, give me another chance. Give *us* another chance."

He waited for her response for what felt like forever, even though he logically knew it could only have been a minute or so. Her face had changed, become unreadable even to someone like him who was used to studying every nuance of expression for answers. Finally, she took in a breath and spoke.

"I can't make a decision about something like that here and now."

He took solace in the fact that it wasn't a direct no.

"I accept that. Look, right now it's enough that you're prepared to think about it."

"I need to get inside. They'll be starting soon."

She pushed past him and he let her go. It would probably be too much to expect her to sit with him. Nolan watched her go in the front doors and started, more slowly, to follow. He didn't care if he stood at the back of the hall for the duration of the pageant, but he would be there for JJ. As he made his way to the door, he saw a shadow detach itself from the bushes near the road. Nolan watched as the man walked toward the parking area. There was something about the shape and size of the man, and the way he moved, that was vaguely familiar. In a rush, Nolan remembered the person he'd seen on the road near Raina's house.

Every sense in his body went on full alert. He followed the man to the lot where he saw the guy draw to a halt by Raina's car.

"Can I help you?" he called out and was surprised when the guy wheeled around to face him rather than run away.

The man's face might once have been handsome, Nolan thought, but the dissipation wrought by hard living, no doubt compounded by too much alcohol judging by the smell coming from him right now, had left its mark.

"I know you," the man said. "Seen you sniffing around Raina's place. She's a fine piece of ass, isn't she?"

Nolan's hands curled into fists at the familiar way the man spoke about Raina.

"What's it to you?" he demanded.

The guy laughed. "She hasn't told you about me, has she? Her dirty little secret."

Suddenly it all started to slip into place. This guy was Raina's ex—and JJ's father. Nolan instinctively wanted to shield them from this guy—to make sure he didn't touch or tarnish their lives again. But, last he checked, murder was still illegal in the state of Texas.

"I know about you," Nolan said, taking scant satisfaction in pricking Jeb Pickering's bubble of confidence. This was the man who'd left Raina's wrist looking black and blue. Nolan itched to deliver a dose of the same thing to the bastard but he knew there were ways and means of dealing with lowlifes like him—and he was going to make sure he never hurt Raina again. "You're not wanted here. Get on your way."

"I got every right to be here. More right 'n you, anyways. JJ's my boy. Not yours."

Jeb's stance altered and he drew himself up to his full height in an effort to intimidate Nolan. While the guy had an inch or two on him, Nolan knew that if it came to it, he'd still best Pickering in a fight. That, however, would be a last resort.

"Now you want to claim him?" Nolan sneered. "A bit late, isn't it?"

"It's never too late," Jeb challenged in return.

"It is when you're a no-good waste of time. You think you're a man but you're nothing. A real man doesn't treat a woman the way you've treated Raina."

Jeb's expression grew ugly under the lamp light, his mouth twisting into a harsh line. "You don't know nothing 'bout what happened."

"I know enough."

The look on Jeb's face changed again, going from belligerent to sly in one breath.

"A man can change his mind, can't he? Although—" he paused and rubbed at the stubble on his chin "—I guess that would mess up your plans, wouldn't it?"

"My plans?"

Nolan inwardly cursed himself for falling into Jeb's verbal trap.

"Yeah, your plans with my girl and my son."

"Look, you might be his biological father but be honest, that's where your attachment to JJ begins and ends. As for Raina, she's not your girl. Not anymore."

"Ah, but she's not yours either, is she? Not yet."

Jeb looked smug and Nolan's hands itched to wipe that expression off his face.

"Besides," Jeb continued. "She owes me."

Nolan shook his head. "I don't see how she owes you anything."

"Money, doofus. She owes me money. We have, what you would say, an agreement."

"Haven't you already taken enough from her? What kind of man are you anyway, constantly leeching off a woman that way?"

The insult fell on deaf ears. "I'm here to get what's mine. Mind you, since you're the one who has the hots for Rai, maybe *you* should be the one paying me."

He could imagine the gears grinding in the back of Jeb's mind as the man took in Nolan's appearance, the quality of his coat, the expensive haircut and his handmade boots. Since money was the man's major motivator, Nolan hoped that maybe he could save Raina the additional pressure of ever having to see Jeb again. Maybe.

"How much?" Nolan demanded.

"Look, man, this is between Raina and me," Jeb started, rocking back on his feet slightly. "But if you wanted to pay what she owes me—hell, I'm an equal opportunity kind of guy. Your money is as good as hers."

"If I give you anything, you have to give me your word, such as it is, that you won't bother Raina again."

"Hey, man, no need to insult me," Jeb protested, suddenly the picture of a man affronted when his integrity has been called into question. But then he laughed. It was an ugly sound that revealed his true avaricious character. "Whatever. When can you pay me?"

"First you have to tell me how much."

Jeb named a figure and Nolan didn't so much as bat an eyelid. "I can do that. Give me your bank account details."

"I don't have no bank account, man. I need cash and I need it now."

"I can get it to you tomorrow night. But on one condition."

"What's that?"

"That you get away from here now and stay away from Raina and JJ."

"It's not like I want to see them," Jeb scowled. "She owes me, is all. But, yeah, I'll do as you say. She won't see me—tonight anyway."

"Good. But if I hear that she's caught so much as a glimpse of you after our talk tonight, the deal's off." Nolan glared at him to make his point clear. "And I'll make sure she doesn't give you anything either."

Jeb looked at him, as if trying to figure out whether Nolan could influence Raina that much. Obviously he decided that Nolan could. He lifted his chin in acceptance of the terms.

"Where d'you want to meet?"

Nolan named a parking lot in back of some buildings downtown. Jeb nodded. "I know it. I'll be there. Six o'clock tomorrow night. Don't be late or the deal's off and I'm back to my original plan."

"Oh, I'll be on time, don't you worry about that," Nolan affirmed, staying outside to watch Jeb as he headed off down the street and faded from sight.

Nolan went back to the hall. The lights gleaming on the front porch were a welcome contrast to the darkness of the man he'd just seen leave. He wondered what the hell Raina had ever seen in Jeb Pickering, but then again, knowing her even as little as he did, he could see why the lost boy inside Jeb would appeal to her nature to nurture and mend what was broken. She certainly had mended what was broken within him, Nolan thought, and made him dream of a new future.

He quietly let himself into the hall and scanned the rows of seats, trying to spot Raina. There she was. Again that familiar wave of protectiveness swept through him. Dealing with Jeb would be an unpleasant business, but he'd do whatever it took to keep Raina safe from that creep and anything or anyone else that threatened her. Raina and JJ both.

As if she'd sensed his presence, she turned and their eyes met. She gave him a tentative smile and waved him to come toward her. Nolan realized she'd saved him a seat. The knowledge eased loose the knot he'd been carrying in his chest since she'd confronted him and told him to get lost, and for the first time in a long time, Nolan admitted he felt hope.

Twelve

From the moment Nolan sat down next to her, Raina felt every nerve and cell in her body become attuned to his nearness. The seats were close together so his broad shoulder brushed against hers. In the end, it was easier to give in to the occasional contact and stop trying to hold herself apart from him.

Who was she kidding anyway? Yes, she was still mad at him and, yes, she still felt betrayed, but he'd extended an olive branch tonight. While her first instinct had been to reject it, and him, in an attempt to save herself from any further hurt or heartbreak, didn't she owe it to herself to give him another chance? If what he said was true, and he'd quit Samson Oil, maybe that was the genuine measure of the man himself.

She glanced toward him and caught him looking back at her. His brown eyes were alight with joy and she felt her body relax even more.

"Our Spider-Man is doing great, don't you think?" he whispered to her, leaning in closer.

Her nostrils flared as his scent wafted toward her, making her insides twist with suppressed need. It was all she could do to smile and nod an acknowledgment and return her eyes to the stage where JJ stood as tall and proud as he could, his little face turned to the crowd and his gaze searching for her among the many faces. She saw the moment he picked her out in the crowd and he beamed at her, and then his eyes drifted to where Nolan sat beside her and she thought JJ's face might split with happiness.

She felt a telltale prickle of tears in her eyes. She'd tried so darn hard to be everything that JJ had needed in his young life. But his obvious joy at having Nolan present made her realize that she couldn't be all things to her son, no matter what she did. Not being able to ensure he had the best of everything life had to offer frustrated her. She wanted him to have it all.

If Nolan's words were true, if he was really falling in love with her, then she had to know how he felt about JJ, too. They were a package deal.

But what of the wife and child she'd heard mention of earlier this week? How could she casually bring that up in conversation without it sounding as if she'd been snooping into his life? Of course, she rationalized, she had a right to snoop—she had more than herself to consider—but snooping had never been her thing. She'd always been a "live and let live" type of person, someone who tried to always see the good in people.

But hadn't that very facet of her personality caused her to make some of the worst decisions in her life, as well? Decisions like Jeb and the loser boyfriends she'd had before him? No—no matter which way she looked at it, she couldn't regret her time with Jeb no matter how much it had cost her and how much heartache he'd wrought. Without him, she wouldn't have had JJ. Becoming a parent had made her realize just what her father had sacrificed for her all these years and deepened her love for him a thousandfold. Her dad had worked hard to make up for her mother's abandonment, and while he'd had lady friends come and go through the years, Raina had never felt as if she'd lacked for not having her mother with her growing up.

Which brought her to even more questions. Was it in JJ's best interests for her to keep allowing Nolan access to them both if he was going to abandon them like he might have done already with his own family? Raina had learned the hard way, time and time again, what abandonment felt like, how much it hurt. Could she even consider risking that for JJ? He was still so young. Still so reliant on her to protect him.

And what of Nolan's wife? Was she someone Raina had met before? Someone she came across in her day-to-day life? She hated the thought that for some poor soul she might become the other woman.

Her mind was whirling with so many worries that she barely noticed the pageant was up to the final number. The children were singing "Silent Night" and the audience had joined in. Beside her, the sound of Nolan's tenor forced her attention back to the present. Sometimes, she reminded herself, you simply had to let go and let God. Maybe it really was as simple as that.

She felt herself begin to relax a little as she joined in for the final lines of the carol. But then a jarring thought sideswiped her. For all her ponderings she hadn't stopped to consider the situation with Jeb or the very large sum of money she had in her purse right now.

With the pageant over, people began to rise from their seats and jostle one another on the way to the main doors. Raina felt Nolan's hand at her elbow, steadying her in the crush as they filed out of their row of seats. Raina turned to him.

"I have to go out the back and collect JJ. Please don't rush off. I know he's going to want to see you."

"And you? Do you want to see me?" Nolan asked, pulling Raina to one side so the crowd could eddy past them without bumping them again.

"I'll be honest—I really don't know. Part of me says, yes, but—"

"I understand. If you'd rather, you can make my apologies to JJ."

She could see the hurt in his eyes, watched the light in them dim a little. It made up her mind.

"Come back to our house for a hot chocolate with JJ. He's going to take some time to unwind before getting off to bed tonight anyway."

Nolan looked at her and she saw the slight curl at the edges of his lips. "Are you sure? I understand if you—"

"No." It was her turn to interrupt him. "I'm sure. Look, he's waiting. I'll see you back at the house, okay?"

"I'll wait for you in the parking lot," Nolan said in a voice that brooked no argument. "And I'll follow you home."

Knowing he'd be there, waiting in the darkness outside, made Raina feel warm inside. And when Jeb showed up for his money, either outside the hall or later, back at her house, she'd deal with it then. Actually, thinking about it, having Nolan handy might make the whole process go more smoothly. She doubted Jeb would try anything stupid with another person there.

"Okay, that's good of you. Thank you."

Later, with JJ in tow and wrapped up again in his winter coat and beanie, they walked quickly to the car. As good as his word, Nolan had pulled up his SUV alongside hers and was waiting in the frigid air.

"Did you see me, No'an?" JJ asked excitedly as they approached the car.

"I did, champ. You were great."

Her little boy's smile made Raina glad she'd asked Nolan back to the house. JJ had had enough of her short-tempered company this week. Goodness only knew, if Nolan hadn't been there tonight, she wouldn't have thought twice about taking JJ home—no doubt kicking and screaming—over the costume issue.

She looked around the parking lot for Jeb. But among all the families loading their preschoolers into their cars and saying bye to their friends, there was no sign of him. Maybe he'd turn up at the house, she decided as she drove along the road toward home. She flicked her eyes to the rearview mirror, reassured by the sight of Nolan's vehicle following her at a safe distance. She was all over the place as far as he was concerned. If only she could trust her heart and they could discover exactly where this complicated relationship of theirs could go. But she'd trusted her heart before and look where that had landed her. She didn't want to ever go through that again.

At the house, Nolan offered to supervise JJ as he changed into his pajamas while she made the hot chocolate. Raina gratefully accepted. As she heated milk on her stove she could hear JJ's excited tones tempered by Nolan's calmer deeper voice down the hall and closed her eyes for just a moment, wondering what it might be like if this were to become a regular, even daily event. How did that make her feel?

A commotion at the kitchen door made her turn as she started to fill the mugs. Nolan had given JJ a piggyback ride from his bedroom and the two of them were laughing. Raina couldn't help but join in.

"Who wants marshmallows?" she asked as she finished pouring the hot drinks.

"Me!" JJ crowed from his perch. "And No'an, too."

Raina looked to Nolan for confirmation. "Are you a marshmallow man?"

"Through and through," he said.

His word were simple at face value but she found herself left wondering if he'd meant more by that. She had to stop overthinking everything. It was time to just let some things find their natural course. She dropped marshmallows in each of the mugs and put them on a tray to carry through to the sitting room.

"Let me take that for you," Nolan offered, swinging JJ down to the floor.

"Thanks."

Raina followed Nolan and JJ and relished just how good it felt to share something as simple as carrying a tray, rather than being responsible for everything herself. But even so, she couldn't allow herself to simply give in to the comfort of this moment. Nolan still had secrets and until he was prepared to share them with her, she had to guard her heart.

Even as she thought it, she knew it was too late. Her heart was already a lost cause when it came to this man. Had been from the moment he'd kissed her. It was why discovering his subterfuge had been so painful.

She watched from the door as Nolan encouraged JJ to kneel on the floor by the coffee table to sip his drink. Obviously sensing her scrutiny, he looked up.

"You okay?" he asked.

She smiled and nodded. "I think so," she answered, and stepped forward to accept the mug he held out for her.

It wasn't long before JJ was drooping with exhaustion. To Raina's surprise he made no argument when she said it was bedtime. He asked to be carried to bed and she lifted him comfortably into her arms and held him close as she went down the hallway to his room. It was a constant marvel to her that this growing child had come from her body. A marvel and a precious gift.

So much responsibility came with parenthood. She had to be certain she was making the right decisions for herself, sure, but for JJ most of all. He deserved only the very best in life. Did that include a second chance with Nolan? she wondered as she supervised JJ brushing his teeth and then carried him to his bed.

JJ was out like a light before she'd even made it to his bedroom. She left the door ajar for him so the nightlight in the hallway could provide enough light should he stir, and she walked slowly back toward the living room. Nolan was sitting on the couch, his mug on the table in front of him.

"Your hot chocolate is cold," he commented. "Can I reheat it for you?"

She shook her head. "It's okay, I'm used to that."

A distant look passed through his eyes as he nodded and gave a short laugh. "Yeah, I bet. Seems that when you have kids nothing is ever eaten or drunk hot or chilled, right? Room temperature is your best friend."

Was he talking about his own child, his own life? He seemed to understand what it was like. Raina couldn't speak for fear that she'd just come straight out and ask him about the little she'd overheard about his wife and kid, but a sense of self-preservation made her hold her tongue. She wasn't even sure that she wanted to know. She knew that made her sound selfish, at least in her own mind.

She drank her lukewarm chocolate and let Nolan steer the conversation to a review of the evening's performance. And while she laughed and talked and agreed with him, she found herself thinking how very much she wished this kind of evening could become a regular event for them. She looked at the clock, startled to see that another full hour had passed since she'd put JJ to bed.

Nolan followed her gaze and made an exclamation. "I'm sorry, I'm keeping you up."

Raina felt a flush of heat and awareness suffuse her body, along with a longing that when she went to bed, they could go together. She shoved the thought to the back of her mind. It was ridiculous. She needed to get her crazy hormones under control. Desire was clouding rationality, and it was that very rationality that got her through every day without falling apart. If she lost that, where would she be?

"Thanks for coming tonight," she said, standing up and putting the mugs on the tray to return them to the kitchen.

Nolan stood also and reached once more for the tray. His fingers brushed hers and her already jangling nerves surged to awareness, making her jerk the tray away.

"It's okay, I can manage," she insisted before turning away from him before he could see the rush of color that stained her cheeks.

Raina set the tray down on the kitchen counter and looked at her reflection in the dark window above. This was ridiculous. She'd barely seen him in the past week and a half and now she was a jittering mass of contradictions in his company. She'd told herself she was better off without him, that she didn't need a man like him in her life, but no matter what her head said, her body told a different story. Even now her breathing was slightly ragged and she felt aware of every brush of her clothing over her sensitized skin. If this was how she reacted when he did nothing more than touch her with a fingertip, she'd be a complete and utter mess if they went any further.

"Raina? You okay? I'm heading off now. Thanks for the drink."

She took a steadying breath and went back to the sitting room.

"You're welcome and thanks again for defusing that

situation with JJ before the pageant. I couldn't have done that without you."

"Only too happy to help out."

He walked toward the door and Raina followed. In the entranceway he paused a moment and then turned to face her.

"Raina, I meant what I said to you earlier tonight. Can I hope that you'll give me another chance to prove to you that I'm not all bad?"

Raina gave him a twisted smile. "I don't have a particularly good track record with bad men."

He smiled back in return but she could see the hurt in his eyes. The knowledge that she was categorizing him with the other deadbeats she'd fallen for in the past.

"Then let's set the record straight, together," he murmured and leaned forward.

She hadn't known he was going to kiss her, at least not consciously. But while her mind may have been slow on the uptake, her body certainly wasn't. She leaned into him, meeting him more than halfway and closing the gap between them. His arms wrapped around her, one hand lifting to spread through her hair.

The second his lips touched hers, she knew she was lost. What was life for if you couldn't take second chances? His lips upon hers were electric, sending a pulse of longing through her body that made her tremble in response. He tasted of hot chocolate and more. Of something darker, spicier, deeper and more forbidden. Logic told her she should pull back, end this. End all of it. But logic took a backseat to the sensation and the promise that poured through her body at this gentlest of caresses.

Raina raised her hands to Nolan's chest. Was it a subconscious attempt to keep some barrier between them, or was it so she could feel the hard strength of his lean muscles beneath the finely woven cotton of his shirt? Her hands tingled as she touched him, as her fingers spread out and her palms soaked up his heat. She ached to feel his skin, to touch him all over, but she daren't ask him to stay. It was too soon. Too much. And she still had far too many questions.

When Nolan pulled back and let his hands drop away from her, Raina felt physically bereft.

"I'll call you tomorrow, okay?" he said, stepping away and opening the front door.

Words failing her, Raina could only nod. After he'd closed the door behind him she stood there for several minutes, the fingertips of one hand pressed to her lips as if she could hold on to the moment—the sweetness, the promise—they'd just shared. But, like everything good in her life, the sensation was a fleeting one, gone before she heard his car start up outside and pull away from the curb.

She wanted him. She knew that. Acknowledged it with an honesty that brought tears to her eyes. But could she have him? Dare she?

Only time would tell.

Thirteen

If the staff at the sheriff's office thought that Nolan looked like someone who'd pulled an all-nighter then that's probably because he had. When he caught sight of his reflection in the outer doors, the red eyes and scruffy jaw, he grimaced. Certainly not his usual *GQ*-style appearance but then it wouldn't be the first time Nolan had looked a bit frayed around the edges.

He'd never felt quite as invested in the result of his work as he had with what he'd done last night. The work itself, and his reasons for doing it, had made one thing abundantly clear to him. He wasn't falling in love with Raina Patterson. He was already there. He loved her. There was no question about it. Yes, it was fast; yes, it had surprised him; and, yes, he'd fought it. But it's what had kept him going at about two this morning when he was questioning his sanity in finding out all there was to know about Jeb Pickering.

Raina was his reason for being here—both at the sheriff's office and in Royal altogether. While his work had sent him here, she was what would keep him. He only needed to convince her of that fact. A cakewalk, right? He snorted under his breath and earned a stern glance from a passing deputy.

"Can I help you, sir?" a woman behind the front counter asked.

"Yes, I know I don't have an appointment but I need to see the sheriff, if he's in. It's urgent."

"Just about every man coming in to see the sheriff says the same thing," she answered with a roll of her eyes. "Your name?"

Nolan gave it and thought he saw a glimpse of recognition in the woman's eyes.

"Howard Dane's boy?"

He nodded. He might be a grown man but he'd always be his father's son in this town—and proud of it, he realized. "Yes, he's my dad."

The receptionist nodded. "Take a seat over there. I'll see if Sheriff Battle's available."

Nolan sat down on a hard vinyl-covered seat against the wall and drummed his fingers on his leg. He was lucky he didn't have to wait long.

"Nolan Dane?" The sheriff had come out to the reception area himself. "Welcome home."

"Thanks," Nolan answered, rising to his feet and offering his hand.

"What brings you to my office?"

"Can we talk in private?"

"Sure, c'mon back."

Once they were seated in a private room, Nolan didn't waste any time.

"I have information on a man named Jeb Pickering. He's got a long list of convictions for petty crime but right now he's wanted in New Mexico on third-degree felony charges."

"Tell me more," Sheriff Battle said, leaning forward with his elbows on the desk between them.

"He's the ex-partner of Raina Patterson, who runs Priceless out at the Courtyard."

The sheriff nodded. "Yeah, I know her. Lost her store in town in the tornado. Brave woman. Has a little boy. He'd be about three now, I guess."

Nolan was impressed that the man could recall one of the people of Royal so easily, but then again that's probably why Nate Battle was reelected each term. He cared. Nolan was counting on that to help him rid Raina of Jeb's shadow forever.

"That's the one. Pickering skipped out on her but keeps coming back for handouts. Seems he has a bit of trouble with gambling and drinking."

"Not the best of combinations but not necessarily a crime, unfortunately."

"No," Nolan agreed. "However, we can now add manslaughter while driving under the influence of alcohol and skipping bail to his list of charms."

The sheriff let out a low whistle. "I see. And you know this how?"

Nolan quickly explained, showing the sheriff the information he'd gathered. After reading it carefully, the sheriff looked up.

"D'you know where he is now?"

"Not exactly, but I know where he'll be tonight."

The anger he was feeling at Jeb Pickering's callous disregard of life added cold hard inflection to his words as Nolan outlined his confrontation with Pickering last night.

"So he thinks you'll be there to give him money so he can head on his way out of state again." The sheriff nodded. "I think we can work with you."

"I was hoping you'd say that." Nolan smiled and leaned back in his chair.

"Give me the details and I'll get a couple of my men together, and I'll alert the New Mexico authorities that their chicken will be coming home to roost."

Nolan stamped his feet against the cold as he waited in the parking area for Jeb to show. So far Nolan hadn't seen a sign of anyone, although he had every confidence that Nate Battle and his men were nearby.

The skitter of a stone on the pavement made Nolan turn around.

"Pickering," he acknowledged as the man slipped out from the shadows.

"You got my money?"

Nolan ignored his request. "I've been doing a bit of research on you, man. It seems you're a wanted criminal."

Jeb's face turned nasty. "What the hell do you know? I've been doing a bit of research of my own. You're just some fancy-pants lawyer who couldn't even keep his wife and son alive. Now give me my money," he demanded as he yanked one hand from his pocket and shoved it in Nolan's direction.

Nolan fought to ignore the man's gibe but even so, it cut deep. The truth always did. He forced himself to focus—to do what was right for Raina. Yes, he might not have been able to save Bennett and Carole, but he'd be damned if he ever saw another person he loved hurt when he could do something about it.

He took a step closer to Jeb. "Turn yourself in, man. You know the authorities are going to catch up with you sooner or later."

"Not if I get to Mexico they won't. With that money I reckon I can disappear for a while."

"Oh, you'll disappear for a while, all right," Nolan

agreed as he spied Nate Battle and a couple of his deputies move silently up behind Jeb.

Jeb grinned, but then he realized that Nolan's words had held a double entendre. "Whaddya mean?"

"I mean there is no money. Not from me and not from Raina either."

Jeb started to swear and launched himself forward at Nolan, both fists now swinging in fury. Nate and his deputies closed the distance between them and wrestled him to the ground, but not before a punch caught the edge of Nolan's jaw making his head snap back. But one shot was all the other man got and it was with a great deal of satisfaction that Nolan watched the deputies cuff Jeb and haul him to his feet to read him his rights then lead him to their car—as he loudly and energetically protested the whole way.

"I think we can add resisting arrest to his list of charges, don't you?" Nate Battle commented as he straightened his jacket.

"Yeah," Nolan said, rubbing his fingers along his jaw where Jeb's fist had connected.

"You want to press charges for that?"

"No." Nolan shook his head. "I'm pretty sure he has enough charges against him now to ensure that he won't bother Raina again."

The sheriff gave him a piercing look. "Like that is it? You're soft on Raina Patterson?"

Nolan nodded.

Nate reached out a hand to Nolan. "As I said this morning, good to have you back in Royal."

Nolan shook the sheriff's hand. "Thanks. It really is good to be back."

"I guess we'll be seeing more of you."

"If you mean, am I staying in town, the answer is yes. And I'm rejoining dad's practice, too."

"That's good. We need men like you and your dad fighting for the vulnerable people in this town."

With that, Nate tipped his hat and turned and walked toward his car.

Nolan stood there in the darkness, oblivious now to the cold that whipped around him. Home. He really was home again and he had the approval of the sheriff. It probably didn't get much better than that in terms of acceptance. There was just one more obstacle to overcome. Raina. He'd taken care of her past, now he needed to share his own. And for the life of him, he didn't know how he was supposed to do this right.

Raina checked the floor safe in the shop for the umpteenth time to reassure herself the money she was holding for Jeb was still there. Well, where else would it be? She closed the door and spun the dial before pulling the trap door down over it again. It had been a couple of days since she'd promised him she'd have the money ready. It wasn't like him not to show and the waiting was making her jumpy.

Even his phone calls and texts had stopped. So what on earth had happened to him? She didn't dare hope that he'd left and forgotten all about it. That wasn't his style at all.

Raina got to her feet and went over to the cheval mirror she had propped in the corner of her small office and checked her appearance. Nolan was picking her up soon and taking her out for dinner. Her dad had JJ at his place for one of their much anticipated Saturday nights together and for some stupid reason Raina felt more nervous about tonight than she had on her very first date with a boy.

This is Nolan, she kept telling herself. *You know him. You trust him...mostly.* She shook her head. She trusted him, she just didn't know everything she needed to know about him yet. There was a difference. Of course he had secrets, so did she, didn't she? She sighed. Maybe that was her trouble. She trusted too darn easily.

She studied her reflection in the mirror. The long floral skirt she'd teamed with a pair of high black boots made her feel feminine and pretty, although after a day on her feet, her toes were beginning to complain. It'd be worth it, she'd told herself as she examined her reflection and smoothed the soft sweater she'd chosen over her hips. She didn't often wear black but the contrast between the sweater and her creamy skin brought out the light in her eyes. Noticing her makeup could definitely do with a touch-up, she grabbed her makeup bag from her purse and made a few running repairs, eager to look her best for the man who continued to send her pulse flying.

The bell chimed out front and she quickly shoved her makeup bag back into her purse and went out into the shop, a smile already stretching her lips.

"Nolan, you're early!" she exclaimed.

"Would it sound ridiculous if I said I couldn't wait to see you?"

He bent and kissed her cheek and even though the touch was about as innocent as you could get, Raina immediately felt her body flare to aching life. She wanted him so much and it was quite clear to her that he felt the same way.

But why didn't he tell her about his wife and son?

Oh, sure, she could come right out and ask him, but she strongly felt that this was Nolan's story to tell on his own terms—even if waiting didn't sit comfortably with her. She'd learned the hard way not to push a man for the truth. In the past, and with Jeb in particular, men had only told her what they thought she wanted to hear. She didn't want to travel down that road with Nolan. He'd tell her about his family when he was ready, she reminded herself for the umpteenth time.

She pushed the niggling thoughts to the back of her mind, determined to enjoy his company tonight.

"I've been looking forward to tonight, too."

"Is there anything I can do to help you lock up?" Nolan asked.

"No, I'm just about finished. It's been quiet today. I guess not everyone wants to buy antiques for Christmas."

"I'd say that was a shame but if it means we get to spend more time together, who am I to complain?"

Nolan smiled at her but Raina's attention was caught by a dark bruise on the edge of his jaw. She raised a hand and gently touched the mark with her fingertips.

"What on earth have you been up to to get this?" she asked.

Nolan grabbed her hand and kissed her fingertips before letting it go again. "It's nothing. Something just flew up and hit me when I wasn't expecting it."

She searched his face, but he just smiled at her in return.

"Are you ready to go? We can get a drink before the movies if we leave now."

"Sure," she shrugged. "I doubt I'll get any last-minute customers at this stage of the day."

Raina grabbed her jacket and set the alarm system before they left through the front door. She shivered as the cold air outside cut through her.

"It almost feels as if it could snow," she commented as Nolan held open his car door for her and helped her up into the SUV.

"Yeah, it might. But even if it does, I doubt it'll stick. You know what it's like around here this time of year."

They made small talk in the car, mostly discussing JJ and how excited he was about Christmas being only six days away. Nolan was good company, the best male company she'd ever had, she decided. If only he'd open up about his past.

The movie was a comedy, and Raina was glad because she loved to hear Nolan laugh—which he did, loudly and often. Afterward, they walked to a nearby Italian place she'd never been to before. The proprietors greeted Nolan like a long lost son and she didn't miss the glance that passed between the Italian couple when Nolan introduced her.

They were shown to a secluded table with low lighting and the ubiquitous red checkered tablecloth and a candle inserted in a used Chianti bottle.

"This is lovely," Raina commented as they studied their menus. "Do you come here often?"

"Not in a long time," he admitted. "It used to be a favorite."

A favorite with his wife perhaps? Maybe that explained the owners' slightly uncomfortable expressions when he'd introduced her.

"So, can you recommend anything?"

"Let's see," Nolan drawled, running his eyes across the menu card. "The veal scalloppini is always good, especially if you're not crazy about pasta. Hell, I didn't think. You do like Italian food, don't you? I just assumed—"

"I love Italian food, and the scalloppini sounds perfect," she hastened to reassure him.

"Okay. What about an appetizer?" he prompted.

"You choose. I'm pretty much okay with everything."

He nodded and beckoned the waiter over, ordering them a platter of antipasto to start, followed by the veal and a bottle of Chianti to go with it.

Raina was feeling decidedly mellow by the end of the evening. The movie, the food and the company had all been incredible, and when Nolan drove back to her house she knew what her next step was.

"Will you come inside?" she asked as they sat in the car in the pitch-dark night.

"I'd like that," Nolan agreed, and together they walked up the front path to her house.

Inside, she hung their coats up and led him to the sitting room. Her heart was beating double time. She knew what she wanted, but was it what he wanted, too?

"Did you want a nightcap, or a coffee?"

Nolan only shook his head and reached for her, pulling her into his arms. "No, I only want you."

"Then we're in agreement," she said softly, feeling a run of excitement deep inside. "Because I want you, too."

She cupped his face and pulled it down to hers and kissed him with all the pent-up longing she'd harbored since their kiss on Thursday night. Instantly her body leaped to life, her nipples tightening into hard nubs and her breasts growing full and heavy. She pressed against his chest, as if that could somehow ease the aching demand, but instead it only heightened it.

Nolan's hands splayed across her back, holding her to him as if they could be molded together forever. One hand drifted to her lower back and pulled her body more firmly against his. The hard ridge of his arousal pressed against her, sending a thrill of anticipation throughout her entire body and ending in a pulse of longing that centered at her core.

"I want to touch you," she whispered against his mouth. "All of you."

She tugged at his shirt, pulling it from the waistband of his trousers and pushing her hands underneath. His skin was smooth and hot, and he shuddered at her touch. Raina forced herself to draw away slightly so she could work his buttons loose. Eventually she succeeded and she pushed the fabric wide open, exposing his tanned skin. A light dusting of hair peppered his chest before narrowing in a tempting path down his abdomen and lower. She traced that line with her fingers and felt his stomach muscles contract beneath her touch.

"Raina, I—"

Whatever he'd been about to say was lost as she leaned forward and pressed her lips to one nipple, her tongue swirling around the smooth disc and teasing its tip into a taut bud. She raked her nails lightly across the other, eliciting a groan of need from deep inside him. The sound gave her a sense of power and she took her time exploring his upper body with her hands, her mouth, her tongue. When Nolan pulled her up to kiss him again, she was one hot mess of need, and when his hands drifted to the waistband of her top she didn't hesitate to let him remove it for her.

Nolan backed her toward the couch and gently guided her down before joining her there. He held himself up on one elbow as he traced the lacy cup of her bra. His eyes looked darker than usual, his pupils almost consuming the brown of his irises, and a light flush of color stained his cheekbones.

"You are so beautiful," he murmured before leaning down and tracing a line in the valley of her breasts with his tongue.

It was what she wanted and yet it still wasn't enough. Raina squirmed against him, desperate to ease the insistent demand of her body. Nolan reached behind her, unsnapped the clasp of her bra and gently tugged the garment away from her before dropping it to the carpet.

For a moment Raina felt self-conscious. She had stretch marks all over her body, silvered now, but a continuing reminder of the son she'd borne. But her insecurity soon vanished as Nolan paid homage to her breasts, teasing first one tip, then the other, with his mouth and tongue. As he drew one into his mouth and suckled hard, she felt a spear of pleasure drive through her body, almost sending her over the edge. She'd never felt so responsive.

She murmured his name as he worked his way down, tracing the lines of her rib cage with his strong fingers and following each touch with a kiss, a lick, a suck of his mouth. Her nerves were screaming for more and she squirmed under his sensual assault. She'd never felt this much before. Never wanted another human being like she wanted him.

Her body felt empty, demanding to be filled, to be led to the precipice of the pleasure she knew she'd find under his touch. Nolan pulled away and she made a sound of protest, which he silenced with a swift kiss.

"Just making you more comfortable," he said, and then he reached for her boots.

He undid first one, then the other, easing them off her feet and peeling away her stockings and tossing them to the floor to join her top and her bra. When Nolan reached for the fastening on the side of her skirt and eased the zipper down, she lifted her hips, allowing him to slide the garment off.

Dressed only in her panties, she was assailed by a sense of awkwardness and moved her hands in an attempt to cover herself. Nolan merely caught her wrists in gentle fingers and pulled her hands away.

"Don't," he admonished. "I meant what I said before. You're beautiful. Every. Inch. Of you." He punctuated his words with a kiss on her belly. Her hips. The edge of her panties.

Raina let her head drop back against the arm of the couch and closed her eyes, giving herself over to the delicious sensations that poured through her. One moment Nolan's hands and mouth were at the edge of her panties and the next her panties were gone and she could feel the heat of his breath against the soft skin of her inner thighs.

He pressed a wet kiss against her skin, and then blew out cool air. She shivered as anticipation threatened to destroy her mind even as her body coiled in hope and eagerness, awaiting his next touch. She wasn't disappointed. His fingers traced a delicious line from her hip to her groin and back again before moving ever so slowly lower.

She knew she was wet and ready for him and yet when his fingers parted her outer lips and traced the entrance of her body she almost jolted right up off the couch.

"Too much?" he asked softly.

"No, not too much. Never too much," she gasped.

She forced herself to relax and let her thighs fall open, giving him easier access to the secrets of her body. When he eased one finger inside her she murmured her approval and clenched against him involuntarily, sending delight spiraling outward from where he touched.

"You feel so good," Nolan said, his voice growing huskier by the minute.

"You make me feel so much," Raina countered breathlessly.

She could feel her climax hovering just on the periphery and knew, without a doubt, that it wouldn't take much more to send her on a trajectory of pleasure that would shatter her into a million pieces. Nolan eased his finger from her body and then reentered her with two. She loved the sense of fullness it gave her, and as he brushed against that magical part of her, she felt the first pull of orgasm.

Her last rational thought was of his mouth closing over her, of his tongue rolling around the tight bead of nerve endings at her center and of the draw of his mouth as he pushed her gently over the edge and tumbling headlong into bliss.

Nolan gathered her into his arms as the final waves of satisfaction petered away into lassitude, and he lifted her off the couch. She made no protest as he carried her down the hallway and deposited her in her bed, but it wasn't until he pulled the comforter up over her naked body that she realized he didn't intend to join her there, or stay.

"Nolan?" she asked, reaching out for him. "We haven't finished."

He bent and pressed his lips to hers. "We have—for tonight."

"But you… I…" She was lost for words to describe the imbalance of what had happened.

"It's okay. Now sleep. Tomorrow's another day. I'll let myself out."

This wasn't how she'd imagined things ending tonight at all, Raina thought as she lay in the darkness and heard the front door close, shortly followed by the sound of Nolan's car driving away. And, while her body was sated, she still felt as though an essential ingredient was missing. She reached across the vacant expanse of her bed and realized that she already missed him. And still she didn't have the truth.

Fourteen

Raina spent the next few days in a blur of confusion about her feelings for Nolan. Their evening together had been wonderful, truly so. And he'd made her feel cherished and special and all those things that she'd decided, after Jeb, were nonnegotiable. But high on her list was honesty, too. Was withholding things about himself the same as being dishonest? She began to worry that the longer it took, the less likely it was she was going to hear about his past from him. And Raina knew she didn't want to hear it from anyone else.

Even so, it didn't stop her from looking forward to seeing him as she had at lunch on Monday, and then for a quick coffee yesterday afternoon. Her father had cautioned her about rushing into things too fast, with a reminder about where that had left her the last time, and she'd acknowledged his concerns. After all, hadn't he been the one to stand by her through all the fallout from each previous disastrous relationship?

The thought brought her back to Jeb. There had still been no contact from him and when she attempted to call his cell phone, it was disconnected.

At least there were still some things in her life she kept a handle on. She smiled to herself as she adjusted the Christmas display in her store window. The antique Santa and the child's sled had garnered a great deal of comment from passersby, bringing them into the store and boosting her small-ticket item sales quite comfortably. And the sled itself had sold, too—with the new owner planning to pick it up before New Year's Eve.

All in all, her December sales had been very strong. Factoring in the success of her craft lessons, things were definitely looking up for the New Year. Which reminded her, she needed to finalize the newsletter she'd be sending out with the new classes and timetables for January.

Outside the store, a car pulled up in the parking area and Raina noticed a young woman alight. She recognized the petite blonde instantly—Clare Connelly. Raina waved as Clare started to walk toward Priceless.

"Good morning," Raina said with a welcoming smile as she opened the door for her. "Have a day off?"

Clare's role as chief pediatric nurse at Royal Memorial Hospital kept her very busy but if anyone could handle busyness with a liberal dose of chaos, it was Clare. Her no-nonsense approach to her work was well-known around Royal and she held the respect of everyone who'd had babies under her care.

"I'm on a late shift tonight but I needed to get some last-minute Christmas shopping done. I need something special for my elderly neighbor. She's such a darling."

"Does she collect anything in particular?" Raina asked as they walked deeper into the store.

Clare wrinkled her brow in concentration. "Not anything specific. Do you mind if I look around for a bit? I'm not 100 percent sure of what I want but I'm hoping I'll recognize what I'm looking for when I see it."

"Sure," Raina said with a smile. "Holler if you need me. I'll just be out back, okay?"

"Thanks," Clare answered as she turned away with a distracted look on her face.

It wasn't like Clare to be indecisive, Raina thought as she pottered around in the back of the store, wielding her dusting cloth and giving some of the larger pieces of furniture a rub with furniture oil. After a few minutes, she looked up at Clare, who'd barely moved from where she left her. The other woman was staring blankly at a Royal Albert tea set as if she was waiting for some genie to waft out of the teapot's spout or something.

Raina worked her way back toward Clare.

"Are you sure I can't help you find something?"

Clare started and gasped in surprise. "Oh, I'm sorry. I was a million miles away. Yes," she said on a sigh. "I would be glad of your help. I know my neighbor has a thimble collection that she's added to ever since she was a little girl. She used to be quite skillful with a needle and thread from what I understand, and most of the thimbles are well used, but her eyesight's deteriorated as she's grown older, and she's developed arthritis and can't work with her hands anymore."

"That's a shame," Raina sympathized. "We have some beautiful handcrafted lace and linen doilies here from the early 1900s. Do you think she'd be interested in them?"

"They sound gorgeous. Show me."

Raina brought Clare over to a large mahogany sideboard and glass-fronted hutch that she used to showcase several of her better pieces of china. She slid open a drawer and removed a tissue-wrapped package. Her hand shook a little as she remembered the last time she'd handled the doilies, and how she'd almost used one to mop ice cream off the front of Nolan's trousers. A smile curved her lips at the memory. How much further had they come since then? Raina unwrapped the tissue and spread the doilies on the gleaming wooden surface of the sideboard.

"They're rather beautiful, don't you think?"

Each one had a round, finely woven linen center and a painstakingly created lace edge. There were four in total, each one slightly different in pattern from the other but with a floral theme that took Raina's breath away every time she looked at them. Such craftsmanship, such patience. She envied the woman who'd created them because she doubted she would ever have been able to have produced such exquisite work.

"They're gorgeous! And they're perfect. Thank you. I should have known you'd find exactly what I needed," Clare said on a note of relief.

"It's my job to make sure you do." Raina smiled back at her. "Clare, I hope you don't mind me saying this, but you don't seem yourself. Is everything okay?"

"Oh, it's nothing in particular. I'm just really stressed with the reorganization of the neonatal unit at the hospital. I'm sure the pressure will drop a little once the new wing is open next month. It's been a tough year."

Raina nodded. "But we're getting through it."

Clare looked at her and smiled. "Yes, we are. We're nothing if not determined, right?"

Raina smiled back. "Would you like me to gift wrap the doilies for you?"

"Would you? That would save me the bother, thank you."

"Come on over to the counter...unless you'd like to keep browsing?"

"Maybe I'll come in some other time and have a good poke around. Perhaps a day when I'm a bit less distracted," Clare laughed.

"Good idea," Raina agreed and walked over to the counter where she rewrapped the doilies in fresh tissue and put them in a gold box that she covered in a vibrant Christmas paper. "There you are," she said as she finished tying a red bow around the box.

"That looks far better than anything I would have done," Clare said admiringly.

"I get a bit more practice. I'm sure you can still diaper and swaddle a baby faster and more effectively than I ever could."

"You could be right," Clare conceded. "How is JJ?"

"He's doing really great, thanks. Of course he can barely sleep for counting the nights until Christmas."

"Good thing there are only two more to go."

"For my sake as well as JJ's," Raina agreed vehemently.

A thought occurred to Raina. She knew Clare was about the same age as Nolan and probably went to the local high school at around the same time as he would have. She'd told herself she wouldn't probe into his past, but with the opportunity presenting itself, maybe it was time she did a little poking around.

"Say, do you remember Nolan Dane?"

"Nolan? Yeah, sure. Why?"

"You know he was working on behalf of Samson Oil, don't you?"

Clare's mouth twisted into moue of distaste. "Yeah, I know. Seems like Royal is evenly divided about whether Samson Oil is a good thing or not."

Raina nodded. "I know. But he resigned from that position. He's going back to family law."

Clare's face brightened. "Is he? That's great. I know everyone around here was so shocked when he left. Of course, it was totally understandable after what he'd been through but no one really expected him to leave. He'd always been so woven into the fabric of Royal, y'know? Excelled at high school—popular and great at sports. It didn't matter what he put his hand to, he did it brilliantly. Our Nolan was quite the golden boy but never arrogant about it. Everyone liked him."

"What he'd been through?" Raina prompted, even though her stomach curled at what she might be told. Being nosy like this was wrong on so many levels—what if she didn't like what she heard? Raina forced herself to clear her mind of anxiety. Yes, this was Nolan's tale to tell, but to be honest, she was done with waiting. She wanted to know. And she'd have to take whatever she heard and deal with it.

"Oh, you don't know, do you? I keep forgetting that you didn't grow up here. That's a compliment by the way," Clare said with a warm smile. "Like I said, Nolan was always a high achiever but so was Carole, his high school sweetheart. They went to college together and then on to law school. Once they got their degrees they came back to Royal and married, and a year later they had a little boy, Bennett. Nolan and Carole were the couple everyone wanted to emulate. They were successful, sure, but they were also so in love. You couldn't look at them without feeling it."

Raina felt each one of Clare's words as if it was a physical blow but she tried hard not to linger on the pain. He'd had a life before she'd met him. So what on earth had gone wrong?

Clare continued, oblivious to the turmoil Raina was going through. "Carole returned to work soon after Bennett was born and I think he was about eighteen months old when it happened."

Raina hesitated to ask but couldn't help herself. "What happened?"

"It was awful. Apparently Nolan used to take Bennett to day care each morning as part of their routine. This particular day he heard that one of his clients had been severely beaten by her husband the night before. She called and asked him to come into the hospital to see her early, so he did. Of course that meant that Carole had to take Bennett to day care. Trouble was, she was in the middle of some really important negotiations her firm was handling at the same time and apparently she got paged while she was driving. She called her office and completely forgot Bennett was in the back of her car. They think he'd probably fallen asleep, too. Carole drove straight to her office and went to work. It was July and her car was parked in direct sunlight. Bennett died of heat exhaustion."

Raina gasped in horror. She'd heard of forgotten baby syndrome and, while she'd never understood it, she could only imagine how unbelievably awful it would be to have it happen to you.

"Did no one at the day care call to see where the baby was?" she asked.

"Apparently they had a new staff member on and they failed to figure it out at first. It wasn't until lunchtime that someone mentioned him. By then it was too late. Of course, the police were sympathetic but they had to bring charges of manslaughter and felony child abuse. It was just an awful time and it divided a lot of the people here.

"Poor Carole, she couldn't live with what she'd done. Before their case even got to court she took her life. Six months after that Nolan was gone, too—to LA, where he's been ever since."

"No wonder he didn't come back," Raina sympathized. "It must have been awful for him to lose them both."

Clare nodded. "It was a sad time for everyone who knew them but, of course, most of all for him."

The old grandfather clock near the front door chimed the hour and Clare glanced at it in consternation.

"Oh, heck, is that the time? I really need to get going. Thanks so much for the help with the Christmas gift,

Raina. I really appreciate it." She cocked her head and looked at Raina with a funny expression on her face. "You know, you actually look a bit like Carole. Same coloring and similar features. You could almost have passed for sisters. She was beautiful, too. Thanks again!"

Clare was gone in a whirlwind of movement, leaving Raina alone with her thoughts. Her heart ached for Nolan's loss. She didn't even want to begin to imagine what it would be like to lose JJ; just thinking about it was enough to bring tears to her eyes. But hearing Nolan's story brought a lot of things into sharper focus. Like his confidence and ability with her son and his patience. Those were all characteristics of someone who was used to being with a child.

She could almost understand him keeping his past to himself, but for one thing—her similarity to his late and obviously much beloved wife. Was that why he thought he was falling in love with *her*? Was it simply that she and JJ represented all that he'd lost? Were they merely substitutes for the wife and son that had been torn so tragically from his life?

It was impossible to know for sure, at least until he really talked to her. But how could she encourage him to do that? And what would she do if her fears were well-founded? Could she turn him away? It would break her heart if she did, and wouldn't she be breaking his all over again, too? He'd already lost his wife and son. But, she asked herself, could she live her life with him, knowing that he didn't love her for herself, but instead loved her for what she represented to him?

She'd promised herself to never again put herself last in a relationship—that things needed to be on an equal footing or no footing at all. She wouldn't settle for being second best. Which left her where, exactly, with Nolan?

Raina groaned out loud and squeezed her eyes shut. What on earth was she going to do?

Nolan walked up the path to Raina's house on Christmas Eve, ready to collect her and JJ to take them to the service at the nearby church. He'd debated with himself, long and hard, before accepting Raina's invitation to go with them. The last time he'd been here in Royal at Christmas, both Carole and Bennett had been alive. Bennett had been a year old and had been a complete handful in church. Not quite walking but active enough to want to be kept busy through the entire service. The memories were still so bittersweet and painful and yet, today at least, thinking about that time didn't bring the searing shaft of pain it used to. He missed them so very much, but he'd learned he needed to move forward with his life a long time ago. The irony that his moving forward had brought him full circle, and back home, wasn't lost on him.

From the other side of the front door, Nolan could hear JJ's excited chatter as he and Raina got ready. After he rapped his knuckles on the door, JJ's excited shout of "No'an!" came through clear as a bell. Nolan felt his lips turn up in a smile that dispelled any of the lingering doubt or sorrow he'd felt about attending the service tonight. He couldn't help but admit it. It was more than nice to be wanted.

And he wanted in return. Raina opened the door wearing a vibrant red wool coat that complemented her fair skin and dark hair perfectly. He took in her appearance and a jolt of lust rocked him. Since he'd left her in her bed last Saturday, he'd been walking around in a state of semiarousal that had tormented and excited him in equal proportions. He'd wanted nothing more than to make love with Raina that night, to stay wrapped in the comfort of her arms and her body through the dark hours and to wake with her in the morning and know that she was his. But he felt their relationship was still so new, so tenuous, that he'd needed to at least try to take things slower. To allow her time to ease into what he hoped would be their future together before taking what he knew would be an almighty step for them both.

Raina had been hurt before, badly. And he'd hurt her, too. He knew it and regretted it with almost every waking thought. So it was up to him to re-earn her respect. To give her space and time to know that she could love him as much as he already knew he loved her. Which, in a nutshell, meant a whole lot of self-denial on his part. Still, he reminded himself, it didn't hurt a man to be prepared. He patted his jacket pocket and felt the small parcel there. He'd carried it around for a couple of days now, debating when would be the right time, keeping it with him always should the opportunity present itself.

"No'an!" JJ launched himself through the front door and off the top step straight into Nolan's arms.

Nolan caught the little boy and swung him in the air, laughing even as Raina chided the boy for not saying hello properly. After whirling a giggling JJ around Nolan tucked him up on one hip and smiled at Raina.

"Good evening. I take it you're both ready?" he said on a laugh.

"As ready as we'll ever be," Raina said and smiled back.

"No'an! Santa's coming tonight!" JJ squealed excitedly.

"So I hear," Nolan replied, giving the little boy his full attention. "Have you been a good boy all year, JJ?"

For a moment JJ's forehead wrinkled in a frown, then his expression smoothed. "Yup!"

"Then I guess tomorrow morning will be a whole lot of fun for you, won't it?"

"Yup." JJ leaned a little closer to Nolan and cupped a small hand in front of Nolan's ear. "Mommy has a present for you," he whispered loudly. "It's a secret."

Nolan looked at Raina, who was rolling her eyes.

"JJ Patterson, what did I tell you about secrets?"

"That you're not suppos'ta tell other people?"

"That's right."

"But No'an's not other people," JJ protested.

Raina's eyes met Nolan's and the look they shared deepened into something else. Something that made Nolan's heart swell on a note of hope.

"No, honey. Nolan's not other people. He's much more than that."

Silence stretched between them. Nolan wished he could do nothing else but kiss Raina right now. Long and hard and deep. He wanted to demand from her what "more than that" meant to her. But he had to satisfy himself with waiting. Down the street, they heard the church bells begin to chime.

"We'd better get going."

He carried JJ toward his SUV but Raina remained on the front path.

"Shouldn't we take my car? I have JJ's seat in there," she said.

Nolan opened the rear door of the SUV and gestured to the new car seat he'd had installed a couple of days ago.

"You bought a car seat?" she asked, her voice incredulous.

"I thought I ought to," he said simply. "Brand-new and ready for a test drive. How about it, champ?" he asked JJ. "You ready to hop in?"

In answer, JJ scrambled into the car seat and waited to be buckled in.

"You want to check he's secure?" Nolan asked Raina,

who was standing on the sidewalk, a bemused expression on her face.

"No, it's okay. I… I trust you."

The words were simple enough in their expression but they meant the world to Nolan. Now he had only to prove to her that she could trust him in all things—not only with her precious son, but with her heart, as well.

The service at the nearby church was well attended and, given that the congregation was primarily young families, it was kept simple and sweet and involved the children for much of it. He didn't miss the pointed glances Raina received from several people when they saw her at his side. The only sign that she'd noticed anything was the faintest of blushes on her cheeks.

But when the service was over, it was the words of one of the older parishioners that really made her blush.

"Raina Patterson, good to see you've seen sense and have found yourself a decent young man," the old woman said as they left the church with JJ holding both their hands between them.

"Mrs. Baker, Merry Christmas to you," Raina replied courteously, but Nolan could see she was embarrassed by the attention. "This is Nolan Dane. You might have heard of his father, Howard Dane?"

The old lady eyed Nolan up and down as if he was a prime cut of meat before smiling and giving him the benefit of the twinkle in her eye. "I remember teaching your father. He was quite the rascal in his day. Are you a rascal, young man?"

Nolan heard Raina's sharp intake of breath and laughed before replying. "Only when absolutely necessary, ma'am."

Mrs. Baker snorted. "Humph. Cheeky. Just like your father." She leaned across and whispered in Raina's ear. "I'd hold on to this one if I was you, young lady. Good men are hard to find."

Raina was clearly speechless and could do no more than nod. Nolan reached down and gave the old lady a kiss on her wrinkled cheek.

"Merry Christmas, Mrs. Baker. I'll pass your regards on to my dad."

"You do that, young man. You do that."

By the time they left the church and headed home, JJ was still wide-awake and more pumped up than ever. As they arrived at Raina's place, she turned to Nolan, her blue eyes troubled.

"I'm sorry about that, back at the church."

"What for? I enjoyed it."

He held her gaze and watched as the concern faded from her face.

"Hot choclik time!" JJ announced from the backseat.

"Are you coming in for a hot drink?" Raina offered.

"Just try and hold me back."

Inside, Raina put on the TV and tuned in to a channel showing Santa's progress from the North Pole. JJ sat and watched the radar blip on the screen as if his life depended on it.

"Straight to bed after your hot chocolate, JJ."

"Can I stay up and see Santa, Mommy. Please? I be good," JJ pleaded.

"Hey, champ, Santa's a bit of a shy guy. He won't come unless you're tucked up in bed and fast asleep," Nolan answered.

"He won't?" JJ's eyes grew huge.

Nolan assumed a solemn expression and shook his head. "Why don't you come up here and sit with me and tell me what you want for Christmas."

Raina threw Nolan a grateful look. "I'll be right back."

Nolan watched her go through to the kitchen, his eyes caught by the gentle sway of her hips as she walked. Her skirt was not so tight as to be indecent, but not so loose as to hide the perfect shape of her either.

"No'an, you listening to me?" JJ's voice broke through his thoughts.

"Sorry, champ. Yep, I'm listening. What did you ask Santa for?"

"I tol' Santa I want one thing more'n anything else."

"And what's that?"

"It's secret," JJ said with a little frown on his forehead. "Can't tell secrets."

"What about if you just whisper it to me. Like you did before."

JJ mulled over Nolan's suggestion and then got up onto his knees and, leaning against Nolan's shoulder, said in his ear. "I aks'd for you to be my daddy."

Nolan's heart skipped a few beats in his chest. As JJ settled back down beside him he put an arm around the little guy's shoulders to give him a hug. His eyes stung with emotion and the enormity of what JJ had just said.

A rattle of mugs on a tray made him realize that Raina had returned to the room and that she'd overheard JJ's wish for Christmas. She was staring at Nolan, her expression a combination of shock and yearning and something else he couldn't quite put his finger on. He wished he could read her better. Wished he could be sure that she wanted the same thing that JJ wanted.

He chose his next words very carefully.

"That's a mighty special wish, JJ. Being a daddy is a very precious gift. You know what precious is?"

JJ shook his head.

"It's something that means everything to you."

"Like Spider-Man?"

"Even more than that," Nolan said with a smile. "I hope you get your wish, champ, but it's a mighty tall order for poor old Santa."

* * *

Raina set the tray down on the table and passed JJ his small mug of hot chocolate and Nolan his larger one.

"There you go, guys."

She averted her gaze from the question in Nolan's eyes. It was too soon, she told herself, even though her heart and soul screamed otherwise. And, yes, while there was nothing physically holding them back, there was an emotional minefield between them that still needed to be successfully negotiated. How could she even think about the future when she wasn't sure that Nolan had dealt with the past?

She hadn't been lying earlier this evening when she said she trusted Nolan. He was exactly what Mrs. Baker had said—a good man. But if she was going to commit to him she needed better than good for her and JJ. She wanted all of him—all his scars, all his truths, all his fears as well as his successes. Not just the parts he was willing to share. It had to be everything, or nothing.

She had to be sure he wanted her for herself, not because she reminded him of his dead wife or because JJ gave him back the chance to be a dad when his own son had been so cruelly taken from him. They both deserved more than that. If Nolan could be honest with her, she knew she'd have no further hesitation in giving herself to him with everything she had. Having him in her and JJ's life was a glowing beacon of what their future could be like. Which made the prospect of turning away from it, from Nolan, terrifying in its enormity.

Fifteen

After Raina caught JJ yawning more than once, she hustled the little guy off to bed but he insisted on both Nolan and her tucking him in. It brought tears to her eyes when JJ's little arms wrapped around Nolan's neck and he hugged him tight before snuggling under the covers.

"Sweet dreams, champ," Nolan said gently as he disentangled JJ's arms.

"Love you, No'an" came JJ's sleepy reply.

Raina saw the look of shock on Nolan's face at JJ's words and watched as he smoothed JJ's hair off his forehead and pressed a kiss there.

As she followed Nolan out of the room and down the hall, her mind was in turmoil. It was already too late to protect JJ from heartache if she shut Nolan out of their lives. And did she even want to do that?

"I've got something for JJ in the car. Do you mind if I put it under the tree for him for tomorrow?" Nolan asked when they got to the living room.

"Oh, that's kind of you," she answered. "No, I don't mind at all. He'll be thrilled. But won't you be able to give it to him tomorrow yourself?"

"I'll be with my parents first thing, and after that I'm flying back to LA. There are some things I need to sort out."

Raina couldn't hold back the sound of dismay that escaped her. "Oh, I'd hoped…"

"I will return, Raina. I promise you that," he hastened to reassure her. "I'm taking the time now to pack up my apartment and settle a few matters before I move back here permanently. I'll be back for New Year's Eve."

She forced herself to smile. "I guess I'll have to be satisfied with that then."

He pressed a quick kiss to her lips. "I'll go get JJ's gift."

As Nolan went out to the car, Raina quickly retrieved JJ's gifts from where she'd hidden them in her room and put them under the tree. Once that was done, she sank down onto the sofa. She'd thought that life might get easier as she got older but it seemed that the complications only came in different forms. She had so much to consider. Did she, like JJ, love Nolan, too? The answer came back to her with resounding clarity. Yes, she did. Either way she turned it, it was clear to her that both she and her son had lost their hearts to the man who'd come into their lives so unexpectedly.

She heard Nolan come back into the house and stood as he entered the living room, an enormous wrapped parcel in his arms.

"Wow, that's huge. I hope you haven't gone to too much trouble," she said as she eyed the massive gift.

"No trouble at all. The first Christmas that I can remember, I was about JJ's age and got one of these. I always wanted to do the same for my—"

Raina frowned as his voice broke off. "For your…?"

she prompted. Maybe this would give him the opening to tell her everything.

"For another three-year-old," Nolan said on a rush of words. "It's a Spider-Man bike, with training wheels. It might still be a bit big for him but the seat and handle bars are adjustable and JJ's tall for his age. Anyway, I hope he likes it."

"He'll love it, but, Nolan, it's too much."

"No." He shook his head. "Where kids are concerned, it's never too much."

There was now a bleak note to his voice that Raina couldn't miss. She realized the holidays must be so hard for him and stepped forward to comfort him without giving it a second thought. Her arms slid around Nolan's waist and she reached up to kiss him gently on the lips.

"Thank you," she said simply. She studied him carefully, her eyes roaming his serious face with his beautiful brown eyes and straight blade of a nose. And those lips. She wanted to taste those lips again. She wanted… oh, she wanted so much more than that. "Will you stay with me tonight?"

Nolan's face grew even more serious than before. "Raina, I—" He shook his head. "I don't think that's a good idea just now."

"Please, Nolan. You could still stay with me a while tonight, couldn't you?"

Did she sound too needy? Too desperate? She hoped not. Raina held her breath, waiting for Nolan's reply.

"Yes, I'd like that."

"Then that makes two of us," she said with a slow smile spreading across her face.

Nolan kissed her. This kiss so different from the last. It was as if Nolan was trying to imprint himself on her, get lost in her, perhaps. Whatever it was, she welcomed him with equal fervor, her lips parting under his possession like the petals of a flower opening for the sun. Desire licked along her veins like wildfire and with it her body came to aching life.

Her breasts felt full and swollen in the cups of her bra, her nipples wildly sensitive against the lace. Nolan continued to kiss her like a man trying to lose himself in sensation, and Raina was only too willing to meet him head-on, matching his passion with her own.

She yanked his sweater up in the back and shoved her hands underneath, her palms flat on the warm smooth skin of his back. She stroked upward along the muscles that ran parallel to his spine then lightly scraped her nails down again. He shuddered in her arms, a groan coming from his mouth as he tore his lips from hers.

"Raina, I want you so much. I never thought I…" His voice trailed away and Raina pressed another kiss to his lips.

"Me either," she whispered softly against his mouth. "Make love with me, Nolan."

His pupils flared, making his eyes look darker, hungrier than she'd ever seen them. A shiver of need ran through her. Nolan was always so in control, so self-assured. She wanted to see him lose that control tonight, and she wanted to be the reason for it.

"Are you sure, Raina? There're things I haven't—"

Not tonight, not now, she decided. She didn't want another woman in bed with them tonight. Instead, she kissed him again. "I'm sure. I don't think I can say it any clearer than that."

A smile tugged at the corners of his beautiful lips. "I guess not," he agreed.

She shook her head and gave a small laugh. Even with her blood pumping through her body, her lips swollen from his kiss and her senses focused on the pleasure she knew she would attain with this man, he could make her laugh. It was a gift, she realized.

"Let's stop talking. Start doing," she urged, curling her fingers and embedding her nails in his back more firmly.

"Whatever the lady wants."

She led him to her bedroom where she gently closed the door behind them and flowed into his arms as if she belonged nowhere else in the world. And, right here, right now, she didn't.

His lips were teasingly gentle when they kissed this time. He made a sweet exploration of her mouth, her jaw, the sensitive cord of muscle down the side of her neck. She moaned as his lips burned a trail to the neckline of her blouse. He brought his hands up between them, his fingers busily plucking her buttons undone until he could ease the fabric aside. He pushed it off her shoulders and let her blouse drop to the bedroom floor.

Raina watched his face as he looked at her. The desire reflected there was tempered with a look of awe that made her feel invincible. As if his world, his attention, began and ended with her and no one else. This was what she'd always craved. A bond between two people that was so perfect that nothing could tear it apart.

Nolan eyes met hers and she quivered a little at the intensity of his gaze.

"I love you, Raina Patterson. I want you to know that before I show you just how much it's true."

She parted her lips to speak, but no words came out. Emotion closed her throat, making it impossible to speak, but he didn't appear to mind that at all as he slid his hands to her waist and skimmed them upward, his fingertips brushing her rib cage and sending goose bumps all over her skin.

He only took a second to size up the bed behind them. The double bed was small, but more than sufficient for their purposes, he thought as he backed Raina toward the mattress and guided her down onto it.

He eased himself over her body and, propping himself up with one elbow, began to trace featherlight designs on her skin with his fingertips, punctuating them with a kiss, a nibble, a swipe of his tongue. She quivered underneath his onslaught and he could see her pebbled nipples against the soft pink lace of her bra. He'd never been a big fan of pink, but right now it was most definitely his favorite color. Nolan bent to cover one tip with his mouth, sucking hard through the delicate lace. Raina's fingers threaded roughly through his hair and she held him to her. She arched her back, thrusting herself upward. Unabashedly offering herself to him.

Nolan released her nipple and traced the outline of her bra with his tongue. With his free hand he reached to cup her other breast before sliding his hand around to the back and unsnapping the fastening. The garment fell away from her body and he slowly guided the straps down her arms, taking his time, worshipping every inch of her as he did so. She shook beneath him as he paid homage to her beauty, to each scar he discovered, each stretch mark, every curve. When he got to her skirt, Raina lifted her hips so he could ease it from her and expose the delicate pink lace panties that matched the bra he'd already discarded somewhere on the floor.

Her body went rigid as he traced the edges of her panty line, his fingers lingering a moment in the hollow at the top of her thigh, eliciting a moan of delight from Raina. He bent closer to her, inhaling the musky sweet scent that was her signature, and nuzzled at her mound. He was rewarded with a gasp, her hands now at his shoulders, her fingers tightening until he could feel the imprint of her nails on his skin.

"I want to taste you, again," he murmured, nuzzling her.

"I'm yours," Raina replied, her voice strained and her body now as taut as a bow beneath him.

He whisked the last remaining barrier from her body and nestled lower between her legs, his fingers at the top of her thighs, pressing gently into her pale flesh and parting her legs that little bit more. When he sank down and teased her glistening flesh with a flick of his tongue, she moaned again—the sound almost enough to make him want to dispense with this foreplay and race straight to the main event. Inside his jeans his erection strained against the restriction of his clothing. He pressed his hips against the mattress in an attempt to relieve his body's demands but it was a short-lived respite.

To distract himself, he focused solely on the woman in his arms, intent on bringing her the kind of pleasure he dreamed of having the right to give her every day of her life. The taste and scent of her body filled him, exciting him to higher levels and driving him to see her every need fulfilled. He sensed that this—making love here in her bed—was the only time she wasn't holding back. Here in the sanctuary of her room, she was his alone and so he paid homage to the privilege she bestowed upon him. Loving her with every cell in his body until she arched beneath him, her body locked in paroxysms of pleasure before softening and sinking back down into the mattress.

Nolan swiftly stripped himself of his clothes and returned to her. His arousal demanded satisfaction but he waited until Raina's eyes cleared, until she was with him 100 percent.

"How do you do that?" she asked, sounding dazed.

"Give you pleasure, you mean?"

"Yes, that."

"I do it from my heart, Raina. I love you. It's that simple."

And with that, he eased his length within her, hissing a little between his teeth as her swollen wet sheath gripped him. It was almost more than he could stand but still he held himself in check. Raina's eyes were a glittering blue, punctuated by wildly dilated pupils. She met his gaze and reached for him, her hands gripping his hips and pulling him to her. He sank deeper into her body, deeper into pleasure, deeper into love, and with every stroke, every withdrawal, he affirmed that love until they both tumbled headlong into satisfaction.

Nolan watched Raina as she slept. They'd been about as close as two people could be. He didn't want to screw this up. It was too precious. Too important to him. He thought about the small package that was nestled at the bottom of his jacket pocket and the note he'd written to go with it.

The logical side of his brain told him that it was too soon to give it to her, but every other cell in his body told him to do it now. The thing was, he was ready—more than ready—to take the next step with her, to make her his forever. But was she? One word began to echo in the back of his mind. *Time*. He had to give her more time. And, he realized, he had to let her come to her decision at her own pace, without undue pressure from him.

Already he wished he didn't have to return to LA. There wouldn't be much to do. He'd barely existed when he'd lived there and he could tie up the loose ends within the week. Would a week be enough for Raina? Would it give her the time he felt she needed to be certain about them both and give them a chance to forge a future together? He certainly hoped so. And when he came back he needed to face his final demons. He needed to tell Raina about Carole and Bennett. He didn't want any secrets between them any longer. It had been one thing to convince himself that it was okay to hide his past, to bury it where it didn't hurt anymore, but Raina deserved to know everything and she deserved to know it from him.

Nolan eased from the bed and felt around in the dark for his clothes before slipping into the bathroom and quickly getting dressed. It was still pitch-dark outside and the sun wouldn't be up for at least another hour. Maybe it was wrong to be leaving her like this—letting her wake alone after all they'd shared together. But he also respected that she would need her space.

And then there was JJ to consider, as well. The little boy's Christmas wish had plucked at Nolan's heart and he'd wished he'd had the right to tell JJ that his wish could come true. He loved the child as if he was his own, there were no two ways about it. He wanted them both in his life but the decision lay firmly in Raina's gentle but capable hands.

Once he was dressed, Nolan walked through the house to the sitting room. The tree lights glittered with their myriad colors, making the small room look exotic and exciting. He knew it wouldn't be long before JJ wakened and raced to see what Santa had brought him. He wished he could be here to see JJ open his gifts, but with any luck he'd be able to share that delight with the little guy next year, and hopefully every year after that.

Nolan's heavy winter jacket lay over the back of an armchair where he'd discarded it last night. He reached into the pocket and pulled out the small gift and the envelope with the note he'd written for Raina before picking her and JJ up last night. He placed them under the tree, in among the gifts for JJ, then quietly let himself out of the house and into the burgeoning dawn.

Sixteen

"Santa's been here, Mommy. Wake up! Santa's been here!"

Raina opened one bleary eye then the other as JJ's joyful cries dragged her from sleep. She reached for Nolan, wondering how on earth they were going to explain his being there in bed with her, but her hand came up empty, the sheets cold beneath her touch. Raina quickly dragged on her nightgown and a robe and went to the living room where JJ was excitedly hopping from one foot to the other and staring at the bounty under the Christmas tree.

"Merry Christmas, JJ," she said, scooping her son up for a cuddle and a kiss. As she expected, he squirmed in her arms wanting to be put down to get to the serious business of opening gifts. "Remember the rules, JJ. Only one gift now. Granddad will be here to have breakfast with us and you can open all the rest then."

"Just one, Mommy?" JJ asked plaintively.

Raina held firm. She'd explained this all to JJ more than once in the days leading up to Christmas.

"How about you phone Granddad and let him know you're awake? He can let you know what time he'll be here."

JJ raced to do as she'd suggested, pressing the speed dial button on the phone Raina had taught him to use. After a brief conversation, he ran back to the Christmas tree. "Ten minnit!" he announced, hopping from one foot to the other.

"Great, now which gift are you going to open first?"

JJ zeroed in on the massive present Nolan had left under the tree for him. "This one," he said, and began tearing the paper off it immediately.

His squeal of delight was ear piercing when he saw the picture on the box. Raina hastened to help him open it and lift the bike out. There was a little assembly required but thankfully it only took a few minutes. Even better, Raina's dad arrived to do it all for her. He raised an eyebrow in her direction when he saw the bike, knowing it wasn't something she'd been able to afford for her son.

"It's from a friend, Dad," Raina said in explanation.

"Fancy wheels from a fancy man," he commented with a brusque nod, his eyes not budging from her face.

Raina felt the heat of a blush rise in her cheeks and she turned away from her father's piercing gaze.

"Now that you're here, I'll go and grab my shower and get dressed. Then I'll make us all breakfast, okay?"

Without waiting for a response, Raina flew down the hall toward the bathroom. She closed the door behind her and leaned against it for a few seconds, willing her blush to subside. Her father knew her too well. She'd seen that look on his face when she'd believed herself in love before. But this time it was different, she told herself. This time it was real.

Thankfully, her father didn't seem inclined to say any more on the subject, and after they'd had breakfast and opened all the presents under the tree, he went back to his place. Raina started to clean up the mess of wrapping paper and boxes that JJ had strewn all over the room in his exuberance. She'd hoped that he'd have happy memories of this day. Goodness knew she'd tried really hard to make it so. Right now, he was in his room, playing with some of his new toys until Raina could take him outside on the sidewalk with the new bike.

Raina almost missed the small parcel and envelope that had been placed at the tree's base. In fact it was already in her hand with the fistful of discarded paper when she felt it. After sorting through the paper and putting it in the trash bag, she sat down and looked at the items in her hand. Her pulse raced as she examined the small wrapped cube and the simple white envelope that accompanied it. Her name was written in bold black script across the front of the envelope and she traced the letters with a fingertip.

It wasn't her father's handwriting, which left only one other person who could have left it there—Nolan. Butterflies swarmed in her stomach, their tiny wings brushing against her nerves and making her hands tremble. What was this? Despite his words last night, could it be a farewell perhaps, or something else? There was only one way to find out but suddenly Raina found the prospect of reading whatever he had written more daunting than anything she'd ever done before.

Eventually she dragged in a deep breath and slid her finger under the flap of the envelope, tearing it open with a jagged edge. There was a single slip of paper inside, which she took out and unfolded.

Dear Raina,
I know we've only known one another a very short time, but believe me when I say that I'm very serious about wanting you in my life. I guess by now you've

realized that I have something very special to ask you. I wanted to ask you last night, but I know you probably need more time to think about this and to be sure, so I'm giving you this next week—unencumbered by my presence—to consider what we mean to one another and particularly what I mean to you.

For my part, I know I don't want to spend the rest of my life without you by my side. I've learned, the hard way, that the special things in life can be torn from you at a moment's notice and that we need to reach out and grasp those gifts when we can—to cherish them and hold them dear to us, the way I want to cherish and hold you.

I only hope that you want the same as I do and that you'll let me be there with you and JJ, loving and supporting you both for as long as you'll let me. Nothing would give me greater pride or pleasure.

I'll be home on New Year's Eve and I'd be honored if you'd accompany me to the Texas Cattleman's Club function that night. You can give me your answer then. In the meantime, I would like you to open my Christmas gift to you and know that it comes from my heart and with my very best intentions.

All my love,
Nolan

Raina's fingers were wrapped tight around the small box in her hand, so tight that her knuckles whitened and her palms began to ache from the imprint of the edges of the box. Did he mean to ask her to marry him? Black spots began to swim in front of Raina's eyes and she realized she was holding her breath. She forced herself to breathe in and out, and again, until the spots receded.

Panic clawed at her throat. She'd thought she was ready for this but she so wasn't. They'd met less than four weeks ago. How could he be so certain she was what he wanted? How could she when she knew he still hadn't told her about the sadness of his past? There was still so much unsaid between them. The details of her past, of his. But did any of that matter when they loved each other?

Droplets of water dripped onto the sheet of paper in her hand and Raina realized she was weeping. The words on the paper blurred and she quickly refolded the sheet and shoved it back in the envelope. All the while, her heart urged her to take a risk on love again and her mind shrieked its horror in the background.

She'd taken risks on love before and she still bore the emotional scars from that. How on earth could she even contemplate marriage, if that was indeed what Nolan was suggesting, based on her track record with men? Hadn't it been a crazy, hormone-driven attraction that had seen her hook-up with Jeb in the first place? She'd been twenty-six, going on twenty-seven. Hardly a child by any means. She should have known better then—and she certainly knew better now.

Sure, deep down, she knew that Nolan was different from Jeb and the others she'd dated before him. But there was still that niggling sense of not knowing exactly where she stood with Nolan.

JJ would be thrilled at the chance to call Nolan Daddy. She knew that. But she had to be careful. She'd fought Jeb and beaten a tornado to give JJ a stable and secure home, a safe and happy childhood. She couldn't risk throwing that all away. Not now.

A voice in the back of her head reminded her that Nolan had acknowledged his initial deceit, that he'd apologized and done his best to make it up to her. That he'd even re-signed from his job over it. Surely those were not the actions of a man who would stomp all over her heart and then walk away. He said he was back in Royal for good now. And she knew he meant it.

A kernel of hope began to bloom inside her until she reminded herself of the money that still sat in the safe back at Priceless and of the fact that Jeb probably still wanted it. While her ex certainly appeared to have dropped off the radar for now, who knew when he'd be back next or what his demands would be? How would Nolan react then? Would he be prepared to accept Raina with all her baggage?

"Mommy? Can we go outside now?"

JJ interrupted her jangled thoughts and Raina latched on to the chance to distract herself.

"Sure, honey," she said, shoving the envelope and the still-wrapped box in a drawer in the sideboard. She'd deal with it later. Maybe. "Let's get our coats on, okay?"

"Yippee!"

It was New Year's Eve and Raina was still in a quandary about Nolan's letter and the box that sat untouched in the drawer of her sideboard. She'd missed him this week. More because she'd known he was so far away. But he was back today and she'd alternately been filled with excitement and with a major case of the jitters.

"G'anddad's here!" JJ announced from where he'd been watching at the front window for his grandfather to pick him up and take him back to the trailer park to see in the New Year.

"Go and get your bag then, JJ," Raina suggested with a smile, turning away from the mirror where she'd been fussing with her hair for about the seventh time already that evening.

She went to the front door and opened it wide.

"You all right, girlie?" her dad asked, stomping his feet on the step before coming inside.

Raina welcomed her father with a huge hug and inhaled the special scents of his forbidden cigars and Old Spice.

"Yeah, Dad, I'm fine. Just glad to see you."

Her father gave her a sharp look and a small nod. "I heard some interesting news today. About your young man."

"My young...? You mean Nolan?"

"He's why I'm sitting for you tonight, isn't he?"

Raina felt the heat of a blush warm her cheeks and nodded. "Yes, he's taking me out tonight. What did you hear?"

Please don't let it be something bad, she wished with all her heart.

"Has to do with that no good piece of sh—"

"Dad! No swearing," Raina interrupted, glancing toward JJ.

"Well, you know who I mean."

"Jeb?"

"Who else?"

"What has Nolan got to do with Jeb?"

Her Dad gave her a sly smile. "Seems your young man arranged a meeting with the lowlife. Got him arrested and put away. Turns out he was wanted for third-degree felony over in New Mexico. Killed someone while driving under the influence and fled the scene, then jumped bail after that."

"But...how...when?" Raina was at a loss for words. How on earth would Nolan have known who Jeb was, let alone arranged for him to be arrested?

"Happened the night after the pageant, apparently. According to my poker buddy at the sheriff's office, Nolan offered him money to stay away from you, permanently. A goodly sum, so I'm told. That scumbag couldn't resist, of course, but it turns out he was dealing with the wrong person. Nolan apparently used his contacts to find out a bit more about who he was dealing with, and took his information to Sheriff Battle, who was only too pleased to oblige and take that waste of space off the streets. Apparently he put up a bit of a fight."

Did that explain the bruise on Nolan's face? Hard on the heels of that question came the realization that Jeb was in jail. Relief warred with confusion in Raina's mind.

"Anyways, doesn't sound like Jeb's going to be a problem for you again. You can thank your young man for that. I certainly plan to the next time I see him." Her dad fixed her with a steely look. "And I will see him a next time, won't I?"

"I... I don't know, Dad. I'm not sure I'm ready."

Her father harrumphed and pulled her into his arms for another hug. "You'll know when you're ready, my girlie. You'll know in your heart."

"But, Dad, we haven't known each other long en—"

"Time isn't what's important here. What you gotta ask yourself is what would your life be like without him in it."

Raina tipped her head to look up at her father. He'd had plenty of lady friends since her mom had left them, but never anyone who stuck around. "Is that what you asked yourself?"

He nodded. "I did, and I never got lucky enough to meet the lady I'd miss forever. Well, not yet anyway," he concluded with a twinkle in his blue eyes. "Now, where's that grandson of mine?"

After JJ and her dad had gone, Raina paced the living room floor, weighing her father's words and the news that Jeb was in jail. The relief she felt was slow to sink in, but bit by bit, the realization that she no longer had to worry about a random knock at her front door or being accosted on the street or receiving yet another late-night phone call or text began to seem real. A feeling of liberation filled her, a sense of freedom she hadn't known in a very long time—and she owed it all to Nolan.

What kind of man did what he'd done? A good man. An honest one. A man who was reliable and forthright and who looked after what was his to the very best of his ability and who wasn't afraid to ask for help when he couldn't do it alone. He'd protected her from harm, even when she hadn't asked for it. And she knew, deep in her heart, that Nolan would move mountains for her if she needed him to.

No matter which way she looked at it, Nolan Dane was a better person than she'd wanted to believe. She'd been so scarred by the actions of her past that she'd let them hold her back when she was being offered a chance to make a new start, a new beginning—filled with the kind of love she'd always dreamed of.

The sound of a car door slamming announced Nolan's arrival. Raina quickly grabbed the wrapped box from the drawer and slipped it into her evening purse.

He'd given her this week and she'd thought long and hard. And she'd reached her decision.

Seventeen

Nolan strode confidently up the path to the house and felt his heart lift when he saw the front door open to reveal Raina standing there, waiting for him. He'd missed her both physically and mentally. He'd lost track of the number of times he'd picked up the phone to call her, only to remind himself that he was giving her space to think.

Now the time had come for what he hoped would be the answer he'd been waiting for. Despite his eagerness, he wouldn't push. He understood her vulnerability, even though she projected such a staunch and strong face to the world. She needed to come to him on her own terms.

Framed in the doorway, she smiled nervously down at him. He bounded up the front steps to greet her the way he'd been waiting to do from the moment he'd left her bed, and she slid easily into his arms and lifted her face for his kiss. He kept it short and sweet, denying the nearly overwhelming urge he had to forget the night ahead and to simply sweep her off her feet, take her into her bedroom and pick up where they'd left off a week ago.

"I've missed you," he said simply, as he forced himself to release her.

She gave him a shy smile. "I've missed you, too."

"You look beautiful."

"Thank you."

Her cheeks flushed a delicate pink beneath the subtle makeup she wore and Nolan felt his heart squeeze in response. There was nothing he didn't love about her. He only hoped she'd let him tell her that every day now for the rest of their lives.

"You left without opening your Christmas gift," Raina said, reaching behind her to the hall table and passing a long slender parcel to him.

Nolan looked at it in surprise. This was the secret JJ had whispered to him about. "Can I open it now?"

"Sure," she teased, "unless you want to wait until next year."

He tore away the wrapping and instantly recognized the case he'd coveted a few weeks ago. He opened the lid and revealed the writing set inside. Nolan was staggered. Not just by the beauty of the gift, but by her thoughtfulness in giving it to him.

"It's old, of course," she said, sounding worried, "but in excellent condition. I remembered you looking at it and I thought—"

"I love it. Thank you, it's perfect."

He leaned forward to kiss her again. She was flushed when he finally let her go.

"Oh, you like it? Well…that's good then."

He smiled; she still sounded as if he'd knocked her off-kilter. She could barely meet his eyes as she reached into the cupboard behind her for her coat. He helped her into it, taking a moment to inhale the fresh herbal scent of her hair as she lifted it over her collar. He imagined his face buried in that sweet softness again and, as his body throbbed in response, was forced to turn his mind to other things.

"Shall we go?" Raina asked.

Surprised, because he'd hoped they'd talk about the gift he'd left for her before they headed out tonight, Nolan inclined his head. "My chariot awaits," he replied, gesturing for her to take his arm.

She locked the door behind her and they headed to the car where he stowed the writing set safely in the back. The journey to the Texas Cattleman's Club was conducted in silence, briefly punctuated by Raina asking how his trip to LA had gone. By the time Nolan handed his car keys to the valet outside the club, his stomach was a ball of nerves. Still not one word about his letter or his gift. He reminded himself that he was the one who'd set the parameters here. It had been his choice to leave her for this week and give her space and time to think about their future, if indeed they had one.

They circulated among the crowd, stopping and chatting here and there. The club was a large, rambling single-story building made of dark stone and wood that had originally been built in the early 1900s. The interior decor still reflected its Old World men's club heritage, with hunting trophies and historical artifacts adorning the paneled walls but, Nolan noticed, the ceiling had been lifted during the repairs after the tornado, giving the club an airier feel about it, and the colors were brighter and lighter than before. Overall the renovations better reflected the now mixed gender culture of what had long been solely a male domain.

In the great room, the mood was vibrant and celebratory, but Nolan knew he couldn't relax and celebrate until he had the answers he sought. During a lull in conversation with a group of his old high school buddies, Nolan tucked Raina closer to his side and drew her away to a quiet alcove he'd spied.

"Tired of the party already?" Raina teased.

Her cheeks were still softly flushed and her blue eyes sparkled, but he sensed that she was nervous. Possibly even as nervous as he was.

He smiled in response—it was now or·never. "Actually, I was wondering what you thought of my Christmas gift."

The smile on Raina's face froze for a moment, before disappearing altogether and Nolan felt his hopes for the future slide inexorably out of his grasp. She reached into her small purse and pulled out the gift he'd left for her under the tree. His stomach dipped as he realized she hadn't even unwrapped it.

Raina looked up at him and he braced himself for the rejection he was sure was coming his way.

"I…" She stopped and chewed at her lower lip for a moment before continuing. "I didn't want to unwrap it without you there. You mentioned intentions in your letter. I need to know exactly what those are, Nolan."

It wasn't what he'd been expecting her to say and for a moment he was lost for words. But then the logical side of his brain kicked in and processed what she'd said. She wasn't rejecting him. She simply needed more reassurance. At least he hoped that's what was happening. He'd felt adrift like this once before in his life and he'd hated every second of it. It was why he'd been so reluctant to embrace the idea of sharing his life with anyone again. But he'd realized that he had to let himself be a little vulnerable if he wanted Raina to trust him. Trust him and love him.

"You know I love you, Raina, don't you?" he asked and felt a tentative swell of hope when she nodded. "I got off on the wrong foot with you to begin with and I can't apologize enough for that. The man I was then, the one who thought he could approach someone with an ulterior motive and damn the consequences—he's not the man I'm meant to be, nor the man I ever wanted to be. Do you believe me when I say that, too?"

Again she nodded and again he felt the tightness ease inside him that little bit more. Nolan led Raina over to a pair of chairs set against the wall in the alcove. They were surrounded by the noise and celebration of the crowd, and yet at the same time they were isolated. Locked in their own private space.

"I walked away from my life once," he began anew. "Things became more than I could bear and I had to leave or lose myself completely. I found a new way of living with myself. Unfortunately it didn't make me a very decent man.

"I like to think that everything in life eventually comes full circle and that fate took a hand in bringing me back to Royal. I wasn't ready to come back, I'll be honest with you about that. And I definitely wasn't ready to fall in love. But I did. Coming home has given me a new start— a chance to lead a good decent life again, a life I want to share with you and JJ, if you'll let me.

"I love you," he repeated and took both her hands in his, bringing them up to his lips to kiss her knuckles.

"I know you love me. I believe you, Nolan," Raina answered him quietly. "My father told me what you did with Jeb. Until I heard what he said and what you'd done, I think I was too afraid to trust my heart and let myself admit that I love you, too." She pressed one hand against his chest. "I know you have a good and decent heart, Nolan, and your actions have proved that to me when I wouldn't listen to what I really wanted to hear. You see, I don't have such a great track record with men. I don't tend to choose the stayers, or the reliable guys. In some ways I think I was just waiting for you to fail at the first hurdle because that would let me let you go."

"And I did fail. I failed you terribly."

"That's in the past, Nolan. You've more than made amends for that. You were acting for your client and, to be honest, even I can see now that you had no other option than to do the best for him at the time."

She looked up at him and Nolan saw tears swimming in her exquisite blue eyes. The sight made his heart wrench at the knowledge he'd put those tears there.

"Raina—" he started, but she put her fingertips to his lips.

"Shh, let me finish. You did what was right at the time, the same way you did what was right when you resigned your position with Samson Oil. I know that now." She took in a deep breath and her voice was so soft when she next spoke, Nolan could barely hear her. "I also know about Carole and Bennett."

The names struck him like a physical blow. "I planned to tell you, eventually," he said, his voice raspy with emotion. "It was more difficult than I thought."

"It's okay, Nolan. I understand that it's probably too painful for you to talk about them. For a while I've held that against you as another secret you were keeping from me. But I've let that go. Even so, there's still something that worries me. Something I need to ask you."

"Ask," he demanded.

"Do you love me and JJ because we remind you of your wife and son?"

Nolan felt her gaze lock on him with an intensity that showed him that everything now relied upon his response. He pushed aside the pain and the hurt, and chose his words carefully. His future happiness depended on how he said this.

"Raina, I will always love Carole and Bennett." His voice cracked on their names and he halted for a moment, closed his eyes and drew in a deep breath. "But they're gone. Losing them— I thought I'd never love again. That I never could. It wasn't just the pain of losing them, it was the risk of putting myself back out there again. Of maybe losing what little I had left of them, as well, if I let someone else into my heart.

"Meeting you has taught me that it's possible to love again without diminishing what I had with Carole, and trust me, I never thought I'd even want to feel about anyone the way I feel about you. You're so strong and so resilient. Life has battered you down and still you've shown your strengths by getting back up and moving forward. You haven't just been an example to me, you've opened my eyes to who I should be and shown me that I can loosen my grip on the past. Doing so allows me to think of a future. It's a future I want with you."

She nodded but remained silent. He looked down at the little packet in her hands.

"Will you open it now?" he asked.

His heart hammered in his chest. She could still return it to him. And he'd accept it and let her go if that was what she really wanted, even though the very thought threatened to tear his heart in two. He held his breath until she'd worked loose the tape that bound the wrapping, exposing the ring box. She lifted the lid and gasped. Inside, nestled against a dark velvet bed, lay his promise to her—a cushion-cut blue diamond edged with brilliant white diamonds and set in delicate platinum scrollwork.

Nolan dropped to one knee on the floor in front of her and lifted the ring from the box, offering it to her.

"Raina Patterson, will you do me the honor of becoming my wife? Will you let me be your husband for eternity and be a father to JJ and any other children we might be lucky enough to have?"

She appeared lost for words until he heard her choke on a sob. Tears rolled down her face but none of that mattered when he heard the words she was so desperately working to get out of her throat.

"Yes. Yes. Yes," she said repeatedly through her tears.

Nolan took her hand, slid the ring onto her finger and stood, pulling her to her feet. Raina lifted her face to his.

"I love you, Nolan. So very much. I was scared, I'll admit it. And probably too quick to look for reasons not to love you. I didn't want you to be able to hurt me and I didn't trust my own judgment anymore. But I do now. I love you and I'd be the happiest woman in the world to marry you. I'm so lucky to have you."

"I'm the lucky one, Raina. I never expected to be given another chance at love and life the way I have with you. And I want to spend the rest of my life showing you how much you mean to me."

He kissed her and, in her arms, found the sense of belonging that had been missing from his world for far too long. Her lips were sweet and tender and tasted of the promise of a future he never dreamed he'd want again. And yet, with Raina, he knew the future would be truly wonderful and that it was something he wanted to grasp with both hands and hold on to and cherish forever.

"They'll be doing the fireworks soon," he commented as they came up for air and he saw the crowd thinning in the great room as people started to move outdoors for the display. "Did you want to go outside to watch?"

Raina shook her head. "No, let's go home instead… and make our own."

* * * * *

"This is the one."

The minute she put on the wedding gown, Natalie knew it. Delicate silver-stitched designs looked like snowflakes dancing across the fabric. It was the most beautiful dress she'd ever seen, and she'd seen hundreds of brides come through her chapel.

It was perfect. Everything she'd ever wanted.

Natalie swallowed hard. Everything she'd ever wanted *for the bride*, she corrected herself.

Quickly she turned to Colin. He said nothing as he walked toward her. Did he hate it?

She felt her chest tighten. He wasn't looking at the gown. He was looking at her. The intensity of his gaze made her insides turn molten. Her knees started trembling.

Just when she thought she couldn't bear his gaze any longer, she turned back around. But this time she caught his reflection in the mirror beside her. Maybe it was the confusion of playing the part of the bride. . .but for one moment he looked like a groom.

Her groom.

* * *

A White Wedding Christmas
is part of the Brides and Belles series: Wedding planning is their business. . .and their pleasure

A WHITE WEDDING CHRISTMAS

BY
ANDREA LAURENCE

Published in Great Britain 2015
by Mills & Boon, an imprint of Harlequin (UK) Limited,
Eton House, 18-24 Paradise Road, Richmond, Surrey, TW9 1SR

© 2015 Andrea Laurence

ISBN: 978-0-263-25289-7

51-1215

Harlequin (UK) Limited's policy is to use papers that are natural, renewable and recyclable products and made from wood grown in sustainable forests. The logging and manufacturing processes conform to the legal environmental regulations of the country of origin.

Printed and bound in Spain
by CPI, Barcelona

Andrea Laurence is an award-winning author of contemporary romance for Mills & Boon Desire and paranormal romance for Mills & Boon Nocturne. She has been a lover of reading and writing stories since she learned to read at a young age. She always dreamed of seeing her work in print and is thrilled to share her special blend of sensuality and dry, sarcastic humor with the world.

A dedicated West Coast girl transplanted into the Deep South, Andrea is working on her own happily-ever-after with her boyfriend and their collection of animals, including a Siberian husky that sheds like nobody's business. If you enjoy Colin and Natalie's story, tell her by visiting her website, www.andrealaurence.com; like her fan page at facebook.com/authorandrealaurence; or follow her on Twitter, @andrea_laurence.

To Diet Coke & Jelly Belly—

A lot of people have supported me throughout my career and over the course of my multiple releases, I've done my best to thank them all. Now that I have, it would be remiss if I failed to thank the two crucial elements of my daily word count: caffeine and sugar. My preferred delivery methods are Diet Coke and Jelly Belly jelly beans (strawberry margarita, pear and coconut, to be precise). They have helped me overcome plot challenges and allowed me to keep up with my insane deadline schedule.

Prologue

A lot had changed in the past fourteen years.

Fourteen years ago, Natalie and her best friend, Lily, were inseparable, and Lily's older brother Colin was the tasty treat Natalie had craved since she was fifteen. Now, Lily was about to get married and their engagement party was being held at the large, sprawling estate of her brother.

He'd come a long way since she saw him last. She'd watched, smitten, as he'd evolved into the cool college guy, and when Lily and Colin's parents died suddenly, Natalie had watched him turn into the responsible guardian of his younger sister and the head of his father's company. He'd been more untouchable then than ever before.

Lily and Natalie hadn't seen much of each other over the past few years. Natalie had gone to college at the

University of Tennessee and Lily had drifted aimlessly. They exchanged the occasional emails and Facebook likes, but they hadn't really talked in a long time. She'd been surprised when Lily called her at From This Moment, the wedding company Natalie co-owned, with a request.

A quickie wedding. Before Christmas, if possible. It had been early November at the time, and From This Moment usually had at least fourteen months of weddings scheduled in advance. But they closed at Christmas and for a friend, she and the other three ladies that owned and operated the wedding chapel agreed to squeeze one more wedding in before the holiday.

Natalie's invitation for the engagement party arrived the next day and now, here she was, in a cocktail dress, milling around Colin's huge house filled with people she didn't know.

That wasn't entirely true. She knew the bride. And when her gaze met the golden hazel eyes she'd fantasized about as a teenager, she remembered she knew a second person at the party, too.

"Natalie?" Colin said, crossing a room full of people to see her.

It took her a moment to even find the words to respond. This wasn't the boy she remembered from her youth. He'd grown into a man with broad shoulders that filled out his expensive suit coat, a tanned complexion with eyes that crinkled as he smiled and a five-o'clock shadow that any teenager would've been proud to grow.

"It is you," he said with a grin before he moved in for a hug.

Natalie steadied herself for the familiar embrace. Not everything had changed. Colin had always been a hugger. As a smitten teen, she'd both loved and hated those hugs. There was a thrill that ran down her spine from being so close; a tingle danced across her skin as it brushed his. Now, just as she did then, she closed her eyes and breathed in the scent of him. He smelled better than he did back when he wore cheap drugstore cologne, but even then, she'd loved it.

"How are you, Colin?" she asked as they parted. Natalie hoped her cheeks weren't flushing red. They felt hot, but that could just be the wine she'd been drinking steadily since she got to the party.

"I'm great. Busy with the landscaping business, as always."

"Right." Natalie nodded. "You're still running your dad's company, aren't you?"

He nodded, a hint of suppressed sadness lighting in his eyes for just a moment. *Good going, Natalie, remind him of his dead parents straight off.*

"I'm so glad you were able to fit Lily's wedding in at your facility. She was adamant that the wedding happen there."

"It's the best," Natalie said and it was true. There was no other place like their chapel in Nashville, Tennessee, or anywhere else she knew of. They were one of a kind, providing everything a couple needed for a wedding at one location.

"Good. I want the best for Lily's big day. You look amazing, by the way. Natalie is all grown up," Colin noted.

Natalie detected a hint of appreciation in his eyes as his gaze raked over the formfitting blue dress her business partner Amelia had forced her into wearing tonight. Now she was happy her fashion-conscious friend had dressed her up for the night. She glanced at Colin's left hand—no ring. At one point, she'd heard he was married, but it must not have worked out. Shocker. That left the possibilities open for a more interesting evening than she'd first anticipated tonight.

"I'm nearly thirty now, you know. I'm not a teenager."

Colin let out a ragged breath and forced his gaze back up to her face. "Thank goodness. I'd feel like a dirty old man right now if you were."

Natalie's eyebrow went up curiously. He *was* into her. The unobtainable fantasy might actually be within her grasp. Perhaps now was the time to make the leap she'd always been too chicken to make before. "You know, I have a confession to make." She leaned into him, resting a hand on his shoulder. "I was totally infatuated with you when we were kids."

Colin grinned wide. "Were you, now?"

"Oh yes." And she wouldn't mind letting those old fantasies run wild for a night. "You know, the party is starting to wind down. Would you be interested in getting out of here and finding someplace quiet where we could talk and catch up?"

Natalie said the words casually, but her body language read anything but. She watched as Colin swallowed hard, the muscles in his throat working up and down as he considered her offer. It was bold, and she knew it, but she might not have another chance to get a taste of Colin Russell.

"I'd love to catch up, Natalie, but unfortunately I can't."

Natalie took a big sip of her wine, finishing her glass, and nodded, trying to cover the painful flinch at his rejection. Suddenly she was sixteen again and felt just as unworthy of Colin's attentions as ever. Whatever.

"Well, that's a shame. I'll see you around then," she said, shrugging it off as though it was nothing but a casual offer. Turning on her heel with a sly smile, she made her way through the crowd and fled the party before she had to face any more embarrassment.

One

Putting together a decent wedding in a month was nearly impossible, even with someone as capable as Natalie handling things. Certain things took time, like printing invitations, ordering wedding dresses, coordinating with vendors... Fortunately at From This Moment wedding chapel, she and her co-owners and friends handled most of the work.

"Thank you for squeezing this last wedding in," Natalie said as they sat around the conference room table at their Monday morning staff meeting. "I know you all would much rather be starting your holiday celebrations."

"It's fine," Bree Harper, the photographer, insisted. "Ian and I aren't leaving for Aspen until the following week."

"It gives me something to do until Julian can fly back

from Hollywood," Gretchen McAlister added. "We're driving up to Louisville to spend the holidays with his family, and working another wedding will keep me from worrying about the trip."

"You've already met his family, Gretchen. Why are you nervous?"

"Because this time I'm his fiancée," Gretchen said, looking down in amazement at the ring he'd just given to her last week.

Natalie tried not to notice that all of her formerly single friends were now paired off. Gretchen and Bree were engaged. Amelia was married and pregnant. At one time, they had all been able to commiserate about their singleness, but now, it was just Natalie who went home alone each night. And she was okay with that. She anticipated a lifetime of going home alone. It's just that the status quo had changed so quickly for them all. The past year had been a whirlwind of romance for the ladies at From This Moment.

Despite the fact that she was a wedding planner, Natalie didn't actually believe in any of that stuff. She got into the industry with her friends because they'd asked her to, for one thing. For the other, it was an amazingly lucrative business. Despite the dismal marriage statistics, people seemed happy to take the leap, shelling out thousands of dollars, only to shell out more to their divorce attorneys at some point down the road.

As far as Natalie was concerned, every couple who walked through the door was doomed. The least she could do was give them a wedding to remember. She'd do her best to orchestrate a perfect day they could look back on. It was all downhill from there, anyway.

"I'll have the digital invitations ready by tomorrow.

Do you have the list of email addresses for me to send them out?" Gretchen asked.

Natalie snapped out of her thoughts and looked down at her tablet. "Yes, I have the list here." Normally, e-invites were out of the question for a formal wedding, but there just wasn't time to get paper ones designed, printed, addressed, mailed and gather RSVPs in a month's time.

"We're doing a winter wonderland theme, you said?" Amelia asked.

"That's what Lily mentioned. She was pretty vague about the whole thing. I've got an appointment with them on the calendar for this afternoon, so we'll start firming everything up then. Bree, you're doing engagement photos on Friday morning, right?"

"Yep," Bree said. "They wanted to take their shots at the groom's motorcycle shop downtown."

Natalie had known Lily a long time, but her choice in a future husband was a surprise even to her. Frankie owned a custom motorcycle shop. He was a flannel-wearing, bushy-bearded, tattooed hipster who looked more like a biker raised by lumberjacks than a successful businessman. Definitely not who Natalie would have picked for her best friend, and she was pretty sure he was not who Colin would've picked for Lily, either.

He seemed like a nice guy, though, and even Natalie could see that under the tattoos and hair, the guy was completely hormone pair-bonded to Lily. She wouldn't say they were in love because she didn't believe in love. But they were definitely pair-bonded. Biology was a powerful thing in its drive to continue the species. They could hardly keep their hands off each other at the engagement party.

"Okay. If that's all for this morning," Bree said, "I'm going to head to the lab and finish processing Saturday's wedding photos."

Natalie looked over her checklist. "Yep, that's it."

Bree and Amelia got up, filing out of the conference room, but Gretchen loitered by the table. She watched Natalie for a moment with a curious expression on her face. "What's going on with you? You seem distracted. Grumpier than usual."

That was sweet of her to point out. She knew she wasn't that pleasant this time of year, but she didn't need her friends reminding her of it. "Nothing is going on with me."

Gretchen crossed her arms over her chest and gave Natalie a look that told her she was going to stand there until she spilled.

"Christmas is coming." That pretty much said it all.

"What is this, *Game of Thrones*? Of course Christmas is coming. It's almost December, honey, and it's one of the more predictable holidays."

Natalie set down her tablet and frowned. Each year, the holidays were a challenge for her. Normally, she would try going on a trip to avoid all of it, but with the late wedding, she didn't have time. Staying home meant she'd have to resort to being a shut-in. She certainly wasn't interested in spending it with one of her parents and their latest spouses. The last time she did that, she'd called her mother's third husband by her second husband's name and that made for an awkward evening.

Natalie leaned back in the conference room chair and sighed. "It's bothering me more than usual this year." And it was. She didn't know why, but it was. Maybe it was the combination of all her friends being blissfully in love colliding with the holidays that was making it doubly painful.

"Are you taking a trip or staying home?" Gretchen asked.

"I'm staying home. I was considering a trip to Buenos Aires, but I don't have time. We squeezed Lily's last-minute wedding in on the Saturday before Christmas, so I'll be involved in that and not able to do the normal end-of-year paperwork until it's over."

"You're not planning to work over the shutdown, are you?" Gretchen planted her hands on her hips. "You don't have to celebrate, but by damn, you've got to take the time off, Natalie. You work seven days a week sometimes."

Natalie dismissed her concerns. Working didn't bother her as much as being idle. She didn't have a family to go home to each night or piles of laundry or housework that a man or child generated faster than she could clean. She liked her job. "I don't work the late hours you and Amelia do. I'm never here until midnight."

"It doesn't matter. You're still putting in too much time. You need to get away from all of this. Maybe go to a tropical island and have a fling with a sexy stranger."

At that, Natalie snorted. "I'm sorry, but a man is not the answer to my problems. That actually makes it worse."

"I'm not saying fall in love and marry the guy. I'm just saying to keep him locked in your hotel suite until the last New Year's firework explodes. What can a night or two of hot sex hurt?"

Natalie looked up at Gretchen and realized what was really bothering her. Colin's rejection from the night of the engagement party still stung. She hadn't told anyone about it, but if she didn't give Gretchen a good reason now, she'd ride her about it until the New Year. "It can hurt plenty when the guy you throw yourself at is your best friend's brother and he turns you down flat."

Gretchen's mouth dropped open and she sunk back down into her seat. "What? When did this happen?"

Natalie took a big sip of her soy chai latte before she answered. "I had too much chardonnay at Lily's engagement party and thought I'd take a chance on the big brother I'd lusted over since I'd hit puberty. To put it nicely, he declined. End of story. So no, I'm not really in the mood for a fling, either."

"Well that sucks," Gretchen noted.

"That's one way of putting it."

"On the plus side, you won't really have to see him again until the wedding day, right? Then you'll be too busy to care."

"Yep. I'll make sure I look extra good that day so he'll see what he missed."

"That's my girl. I'm going to go get these email invitations out."

Natalie nodded and watched Gretchen leave the room. She picked up her tablet and her drink, following her out the door to her office. Settling in at her desk, she pulled out a new file folder and wrote *Russell-Watson Wedding* on the tab. She needed to get everything prepared for their preliminary meeting this afternoon.

Staying busy would keep Christmas, and Colin, off her mind.

Colin pulled into the parking lot at From This Moment, his gaze instantly scanning over the lackluster shrubs out front. He knew it was winter, but they could certainly use a little more pizzazz for curb appeal.

He parked and went inside the facility. Stepping through the front doors, he knew instantly why Lily had insisted on marrying here. Their box holly hedges might have left something to be desired, but their focus was clearly on the interior. The inside was stunning with high ceilings, crystal chandeliers, tall fresh flower arrangements on the entryway table and arched entryways leading to various wings of the building. Mom would've loved it.

He looked down at his watch. It was a minute to one, so he was right on time for the appointment. Colin felt a little silly coming here today. Weddings weren't exactly his forte, but he was stepping up in his parents' place. When he'd married a year and a half ago, it had been a quick courthouse affair. If they'd opted for something more glamorous, he would've let Pam take the lead. Pam wasn't interested in that, though, and apparently, neither was his sister, Lily.

If she'd had her way, she and Frankie would've gone down to the courthouse, too. There was no reason to rush the nuptials, like Colin and Pam, but Lily just wanted to be done. She loved Frankie and she wanted to be Mrs. Watson as soon as possible. Colin had had to twist her arm into having an actual wedding, reminding her that their mother would be rolling over in her grave if she knew what Lily was planning.

She'd finally agreed under two circumstances: one, that the wedding be at Natalie's facility. Two, that he handle all the details. He insisted on the wedding, he'd offered to pay for it; he could make all the decisions.

Lily intended to show up in a white dress on the big day and that was about it.

Colin wasn't certain how he'd managed to be around so many women who weren't interested in big weddings. Pam hadn't wanted to marry at all. Hell, if it hadn't been for the baby and his insistence, she wouldn't have accepted the proposal. In retrospect, he realized why she was so hesitant, but with Lily, it just seemed to be a general disinterest in tradition.

He didn't understand it. Their parents had been very traditional people. Old-fashioned, you might even say. When they died in a car accident, Colin had tried to keep the traditions alive for Lily's sake. He'd never imagined he would end up raising his younger sister when he was only nineteen, but he was determined to do a good job and not disappoint his parents' memory.

Lily was just not that concerned. To her, the past was the past and she wasn't going to get hung up on things like that. Formal weddings fell into the bucket of silly traditions that didn't matter much to her. But it mattered to him, so she'd relented.

Colin heard a door open down one of the hallways and a moment later he found himself once again face-to-face with Natalie Sharpe. She stopped short in the archway of the foyer, clutching a tablet to her gray silk blouse. Even as a teenager, she'd had a classic beauty about her. Her creamy skin and high cheekbones had drawn his attention even when she was sporting braces. He'd suppressed any attraction he might have had for his little sister's friend, but he'd always thought she would grow up into a beautiful woman. At the party, his suspicions had been confirmed. And better yet, she'd looked at him with a seductive smile and an openness he hadn't expected. They weren't kids anymore, but there were other complications that had made it impossible to take her up on her offer, as much as he regretted it.

Today, the look on her face was a far cry from that night. Her pink lips were parted in concern, a frown lining her brow. Then she took a breath and shook it off. She tried to hide her emotions under a mask of professionalism, but he could tell she wasn't pleased to see him.

"Colin? I wasn't expecting to see you today. Is something going on with Lily?"

"Lots of things are going on with Lily," he replied, "but not what you're implying. She's fine. She's just not interested in the details."

Natalie swung her dark ponytail over her shoulder, her nose wrinkling. "What do you mean?"

"I mean, she told me this is my show and I'm to plan it however I see fit. So here I am," he added, holding out his arms.

He watched Natalie try to process the news. Apparently Lily hadn't given her a heads-up, but why would she? He doubted Lily knew about their encounter at the engagement party. She wasn't the kind of girl to give much thought to how her choices would affect other people.

"I know this is an unusual arrangement, but Lily is an unusual woman, as you know."

That seemed to snap Natalie out of her fog. She nodded curtly and extended her arm. "Of course. Come this way to my office and we can discuss the details."

Colin followed behind her, appreciating the snug fit of her pants over the curve of her hips and rear. She was wearing a pair of low heels that gave just enough lift to flatter her figure. It was a shame she walked in such a stiff, robotic way. He wouldn't mind seeing those hips sway a little bit, but he knew Natalie was too uptight for that. She'd always been a sharp contrast to his free-spirited sister—no-nonsense, practical, serious. She walked like she was marching into battle, even if it was a simple trip down the hallway.

After their encounter at the engagement party, he'd started to wonder if there was a more relaxed, sensual side to her that he hadn't had the pleasure of knowing about. He could only imagine what she could be like if she took down that tight ponytail, had a glass of wine and relaxed for once.

He got the feeling he would know all about that if he'd accepted her offer at the party. Unfortunately, his rocky on-again, off-again relationship with Rachel had been *on* that night. As much as he might have wanted to spend private time with Natalie, he couldn't. Colin was not the kind of man who cheated, even on a rocky relationship. Especially after what had happened with Pam.

After realizing how much more he was attracted to Natalie than the woman he was dating, he'd broken it off with Rachel for good. He was hopeful that now that he was a free man, he might get a second chance with Natalie. So far the reception was cold, but he hoped she'd thaw to his charms in time.

He followed her into her office and took a seat in the guest chair. Her office was pleasantly decorated, but extremely tidy and organized. He could tell every knick-knack had its place, every file had a home.

"Can I get you something to drink? We have bottled water, some sparkling juices and ginger ale."

That was an unexpected option. "Why do you have ginger ale?"

"Sometimes the bride's father gets a little queasy when he sees the estimate."

Colin laughed. "Water would be great. I'm not that worried about the bill."

Natalie got up, pulling two bottles of water out of the small stainless steel refrigerator tucked into her built-in bookshelves. "On that topic, what number makes you comfortable in terms of budget for the wedding?" she asked as she handed him a bottle.

Colin's fingers brushed over hers as he took the bottle from her hand. There was a spark as they touched, making his skin prickle with pins and needles as he pulled away. He clutched the icy cold water in his hand to dull the sensation and tried to focus on the conversation, instead of his reaction to a simple touch. "Like I said, I'm not that worried about it. My landscaping company has become extremely successful, and I want this to be an event that my parents would've thrown for Lily if they were alive. I don't think we need ridiculous extras like ice bars with martini luges, but in terms of food and decor, I'm all in. A pretty room, pretty flowers, good food, cake, music. The basics."

Natalie had hovered near her chair after handing him the water, making him wonder if she'd been affected by their touch, too. After listening to him, she nodded curtly and sat down. She reached for her tablet and started making careful notes. "How many guests are you anticipating? Lily provided me a list of emails, but we weren't sure of the final total."

"Probably about a hundred and fifty people. We've

got a lot of family and friends of my parents that would attend, but Frankie doesn't have many people nearby."

He watched her tap rapidly at her screen. "When I spoke with Lily, I suggested a winter wonderland theme and she seemed to like that. Is that agreeable?"

"Whatever she wants." Colin had no clue what a winter wonderland wedding would even entail. White, he supposed. Maybe some fake snow like the kind that surrounded Santa at the mall?

"Okay. Any other requests? Would you prefer a DJ or a band for the reception?"

That was one thing he had an answer for. "I'd like a string quartet, actually. Our mother played the violin and I think that would be a nice nod to her. At least for the ceremony. For the reception, we probably need something more upbeat so that Lily and her friends can dance and have a good time."

"How about a swing band? There's a great one locally that we've used a couple times."

"That would work. I think she mentioned going swing dancing at some club a few weeks back."

Natalie nodded and finally set down her tablet. "I'm going to have Amelia put together a suggested menu and some cake designs. Gretchen will do a display of the tablescape for your approval. I'll speak with our floral vendor to see what she recommends for the winter wonderland theme. We'll come up with a whole wedding motif with some options and we'll bring you back to review and approve all the final choices. We should probably have something together by tomorrow afternoon."

She certainly knew what she was doing and had this whole thing down to a science. That was good because Colin wasn't entirely sure what a tablescape even was.

He was frankly expecting this process to be a lot more painful, but perhaps that was the benefit of an all-in-one facility. "That all sounds great. Why don't you firm up those details with the other ladies and maybe we can meet for dinner tomorrow night to discuss it?"

Natalie's dark gaze snapped up from her tablet to meet his. "Dinner won't be necessary. We can set up another appointment if your schedule allows."

Colin tried not to look disappointed at her quick dismissal of dinner. He supposed he deserved that after he'd done the same to her last week. Perhaps she was just angry with him over it. If he could convince her to meet with him, maybe she could relax and he could explain to her what had happened that night. He got the distinct impression she wouldn't discuss it here at work.

"If not dinner, how about I just stop by here tomorrow evening? Do you mind staying past your usual time?"

Natalie snorted delicately and eased up out of her chair. "There's no usual time in this business. We work pretty much around the clock. What time should I expect you?"

"About six."

"Great," she said, offering her hand to him over the desk.

Colin was anxious to touch her again and see if he had the same reaction to her this time. He took her hand, enveloping it in his own and trying not to think about how soft her skin felt against his. There was another sizzle of awareness and this time, it traveled up his arm as he held her hand, making him all the more sorry she'd turned down his dinner invitation. He'd never had that instant of a reaction just by touching someone. He had this urge to lean into her and draw the scent of her perfume into his lungs even as the coil of desire in his gut tightened with every second they touched. What would it be like to actually kiss her?

He had been right before when he thought Natalie was caught off guard by their connection. He was certain he wasn't the only one to feel it. Colin watched as Natalie avoided his gaze, swallowed hard and gently extracted her hand from his. "Six it is."

Two

Discuss it over dinner? *Dinner!* Natalie was still steaming about her meeting with Colin the next afternoon. As she pulled together the portfolio for his review, she couldn't help replaying the conversation in her mind.

That look in his eye. The way he'd held her hand. Dinner! He was hitting on her. What was that about? Natalie was sorry, but that ship had sailed. Who was he to reject her, then come back a week later and change his mind? He had his shot and he blew it.

As she added the suggested menu to the file, she felt her bravado deflate a little. Natalie would be lying if she said she didn't want to take him up on the offer. She really, really did. But a girl had to draw the line somewhere. Her pride was at stake and if she came running just because he'd changed his mind, she'd look needy. She was anything but needy.

He had passed up on a one-night stand and what was done, was done. Now that she knew they were working together on the wedding plans, it was just as well. She didn't like to mix business with pleasure.

Natalie looked at the clock on her computer. It was almost six. The rest of the facility was dark and quiet. It was Tuesday, so the others were all off today. Natalie was supposed to be off, too, but she usually came into the office anyway. When it was quiet, she could catch up on paperwork and filing, talk with their vendors and answer the phone in case a client called. Or stopped by, as the case was tonight.

She slid open the desk drawer where she kept all her toiletries. Pulling out a small hand mirror, she checked her teeth for lipstick, smoothed her hand over her hair and admired her overall look. She found her compact to apply powder to the shinier areas and reapplied her lipstick. She may have put a little extra effort into her appearance today. Not to impress Colin. Not really. She did it more to torture him. Her pride stung from his re-buffing and she wanted him to suffer just a little bit, too.

Satisfied, she slipped her things back into the drawer. A soft door chime sounded a moment later and she knew that he'd arrived. She stood, taking a deep breath and willing herself to ignore her attraction to him. This was about work. Work. And anytime she thought dif-ferently, she needed to remind herself how she'd felt when he rejected her.

Natalie walked quickly down the hallway to the lobby. She found Colin waiting for her there. At the party and at their meeting yesterday, he'd been wearing a suit, but tonight, he was wearing a tight T-shirt and khakis. She watched the muscles of his broad shoulders move beneath the fabric as he slipped out of his winter coat, hanging it on the rack by the door.

When he turned to face her, she was blindsided by his bright smile and defined forearms. When he wore his suit, it was easy to forget he wasn't just a CEO, he was also a landscaper. She'd wager he rarely got dirt under his nails these days, but he still had the muscular arms and chest of a man who could move the earth with brute strength.

Colin looked down, seemingly following her gaze. "Do you like the shirt? We just had them made up for all the staff to wear when they're out on job sites."

Honestly, she hadn't paid much attention to the shirt, but talking about that was certainly better than admitting she was lusting over his hard pecs. "It's very nice," she said with a polite smile. "I like the dark green color." And she did. It had the Russell Landscaping logo in white on the front. It looked nice on him. Especially the fact that it looked painted on.

"Me, too. You didn't call to say there was an issue, so I assume you have the wedding plans ready?"

"I do. Come on back to my office and I'll show you what we've pulled together."

They turned and walked down the hallway, side by side. She couldn't help but notice that Colin had gently rested a guiding hand at the small of her back as she slipped into the office ahead of him. It was a faint touch, and yet she could still feel the heat of it through her clothes. Goose bumps raised up across her forearms when he pulled away, leaving her cold. It was an unexpected touch and yet she had to admit she was a little disappointed it was so quick. Despite their years apart, her reaction to Colin had only grown along with his biceps. Unfortunately, those little thrills were all she'd allow herself to have. She was first and foremost a professional.

They settled into her office and Natalie pulled out the trifold portfolio she used for these meetings. She unfolded it, showing all the images and options for their wedding. Focusing on work was her best strategy for dealing with her attraction to Colin.

"Let's start with the menu," she began. "Amelia, our caterer, would normally do up to three entrees for a wedding this size, but with such short notice, we really don't have time for attendees to select their meals. Instead, she put together a surf and turf option that should make everyone happy. Option one pairs her very popular beef tenderloin with a crab cake. You also have the choice of doing a bourbon-glazed salmon, or a chicken option instead if you think fish might be a problem for your guests."

She watched Colin look over the options thoughtfully. She liked the way his brow drew together as he thought. Staring down at the portfolio, she could see how long and thick his eyelashes were. Most women would kill for lashes like those.

"What would you choose?" he asked, unaware of her intense study of his face.

"The crab cake," Natalie said without hesitation. "They're almost all crab, with a crisp outside and a spicy remoulade. They're amazing."

"Okay, that sounds great. Let's go with that."

Natalie checked off his selection. "For the cake, she put together three concept designs." She went into detail on each, explaining the decorations and how it fit with the theme.

When she was finally done, he asked again, "Which one of these cakes would you choose?"

Natalie wasn't used to this. Most brides knew exactly what they wanted. Looking down at the three concept sketches for the cake, she pointed out the second option. "I'd choose this one. It will be all white with an iridescent shimmer to the fondant. Amelia will make silver gum paste snowflakes and when they wrap around the cake it will be really enchanting."

"Let's go with that one. What about cake flavors?"

"You won't make that decision today. If you can come Thursday, Amelia will set up a tasting session. She's doing a couple other appointments that day, so that would work best. Do you think Lily would be interested in coming to that?"

"I can work that out. I doubt Lily will join me, but I'll ask. I'm sure cake is cake in her eyes."

Natalie just didn't understand her friend at all. Natalie had no interest in marriage, therefore no interest in a wedding. But Lily should at least have the party she wanted and enjoy it. It didn't make sense to hand that over to someone else. Her inner control freak couldn't imagine someone else planning her wedding. If by some twist of fate, she was lobotomized and agreed to marry someone, she would control every last detail.

"Okay." Natalie noted the appointment in her tablet so Amelia could follow up with him on a time for Thursday. From there, they looked at some floral concepts and bouquet options. With each of them, he asked Natalie's opinion and went with that. Sitting across from her was a sexy, intelligent, wealthy, thoughtful and agreeable man. If she *was* the kind to marry, she'd crawl into his lap right now. Whoever did land Colin would be very lucky. At least for a while.

Everything flowed easily from there. Without much debate, they'd settled on assorted tall and low arrangements with a mix of white flowers including rose, ranunculus, stephanotis and hydrangea. It was everything she would've chosen and probably as close as she'd get to having a wedding without having to get married.

"Now that we've handled all that, the last thing I want to do is to take you to the table setup Gretchen put together."

They left her office and walked down to the storage room. She kept waiting for him to touch her again, but she was disappointed this time. Opening the doors, she let him inside ahead of her and followed him in. In their storage room, amongst the shelves of glassware, plates, silver vases and cake stands, they had one round dinner table set up. There, Gretchen put together mock-ups of the reception tables for brides to better visualize them and make changes.

"Gretchen has selected a soft white tablecloth with a delicate silver overlay of tiny beaded snowflakes. We'd carry the white and silver into the dishes with the silver chargers, silver-rimmed white china, and then use silver-and-glass centerpieces in a variety of heights. We'll bring in tasteful touches of sparkle with some crystals on white manzanita branches and lots of candles."

Colin ran the tip of his finger over a silver snowflake and nodded. "It all looks great to me. Very pretty. Gretchen has done a very nice job with it."

Natalie made a note in her tablet and shook her head with amazement. "You're the easiest client I've ever had. I refuse to believe it's really that easy. What are you hiding from me?"

Colin looked at her with a confused expression. "I'm not hiding anything. I know it isn't what you're used to, but really, I'm putting this wedding in your capable hands."

He placed his hand on her shoulder as he spoke. She could feel the heat radiating through the thin fabric of her cashmere sweater, making her want to pull at the collar as her internal temperature started to climb.

"You knew my parents. You know Lily. You've got the experience and the eye for this kind of thing. Aside from the discussion about flowers, I've had no clue what you were talking about most of the time. I just trust you to do a great job and I'll write the check."

Natalie tried not to frown. Her heated blood wasn't enough for her to ignore his words. He was counting on her. That was a lot of pressure. She knew she could pull it off beautifully, but he had an awful lot of confidence in her for a girl he hadn't seen since she wore a retainer to bed. "So would you rather just skip the cake tasting?"

"Oh no," he said with a smile that made her knees soften beneath her. "I have a massive sweet tooth, so I'm doing that for sure."

Natalie wasn't sure how much her body could take of being in close proximity to Colin as friends. She wanted to run her hand up his tanned, muscular forearm and rub against him like a cat. While she enjoyed indulging her sexuality from time to time, she didn't have a reaction like this to just any guy. It was unnerving and *so* inappropriate. This wedding couldn't come fast enough.

* * *

"Thank you for all your help with this," Colin said as Natalie closed up and they walked toward the door.

"That's what I do," she said with the same polite smile that was starting to make him crazy. He missed her real one. He remembered her carefree smile from her younger days and her seductive smile from the engagement party. This polite, blank smile meant nothing to him.

"No, really. You and your business partners are going out of your way to make this wedding happen. I don't know how to thank you."

Natalie pressed the alarm code and they stepped outside where she locked the door. "You and Lily are like family to me. Of course we'd do everything we could. Anyway, it's not like we're doing it for free. You're paying us for our time, so no worries."

Their cars were the only two in the parking lot, so he walked her over to the cherry-red two-seat Miata convertible. Had there been another car in the lot, he never would've guessed this belonged to Natalie. It had a hint of wild abandon that didn't seem to align with the precise and businesslike Natalie he knew. It convinced him more than ever that there was another side to her that he desperately wanted to see.

"Let me take you to dinner tonight," he said, nearly surprising himself with the suddenness of it.

Natalie's dark brown eyes widened. "I really can't, Colin, but I appreciate the offer."

Two up at bats, two strikeouts. "Even just as friends?"

Her gaze flicked over his face and she shook her head. "You and I both know it wouldn't be as friends."

Turning away, Natalie unlocked her car and opened the door to toss her bag inside.

"I think that's unfair."

"Not really. Listen, Colin, I'm sorry about the other night at the party. I'd been hit by a big dose of nostalgia and too much wine and thought that indulging those old teenage fantasies was a good idea. But by the light of day, I know it was silly of me. So thank you for having some sense and keeping me from doing something that would've made this whole planning process that much more awkward."

"Don't thank me," Colin argued. "I've regretted that decision every night since it happened."

Natalie's mouth fell agape, her dark eyes searching his face for something. "Don't," she said at last. "It was the right choice."

"It was at the time, but only because it had to be. Natalie, I—"

"Don't," Natalie insisted. "There's no reason to explain yourself. You made the decision you needed to make and it was the right one. No big deal. I'd like to just put that whole exchange behind us. The truth is that I'm really not the right kind of woman for you."

Colin wasn't sure if she truly meant what she said or if she was just angry with him, but he was curious what she meant by that. He was bad enough at choosing women. Maybe she knew something he didn't. "What kind of woman is that?"

"The kind that's going to have any sort of future with you. At the party, I was just after a night of fun, nothing serious. You're a serious kind of guy. Since you were a teenager, you were on the express train to marriage and kids. I'm on a completely different track."

They hadn't really been around each other long enough for Colin to think much past the ache of desire she seemed to constantly rouse in him. But if what she said was true, she was right. He wanted all those things. If she didn't, there wasn't much point in pursuing her. His groin felt otherwise, but it would get on board eventually.

"Well, I appreciate you laying that out for me. Not all women are as forthcoming." Pam had been, but for some reason he'd refused to listen. This time he knew better than to try to twist a woman's will. It didn't work. "Just friends, then," he said.

Natalie smiled with more warmth than before, and she seemed to relax for the first time since he'd arrived. "Friends is great."

"All right," he said. "Good night." Colin leaned in to give Natalie a quick hug goodbye. At least that was the idea.

Once he had his arms wrapped around her and her cheek pressed to his, it was harder to let go than he expected. Finally, he forced himself back, dropping his hands at his sides and breaking the connection he'd quickly come to crave. And yet, he couldn't get himself to say good-night and go back to his truck. "Listen, before you go can I ask you about something?"

"Sure," she said, although there was a hesitation in her voice that made him think she'd much rather flee than continue talking to him in the cold. She must not think he'd taken the hint.

"I'm thinking about giving Lily and Frankie the old house as a wedding present."

"The house you and Lily grew up in?" she asked with raised brows.

"Yes. It's been sitting mostly empty the last few years. Lily has been living with Frankie in the little apartment over his motorcycle shop. They seem to think that's great, but they're going to need more space if they want to start a family."

"That's a pretty amazing wedding present. Not many people register for a house."

Colin shrugged. "I don't need it. I have my place. It's paid for, so all they'd have to worry about are taxes and insurance. The only problem is that it needs to be cleaned out. I never had the heart to go through all of Mom's and Dad's things. I want to clear all that out and get it ready for the newlyweds to make a fresh start there."

Natalie nodded as he explained. "That sounds like a good plan. What does it have to do with me?"

"Well," Colin said with an uncharacteristically sheepish smile, "I was wondering if you would be interested in helping me."

She flinched at first, covering her reaction by shuffling her feet in the cold. "I don't know that I'll be much help to you, Colin. For one thing, I'm a wedding planner, not an interior decorator. And for another thing, I work most of the weekends with weddings. I don't have a lot of free time."

"I know," he said, "and I'm not expecting any heavy lifting on your part. I was thinking more of your organizational skills and keen aesthetic eye. It seems to me like you could spot a quality piece of furniture or artwork that's worth keeping amongst the piles of eighties-style recliners."

There was a light of amusement in her eyes as she

listened to him speak. "You're completely in over your head with this one, aren't you?"

"You have no idea. My business is landscaping, and that's the one thing at the house that doesn't need any work. I overhauled it a few years ago and I've had it maintained, so the outside is fine. It's just the inside. I also thought it would be nice to decorate the house for Christmas since they get back from their honeymoon on Christmas Eve. That way it will be ready to go for the holidays."

The twinkle in her eye faded. "I'm no good with Christmas, Colin. I might be able to help you with some of the furniture and keepsakes, but you're on your own when it comes to the holidays."

That made Colin frown. Most people enjoyed decorating for Christmas. Why was she so opposed to it? In his eyes it wasn't much different from decorating for a wedding. He wasn't about to push that point, however. "Fair enough. I'm sure I can handle that part on my own. Do you have plans tonight?"

Natalie sighed and shook her head. "I'm *not* going out with you, Colin."

He held up his hands in surrender. "I didn't ask you out. I asked if you were busy. I thought if you weren't busy, I'd take you by the old house tonight. I know you don't have a lot of free time, so if you could just take a walk through with me this evening and give me some ideas, I could get started on it."

"Oh," she said, looking sheepish.

"I mean, I could just pay a crew to come and clean out the house and put everything in storage, but I hate to do that. Some things are more important than others, and I'll want to keep some of it. Putting everything in storage just delays the inevitable. I could use your help, even if for just tonight."

Natalie sighed and eventually nodded. "Sure. I have some time tonight."

"Great. We'll take my car and I'll bring you back when we're done," Colin said.

He got the distinct impression that if he let Natalie get in her car, she'd end up driving somewhere other than their old neighborhood, or make some excuse for a quick getaway. He supposed that most men agreed to just being friends, but secretly hoped for more. Colin meant what he'd said and since she'd agreed, there was no need to slink away with his tail between his legs.

Holding out his arm, he ushered her reluctantly over to his Russell Landscaping truck. The Platinum series F-250 wasn't a work truck, it was more for advertising, although he did get it dirty from time to time. It was dark green, like their shirts, with the company logo and information emblazoned on the side.

He held the passenger door open for her, a step automatically unfolding along the side of the truck. Colin held her hand as she climbed inside, then slammed the door shut.

"Do you mind if we listen to some music on the way?" she asked.

Colin figured that she wanted music to avoid idle conversation, but he didn't mind. "Sure." He turned on the radio, which started playing music from the holiday station he'd had on last.

"Can I change it to the country channel?"

"I don't care, although you don't strike me as a country girl," he noted.

"I was born and raised in Nashville, you know. When

I was a kid, my dad would take me to see performances at the Grand Ole Opry. It's always stuck with me." She changed the station and the new Blake Wright song came on. "Ooh. I love this song. He's going to be doing a show at the Opry in two weeks. It's sold out, though."

Colin noted that information and put it in his back pocket. From there, it wasn't a long drive to the old neighborhood, just a few miles on the highway. Blake had just finished singing when they arrived.

They had grown up in a nice area—big homes on big lots designed for middle-class families. His parents honestly couldn't really afford their house when they had first bought it, but his father had insisted that they get the home they wanted to have forever. His parents had wanted a place to both raise their children and entertain potential clients, and appearances counted. If that meant a few lean years while the landscaping business built up, so be it.

The neighborhood was still nice and the homes had retained an excellent property value. It wasn't as flashy or trendy with the Nashville wealthy like Colin's current neighborhood, but it was a home most people would be happy to have.

As they pulled into the driveway, Natalie leaned forward and eyed the house through the windshield with a soft smile. "I've always loved this house," she admitted. "I can't believe how big the magnolia trees have gotten."

Colin's father had planted crepe myrtles lining the front walkway and magnolia trees flanking the yard. When he was a kid they were barely big enough to provide enough shade to play beneath them. Now the magnolias were as tall as the two-story roofline. "I've maintained the yard over the years," he said proudly. "I knew how important that was for Dad."

It was too dark to really get a good look at the outside, even with the lights on, so he opened the garage door and opted to take her in through there. His father's tool bench and chest still sat along the rear wall. A shed in the back housed all the gardening supplies and equipment. He hadn't had the heart to move any of that stuff before, but like the rest of it, he knew it was time.

They entered into the kitchen from the garage. Natalie instantly moved over to the breakfast bar, settling onto one of the barstools where she and Lily used to sit and do their homework together.

He could almost envision her with the braces and the braids again, but he much preferred Natalie as she was now. She smiled as she looked around the house, obviously as fond of his childhood home as he was. He wanted to walk up behind her to look at it the same way she was. Maybe rub the tension from her tight shoulders.

But he wouldn't. It had taken convincing to get her here. He wasn't about to run her off so quickly by pushing the boundaries of their newly established friendship. Eventually, it would be easier to ignore the swell of her breasts as they pressed against her sweater or the luminous curve of her cheek. Until then, he smoothed his hands over the granite countertop and let the cold stone cool his ardor.

"How long has it been since you've lived here, Colin? It seems pretty tidy."

"It's been about three years since I lived here full-time. Lily used it as a home base on and off for a while, but no one has really lived here for a year at least. I have a service come clean and I stop in periodically to check on the place."

"So many memories." She slipped off the stool and went into the living room. He followed her there, watching her look around at the vaulted ceilings. Natalie pointed at the loft that overlooked the living room. "I used to love hanging out up there, listening to CDs and playing on the computer."

That made him smile. The girls had always been sprawled out on the rug or lying across the futon up there, messing around on the weekends. Natalie had spent a lot of time at the house when they were younger. Her own house was only the next block over, but things had been pretty volatile leading up to her parents' divorce. While he hated that her parents split up, it had been nice to have her around, especially after his own parents died. Colin had been too busy trying to take care of everything and suddenly be a grown-up. Natalie had been there for Lily in a way he hadn't.

"Lily is very lucky to have a brother like you," she said, conflicting with his own thoughts. "I'm sure she'll love the house. It's perfect for starting a family. Just one thing, though."

"What's that?"

Natalie looked at him and smiled. "The house is exactly the same as it was the last time I was here ten years ago, and things were dated then. You've got some work ahead of you, mister."

Three

After a few hours at the house, Colin insisted on ordering pizza and Natalie finally acquiesced. That wasn't a dinner date, technically, and she was starving. She wasn't sure that he had put the idea of them being more than friends to bed—honestly neither had she—but they'd get there. As with all attractions, the chemical reactions would fade, the hormones would quiet and things would be fine. With a wedding and the house to focus on, she was certain it would happen sooner rather than later.

While he dealt with ordering their food, she slipped out onto the back deck and sat down in one of the old patio chairs. The air was cold and still, but it felt good to breathe it in.

She was exhausted. They'd gone through every room, talking over pieces to keep, things to donate and what renovations were needed. It wasn't just that, though. It was the memories and emotions tied to the place that were getting to her. Nearly every room in the house held some kind of significance to her. Even though Lily and Colin's parents had been dead for nearly thirteen years now, Natalie understood why Colin had been so reluctant to change things. It was like messing with the past somehow.

Her parents' marriage had dissolved when she was fourteen. The year or so leading up to it had been even more rough on her than what followed. Lily's house had been her sanctuary from the yelling. After school, on the weekends, sleepovers…she was almost always here. Some of her happiest memories were in this place. Colin and Lily's parents didn't mind having her around. She suspected that they knew what was going on at her house and were happy to shelter her from the brunt of it.

Unfortunately, they couldn't protect her from everything. There was nothing they could do to keep Natalie's father from walking out on Christmas day. They weren't there to hold Natalie's hand as her parents fought it out in court for two years, then each remarried again and again, looking for something in another person they couldn't seem to find.

Her friends joked that Natalie was jaded about relationships, but she had a right to be. She rarely saw them succeed. Why would she put herself through that just because there was this societal pressure to do it? She could see the icy water and jagged rocks below; why would she jump off the bridge with everyone else?

She heard the doorbell and a moment later, Colin called her from the kitchen. "Soup's on!"

Reluctantly, Natalie got back up and went inside the

house to face Colin and the memories there. She found a piping hot pizza sitting on the kitchen island beside a bottle of white wine. "Did they deliver the wine, too?" she asked drily. The addition of wine to the pizza made this meal feel more suspiciously like the date she'd declined earlier. "If they do, I need their number. Wine delivery is an underserved market."

"No, it was in the wine chiller," he said as though it was just the most convenient beverage available. "I lived here for a few weeks after I broke up with Pam. It was left over."

Natalie had learned from Lily that Colin got a divorce earlier this year, but she didn't know much about the details. Their wedding had been a quiet affair and their divorce had been even quieter. All she did hear was that they had a son together. "I'm sorry to hear about your divorce. Do you still get to see your son pretty often?"

The pleasant smile slipped from his face. He jerked the cork out of the wine bottle and sighed heavily. "I don't have a son."

Natalie knew immediately that she had treaded into some unpleasant territory. She wasn't quite sure how to back out of it. "Oh. I guess I misheard."

"No. You heard right. Shane was born about six months after we got married." He poured them each a glass of chardonnay. "We divorced because I found out that Shane wasn't my son."

Sometimes Natalie hated being right about relationships. Bad things happened to really good people when the fantasy of love got in the way. She took a large sip of the wine to muffle her discomfort. "I'm sorry to hear that, Colin."

A smile quickly returned to his face, although it seemed a little more forced than before. "Don't be. I did it to myself. Pam had been adamant when we started dating that she didn't want to get married. When she told me she was pregnant, I thought she would change her mind, but she didn't. I think she finally gave in only because I wouldn't let it go. I should've known then that I'd made a mistake by forcing her into it."

Natalie stiffened with a piece of pizza dangling from her hand. She finally released it to the plate and cleared her throat. "Not everyone is meant for marriage," she said. "Too many people do it just because they think that's what they're supposed to do."

"If someone doesn't want to get married, they shouldn't. It's not fair to their partner."

She slid another slice of pizza onto his plate. Instead of opting for the perfectly good dining room table, Natalie returned to her perch at the breakfast bar. That's where she'd always eaten at Lily's house. "That's why I've made it a policy to be honest up front."

Colin followed suit, handing her a napkin and sliding onto the stool beside her. "And I appreciate that, especially after what happened with Pam. You're right though. I'm the kind of guy that is meant for marriage. I've just got to learn to make better choices in women," he said. Pam had been his most serious relationship, but he had a string of others that failed for different reasons. "My instincts always seem to be wrong."

Natalie took a bite of her pizza and chewed thoughtfully. She had dodged a bullet when Colin turned her down at the engagement party. She'd only been looking for a night of nostalgic indulgence, but he was the kind of guy who wanted more. More wasn't something she could give him. She was a bad choice, too. Not lie-about-the-paternity-of-your-child bad, but definitely not the traditional, marrying kind he needed.

"Your sister doesn't seem to want to get married," Natalie noted, sending the conversation in a different direction. She'd never seen a more reluctant bride. That kind of woman wouldn't normally bother with a place like From This Moment.

"Actually, she's very eager to marry. It's the wedding and the hoopla she can do without."

"That's an interesting reversal. A lot of women are more obsessed with the wedding day than the actual marriage."

"I think she'll appreciate it later, despite how much she squirms now. Eloping at the courthouse was very underwhelming. We said the same words, ended up just as legally joined in marriage, but it was missing a certain something. I want better for my little sister's big day."

"She'll get it," Natalie said with confidence. "We're the best."

They ate quietly for a few moments before Colin finished his slice and spoke up. "See," he said as he reached for another piece and grinned. "I told you that you'd have dinner with me eventually."

Natalie snorted softly, relieved to see the happier Colin return. "Oh, no," she argued with a smile. "This does not count, even if you add wine. Having dinner together implies a date. This is not a date."

Colin leaned his elbows on the counter and narrowed his eyes at her. "Since we're sharing tonight, do you mind telling me why you were so unhappy to see me yesterday at the chapel?"

"I wouldn't say unhappy. I would say surprised. I expected Lily. And considering what happened the last time I saw you, I was feeling a little embarrassed."

"Why?"

"Because I hit on you and failed miserably. It was stupid of me. It was a momentary weakness fueled by wine and abstinence. And since you passed up the chance, this is definitely not a date. We're on a nondate eating pizza at your childhood home."

A knowing grin spread across Colin's face, making Natalie curious, nervous and making her flush at the same time. "So that's what it's really about," he said with a finger pointed in her direction. "You were upset because I turned you down that night at the party."

Natalie's cheeks flamed at the accusation. "Not at all. I'm relieved, really." She took a large sip of her wine and hoped that sounded convincing enough.

"You can say that, but I know it isn't true. You couldn't get out of the house fast enough that night."

"I had an early day the next morning."

Colin raised his brow in question. He didn't believe a word she said. Neither did she.

"Okay, fine. So what?" she challenged. "So what if I'm holding it against you? I'm allowed to have feelings about your rejection."

"Of course you're allowed to have feelings. But I didn't reject you, Natalie."

"Oh really? What would you call it?"

Colin turned in his seat to face her, his palms resting on each knee. "I would call it being the good guy even when I didn't want to be. You may not have noticed, but I had a date at the party. She was in a corner sulking most of the night. It wasn't really serious and we broke it off the next day, but I couldn't very well ditch her and disappear with you."

Natalie's irritation started to deflate. She slumped in her seat, fingering absentmindedly at her pizza crust. "Oh."

"Oh," he repeated with a chuckle. "Now if you were the kind of woman that *would* date me, you'd be feeling pretty silly right now."

Natalie shook her head. "Even if I were that woman, this is still not a date. You can't just decide to be on a date halfway through an evening together. There's planning and preparation. You'd have to take me someplace nicer than this old kitchen, and I would wear a pretty dress instead of my clothes from work. A date is a whole experience."

"Fair enough," Colin agreed, taking another bite of his pizza. "This isn't a date."

Natalie turned to her food, ignoring the nervous butterflies that were fluttering in her stomach. It wasn't a date, but it certainly felt like one.

They cleaned up the kitchen together and opted to climb in the attic to take a look at what was up there before they called it a night. Colin's father had had the attic finished when they moved in, so the space was a little dusty, but it wasn't the treacherous, cobweb-filled space most attics were.

"Wow," Natalie said as she reached the top of the stairs. "There's a lot of stuff up here."

She was right. Colin looked around, feeling a little intimidated by the project he'd put on himself. He'd put all this off for too long, though. Giving the house to Lily and Frankie was the right thing to do and the motivation he needed to actually get it done.

He reached for a plastic tote and peeked inside. It was filled with old Christmas decorations. After further investigation, he realized that was what the majority of the items were. "My parents always went all out at Christmas," he said. "I think we've found their stash."

There were boxes of garland, lights, ornaments and lawn fixtures. A five-foot, light-up Santa stood in the corner beside a few white wooden reindeer that lit up and moved.

"This is what you were looking for, right?" Natalie asked. "You said you wanted to decorate the house for the holidays."

He nodded and picked up a copy of *A Visit From St. Nicholas* from one of the boxes. His father had read that to them every year on Christmas Eve, even when he and his sister were far too old for that sort of thing. In the years since they'd passed, Colin would've given anything to sit and listen to his father read that to him again.

"This is perfect," he said. "I have to go through all this to see what still works, but it's a great start. I'll just have to get a tree for the living room. What do you think?"

Natalie shrugged. "I told you before, I'm not much of an expert on Christmas."

He'd forgotten. "So, what's that about, Grinch?"

"Ha-ha," she mocked, heading toward the stairs.

Colin snatched an old Santa's hat out of a box and followed her down. He slipped it on. "Ho-ho-ho!" he shouted in his jolliest voice. "Little girl, tell Santa why you don't like Christmas. Did I forget the pony you asked for?"

Natalie stopped on the landing and turned around to look at him. She tried to hide her smirk with her hand, but the light in her eyes gave away her amusement. "You look like an idiot."

"Come on," he insisted. "We've already talked about my matrimonial betrayal. It can't be a bigger downer than that."

"Pretty close," Natalie said, crossing her arms defensively over her chest. "My dad left on Christmas day."

The smile faded from his face. He pulled off the Santa hat. "I didn't know about that."

"Why would you? I'm sure you were spared the messy details."

"What happened?"

"I'm not entirely sure. They'd been fighting a bunch leading up to Christmas, but I think they were trying to hold it together through the holidays. That morning, we opened presents and had breakfast, the same as usual. Then, as I sat in the living room playing with my new Nintendo, I heard some shouting and doors slamming. The next thing I know, my dad is standing in the living room with his suitcases. He just moved out right then. I haven't celebrated Christmas since that day."

"You haven't celebrated at all? In fifteen years?"

"Nope. I silently protested for a few holidays, passed between parents, but once I went to college, it was done. No decorations, no presents, no Christmas carols."

He was almost sorry he'd asked. So many of Colin's favorite memories had revolved around the holidays with his parents. Even after they died, Christmas couldn't be ruined. He just worked that much harder to make it special for Lily. He'd always dreamed of the day he'd celebrate the holidays with his own family. He'd gotten a taste of it when they celebrated Shane's first Christmas, but not long after that, he learned the truth about his son's real father.

"That's the saddest thing I've ever heard." And coming from a guy whose life had fallen apart in the past year, that was saying a lot.

"Divorce happens," Natalie said. A distant, almost ambivalent look settled on her face. She continued down the stairs to the ground floor. "It happens to hundreds of couples every day. It happened to you. Heck, it's happened to my mother three times. She's on her fourth husband. My sad story isn't that uncommon."

"I actually wasn't talking about the divorce." Colin stepped down onto the first-floor landing and reached out to grip the railing. "I mean, I'm sure it was awful for you to live through your parents' split. I just hate that it ruined Christmas for you. Christmas is such a special time. It's about family and friends, magic and togetherness. It's a good thing we've decided to just be friends because I could never be with someone who didn't like Christmas."

"Really? It's that important?"

"Yep. I look forward to it all year. I couldn't imagine not celebrating."

"It's easier than you think. I stay busy with work or I try to travel."

Colin could only shake his head. She wasn't interested in long-term relationships or holidays, both things most people seemed to want or enjoy. Her parents' divorce must've hit at a crucial age for her. He couldn't help reaching out to put a soothing arm around her shoulder. "You shouldn't let your parents' crap ruin your chances for having a happy holiday for the rest of your life."

"I don't miss it," she said, shying away from his touch, although she didn't meet his eyes when she said it.

He didn't fully believe her. Just like he didn't believe her when she said she wasn't interested in going on a date with him. She did want to, she was just stubborn and afraid of intimacy. As much as he might be drawn to Natalie, he wasn't going to put himself in that boat again. He was tired of butting his head against relationship brick walls. But even if they were just friends, he couldn't let the Christmas thing slide. It was a challenge unlike any he'd had in a while.

"I think I could make you like Christmas again."

Natalie turned on her heel to look at him. Her eyebrow was arched curiously. "No, you can't."

"You don't have much faith in me. I can do anything I put my mind to."

"Be serious, Colin."

"I am serious," he argued.

"You can't make me like Christmas. That would take a lobotomy. Or a bout of amnesia. It won't happen otherwise."

He took a step closer, moving into her space. "If you're so confident, why don't we wager on it?"

Her dark eyes widened at him and she stepped back. "What? No. That's silly."

"Hmm…" Colin said, leaning in. "Sounds to me like you're too chicken to let me try. You know you'll lose the bet."

Natalie took another step backward until her back

was pressed against the front door. "I'm not scared. I'm just not interested in playing your little game."

"Come on. If you're so confident, it won't hurt to take me up on it. Name your victor's prize. We're going to be spending a lot of time together the next two weeks. This will make it more...interesting."

Natalie crossed her arms over her chest. "Okay, fine. You're going to lose, so it really doesn't matter. You have until the wedding reception to turn me into a Christmas fan again. If I win the bet, you have to pay for me to spend Christmas next year in Buenos Aires."

"Wow. Steep stakes," Colin said.

Natalie just shrugged it off. "Are you confident or not?"

Nice. Now she'd turned it so he was the chicken. "Of course I'm confident. You've got it. I'll even fly you there first class."

"And what do you want if you win?"

A million different options could've popped into his mind in that moment, but there was only one idea that really stuck with him. "In return, if I win the bet, you owe me...a kiss."

Natalie's eyebrow went up. "That's it? A kiss? I asked for a trip to South America."

Colin smiled. "Yep, that's all I want." It would be a nice little bonus to satisfy his curiosity, but in the end, he was more interested in bringing the magic back to Christmas for her. Everyone needed that in their life. He held out his hand. "Shall we shake on it and make this official?"

Natalie took a cleansing breath and nodded before taking his hand. He enveloped it with his own, noting how cold she was to the touch. She gasped as he held her, her eyes widening. "You're so warm," she said.

"I was about to mention how cold you are. What's the matter? Afraid you're going to lose the bet?"

She gave a soft smile and pulled her hand from his. "Not at all. I'm always cold."

"It *is* Christmastime," Colin noted. "That just means you'll need to bundle up when we go out in search of some Christmas spirit."

She frowned, a crease forming between her brows. "We're both really busy, Colin. What if I just kiss you now? Will you let the whole thing drop?"

Colin propped his palm on the wall over her shoulder and leaned in until they were separated by mere inches. He brought his hand up to cup her cheek, running the pad of this thumb across her full bottom lip. Her lips parted softly, her breath quickening as he got closer. He had been right. She was attracted to him, but that just wasn't enough for her to want more.

"You can kiss me now if you want to," he said. "But there's no way I'm dropping this bet."

His hand fell to his side as a smirk of irritation replaced the expression on her face. This was going to be more fun than he'd expected.

"It's getting late. I'd better get you home."

He pulled away, noting the slight downturn of Natalie's lips as he did. Was she disappointed that he didn't kiss her? He'd never met a woman who sent such conflicting signals before. He got the feeling she didn't know what she wanted.

She didn't need to worry. They might just be friends, but he would kiss her, and soon. Colin had no intention of losing this bet.

Four

Natalie was on pins and needles all day Thursday knowing that Colin would be coming for the cake tasting that afternoon. She was filled with this confusing mix of emotions. First, there was the apprehension over their bet. Colin was determined to get her in the Christmas spirit. Wednesday morning when she'd stepped outside, she found a fresh pine wreath on her front door with a big red velvet bow.

She was tempted to take it down, but she wouldn't. She could withstand his attempts, but she knew the more she resisted, the more she would see of Colin. That filled her with an almost teenage giddiness—the way she used to feel whenever Colin would smile at her when they were kids. It made her feel ridiculous considering nothing was going to happen between the two of them, and frankly, it was distracting her from her work. Thank goodness this weekend's wedding was a smaller affair.

She was about to call the florist to follow up on the bride's last-minute request for a few additional boutonnieres when she noticed a figure lurking in her doorway. It was Gretchen.

Natalie pulled off her earpiece. "Yes?"

"So Tuesday night, I was meeting a friend for dinner on this side of town and I happened to pass by the chapel around nine that night. I noticed your car was still in the parking lot."

Natalie tried not to frown at her coworker. "You know I work late sometimes."

"Yeah, that's what I thought at first, too, but none of the lights were on. Then I noticed on your Outlook calendar that you had a late appointment to discuss the Russell-Watson wedding." A smug grin crossed Gretchen's face.

Natalie rolled her eyes. "It was nothing, so don't turn it into something. We finalized the plans for the wedding, that's all. Then he asked me for help with his wedding present for Lily. He's giving her a house."

"A house? Lord," Gretchen declared with wide eyes. "I mean, I know I'm engaged to a movie star and all, but I have a hard time wrapping my head around how rich people think."

"It's actually the home they grew up in. He asked me to help him fix it up for them."

Gretchen nodded thoughtfully. "Did you help him rearrange some of the bedroom furniture?"

"Ugh, no." Natalie searched around her desk for something to throw, but all she had was a crystal paperweight shaped like a heart. She didn't want to knock

Gretchen unconscious, despite how gratifying it might feel in the moment. "We just walked around and talked about what I'd keep or donate. Nothing scandalous. I'm sorry to disappoint you."

"Well, boo. I was hopeful that this guy would make it up to you for his cruel rebuffing at the engagement party."

"He didn't make it up to me, but he did explain why he'd turned me down. Apparently he had a date that night."

"And now?"

"And now they've broken up. But that doesn't change anything. We're just going to be friends. It's better this way. Things would've just been more…complicated if something had happened."

Gretchen narrowed her gaze at her. "And you helping him with the house now that he's single won't be complicated?"

Natalie swung her ponytail over her shoulder and avoided her coworker's gaze by glancing at her computer screen. There were no critical emails to distract her from the conversation.

"Natalie?"

"No, it won't," she said at last. "It's going to be fine. We've been family friends for years and that isn't going to change. I'm going to handle the wedding and help him with the house and everything will be fine. Great, really. I think it's just the distraction I need to get through the holidays this year."

Gretchen nodded as she talked, but Natalie could tell she wasn't convinced. Frankly, neither was Natalie. Even as she said the words, she was speaking to herself as much as to her friend. She certainly wasn't going to tell her that she was fighting her attraction to Colin like a fireman with a five-alarm inferno. Or that she'd gotten herself roped into a bet that could cost her not only a kiss, but a solid dose of the holidays she had just said she was avoiding.

"Okay, well, whatever helps you get through the holidays, hon."

"Thank you."

"Uh-oh. Speak of the devil," Gretchen said, peeking out Natalie's window.

"He's here?" Natalie said, perking up in her seat, eyes wide with panic. "He's early." She was automatically opening her desk drawer and reaching for her compact when she heard Gretchen's low, evil laugh.

"No, he's not. I lied. I just wanted to see how you'd react. I was right. You're so full of it, your eyeballs should be floating."

Natalie sat back in her chair, the panic quickly replaced by irritation. Her gaze fell on the drawer to the soft foam rose stress ball that the florist had given them. She picked it up and hurled it at Gretchen, who ducked just in time.

"Get out of my office!" she shouted, but Gretchen was already gone. Natalie could hear her cackling down the hallway. Thank goodness there weren't any customers in the facility this morning.

There would be several clients here after lunchtime, though. Amelia had three cake tastings on the schedule today, including with Colin.

Hopefully that would go better than just now. Gretchen had already called her on the ridiculous infatuation that had reignited. Amelia would likely be more tactful. She hoped. Natalie didn't think she'd been that obvious. In the end, nothing *had* happened. They'd finalized plans, she'd helped him with the house and they'd had pizza. They hadn't kissed. She had certainly wanted to.

It was hard to disguise the overwhelming sense of disappointment she felt when they had their near miss. Natalie had been certain he was about to kiss her. She thought maybe dangling that carrot would serve her on two levels: first that they could call off the silly bet, and second, that she'd finally fulfill her youthful fantasy of kissing the dashing and handsome Colin Russell.

Then…nothing. He knew what he was doing. He'd turned up the dial, gotten her primed, then left her hanging. He was not letting her out of the bet. It might be a painful two weeks until the wedding while he tried, but in the end, she'd get a nice trip to Argentina out of it.

Colin was well-intentioned, but he wasn't going to turn her into a jolly ol' elf anytime soon. It wasn't as though she wanted to be a Humbug. She'd tried on several occasions to get into the spirit, but it never worked. The moment the carols started playing in the stores, she felt her soul begin to shrivel inside her. Honey-glazed ham tasted like ash in her mouth.

With her parents' marriages in shambles and no desire to ever start a family of her own, there wasn't anything left to the season but cold weather and commercialism.

That said, she didn't expect Colin to lose this bet quietly. He would try his damnedest, and if last night was any indication, he was willing to play dirty. If that was the case, she needed to as well. It wouldn't be hard to deploy her own distracting countermeasures. The chemistry between them was powerful and could easily derail his focus. She wouldn't have to go too far—a seductive smile and a gentle touch would easily plant something other than visions of sugarplums in his head.

Natalie reached back into the drawer for the mirror she'd sought out earlier. She looked over her hair and re-applied her burgundy lipstick. She repowdered her nose, then slipped everything back into her desk. Glancing down at her outfit, she opted to slip out of her blazer, leaving just the sleeveless burgundy and hunter-green satin shell beneath it. It had a deep V-neck cut, and the necklace she was wearing today would no doubt draw the eye down to the depths of her cleavage.

Finally, she dabbed a bit of perfume behind her ears, on her wrists and just between her collarbones. It was her favorite scent, exotic and complex, bringing to mind perfumed silk tents in the deserts of Arabia. A guy she'd once dated had told her that perfume was like a hook, luring him closer with the promise of sex.

She took a deep breath of the fragrance and smiled. It was playing dirty, but she had a bet to win.

"I brought you a gift."

Colin watched Natalie look up at him from her desk with a startled expression. From the looks of it, she'd been deep into her work and lost track of time. She recovered quickly, sitting back in her chair and pulling off her headset. "Did you? What is it now? A light-up snowman? A three-foot candy cane?"

"Close." He whipped out a box from behind his back and placed it on her desk. "It's peppermint bark from a candy shop downtown."

Natalie smirked at the box, opening it to admire the

contents. "Are you planning to buy your way through this whole bet?"

"Maybe. Either way, it's cheaper than a first-class ticket to Buenos Aires."

"You added the first class part yourself, you know, when you were feeling cocky." She leaned her elbows on the desk and watched him pointedly.

His gaze was drawn to a gold-and-emerald pendant that dangled just at the dip of her neckline. The shadows hinted at the breasts just beyond the necklace. He caught a whiff of her perfume and felt the muscles in his body start to tense. What were they talking about? Cocky. Yes. That was certainly on point. "Do you like the wreath?" he asked, diverting the subject.

"It's lovely," she said, sitting back with a satisfied smile that made him think she was teasing him on purpose.

That was definitely a change from that night at the house. She'd been adamant about being the wrong kind of woman for him and that they should be friends. Now she was almost dangling herself in front of him. He couldn't complain about the view, but he had to question the motivation.

"It makes my entryway smell like a pine forest."

At least she hadn't said Pine-Sol. "You're supposed to say it smells like Christmas."

"I don't know what Christmas is supposed to smell like. When I was a kid, Christmas smelled like burned biscuits and the nasty floral air freshener my mom would spray to keep my grandmother from finding out she was smoking again."

Colin winced at her miserable holiday memories. It sounded as though her Christmas experiences sucked long before her dad left. His next purchase was going to be a mulling spice candle. "That is not what Christmas smells like. It smells like pine and peppermint, spiced cider and baking sugar cookies."

"Maybe in Hallmark stores," she said, pushing up from her chair and glancing at her watch. "But now we need to focus on cake, not sugar cookies."

Colin followed her into a sitting room near the kitchen. It had several comfortable wingback chairs and a loveseat surrounding a coffee table.

"Have a seat." Natalie gestured into the room.

"Are you joining me?" he asked as he passed near to her.

"Oh yes," she said with a coy smile. "I've just got to let Amelia know we're ready."

He stepped inside and Natalie disappeared down the hallway. He was happy to have a moment alone. The smell of her skin mingling with her perfume and that naughty smile was a combination he couldn't take much more of. At least not and keep his hands off her.

Something had definitely changed since Tuesday. Tuesday night, she'd been more open and friendly once he told her why he'd turned her down, but nothing like this. Not even when she'd leaned into him, thinking he was about to kiss her.

Perhaps she was trying to distract him. Did she think that keeping his mind occupied with thoughts of her would shift the focus away from bringing Christmas joy back into her life? This had all happened after the bet, so that had to be it. *Tricky little minx.* That was playing dirty after her big speech about how she wasn't the right kind of woman for him. Well, two could play at that game. If he was right, now that he knew her ploy he'd let her see how far she was willing to push it to win.

No matter what, he wouldn't let himself be ensnared by her feminine charms. They were oil and water that wouldn't mix. But that didn't mean he wouldn't enjoy letting her try. And it didn't mean he'd let himself lose sight of the bet in the process.

He heard a click of heels on wood and a moment later Natalie came back into the room. She settled onto the loveseat beside him. Before he could say anything, the caterer, Amelia, blew in behind her.

"Okay," Amelia said as she carried a silver platter into the room and placed it on the coffee table. "Time for some cake tasting. This is the best part of planning a wedding, I think. Here are five of our most popular cake flavors." She pointed her manicured finger at the different cubes of cake that were stacked into elegant pyramids. "There's a white almond sour cream cake, triple chocolate fudge, red velvet, pistachio and lemon pound cake. In the bowls, we've got an assortment of different fillings along with samples of both my butter-cream and my marshmallow fondant. The cake design you selected will work with either finish, so it's really just a matter of what taste you prefer."

"It all looks wonderful, Amelia. Thanks for putting this together."

"Sure thing. On this card, it has all the flavors listed along with some popular combinations you might like to try. For a wedding of your size, I usually recommend two choices. I can do alternating tiers, so if a guest doesn't one like flavor, they can always try the other. The variety is nice. Plus, it makes it easier to choose if you have more than one you love."

"Great," Colin said, taking the card from her and setting it on the table. He watched as the caterer shot a pointed look at Natalie on the couch beside him.

"And if you don't mind, since Natalie is here with you, I'm going to go clean up in the kitchen. I've got another cake to finish piping tonight."

Colin nodded. He was fine being alone with Natalie. That left the door open for her little games anyway. "That's fine. I'm sure you've got plenty to do. Thanks for fitting me in on such short notice."

"Thanks, Amelia," Natalie said. "If we have any questions about the cake, I'll come get you."

Amelia nodded and slipped out of the room. Colin watched her go, then turned back to the platter in front of them. "Where should we start?"

Natalie picked up the card from the table. "I'd go with Amelia's suggestions. She knows her cake."

"Great. What's first?"

"White almond sour cream cake with lemon curd."

They both selected small squares of cake from the plate, smearing them with a touch of the filling using a small silver butter knife. Colin wasn't a big fan of lemon, but even he had to admit this was one of the best bites of cake he'd ever had.

And it was just the beginning. They tried them all, mixing chocolate cake with chocolate chip mousse, lemon pound cake with raspberry buttercream and red velvet with whipped cream cheese. There were a million different combinations to choose from. He was glad he'd eaten a light lunch because by the time they finished, all the cake was gone and his suit pants were a bit tighter than they'd been when he sat down.

"I don't know how we're going to choose," he said

at last. "It was all great. I don't think there was a single thing I didn't like."

"I told you she did great work."

Colin turned to look at Natalie, noticing she had a bit of buttercream icing in the corner of her mouth. "Uh-oh."

"What?" Natalie asked with concern lining her brow.

"You've got a little…" his voice trailed off as he reached out and wiped the icing away with the pad of his thumb. "…frosting. I got it," he said with a smile.

Natalie looked at the icing on the tip of his thumb. She surprised him by grasping his wrist to keep him from pulling away. With her eyes pinned on his, she leaned in and gently placed his thumb in her mouth. She sucked off the icing, gliding her tongue over his skin. Colin's groin tightened and blood started pumping hard through his veins.

She finally let go, a sweet smile on her face that didn't quite match her bold actions. "I didn't want any to go to waste."

For once in his life, Colin acted without thinking. He lunged for her, capturing her lips with his and clutching at her shoulders. He waited for Natalie to stiffen or struggle away from him, but she didn't. Instead, she brought up her hands to hold his face close to her, as though she was afraid he might pull away too soon.

Her lips were soft and tasted like sweet vanilla buttercream. He'd had plenty of cake today, but he couldn't get enough of her mouth. There was no hesitation in her touch, her tongue gliding along his just as she'd tortured him with his thumb a moment ago.

Finally, he pulled away. It took all his willpower to do it, but he knew he needed to. This was a wedding chapel, not a hotel room. He didn't move far, though. His hand was still resting on Natalie's upper arm, his face mere inches from hers. She was breathing hard, her cheeks flushed as her hands fell into her lap.

He could tell that he'd caught her off guard at first with that kiss, but he didn't care. She'd brought that on herself with her distracting games. If her body was any indicator, she hadn't minded. She'd clung to him, met him measure for measure. For someone who thought they were unsuitable for each other, she'd certainly participated in that kiss.

He just wished he knew that she wanted to, and she wasn't just doing it as a distraction to help her win the bet. There was one way to find out. She wasn't good at hiding her initial emotional responses, so he decided to push a few buttons. "So, what do you think?" he asked.

Natalie looked at him with glassy, wide eyes. "About what?"

"About the cake. I'm thinking definitely the white cake with the lemon, but I'm on the fence about the second choice."

Natalie stiffened, the hazy bliss vanishing in an instant. He could tell that cake was not what she'd had on her mind in that moment. She'd let her little game go too far. He was glad he wasn't the only one affected by it.

"Red velvet," she said. She sniffed delicately and sat back, pulling away from him. Instantly, she'd transformed back into the uptight, efficient wedding planner. "It's a universal flavor. I'm told it's a Christmas classic, so it suits the theme. It's also one of my favorites, so admittedly I'm partial."

"Okay. The choices are made. Thanks for being so… helpful."

Natalie looked at him with a narrowed gaze that softened as the coy smile from earlier returned. "My pleasure."

Five

Monday afternoon, Colin made a stop by Frankie's motorcycle store on his way home from his latest work site.

When he'd first found out that his sister was dating a guy who looked more like a biker than a businessman, he'd been hesitant. Meeting Frankie and visiting his custom bike shop downtown had changed things. Yes, he had more tattoos than Colin could count and several piercings, but he was a talented artisan of his craft. The motorcycles he designed and built were metal masterpieces that earned a high price. Over the past year, Frankie's business had really started to take off. It looked like he and Lily would have a promising future together.

Slipping into the shop, Colin walked past displays of parts, gear and accessories to the counter at the back. Lily was sitting at the counter. Frankie had hired her to run the register, making the business a family affair. Living upstairs from the shop had made it convenient, but he couldn't imagine they had enough space to raise a family there or even stretch their legs.

"Hey, brother of mine," Lily called from the counter. "Can I interest you in a chopper?"

"Very funny." Colin laughed.

Lily came out from behind the counter to give him a hug. "If not for a bike, to what do I owe this visit?"

"Well, I thought you might want to know about some of the wedding plans Natalie and I have put together." Colin had a copy of the design portfolio to show her. He hoped that by showing her the designs, she would start getting more excited about the wedding.

Lily shrugged and drifted back to her post behind the counter. "I'm sure whatever you've chosen will be great."

"At least look at it," Colin said, opening the folder on the counter. "Natalie and her partners have worked really hard on putting together a beautiful wedding for you. We went with the winter wonderland theme you and Natalie discussed. For the cake, we chose alternating tiers of white almond sour cream cake with lemon curd filling and red velvet with cream cheese. Natalie said those were two of their most popular flavors, and they were both really tasty."

"Sounds great," Lily said, sitting back onto her stool. "I have no doubt that it will come together beautifully. As long as I have someone to marry us, it's fine by me. The rest of this is just a bonus."

"Have you ordered a dress yet?"

His sister shook her head. "No."

Colin frowned. "Lily, you don't have a dress?"

"I was just going to pull something from my closet. I have that white dress from my sorority induction ceremony."

"Are you serious? You've got to go get a wedding dress, Lily."

His sister shrugged again, sending Colin's blood pressure higher. He couldn't fathom how she didn't care about any of this. Pam hadn't been very interested in planning their wedding either. Since they were in a hurry, they'd ended up with a courthouse visit without frills. It was a little anticlimactic. He didn't want that for Lily, but she seemed indifferent about the whole thing.

"I've got a job, Colin. Frankie and I work at the shop six days a week. I can't go running around trying on fluffy Cinderella dresses. If you are so concerned with what I'm wearing, you can pick it out. I wear a size six. Natalie and I used to be able to share clothes when we were teenagers. At the engagement party she looked like she might still wear the same size as I do. I'm sure you two can work it out without me."

Colin fought the urge to drop his face into his hands in dismay. "Will you at least go to a dress fitting?"

"Yeah, sure."

"Okay. So we'll get a dress." He pulled out his phone to call Natalie and let her know the bad news. He knew she had been busy over the weekend with a wedding, so he hadn't bothered her with wedding or holiday details. He couldn't wait any longer, though. He was certain this was an important detail and could be the very thing that pushed his cool, calm and collected wedding planner over the edge.

She didn't answer, so he left a quick message on her

phone. When he slipped his phone back into his pocket, he noticed Lily watching him. "What?"

"Your voice changed when you left her a message."

"I was trying to soften the blow," he insisted.

Lily shook her head. "I don't know. That voice sounded like the same voice I remember from when you would tie up the house phone talking to girls in high school. What's going on between you two?"

"Going on?" Colin tried to find the best way to word it. "I don't know. We've spent a lot of time together planning the wedding. Things have been…interesting."

"Are you dating?"

"No," Colin said more confidently. He was determined not to wade into that territory with Natalie. She was beautiful and smart and alluring, but she also had it in her to crush him. "Natalie and I have very different ideas on what constitutes a relationship."

Lily nodded. "Natalie has never been the princess waiting for her prince to save her. She always kept it casual with guys. I take it you're not interested in a booty call. You should consider it. Going from serious relationship to serious relationship isn't working for you either."

Colin did not want to have this conversation with his little sister. Instead, he ignored the kernel of truth in her words. "I am not going to discuss booty calls with you. I can't believe I even said that phrase out loud."

"Have you kissed her?"

He didn't answer right away.

"Colin?"

"Yes, I kissed her."

Lily made a thoughtful clicking sound with her tongue. "Interesting," she said slowly, her hands planted on her hips. "What exactly do you—?"

Colin's phone started to ring at his hip, interrupting her query. He'd never been so relieved to get a call. "I've got to take this," he said, answering the phone and moving to the front of the shop. "Hello?"

"There's no dress?" It was Natalie, her displeasure evident by the flat tone of her query.

"That is correct," he said with a heavy sigh. "And like everything else, she says to just pick something. Lily says she's a size six and that you used to share clothes, so fake it."

"Fake it?" Natalie shrieked into his ear.

"Yep." He didn't know what else to say.

Natalie sat silent on the other end of the line for a moment. "I need to make a few calls. Can you meet me at a bridal salon tonight?"

Colin looked down at his watch. It was already after five. Did they have enough time? "Sure."

"Okay. I'll call you back and let you know where to meet me."

Colin hung up, turning to see a smug look on his sister's face.

"I told you she could handle it."

"That well may be, but she wasn't happy about it." At this point, they'd probably be lucky if Lily didn't go down the aisle in a white trash bag. They had about two weeks to pick the dress, order it, have it come in and do any alterations. He wasn't much of a wedding expert, but he got the feeling it would be a rough road. "What about Frankie? Do I need to dress him, too?"

Lily shook her head and Colin felt a wave of relief wash over him. "He's good. He's got a white suit and picked out a silver bowtie and suspenders to go with the theme."

He should've known a bit of hipster style would make its way into this wedding. Whatever. It was one less person he had to dress.

Returning to the counter, he closed the wedding portfolio. He was anxious to get out of here before Lily started up the conversation about Natalie again. "Okay, well, I'm off to meet Natalie at some bridal salon. Any other surprises you're waiting to tell me until an inopportune time?"

The slight twist of Lily's lips was proof that there was. "Well…" she hesitated. "I kind of forgot about this before, but it should be fine."

Somehow, he doubted that. "What, Lily?"

"Next week, Frankie and I are flying to Las Vegas for a motorcycle convention."

"Next week? Lily, the wedding is next week."

"The wedding isn't until Saturday. We're flying back Friday. No problem."

Colin dropped his forehead into his hand and squeezed at his temples. "What time on Friday? You've got the rehearsal that afternoon and the rehearsal dinner after that."

"Hmm…" she said thoughtfully, reaching for her phone. She flipped through the screens to pull up her calendar. "Our flight is scheduled to arrive in Nashville at one. That should be plenty of time, right?"

"Right." He didn't bother to point out that it was winter and weather delays were a very real concern this time of year. With his luck, she was connecting in Chicago or Detroit. "When do you leave?"

"Monday."

Colin nodded. Well, at the very least, he knew he

could work on the house without worrying about her stopping by and ruining the surprise.

A chime on his phone announced a text. Natalie had sent him the name and address of the bridal shop where they were meeting.

"Anything else I need to know, Lil?"

She smiled innocently, reminding him of the sweet girl with pigtails he remembered growing up. "Nope. That's it."

"Okay," he said, slipping his phone back into his pocket. "I'm off to buy you a wedding dress."

"Good luck," she called to him as he slipped out of the store.

He'd need it.

Natalie swallowed her apprehension as she went into the bridal shop. Not because she had to get Lily a dress at the last minute—that didn't surprise her at all. They were close enough to sample size to buy something out of the shop and alter it.

Really, she was more concerned about trying on wedding dresses. It wasn't for her, she understood that, but it still felt odd. She'd never tried on a wedding dress before, not even for fun. Her mother had sold her wedding dress when her parents divorced.

She knew it was just a dress, but there was something transformative about it. She didn't want to feel that feeling. That was worse than Christmas spirit.

She'd avoided the bulk of Colin's holiday bet by staying busy with a wedding all weekend. But now it was the start of a new week and she had no doubt he would find some way to slip a little Christmas into each day.

In addition to the wreath and the peppermint bark,

she'd also received a Christmas card that played carols when she opened it. A local bakery had delivered a fruitcake to the office on Friday, and a florist had brought a poinsettia on Saturday morning.

What he didn't know was that she'd received plenty of well-meaning holiday gifts throughout the years. That wasn't going to crack her. It just gave her a plant to water every other day.

As she entered the waiting room of the salon, she found Colin and the storekeeper, Ruby, searching through the tall racks of gowns. Ruby looked up as she heard Natalie approach.

"Miss Sharpe! There you are. Mr. Russell and I were looking through a few gowns while we waited."

"Not a problem. Thanks for scheduling us with such late notice."

"This is the bridal business," Ruby said with a dismissive chuckle. "You never know what you'll get. For every girl that orders her gown a year in advance, I get one pregnant and in-a-hurry bride that needs a gown right away. After being in this industry for twenty years, I've learned to keep a good stock of dresses on hand for times like this."

Ruby was good at what she did. Natalie referred a lot of brides to her salon because of it. "Did Colin fill you in on what we need?"

"Yes. He said you need something in a street size six that will fit a winter wonderland theme. He also said the bride won't be here to try them on."

"That's correct. We wear the same size, so I'll try on the dresses in her place."

"Okay. I'd recommend something with a corset back. You don't have a lot of time for alterations and with a corset bodice, you can tighten or loosen it to account for any adjustments in your sizes."

Brilliant. She'd have to remember this in the future for quick-turnaround brides. "Perfect."

"Great. If you'd like to take a seat, Mr. Russell, I'll take Miss Sharpe to the dressing room to try on a few gowns to see what you like."

"Have fun," Colin said, waving casually at her as she was ushered into the back.

She was officially on the other side now. She'd passed the curtain where only brides went. It made her stomach ache.

"I've pulled these three dresses to start with. I think you're pretty close to the sample size, so this should be a decent fit. Which would you like to try first?"

Natalie looked over the gowns with apprehension. She needed to think like Lily. Everything else about the wedding had turned out to be Natalie's choice, but when it came to dresses, it seemed wrong to pick something she liked. "It doesn't matter," she said. "I'm going to let her brother choose."

"Then let's start with the ruched satin gown."

Natalie slipped out of her blouse and pencil skirt and let Ruby slip the gown over her head. She was fully aware how heavy bridal gowns could be, but for some reason, it seemed so much heavier on than she had expected it to.

She held the gown in place as Ruby tightened the corset laces in the back. Looking in the mirror, she admired the fit of the gown. The corset gave her a curvy, seductive shape she hadn't expected. She never felt much like a sex kitten. Her shape had always been a little lanky and boyish in her opinion, but the gown changed that.

The decorative crystals that lined the sweetheart neckline drew the eyes to her enhanced cleavage.

"Do you like the snowflake?"

Natalie narrowed her gaze at her reflection and noticed the crystal design at her hip that looked very much like a snowflake. Perfect for the theme. "It's nice. It's got a good shape and the crystals give it a little shine without being overpowering."

"Let's go show him."

There was more apprehension as Natalie left the dressing room. This wasn't about her, but she wanted to look the best she could when she stepped onto the riser to show him the gown. She focused on her posture and grace as she glided out into the salon.

Her gaze met his the minute she cleared the curtain. His golden hazel eyes raked up and down the length of the gown with the same heat of appreciation she'd seen that night at the engagement party. Natalie felt a flush of heat rise to her cheeks as she stepped onto the pedestal for his inspection.

"It's beautiful," he said. "It's very elegant and you look amazing in it. But I have to say that it's not right for Lily at all."

Natalie sighed and looked down. He was right. "Ruby, do we have one that's a little more whimsical and fun?"

Ruby nodded and helped her down. "I have a few that might work. How fun are we talking?" she asked as they stepped back into the dressing room. "Crazy tulle skirt? Blush- or pink-colored gowns?"

"If she was here, probably all that and more. But she should've shown up herself if she had that strong of an opinion. Let's go for something a little more whimsical, but still classically bridal."

The minute Ruby held up the gown, Natalie knew this dress was the one. It was like something out of a winter fantasy—the gown of the snow queen. It was a fitted, mermaid style with a sweetheart neckline and sheer, full-length sleeves. All across the gown and along the sleeves were delicate white-and-silver-stitched floral designs that looked almost like glittering snowflakes dancing across her skin.

She held her breath as she slipped into the gown and got laced up. Ruby fastened a few buttons at her shoulders and then it was done. It was the most beautiful dress she'd ever seen, and she'd seen hundreds of brides come through the chapel over the years.

"This gown has a matching veil with the same lace trim along the edges. Do you want to go out there with it on?"

"Yes," she said immediately. Natalie wanted to see the dress with the veil. She knew it would make all the difference.

Ruby swiftly pinned her hair up and set the veil's comb in. The veil flowed all the way to floor, longer than even the gown's chapel-length train.

It was perfect. Everything she'd ever wanted.

Natalie swallowed hard. Everything she'd ever wanted *for Lily*, she corrected herself. Planning a wedding in the bride's place was messing with her head.

She headed back out to the salon. This time, she avoided Colin's gaze, focusing on lifting the hem of the skirt to step up on the pedestal. She glanced at herself for only a moment in the three-sided mirror, but even that was enough for the prickle of tears to form in her eyes.

Quickly, she jerked away, turning to face Colin. She covered her tears by fidgeting with her gown and veil.

"What do you think of this one?" Ruby asked.

The long silence forced Natalie to finally meet Colin's gaze. Did he hate it?

Immediately, she knew that was not the case. He was just stunned speechless.

"Colin?"

"Wow," he finally managed. He stood up from the velour settee and walked closer.

Natalie felt her chest grow tighter with every step. He wasn't looking at the gown. Not really. He was looking at her. The intensity of his gaze made her insides turn molten. Her knees started trembling and she was thankful for the full skirt that covered them.

Just when she thought she couldn't bear his gaze any longer, his eyes dropped down to look over the details of the dress. "This is the one. No question."

Natalie took a breath and looked down to examine the dress. "Do you think Lily will like it?"

Colin hesitated a moment, swallowing hard before he spoke. "I do. It will look beautiful on her. I don't think we could find a dress better suited to the theme you've put together." He took a step back and nodded again from a distance. "Let's get this one."

"Wonderful!" Ruby exclaimed. "This one really is lovely."

The older woman went to the counter to write up the slip, completely oblivious to the energy in the room that hummed between Natalie and Colin. Natalie wasn't quite sure how she didn't notice it. It made it hard for

Natalie to breathe. It made the dress feel hot and itchy against her skin even though it was the softest, most delicate fabric ever made.

Colin slipped back down onto the couch with a deep sigh. When he looked up at her again, Natalie knew she wasn't mistaken about any of this. He wanted her. And she wanted him. It was a bad idea, they both knew it, but they couldn't fight it much longer.

She also wanted out of this dress. Right now. Playing bride was a confusing and scary experience. Before Colin or Ruby could say another word, she pulled the veil from her head, leaped down from the pedestal and disappeared behind the curtains into the dressing room as fast as she could.

Six

"I'd like to take you to dinner," Colin said as they walked out of the shop with the gown bagged over his arm. "I'm serious this time. You really bailed me out on this whole dress thing."

It was a lame excuse. It sounded lame to his own ears, but he couldn't do anything about it. There was no way he could look at Natalie, to see her in that dress looking like the most beautiful creature he'd ever set his eyes on, and then let her just get in her car and go home. It no longer mattered if they were incompatible or had no future. The taste of her already lingered on his lips, the heat of her hummed through his veins. He wanted her. End of story.

Natalie stopped and swung her purse strap up onto her shoulder. "Dinner? Not a date?"

This again. You'd think after their kiss, and after the intense moment they'd just shared in the salon, that she wouldn't be so picky about the details. "No, it's not a date, it's a thank-you. I believe that I have yet to meet your stringent qualifications for a date."

Natalie's lips curled into a smile of amusement. He expected her to make an excuse and go home, but instead she nodded. "Dinner sounds great."

Colin opened the door of his truck and hung the gown bag up inside. "How about the Italian place on the corner?"

"That's perfect."

He closed up the truck and they walked down the sidewalk together to the restaurant. Colin had eaten at Moretti's a couple of times and it had always been good. It was rustic Italian cuisine, with a Tuscan feel inside. The walls were a rusty brown with exposed brick, worn wood shelves and tables, warm gold lighting and an entire wall on the far end that was covered in hundreds of wine bottles. It wasn't the fanciest place, but it was a good restaurant for a casual dinner date, or a thank-you dinner as the case was here.

It was a pretty popular place to eat in this area. Typically, Moretti's was super busy, but coming later on a Monday night the restaurant was pretty quiet. There were about a dozen tables with customers when they arrived and no waiting list.

The hostess immediately escorted them to a booth for two near the roaring fireplace. Nashville didn't get very cold in the winter, but with the icy December wind, it was cold enough that the fire would feel amazing after their walk down the street. Colin helped Natalie out of her coat, hanging it on one of the brass hooks mounted to the side of the booth.

The waiter arrived just as they'd settled into their

seats, bringing water and warm bread with olive oil. He offered them the daily menus and left them alone to make their choices. After a bit of deliberation, Natalie chose the angel-hair primavera and Colin, the chicken parmesan. They selected a bottle of cabernet to share and the waiter returned with that immediately.

The first sip immediately warmed Colin's belly and cheeks, reminding him to go slow until he ate some bread. He'd had a quick sandwich around eleven, but he was starving now and wine on an empty stomach might make him say or do something he'd regret, like kissing Natalie again. Or maybe he'd do something he wouldn't regret, but shouldn't do. At the moment, Lily's suggestion that he indulge himself in something casual with Natalie was sounding pretty good. He took a bite of bread as a precaution.

"Well, this is certainly not how I envisioned this evening going," Natalie noted as she tore her own chunk of bread from the loaf.

"It's not bad, is it?"

"No," she admitted. "But when I woke up this morning, I didn't figure I'd be trying on wedding dresses and having dinner with you."

It hadn't been on his radar either, but he was happy with the turn of events. There was something about spending an evening with Natalie that relaxed him after a stressful day. "Did you have plans for tonight that I ruined?"

"Not real plans. I'd anticipated a frozen dinner and a couple chapters of a new book I downloaded."

"I was going to grab takeout and catch up on my DVR. We're an exciting pair. Are you off tomorrow?"

Natalie shrugged, confusing him with her response

to a simple question. "Technically," she clarified. "The chapel is closed on Tuesday and Wednesday, but I usually go in."

"That means you don't get any days off."

"I don't usually work a full day. And I only work half of Sunday to clean up."

Colin shook his head. "You sound as bad as I used to be when I took over Dad's business. I worked eighteen-hour days, seven days a week trying to keep afloat. Is that why you put in so many hours? How's the wedding business?"

If the bill he'd received for the upcoming wedding was any indication, they were doing very well. He'd told her money was no object and she'd believed him. It was well worth it for Lily, but he'd been surprised to see so many digits on the invoice.

"Business is great. That's why it's so hard not to come in. There's always something to do."

"Can't you hire someone to watch the place and answer the phones while you all take time off? Like a receptionist?"

Natalie bit her lip and took a large sip of wine as though she were delaying her response. "I guess we could. Anyways, I'm the only one without a backup, but I'm the only one of us without a life. It's kind of hard to swap out the wedding planner, though. I'm the one with the whole vision of the day and know all the pieces that have to fall into place just perfectly."

"Getting a receptionist isn't the same as getting a backup planner. It just frees you up so you're not answering the phones and filing paperwork all the time. You should look into it. Of course, that would require you not to be such a control freak."

Natalie perked up in her seat. "I am not a control freak."

At that, Colin laughed. "Oh, come on now. Your office is immaculate. You're always stomping around with that headset on, handling every emergency. I'm beginning to think you run a one-stop wedding company because you won't let anyone else do any of it."

She opened her mouth to argue, then stopped. "Maybe I should look into a receptionist," she admitted.

"If you had one, you could spend the next two days with me instead of sitting alone in that lonely office of yours."

Natalie's eyebrow raised in question. "Spend the next two days with you doing what?"

"Working on the house. Helping me decorate. What we discussed last week. I've turned over the reins of the company to my second-in-command to manage our remaining projects through the end of the year so I can focus on what I need to do before the holidays."

"Oh."

That wasn't the enthusiastic response he was hoping for. "Oh, huh? I guess I should sweeten the deal, then. Spending time with me to help your childhood best friend isn't enough incentive."

"Quit it," Natalie chided. "I told you I'd help you with the house. Since I work on weekends, it makes sense to come over tomorrow, you're right. And I will. I was just expecting something else."

"Like what?"

"I don't know…a trip to the Opryland Hotel to look at the Christmas decorations and visit Santa, maybe?"

Opryland! Colin silently cursed and sipped his wine to cover his aggravation. The hotel in central Nashville was practically its own city. They went all out every holiday with massive decorations. They usually built a giant ice village with slides kids could play on. They even hosted the Rockettes' Christmas show. That would've been perfect, but of course he couldn't do it now that she'd brought it up. He refused to be predictable.

There wasn't really time for that, either. When he'd made that impulsive bet, he hadn't given a lot of thought to how much they both worked and how incompatible their schedules were. Between their jobs, working on the house and the wedding, there wasn't much time left to reintroduce Natalie to the holiday magic. He'd find a way, though. He was certain of it.

"I figured it was something related to the bet, although I don't know why you'd bother after that kiss we shared at the cake tasting. I'm not sure the one you'll win will be better than that."

Colin smiled wide. "Are you serious?" he asked.

She looked at him blankly. "Well, yes. It was a pretty good kiss, as kisses go."

"It was an amazing kiss," Colin conceded. "But it won't hold a candle to the kiss I'll get when I win."

Natalie sucked in a ragged breath, her pale skin growing a more peachy-pink tone in the golden candlelight. "I guess as a teenager I never realized how arrogant you were."

"It's not arrogance when it's fact. I intend to make your pulse spike and cheeks flush. I want you to run your fingers through my hair and hold me like you never want to let me go. When I win this bet, I'll kiss you until you're breathless and can't imagine ever kissing anyone else."

He watched Natalie swallow hard and reach a shaky hand out for more wine. He hid away his smile and focused on her so she knew he meant every word.

"Y-you've still g-got to win the bet," she stammered. "I'm pretty sure you've run out of Christmas stuff to mail to the office."

"Don't underestimate me," Colin said. "Those holiday gifts were just to get you in the right mindset." There were a lot of sensory elements to Christmas— the smell of pine and mulling spice, the taste of peppermint and chocolate, the sight of bright lights and colorful poinsettias. "I wanted to…prime the pump, so to speak. When you're ready, that's when I'll move in for the kill."

The waiter arrived with their salads, but Colin had suddenly lost his appetite. He knew what he wanted to taste and it wasn't on the Moretti's menu. A part of him knew it was a mistake to let himself go any further with Natalie, but the other part already knew it was too late. He needed to have her. Knowing nothing would come of it going in, he would be able to compartmentalize it. Just because he rarely had sex for sex's sake didn't mean he couldn't. What they had was a raw, physical attraction, nothing more. Natalie was certainly an enticing incentive to try to start now.

Perhaps if he did, he could focus on something else for a change. He had plenty going on right now, but somehow, Natalie's full bottom lip seemed to occupy all his thoughts.

As they ate, Natalie shifted the conversation to the wedding and his sister, even asking about his business, but he knew neither of them was really interested in talking about that tonight. They just had to get through dinner.

It wasn't until they were halfway through their pasta that she returned to the previous discussion. "I've been thinking," she began. "I think you and I started off on the wrong foot at the engagement party. I'd like us to start over."

"Start over?" He wasn't entirely sure what that meant.

"Yes. When we get done eating, I'm going to once again ask if you'd like to go someplace quiet to talk and catch up. This time, since you're not dating anyone, I hope you'll give a better response."

Was she offering what he thought she was offering? He sincerely hoped so. He finished his wine and busied himself by paying the bill. When the final credit card slip was brought to him, he looked up at Natalie. She was watching him with the sly smile on her face that she'd greeted him with the first time.

"So, Colin," she said softly. "Would you be interested in getting out of here and finding someplace quiet where we could talk and catch up?"

Colin had replayed that moment in his mind several times since the engagement party and now he knew exactly what he wanted to say.

"Your place or mine?"

It turned out to be his place, which was closer. Natalie's heart was pounding as she followed Colin down the hallway and into his kitchen. She'd only been here once before, the night of the engagement party. The house looked quite different tonight. There were no huge catering platters, no skirted tables, no jazz trio. It was just the wide open, modern space he called home.

It actually looked a little plain without everything else. Spartan. Like a model home.

She couldn't help but notice the sharp contrast between it and the warm, welcoming feel of his parents' house. It was about as far as you could get between them. Natalie had no doubt that this was a million-dollar house, but it was far too contemporary in style to suit her.

"May I offer you more wine?" he asked.

"No, thank you," she said, putting her purse down on the white quartz countertop. "I had plenty at dinner." And she had. She was stuffed. Natalie had focused on her food to avoid Colin's heated appraisal and now she regretted it. If she'd fully realized that her fantasies would actually play out after dinner, she would've held back a touch. She didn't exactly feel sexy, full to the gills with pasta, bread and wine.

"May I offer you a tour, then? I'm not sure how much you got to see of the place the other night."

"Not much," Natalie admitted. Since she'd only known the bride and her brother, she hadn't done much socializing. She'd hovered near the bar, people watching most of the evening.

Colin led her out of the sleek kitchen and through the dining room to the two-story open living room with a dramatic marble fireplace that went up to the ceiling. She followed him up the stairs to his loft office, then his bedroom. "This is the best part," he said.

"I bet," Natalie replied with a grin.

"That's not what I meant." He walked past the large bed to a set of French doors. He opened them and stepped out onto a deck.

Natalie went out behind him and stopped short as

she caught a glimpse of the view. They'd driven up a fairly steep hill to get here, she remembered that, but she hadn't realized his house virtually clung to the side of the mountain. While precarious, it offered an amazing view of the city. The lights stretched out as far as the eye could see, competing with the stars that twinkled overhead.

She had a really nice townhouse she liked, but it couldn't hold a candle to this. She could sit out here all night just looking up at the stars and sipping her coffee. Natalie bet it was amazing at sunrise, too.

"So, what do you think?"

Natalie hesitated, trying to find the right words. She turned to Colin, who was leaning against the railing with his arms crossed over his chest. "The deck is amazing."

"What about the rest of the house?"

"It's very nice."

"Nice, huh? You don't like it at all."

Natalie avoided the question by stepping back into the bedroom with him on her heels. "It's a beautiful home, really. The view alone is worth the price you paid for it. The aesthetic is just a little modern for my taste."

Colin nodded. "Me, too. To be honest, Pam picked this place. If I hadn't been so mad about Shane, I probably would've let her keep it."

Natalie stiffened at the mention of his ex-wife and the son who'd turned out not to be his. She still wasn't sure exactly what had happened, but prying seemed rude. Since he brought it up… "Does she ever let you see Shane?"

Colin shook his head once, kind of curt. "No. I think it's better that way though since he's still a baby. If he'd been any older, it would've been harder to help him understand where his daddy was. He's probably forgotten who I am by now."

"I don't know about that," Natalie said, stepping toward him until they were nearly touching. "I know I've never been able to forget about you."

"Is that right?" Colin asked, wrapping his arms around her waist. The pain had faded from his face, replaced only with the light of attraction. "So, did you fantasize about what it would be like to kiss me?"

Natalie smiled. How many nights had she hugged her pillow to her chest and pretended it was Lily's handsome older brother? "An embarrassing number of times," she admitted.

"Did our first kiss live up to those expectations?"

"It did, and then some. Of course, when I was fifteen, I didn't know what was really possible like I do now."

"Oh really?"

"Yes. And now I want more."

Colin didn't hesitate to meet her demand. His mouth met hers, offering her everything she wanted. She ran her fingers through his hair, tugging him closer. Natalie wasn't letting him get away this time. He was all hers tonight. She arched her back, pressing her body against the hard wall of his chest.

He growled against her lips, his hand straying from her waist to glide along her back and hips. He cupped one cheek of her rear through the thin fabric of her skirt, pushing her hips against his until she could feel the firm heat of his desire.

Natalie gasped, pulling from his mouth. "Yeah," she said in a breathy voice. "There's no way I would've imagined a kiss like that."

Pulling back, she reached for the collar of his jacket. She pushed his blazer off his shoulders, letting it fall to the floor. Her palms moved greedily over his broad shoulders and down the front of his chest, touching every inch of the muscles she'd seen in that tight T-shirt. Starting at his collar, she unbuttoned his shirt, exposing the muscles and dark chest chair scattered across them.

Colin stood stiffly as she worked, his hands tightly curled into fists at his sides. When Natalie reached his belt, he sprang into action, grasping her wrists. "That's not really fair, is it?"

"Well," she reasoned, "I've been fantasizing about seeing you naked for years. I think it's only right I shouldn't have to wait any longer."

Colin gathered the hem of her blouse and lifted it slowly over her head. Natalie raised her arms to help him take it off. He cast her shirt onto a nearby chair. "I don't think a few more minutes will kill you."

He focused on her breasts, taking in the sight before covering the satin-clad globes with the palms of his hands. Natalie gasped when he touched her, her nipples hardening and pressing into the restraining fabric. He kneaded her flesh, dipping his head down to taste what spilled over the top of the cups. Colin nipped at her skin, soothing it with the glide of his tongue. Tugging down at her bra, he uncovered her nipples, drawing one, then the next into his mouth.

Natalie groaned, pulling his head closer. The warmth of his mouth on her sensitive flesh built a liquid heat in her core. She wasn't sure how much longer she could take this kind of torture.

"I need you," she gasped. "Please."

In response, Colin sought out the back of her skirt

with his fingers. He unzipped it, letting it slide down over her hips. She stepped out of the skirt and her heels, then let Colin guide her backward through the room until the backs of her legs met with the mattress. She reached behind her, crawling onto the bed.

While Colin watched, she unclasped her bra and tossed it aside, leaving nothing on but her panties. His eyes stayed glued to her as he unfastened his pants and slipped them off with his briefs. He pulled away long enough to retrieve a condom from the bedside stand before he climbed onto the bed.

The heat of his body skimmed over hers. He hovered there, kissing her as one hand roamed across her stomach. It brushed the edge of her panties, slipping beneath to dip his fingers between her thighs. Natalie arched off the bed, gasping before meeting his lips once more. He stroked her again and again, building a tension inside her that she was desperate to release.

Colin waited until she was on the very edge, then he retreated, leaving her panting and dissatisfied. "Just a few more minutes," he reassured her with a teasing grin.

He moved down her body, pulling the panties over her hips and along the length of her legs as he moved. Tossing them aside, he sheathed himself and pressed her thighs apart. He nestled between them and positioned himself perfectly to stroke her core as his hips moved forward and back. He rebuilt the fire in her belly, then, looking her in the eye, shifted his hips and thrust into her.

Natalie cried out, clawing at the blankets beneath her. He started slow, clenching his jaw with restraint, then began moving faster. She drew her legs up, wrapping them around his hips as they flexed, eliciting a low groan deep in Colin's throat.

"Yes," Natalie coaxed as he moved harder and faster inside her.

The release he'd teased at before quickly built up inside her again and this time, she knew she would get what she wanted. She gripped his back, feeling the knot tighten in her belly. "Please," she said.

"As you wish." He thrust hard, grinding his pelvis against her sensitive parts until she screamed out.

"Colin!" she shouted as the tiny fire bursts exploded inside her. Her release pulsated through her whole body, her muscles tightening around him as she shuddered and gasped.

Thrusting again, Colin buried his face in her neck and poured himself into her. "Oh, Natalie," he groaned into her ear.

The sound of her name on his lips sent a shiver down her spine. She wrapped her arms around him as he collapsed against her. She gave him a few minutes to rest and recover before she pushed at his shoulders. "Come on," she said.

"Come where?" He frowned.

"To the shower. You and I are just getting started. I've got fourteen years to make up for."

Seven

Colin was making coffee downstairs the next morning when he heard the heavy footsteps of a sleepy Natalie coming down the stairs. He peeked around the corner in time to see her stumble onto the landing. She'd pulled her messy hair into a ponytail and was wearing her professional office attire, but it was rumpled and definitely looked like a day-two ensemble for her.

He watched as she hesitated at the bottom of the stairs. She looked around nervously, almost like she was searching for an exit route. Was she really trying to sneak out without him seeing her? Yes, there wasn't anything serious between them, but she didn't need to flee the scene of the crime. She started slinking toward the front door, but he wasn't about to let her off so easily.

"Good morning, Natalie," he shouted.

She stiffened at the sound of his voice, and then reluctantly turned and followed the noise toward the kitchen. "Good morning," she said as she rounded the corner.

He loved seeing this unpolished version of her. With her wrinkled clothes, her mussed-up hair and day-old makeup, it was a far cry from the superprofessional and sleek wedding planner at the chapel. It reminded him of just how she'd gotten so messy and made him want to take her back upstairs to see what more damage he could do to her perfect appearance in the bedroom.

From the skittish expression on her face, he doubted he'd get the chance. Last night was likely a one-time event, so he'd have to be content with that. Instead, Colin returned to pouring the coffee he'd made into a mug for each of them. "How do you take your coffee? I have raw sugar, fake sugar, whole milk and hazelnut creamer. Oh, and getting it in a go-cup isn't an option, by the way."

She smiled sheepishly, clearly knowing she'd been caught trying to make a quick getaway. "I promise not to drink on the run. A splash of milk and a spoonful of raw sugar, please."

He nodded and worked on making her the perfect cup. "Would you like to have coffee downstairs or on the deck?"

She looked up at the staircase to the bedroom, which they'd have to pass through to get to the deck. "The kitchen nook is fine," she said, obviously unwilling to risk the pleasurable detour. "I'm sure we missed the best of the sunrise a long time ago."

Colin handed over her mug and followed her to the

table with a plate of toasted English muffins with straw-berry jam and butter. He sat down and picked up one muffin, taking a bite with a loud crunch. He finished chewing and let Natalie sip her coffee before he pressed her about her great escape.

"You seem to be in a hurry this morning. What's the rush?"

Natalie swallowed her sip of coffee and set the mug on the kitchen table. "I was hoping you wouldn't no-tice. It's just that I'm, uh, not used to staying over. I'm sort of a master of the four a.m. vanishing act. I prefer to avoid the awkward morning-after thing."

"You mean coffee and conversation?"

"I suppose," she said with a smile.

"What kept you from leaving last night?" Colin wasn't quite sure what he would've done if he'd woken up and she was gone. He wasn't used to this kind of scenario with a woman. He was a relationship guy, and that usu-ally meant enjoying a nice breakfast after a night together, not cold empty sheets beside him in bed.

"I think it was all the wine we had at dinner on top of the…exercise I got later. When I fell asleep, I slept hard. I didn't so much as move a muscle until I smelled the coffee brewing downstairs."

Colin considered her answer. He tried not to let it hurt his pride that she hadn't stayed because she felt compelled, or even wanted to. "You know, despite what happened last night, we're still friends. I don't want this to change that, so there's no need to run before you turn back into a pumpkin. Do you mind me asking why you feel the need to leave?"

Natalie bit at her lip before nodding. "Like I told you

before, I'm not much on the relationship thing. I like to keep things simple and sweet. Uncomplicated."

What was more complicated than this? Colin couldn't think of anything else. A normal relationship seemed a lot more straightforward. "What does that even mean, Natalie?"

"It means that what we shared last night is all I'm really wanting."

"I get that. And I'm on board with that or I wouldn't have let it go that far last night. I'm just curious as to why you feel this way about guys and relationships in general."

"There's nothing really in it for me after that first night or two because I don't believe in love. I think it's a chemical reaction that's been built up into more. I also don't believe in marriage. I enjoy the occasional companionship, but it's never going to come to any more than that with any man."

Colin listened to her talk, realizing this was worse than he'd thought. It could've just as easily been his ex-wife, Pam, sitting across the table talking to him. Yes, Natalie had said she wasn't the marrying kind, but this was more than just that. She didn't believe in the entire concept. He raised his hand to his head to shake off the déjà vu and the dull throb that had formed at his temple. It was a good thing he knew about her resistance going into this or it could've been a much bigger blow. "A wedding planner that doesn't believe in love or marriage?"

She shrugged. "Just because I don't believe in it doesn't mean that other people can't. I'm organized and I'm detail-oriented. I was made for this kind of work, so why not?"

The whole thing seemed a little preposterous. "So even though you spend all your days helping people get married, you never intend to marry or have a family of your own?"

"No," Natalie said, shaking her head. "You know what I grew up with, Colin. My mother is on the verge of dumping her fourth husband. I've seen too many relationships fall apart to set myself up for that. The heartache, the expense, the legal hassles… I mean, after everything that happened, don't you sometimes wish that you'd never married Pam?"

That wasn't a simple question to answer. He'd spent many nights asking himself the same thing and hadn't quite decided on what he'd choose if he had the power to bend time and do things differently. "Yes and no. Yes, never marrying or even never dating would've been easier on my heart. But more than not getting married, I just wish Shane had been mine. I don't know how long Pam and I would've been able to hold our marriage together, but even if we'd divorced in that case, I'd still have my son. I'd have a piece of the family I want. Now I have nothing but the lost dream of what I could've had. As they say, 'a taste of honey is worse than none at all,' but I wouldn't trade away my time with Shane. The day he was born was the happiest day of my life. And the day I found out he wasn't my son was the worst. I lost my son and I wasn't even allowed to grieve the loss because I never truly had him to begin with."

Natalie frowned into her coffee cup. "That's exactly the kind of heartache I want to stay away from. I can't understand how someone could go through that and be willing to dust themselves off and try again."

"It's called hope. And I can't understand how someone could go through their life alone. Having a family, having children and seeing them grow up is what life is all about."

"Exactly. It's survival of the species, our own biology tricking us into emotional attachments to ensure stability for raising the next generation. Then it fades away and we're left feeling unfulfilled because society has sold us on a romantic ideal that only really exists in movies and books."

Colin could only shake his head. "That's the worst attitude about love I've ever heard."

"I don't force anyone else to subscribe to my ideas. I didn't come up with this overnight, I assure you. I learned the hard way that love is just a biological impulse that people confuse with Hallmark card sentiment. Have you ever noticed that all the fairy tales end when the Prince and Princess get married? That's because the story wouldn't be that exciting if it showed their lives after that. The Prince works too much. The Princess resents that she's constantly picking up his dirty socks and wiping the snotty noses of his children, so she nags at the Prince when he comes home. The Prince has an affair with his secretary. The Princess throws the Prince out of the palace and takes him to court for child support. Not exactly happily ever after."

"Don't ever write children's books," Colin said drily.

"Someone needs to write that book. That way little girls won't grow up believing in something that isn't going to happen. It would save them all a lot of disappointment."

Colin had tasted every inch of Natalie last night and there hadn't been the slightest bitterness, but now, it seemed to seep from every pore. He was frankly stunned by her attitude about love. It was even more deep-seated and angry than Pam's negative ideas. Pam just didn't want the strings of marriage and monogamy. Natalie didn't believe in the entire construct.

"Hopefully you weren't disappointed with last night."

"Of course not. Last night was great, Colin. It was everything that I'd hoped it would be, and more. And by stopping right now, we get to preserve it as the amazing night that it was."

He knew she was right. He could feel it in his bones. But he also couldn't just let this be the end of it. He wouldn't be able to finish dealing with the wedding plans and the house, being so close to her, without being able to touch her again. "What if I wanted another night or two like last night?"

Natalie watched him with a suspicious narrowing of her eyes. "Are you suggesting we have a little holiday fling?"

He shrugged. Colin had never proposed such a thing, so he wasn't entirely sure. "I did bet you that I could put a little jingle in your step. I think the time we spend together would be a lot more fun for us both if we let this attraction between us be what it is. No promise of a future or anything else, and you don't have to dash from the bed like a thief in the night. What do you think?"

"It sounds tempting," she admitted. "I wouldn't mind getting a little more of those toe-curling kisses you promised me. But you have to agree that after the wedding, we part as we started—as old friends. No hard feelings when it's over."

"Okay, it's a deal. I promise not to fall in love with you, Natalie."

"Excellent," she said with a smile before leaning in to plant a soft kiss on his lips. "I don't plan on falling in love with you either."

"So, what do you think?"

Natalie hovered in the doorway of Colin's family home, her mouth agape in shock. It had only been a week since she was in the house, but it had been completely transformed. "Is this the same place?"

Colin smiled. "A lot has happened since you were here. While I have been busy planning Lily's wedding and seducing you, I couldn't just sit around doing nothing all weekend while you were working, you know."

He'd worked magic in Natalie's opinion. A lot of the old furniture and things they didn't want to keep were gone. In their place were new pieces that looked a million times better. There was new paint on the walls, updated light fixtures and window coverings…the place looked better than she ever remembered. "You've worked a miracle."

"I didn't do it alone, I assure you. The Catholic charity came and picked up all the old things we didn't want to keep. I've had contractors in and out all week. We didn't do any major renovations, so it's mostly cosmetic, but I think it turned out nicely."

"Well, what's left for me to do?"

Colin took her hand and led her into the formal dining room. There, in front of the bay window, was a giant Christmas tree. Apparently her plan to distract him with sexual escapades hadn't worked the way she'd thought.

"Colin," she complained, but he raised a hand to silence her.

"Nope. You agreed to go along with the bet. It's not fair if you stonewall my plans. If you're confident enough to win, you're confident enough to decorate a Christmas tree without being affected by the cloying sentimentality of it all."

Natalie sighed. "Okay, fine. We'll trim the tree."

Colin grinned wide. "Great! I got all the decorations down from the attic."

They approached the pile of boxes and plastic totes that were neatly stacked by the wall. He dug around until he found the one with Christmas lights.

"When did you have the time to get a live tree?"

"I went by a tree lot while you went back to your place to shower and change. It took some creative maneuvering to get it into the house, but I was successful. Would you like a drink before we get started?" he asked as he walked into the kitchen.

"Sure. Water would be fine."

"How about some cider?" he called.

Cider? Natalie followed him into the kitchen, where she was assaulted by the scent of warm apple, cinnamon, orange zest and cloves. It was almost exactly like the scented candle she still had sitting on her desk from one of his holiday deliveries. She could hardly believe it, but Colin actually had a small pot of mulled cider simmering on the stove. Sneaky.

She wasn't going to acknowledge it, though. "Some cider would be great," she said. "It's a cold day."

"All right. I'll be right out and we can get started on that tree."

Natalie wandered back into the dining room and stared down the Christmas tree. She hadn't actually been this close to one in a long time. The scent of pine was strong, like the wreath on her door. She'd never had a real tree before. Her mother had always insisted on an artificial tree for convenience and aesthetics. While perfectly shaped and easy to maintain, it was lacking something when compared to a real tree.

The soft melody of music started in another room, growing louder until she could hear Bing Crosby crooning. Before she could say anything, Colin came up to her with a mug of cider and a plate of iced sugar cookies.

"You're kidding, right? Did you seriously bake Christmas cookies?"

"Uh, no," he laughed. "I bought them at a bakery near the tree lot. I didn't have time to do everything."

"You did plenty," she said, trying to ignore Bing's pleas for a white Christmas. "Too much." She sipped gingerly at the hot cider. The taste was amazing, warming her from the inside out. She'd actually never had cider before. It seemed she'd missed out on a lot of the traditional aspects of the holiday by abstaining for so long.

While it was nice, it wasn't going to change how she felt about Christmas in general. Natalie reluctantly set her mug aside and opened the box of Christmas lights. The sooner they got the tree decorated, the sooner she could get out of here.

They fought to untangle multiple strands, wrapping the tree in several sets of multicolored twinkle lights. From there, Colin unpacked boxes of ornaments and handed them one at a time to Natalie to put them on the tree. They were all old and delicate: an assortment of glass balls and Hallmark figurines to mark various family milestones.

"Baby's First Christmas," Natalie read aloud. It was a silver rattle with the year engraved and a festive bow tied around it. "Is this yours?"

Colin nodded. "Yep. My mom always bought a few ornaments each year. This one," he said, holding up Santa in a boat with a fishing pole, "was from the year we went camping and I caught my first fish."

Natalie examined the ornament before adding it to the tree with the others. "That's a sweet tradition."

"There are a lot of memories in these boxes," Colin said. "Good and bad." He unwrapped another ornament with a picture of his parents set between a pair of pewter angel wings.

When he handed it to Natalie, she realized it was a memorial ornament and the picture was one taken right before their accident. It seemed an odd thing to put on the Christmas tree. Why would he decorate with bad memories?

"Put it near the front," Colin instructed. "I always want our parents to be a part of our Christmas celebration."

Natalie gave the ornament a place of honor, feeling herself get a little teary as she looked at the two of them smiling, with no idea what was ahead for them and their children. "I miss them," she said.

Colin nodded. "Me, too." He took a bite of one of the iced snowman cookies. "Mom's were better," he said.

That was true. Mrs. Russell had made excellent cookies. But as much as Natalie didn't like the holidays, she didn't want to bring down the evening Colin planned with sad thoughts. "Do we have many more ornaments?"

The sad look on Colin's face disappeared as he focused on the task of digging through the box. "Just one more." He handed over a crystal dove. "Now we just need some sparkle."

Together, they rolled out the red satin tree skirt with the gold-embroidered poinsettias on it, then they finished off the last decorating touches. Colin climbed onto a ladder to put the gold star on the top of the tree while Natalie wrapped some garland around the branches.

"Okay, I think that's it," Colin said as he climbed down from the ladder and stepped back to admire their handiwork. "Let's turn out the lights and see how it looks."

Natalie watched him walk to the wall and turn out the overhead chandelier for the room. She gasped at the sight of the tree as it glowed in front of the window. The red, green, blue and yellow lights shimmered against the walls and reflected off the glass and tinsel of the tree.

Colin came up behind her and wrapped his arms around her waist. She snuggled into him, feeling herself get sucked into the moment. The tree, the music, the scents of the holidays and Colin's strong embrace… it all came together to create a mood that stirred long-suppressed emotions inside her.

"I think we did a good job," Colin whispered near her ear.

"We did a great job," she countered, earning a kiss on the sensitive skin below her earlobe. It sent a shiver through her body with goose bumps rising up across her flesh.

"Are you cold?" he asked. "I can turn on the gas fireplace and we can drink our cider there. Soak in the ambience."

"Sure," Natalie said. She picked up her cider and the plate of cookies and followed Colin into the living room. Natalie noticed that above the fireplace were a pair of stockings with both Lily's and Frankie's names embroidered on them. There was pine garland with lights draped across the mantel with tall red pillar candles and silk poinsettias. It was perfect.

With the flip of a switch, the fireplace roared to life. Colin settled down on the love seat and Natalie snuggled up beside him. She kicked off her shoes and pulled her knees up to curl against him. It was soothing to lie there with his arm around her, his heartbeat and the Christmas carols combining to create a soundtrack for the evening.

It had been a long time since Natalie had a moment like this. She didn't limit herself to one-night stands, but her relationships had focused more on the physical even if they lasted a few weeks. She hadn't realized how much she missed the comfort of being held. How peaceful it felt to sit with someone and just be together, even without conversation.

Sitting still was a luxury for Natalie. Once they had opened the chapel there was always something to be done, and she liked it that way. Now she was starting to wonder if she liked it that way because it filled the holes and distracted her from what she was missing in her life. Companionship. Partnership. Colin hadn't convinced her to love Christmas again, but he had opened her eyes to what she'd been missing. She could use more time like this to just live life.

Unfortunately, time like this with a man like Colin came with strings. It had only been a few short hours since they'd agreed to a casual fling, but in her heart, Natalie still worried.

While the decisive and successful owner of Russell Landscaping was driven and in control of his large company, the Colin she'd always known was also sentimental and thoughtful on the inside. The business success and the money that came with it were nice, but she could tell that he'd done all that to honor his father's memory. And more than anything, he wanted his own family, and had since he lost his parents. No little fling would change that.

She liked Colin a lot, but even her teenage infatuation couldn't turn it into more than that. More than that didn't exist in her mind. She could feel her hormones raging and her thoughts kept circling back to Colin whether she was with him or not, but that wasn't love. That was biology ensuring they would continue to mate until she conceived. He might be attracted to her now, but she would never be the wife and mother he envisioned sitting around the Christmas tree with their children. She just wasn't built for that.

Natalie knew she had to enjoy her time with Colin, then make sure it came to a swift end before either of them got attached to the idea of the two of them. She was certain that their individual visions of "together" would be radically different.

"That wasn't so bad, was it?" Colin asked.

The question jerked Natalie from her thoughts and brought her back to the here and now, wrapped in Colin's arms. "It wasn't," she admitted. "I have to say that was the most pleasant tree decorating experience I've had in ten years."

"Natalie, have you even decorated a Christmas tree in ten years?"

Of course he'd ask that. "Nope. I appreciate all your efforts, but even if it had been a miserable night, it still would've been the best. So sorry, but you haven't won the bet yet."

Eight

Tomorrow night, Natalie's cell phone screen had read on Wednesday.

Colin followed it up with another text. You and I are going on a date. Per your requirements, you will wear a pretty dress and I will take you someplace nice. I will pick you up at seven.

She ignored the warning bells in her head that insisted a real date fell outside their casual agreement. While going on a date with Colin had the potential to move them forward in a relationship with nowhere to go, it also might do nothing other than provide them both with a nice evening together. She tried not to read too much into it.

Natalie made a point of not staying at work too late on Thursday so she could get home and get ready for their date. She ignored the pointed and curious glare of Gretchen when she announced that she was leaving early. She would deal with that later.

Back at her townhouse, she pored through her closet looking for just the right dress. She settled on a gray-and-silver lace cocktail dress. It was fitted with a low-plunging scalloped V-neckline that enhanced what small bit of cleavage she had. It also had shimmering silver bands that wrapped around the waist, making her boyish figure appear more seductively hourglass-shaped.

Once that was decided, she spent almost a half hour flatironing her hair. She wore it in a ponytail most every day. At work, she liked it off her face, but tonight, she wanted it down and perfect.

The doorbell rang exactly at seven and Natalie tried not to rush toward the door. She took her time, picking up her silver clutch on the way.

"Hello there," Natalie said as she opened the door.

Colin didn't respond immediately. His gaze raked over her body as he struggled to take it all in. Finally, he looked at her and smiled. "I like going on dates with you, pretty dress and all."

She preened a little, taking a spin to show off how good her butt looked in the dress before pulling her black wool dress coat from the closet. "I made a big deal of tonight's requirements so I wanted to hold up my end of the bargain."

Colin held out her jacket to help her into it. "You certainly have. You look amazing tonight."

"Thank you."

"Your chariot awaits," Colin said, gesturing toward a silver Lexus Coupe in the driveway.

"Where's the truck?" she asked.

"I didn't think you'd feel like climbing up into it when you're dressed up. Besides, this car matches your dress. It's fate."

He helped her into the car and they drove through town, bypassing some of the usual date spots and heading toward one of the high-end outdoor shopping plazas in Nashville. "Where are we going?" she asked as they pulled into the crowded parking lot. She made a point of avoiding any major shopping areas in December. She was guaranteed to run into Christmas music, decorations and grumpy people fighting their way through their chore lists.

"You'll see," Colin replied, ignoring her squirming in the seat beside him.

"Is this part of the Christmas bet? Telling me you're taking me on a date, letting me get all dressed up and then taking me to see Santa at the mall is cruel. I can assure you it won't fill me with Christmas spirit. More than likely, it will fill me with impatience and a hint of rage. These heels are pretty and expensive, but I'm not above throwing them at someone."

Colin just laughed at her and pulled up to the valet stand at the curb. "Keep your shoes on. I doubt you'll have need to use them as a weapon. I didn't bring you here for the holiday chaos. I brought you here for the best steak and seafood in Nashville."

"Oh," she said quietly. There *were* some nice restaurants here; it was just hard to think about going to them in mid-December. Natalie waited until Colin opened her door and helped her out of the car. "What's that under your arm?" she asked as they made their way through the maze of shops.

Colin looked down at the neatly wrapped package

beneath his arm and shrugged. "It's just a little some-thing."

Natalie wrinkled her nose in a touch of irritation. She hated surprises, hated not knowing every detail of what was going on in any given situation. Being a wedding planner allowed her to legitimately be a control freak. She wanted to press the issue with him but let the sub-ject go since they were approaching the heavy oak doors of the restaurant. A man opened one for them, welcom-ing them inside the dark and romantic steakhouse. They checked in and were taken back to a private booth away from the main foot traffic of the restaurant.

They ordered their food and a bottle of wine, settling in for a long, leisurely dining experience. "So, now will you tell me what's in the box?"

Colin picked up the shiny silver package. "You mean this box?" he taunted.

"Yes. That's the one."

"Not right now. I have something else to discuss."

Natalie's eyebrow went up. "You do, do you?"

"Yes. I was wondering what you're doing Sunday evening."

Natalie wished she had her tablet with her. "Sunday morning, we clean and break down from Saturday's wedding. I don't think I have plans that night, aside from kicking off my shoes and relaxing for the first time in three days."

"That doesn't sound like it's any fun. I think you should consider coming with me to a Christmas party."

"Oh no," Natalie said, shaking her hand dismissively. "That's okay. I'm not really comfortable at that kind of thing."

"What's there to be uncomfortable about? We'll eat,

drink and mingle. Aside from the reason for the party, you might even forget it's a holiday gathering."

"Yes, but I won't know anyone there. I'm awful at small talk."

"Actually, you'll know everyone. It's Amelia Dixon's party."

"Amelia?" Natalie frowned. "My friend Amelia invited *you* to a Christmas party?"

Colin took a sip of his wine and nodded. "She did. Why are you so surprised? Did she not invite you?"

Honestly, Natalie wasn't sure. She didn't really pay much attention to her mail this time of year if it didn't look like an important bill of some kind. A few folks, Amelia included, always seemed to send her a Christmas card despite her disinterest. If she'd gotten an invite, it was probably in her trash can.

"I typically don't attend Amelia's Christmas party. I'm more curious as to how you got invited. You don't even know her."

"I know her well enough for a little Christmas gathering when I'm dating her close friend."

"Are we dating?" Natalie asked.

"And more importantly," he continued, ignoring her question, "I think she understands you better than you'd like to think. I get the feeling she invited me to make sure you showed up this time."

"I wouldn't be surprised." Amelia had proved in the past that she was a scheming traitor when it came to men. She'd lured Bree to a bar to see Ian after they broke up. Natalie had no doubt she would stoop to similar levels to push her and Colin together *and* get her to come to her annual Christmas soirée. "Despite how much she pesters me, she knows I won't come."

"Well this year, I think you should make an exception and go. With me."

She could feel her defenses weakening. It all sounded nice, and she couldn't wait to see what kind of party Amelia could throw in their big new house with all that entertaining space. But she wished it didn't have to be a Christmas party. The last Christmas party she went to was for kids. Santa was there handing out little presents to all the children, they ate cupcakes and then they made reindeer out of clothespins. She was pretty certain that wasn't what they'd be doing at Amelia and Tyler's. What did adults even do at Christmas parties? "I don't know, Colin."

"It's settled, you're coming." Colin picked up his phone and RSVP'd to Amelia while they were sitting there. Natalie opened her mouth to argue, but it was too late. There was no getting out of it now. Amelia would insist and there would be no squirming.

"Why do you hate me?" Natalie asked as he put his phone away.

"I don't hate you. I like you. A lot. That's why I'm so determined to make the most of our short time together. It also doesn't hurt that it might help me win that kiss." His hazel eyes focused on her across the table, making her blood heat in her veins.

Natalie sighed, trying to dismiss her instant reaction to him. "I've kissed you twenty times. What's so important about *that* kiss?"

"It's The One. The most important kiss of all. Nothing can compare to it, I assure you. But I'll make you a deal," he offered.

"A deal? Does it allow me to skip the Christmas

party? I'll gladly spend that whole night naked in your bed if you'll let me skip the stupid party."

Colin's lips curled up in a smile that dashed her hopes of that negotiation. "While that sounds incredibly tempting, no. You're going to that party with me. But, if you promise to come and not give me grief about it the entire time, I'll let you open this box." He picked up the silver-wrapped box with the snowflake hologram bow and shook it tantalizingly at her.

Considering she was pretty much stuck going to the party anyway, she might as well agree and finally soothe her curiosity about that package. "Okay," Natalie conceded. "I will go with you to the party, and I will not bellyache about it."

"Excellent. Here you go."

Natalie took the box from Colin's hand, shaking it to listen for any telltale clues. No such luck. She'd just have to open it. Peeling away at a corner, she pulled back the wrapping to expose a white gift box. Lifting the lid, she found a Swarovski-crystal-covered case for her tablet.

This wasn't some cheap knockoff they sold at the flea markets. Natalie had done enough weddings to recognize real Swarovski crystal when she saw it. She'd seen covers like these in the hands of Paris Hilton and other celebrities. Out of curiosity, she'd looked it up online once and found far too many zeroes at the end to even consider it. It was impossibly sparkly, each crystal catching the flickering candlelight of the restaurant, and it twinkled like thousands of diamonds in her hands. It cast a reflection on the ceiling like stars overhead.

"Do you like it?" Colin asked.

"Yes, I love it. I've always wanted one, but I don't

think I ever told anyone that. What made you think to buy me something like this?"

"Well," Colin explained, "whenever I see you at the chapel, you've got your iPad in your hands. It's like a third arm you can't live without. It seemed a little boring though. I thought a girl that drove a little red sports car might like a little bling in her life. Besides, jewelry seemed...predictable."

Natalie shook her head. "I'm pretty certain that a fling doesn't call for gifts, much less jewelry. This is too much, really. What is this for?"

"It's your Christmas present. I thought you could make good use of it at your upcoming weddings so I wanted to give it to you early. Besides, we're not supposed to make it to Christmas, so I thought if I was going to give you something, the sooner the better."

"It's perfect," Natalie said. Even as she ran her fingertips over the shining stones, she felt guilty. Not just because he'd bought her a gift, but because Colin had given it to her early because she was too flaky to stick with a relationship for two more weeks. She shouldn't feel bad, though. They'd agreed to the arrangement. It had even been his suggestion, and yet she found herself already dreading this coming to an end. "But you shouldn't have done it. It's too much money."

Colin only shrugged at her complaints. "What is the point of earning all this money if I don't do anything with it? I wanted to buy you something and this is what I came up with. End of discussion."

"I haven't gotten you anything," she argued. And she hadn't. She hadn't bought a Christmas gift in years and she was adamant about not receiving one. Every year she had to remind people she was on the naughty list, so no gifts. It had worked so far. Then Colin came in and started busting down every wall she had, one at a time. Soon, if she wasn't careful, she'd be completely exposed.

Colin reached across the table and took her hand. "You've given me plenty without you even knowing it. The last year has been really hard for me with the divorce and everything else. For the first time since I found out about Shane, I'm excited for what each day holds. That's all because of you."

"That may have been the most amazing bread pudding I've ever had," Natalie said as they stepped out of the restaurant and back into the mingling flow of holiday shoppers.

"It was excellent, I have to admit." He wasn't entirely sure where he wanted to take Natalie next, but he knew he didn't want to rush home. Not because he didn't want to make love to her again, but because he wanted her to take in some of the holiday ambience. This was a shopping center in December, but it wasn't the day-after-Thanksgiving crush. There was rarely a riot over a sale at the Louis Vuitton.

He also wanted to simply spend time with Natalie. He'd meant what he said in the restaurant earlier. For the past year, he'd been going through the motions, trying to figure out what his life was supposed to be like now that he wasn't a husband or a father any longer. It had been easy to focus on work, to center all this attention on expanding Russell Landscaping into Chattanooga and Knoxville.

It wasn't until his sister announced her engagement that he'd snapped out of his fog. Pam may not have been the right woman for him, but there was someone out there who could make him happy. He'd started dating again, unsuccessfully, but he was out there. And then he'd spied Natalie at the engagement party and his heart had nearly stilled in his chest from the shock of how beautiful she'd become.

How had the quiet teenager with the dark braid, the braces and the always-serious expression grown up into such a beauty? The timing was terrible, but Colin had known that he would do whatever he had to do to have Natalie in his life again.

Of course, at the time, Colin hadn't known about her pessimistic stance on love and marriage. That had been like a dousing of ice water. It was cruel for the universe to bring him into contact with such a smart, beautiful, talented woman, then make it impossible for them to have any kind of chance of being together. She even hated Christmas. That was a smack in the face of everything he held dear.

Their night together after the bridal shop had just been a chance to release the unbearable pressure building up. He had been dismayed to wake the next morning and find he wanted Natalie more than ever. Continuing to see each other casually until the wedding was a good idea in theory, but it was prolonging the torture in practice. This date, this night together, would probably do more harm than good in the end. But he couldn't stop himself.

Colin knew he was playing with fire. He hadn't gone into this thinking any of it would happen the way it had, or that he could somehow change Natalie's mind. At least about love and marriage. His determination to help her find her Christmas spirit had made slow progress, but progress nonetheless. He could already see cracks in that facade after only a week of trying.

He could see a similar weakness when she was around him. Her mouth was saying one thing while her body was saying another. When she'd stepped out in that wedding gown, it was like nothing existed but her. As much as she built up her theories about biology interfering in relationships, he could tell she was comfortable around him. Happy. Passionate. If they could both be convinced to take whatever this was beyond the wedding, there would be more between them than just sex.

But would what she was willing to give him be enough to make him happy? Companionship and passion seemed nice, but without love in the mix, it would grow tired, or worse, she might stray, like Pam. Without the commitment of love and marriage, there was no glue to hold two people together. It didn't matter how alluring or wonderful Natalie seemed, she would never be the woman he wanted and needed. But for now, for tonight, none of that mattered. They'd had a nice dinner and he had a bet to win. Reaching out, he took her hand. "How about a stroll to walk some of that dinner off?" he asked.

"I probably need to."

They walked together through the outdoor mall, passing a trio of musicians playing Christmas carols. Farther up ahead, Colin could spy the giant Christmas tree that the mayor had lit the week before. The whole place was decorated. There were white twinkle lights in all the bushes and wrapped around each light post. Near the fountain was a fifteen-foot gold reindeer with a wreath of holly and a cluster of oversize ornaments around his neck.

"The lights are pretty," Natalie admitted as they neared the big tree. "It reminds me of the tree in Rockefeller Center."

"Now why would a Grinch go see the tree in New York?" he asked.

"I was there on business," she insisted. "I went down to see the ice skaters and there it was. It's pretty hard to miss."

They approached the black wrought iron railing that surrounded and protected the tree. It, too, was wrapped in lighted garland and big velvet bows. Colin rested his elbows on the railing and looked up at the big tree. "I think our tree is nicer."

Natalie cozied up beside him and studied the tree more closely. "I think you're right. This tree is kind of impersonal. Ours had a special something."

"Maybe we need hot cider," he suggested.

"No," Natalie groaned, pushing away from the railing. "There is no room left in me for anything, even hot cider."

She reached for his hand and he took hers as they started back to the other end of the shopping center where they'd left his car.

"Thank you for bringing me here tonight," she said. "I've never seen this place decorated for the holidays. It's pretty. And not as crowded and chaotic as I was expecting it to be."

"I'm glad you think so," Colin said with a chuckle. "If you'd have been miserable, it could've set me back days."

"No," Natalie said, coming to a stop. "It's perfect. A great first date, I have to say."

"It's not over yet." As they paused, Colin noticed a decorative sprig of mistletoe hanging from a wire overhead. He couldn't have planned this better if he'd tried. "Uh-oh," he said.

Natalie's eyes grew wide. "What? What's wrong?"

Colin pointed up and Natalie's gaze followed. He took a step closer to her, wrapping his arms around her waist. "That's mistletoe up there. I guess I'm going to have to kiss you."

"Sounds like a hardship," she said. "Christmas is such a burdensome holiday. Shop, eat, decorate, make out... I don't know how you people stand it every year with all these demands on your time."

"Am I wrong or does it sound like you're coming around to Team Christmas?"

Natalie wrapped her arms around his neck and entwined her fingers at his collar. "I wouldn't say I'm that far gone yet. A lot hinges on this kiss, though. I've never been kissed under the mistletoe, so I can't understate how critical this moment is to you potentially winning this bet."

"No pressure," Colin said with a smile. Dipping his head, he pressed his lips to hers. Her mouth was soft and yielding to him. She tasted like the buttery bourbon sauce from the bread pudding and the coffee they'd finished their meal with. He felt her melt into him, his fingertips pressing greedily into her supple curves.

Every time he kissed Natalie, it was like kissing her for the first time. There was a nervous excitement in his chest, tempered by a fierce need in his gut. Combined, it urged him to touch, taste and revel in every sweet inch of her.

As they pulled apart, Colin felt the cold kiss of ice against his skin. Opening his eyes, he saw a flurry of snowflakes falling around them. "It's snowing!" he said in surprise. Nashville did get cold weather, but snow was an unusual and exciting event. "How's that for your first kiss under the mistletoe? I kiss you and it starts to snow."

"Wow, it really is snowing." Natalie took a step back, tipping her face up to the sky. She held out her arms, letting the snowflakes blanket her dark hair and speckle her black coat. She spun around, grinning, until she fell, dizzy, back into Colin's arms. "I guess I haven't been paying enough attention to the weatherman," she admitted when she opened her eyes.

"I'm not sure snow was in the forecast. It must be a little Christmas magic at work." Colin looked around as the other shoppers quickly made their way back to their cars. Not everyone appreciated the shift in the weather. In the South, snow typically ended up turning icy and the roads would get bad pretty quickly. They all had to make an emergency run to the grocery store for milk, bread and toilet paper in case they lost power.

He wasn't worried about any of that. Colin just wanted to be right here, right now, with a flushed and carefree Natalie in his arms. She'd worn her hair down tonight for the first time and it looked like dark silk falling over her shoulders and down her back. The cold had made her cheeks and the tip of her nose pink, accentuating the pale porcelain of her complexion.

But most enticing of all was the light of happiness in her eyes. It was the authentic smile he'd been so desperate to lure out of her. The combination threatened to knock the wind out of him every time he looked at her.

"When I picked you up for our date tonight, I didn't think you could get more beautiful," he admitted. Colin brushed a snowflake from her cheek. "I was wrong. Right this moment, you are the most beautiful woman I've ever laid eyes on."

Natalie tried to avoid his gaze and ignore his compliment. He wasn't sure why she was so uncomfortable hearing the truth. She was beautiful and she needed to believe it.

Instead, with a dismissive shake of her head, she said, "Flattery won't help you win the bet, Colin."

"I'm not trying to win a bet," he said, surprising even himself. "I'm trying to win you."

Nine

"You're here!" Amelia nearly shrieked when she spied Natalie and Colin come through the front door of the sprawling mansion in Belle Meade she and Tyler had bought earlier that year. "I didn't believe it when he said you'd agreed to come."

"It's not a big deal," Natalie muttered as she slipped out of her jacket. "You just saw me this morning."

Amelia took both their coats to hang them in the hall closet. "It's not about seeing you, it's about seeing you at my Christmas party. That's a pretty big deal, considering you've never bothered to come before."

"You always held it at your cramped apartment before," Natalie argued, although Colin doubted that the setting had anything to do with it.

"Whatever," Amelia said dismissively. "The important thing is that both of you are here. Come in. Everyone is in the kitchen, of course. Thousands of square feet and everyone congregates there."

Colin took Natalie's hand and led her away from the nearest exit into the house. It was a massive home, large even by his standards, though it looked as if Amelia and her husband were still trying to accumulate enough furniture to fill it up. They had the place beautifully decorated for the holidays, though. A cluster of multiple-sized Christmas trees with lights sat by the front window like a small indoor forest. A decorated tree that had to be at least fourteen feet tall stood in the two-story family room. Any smaller and it would've been dwarfed by the grand size of the house. The banisters were wrapped with garland and ribbon. There was even holiday music playing in the background. Colin was pleased to drag Natalie to a proper holiday gathering.

"Everyone, this is another of my friends and coworkers, Natalie, and her date, Colin. He owns Russell Landscaping."

A few welcomes and hellos sounded from the crowd of about twenty-five people milling through the kitchen, dining room and keeping room area. He recognized a few of them—the wedding photographer, Bree, and Gretchen, the decorator. Bree was hanging on the arm of a dark-headed guy in a black cashmere sweater. Gretchen was alone despite the huge diamond on her finger. He wasn't sure what that was about.

"What would you like to drink?" Amelia asked, rattling off a long list of options.

"I also have a nice microbrew from a place downtown," Tyler offered, holding up a chilled bottle he pulled from the refrigerator.

"Perfect," Colin said, taking it from his hand. Natalie opted for a white wine that Amelia poured for her.

"Help yourself to something to eat. There's plenty, of course," Amelia said, gesturing to the grand buffet table along the wall.

Plenty was an understatement. The caterer in her had gone wild. He and Natalie perused the table, taking in all their options. There were chafing dishes with hot hors d'oeuvres like barbecued meatballs, chicken wings and fried vegetable eggrolls, platters of cold cheeses, finger sandwiches, crudités, dips and crackers, and more desserts than he could identify.

"She's gone overboard," Natalie said. "This is enough to feed a hundred wedding guests. She's just no good at cooking for small numbers. You'd think being pregnant would slow her down, but she's like a machine in the kitchen."

After surveying everything, they each made a plate and moved over to a sitting area with a low coffee table. They ate and chatted with folks as they milled around. Eventually Gretchen approached with her own plate and sat down with them.

"I'm sorry Julian couldn't be here with you tonight," Natalie said.

Gretchen just smiled and shrugged. "It's okay. He's almost done refilming some scenes the director wanted to change and then he'll be home. We'll have a great first Christmas together even though he missed this."

"Your fiancé is in the movie business?" Colin asked.

Gretchen nodded. "Yes, he's an actor. You've probably heard of him. Julian Cooper?"

Colin hesitated midbite. "Really?"

"I know, right?" Gretchen said. "Not who you'd expect me to be with."

"That's not what I meant," he countered. "I'm sure he's very lucky to have you. I've just never met anyone famous before. Feels odd to be one degree of separation from an action hero."

Gretchen smiled, obviously bolstered by his compliment. "You're also officially four degrees from Kevin Bacon."

Colin laughed and lifted his drink to take another sip.

"Excuse me, did I hear Amelia say you own Russell Landscaping?" the man beside him asked.

Colin turned his attention to his right. "Yes." He held out his hand to shake with the man, turning on his bright, businessman charm. "I'm Colin Russell."

"I'm in the construction business with Bree's father," he explained. "I'd love to talk to you about landscaping at our latest project. We're breaking ground on an apartment complex in the spring and looking for a company to handle that for us."

On cue, Colin pulled out his wallet and handed the man his business card. He lost himself in work discussions, realizing after about ten minutes that both Natalie and Gretchen had disappeared.

"Give me a call and we'll set something up," Colin concluded. "I'm going to hunt down my date."

Getting up, Colin carried his empty plate into the kitchen and got a fresh drink. Amelia was buzzing around with Bree helping her, but the others weren't in there. He wandered back into the living room toward the entry hall. Maybe they'd gone to the restroom as a pair, the way women tended to do.

He'd almost reached the entry when he heard Gretchen's voice. Still cloaked in the dark shadows of the room lit only with Christmas lights, he stopped and listened.

"All right, spill," Gretchen said.

Colin heard a hushing sound and some footsteps across the tile floor of the hallway. "Are you crazy?" Natalie asked in a harsh whisper. "Someone is going to hear you. What if Colin heard you?"

"Come on, Natalie. He's all tied up in talk about shrubs and mulch. It's perfectly safe. Tell me the truth. Bree and I have twenty bucks wagered on your answer."

"You're betting on my love life?"

Colin chuckled at Natalie's outrage. He liked her friends.

"Not exactly. We're betting on your emotional depth. That's probably worse. See, Bree thinks you're a shallow pool and believes your big talk when you go on about love not being real and blah, blah."

"And you?" Natalie asked.

"I think you've changed since you met Colin. You've bebopped around the office for the last week like you're on cloud nine. You've been texting him all the time. You haven't been as cranky. You were even humming a Christmas carol this morning."

"So, I'm in a good mood."

"Natalie, you even forgot about a bridal appointment on your calendar tomorrow morning. Your mind isn't on your work, and I think it's because you've realized you were wrong."

Colin held his breath. He was curious to hear what Natalie was going to say but worried he was going to get caught listening in. He leaned against the wall, casually sipping his beer as though he were just waiting for Natalie's return. Even then, he strained to catch the conversation over the holiday music.

"Wrong about what?"

"Wrong about love. You are in love with Colin. Admit it."

Colin's eyes widened. Would his skeptical Natalie really say such a thing? If she did, it could change everything.

"I am not," she insisted, but her voice wasn't very convincing.

Gretchen seemed to agree. "That's a load of crap. I get that you haven't been in love before, and until recently, neither had I. But when it hits you, you know it. And it's not biology or hormones or anything else. It's love. And you, sister, have fallen into it."

"I don't know, Gretchen. This is all new to me. I'm not sure I would call this love."

"Is he the first thing you think about in the morning and the last thing you think of at night? Is he the person you can't wait to share good news with? Does your busy workday suddenly drag on for hours when you know you'll get to see him that night?"

"Yes. Yes, yes and yes," Natalie said almost groaning. "What am I going to do?"

That wasn't exactly the reaction Colin was hoping for when a woman declared her love for him. Yes, she loved him, but she was miserable about it. Considering this was skeptical Natalie, he supposed that shouldn't surprise him. She'd go down kicking and screaming.

"Just go with it," Gretchen encouraged. "Love is awesome."

That was enough for him. Colin was about to cut it too close if he loitered here any longer. He scooted si-

lently across the plush living room carpeting toward
the kitchen to get something to nibble on and wait for
Natalie's return. While he tried to look calm on the outside, he was anything but.

Could it be true? Was Natalie really in love with him?
It had only been a few short weeks, but they'd technically known each other for years. Stranger things had
happened. If he was honest with himself, he was having feelings for her as well. He could've answered yes
to all of Gretchen's questions. Was that love? He was as
clueless as Natalie there. He'd loved his parents, his son,
but his attempts to fall in love with a woman had failed.

He felt more deeply for Natalie than he had for any
other woman, even Pam. He was mature enough to
admit that whole marriage had been about Shane, not
about love.

Love. Was that what this was?

It could be. It felt different, somehow. Despite everything going on in his life, he was preoccupied with
the brunette who had challenged him at every turn.
She was like quicksand, drawing him in deeper the
more he struggled against her. Colin had gone into this
fling keeping his heart in check, or at least he'd tried
to. Natalie wasn't the kind of woman he could settle
down with and he knew that. But after spending time
with her, he knew this couldn't be just a fling, either.
He wanted more, and if Natalie was honest with herself,
he was certain she wanted more, too. It was just a matter of convincing her not to run the moment her emotions got too serious or complicated. She might believe
in love now, but he got the feeling that getting Natalie
to believe in the beauty and power of a good marriage
would be the challenge of a lifetime.

Colin popped a chocolate mint petit four into his mouth, looking up in time to see Natalie and Gretchen stroll back into the room. Natalie looked a little pale from their revealing discussion, her ashen color enhanced by her black dress.

No, Natalie might be in love with him, but she was anything but happy about it.

"You've been awfully quiet tonight," Colin said as they pulled into her driveway. "You've hardly said a thing since we left Amelia and Tyler's place."

Natalie shrugged it off, although she felt anything but cavalier about the thoughts racing through her head. "I'm just a little distracted tonight," she said. To soothe his concerns, she leaned in and kissed him. "I'm sorry. Would you like to come in?"

"I would," he said with a smile.

They got out of the car and went into her townhouse. Natalie didn't normally feel self-conscious about her place, but after being at Colin's and Amelia's, her little two-story home felt a bit shabby. Or maybe she was just an emotional live wire after everything that happened at the party.

"Nice place," Colin said as he pulled the door shut behind him.

"Thanks. It's nothing fancy, but it suits me." She led him through the ground floor, absentmindedly prattling on about different features. Mentally, she was freaking out, and had been since Gretchen cornered her at the party. Yes, she'd been quiet. She'd been analyzing every moment of the past two weeks. Was it possible that *she* was the one to break their casual arrangement and fall in love with Colin? Surely it hadn't been long enough for something like that to happen. They'd only been out a few times together.

Then again, Gretchen and Julian fell in love in a week. Bree and Ian fell in love again over a long weekend trapped in a cabin. Amelia had given Tyler thirty days to fall in love and they hadn't needed that long.

So it *was* possible. But was it smart?

Her brain told her no. Love equals heartache. But she couldn't stop herself from sinking further into the warm sensation of love. Colin made it so easy by being everything she never knew she always wanted. She wished he hadn't been so charming and thoughtful so it would be easier to fight.

But even if she *was* in love, it didn't change anything. It didn't mean she wanted to get married. Marriages seemed to ruin good relationships. Maybe it was marriage, not love, that was the real problem.

As Natalie turned to look at him, she realized he had an expectant expression on his face. "What?" she asked.

"I just complimented you on your large collection of classic country vinyl albums," he said, gesturing toward the shelf with her stereo and turntable.

Natalie glanced over at her albums and nodded. "My father bought a lot of them for me," she said. "We used to go to thrift stores looking for old records on Saturday afternoons."

"I mentioned it twice before you heard a word I said." Colin chuckled softly. "You're on another planet tonight, aren't you?"

"I am. I'm sorry." Natalie racked her brain for a way to distract him. She certainly wasn't going to tell him how she was feeling. Running her gaze over his sharply tailored suit, she decided to fall back on her earlier distraction tactic—seduction. She wrapped her arms around his waist and looked up at him. "Have I told you just how handsome you look tonight?"

He smiled, all traces of concern disappearing as he looked down at her adoringly. "Not in the last hour or so."

"Well, you do," she said, slipping her hands into his back pockets to grab two solid handfuls of him. "It's enough to make a girl want to throw the bet so she can experience that amazing kiss you've promised."

Colin shook his head. "There's no throwing the bet. You either shed your humbug ways or you don't. Either way, I'm not giving up until you've been converted. I don't care how long it takes."

"Even after I've won?" she asked.

"You bet. I think Christmas in Buenos Aires will be lovely, and I'll see to it that it is."

Natalie laughed. "You're inviting yourself to my vacation prize? I don't recall asking for company."

"I don't recall asking permission. I am paying for the trip, after all."

Natalie twisted her lips in thought. She was both thrilled and terrified by the idea of Colin still being in her life a year from now. She was so confused about all of this, she didn't know what to do. "So if I win the bet, will I ever get this infamous kiss? I don't want to miss out on it."

Colin narrowed his gaze at her. "How about this? How about I give you a little taste of how amazing it will be right now? That should be enough to tide you over until I've won."

She certainly couldn't turn down an offer like that, especially knowing that his talented mouth and hands would distract her from everything else she was worried about. "All right," she agreed. "Lay one on me."

Colin shook his head at her. "Before I do that, I think we'd better adjourn to the bedroom."

"Why is that?" Natalie asked. "It's just a kiss."

"You say that, but this won't be an ordinary kiss. You'll be glad we waited until we're in there, I promise."

"Okay." She wasn't sure if he could deliver on the hype, but she was looking forward to finding out. Taking his hand, she led him up the stairs and down the hallway to her master bedroom.

Her bedroom had been what sold her on the townhouse. The master was spacious with large windows that let in the morning light. Even filled with her furniture, there was plenty of room to move around. "All right," she said, standing beside the bed with her hands on her hips. "Let's get a sampling of this infamous kiss of yours."

Colin moved closer and Natalie couldn't help but tense up. She didn't know what to expect. This wasn't even *the* kiss and she was nervous with anticipation.

"You look like I'm about to eat you alive," he said with an amused smile.

"Sorry," she said, trying to shake the tension out of her arms.

"That's okay." He stopped in front of her, just shy of touching. Instead of leaning in to kiss her, he turned her around and undid the zipper of her dress. He eased it off her shoulders, letting it pool to the floor.

"What are you doing?" she asked, curiously. What kind of kiss required her to be naked?

Leaning in, Colin growled in her ear, "I'm about to eat you alive."

Natalie gasped at the harsh intensity of his words, even as a thrill of need ran through her body. Before she could respond, he unclasped her bra and pulled her panties to the floor. Completely naked, she turned around to complain about the unfairness, but found he was busily ridding himself of his clothing as well. In a few moments, it was all tossed aside and he pulled her close.

"When is the kissing going to start?" she asked.

"You ask too many questions. This isn't a wedding you're in charge of. There are no schedules, tablets and earpieces tonight. Go with it."

"Yes, sir," Natalie said with a sheepish smile. Admittedly, she had trouble letting go and not knowing every aspect of the plan. She didn't think she had anything to worry about here, so she tried to turn off her brain and just let Colin take the lead. That was the whole point tonight, anyway.

His fingers delved into her hair as he leaned in for the kiss. Natalie braced herself for the earth-shattering impact, but at first at least, it was just a kiss. He coaxed her mouth open, letting his tongue slide along hers. His fingers massaged the nape of her neck as he tasted and nibbled at her.

Then she felt him start to pull away. His lips left hers, but technically, they never lost contact with her skin. He planted kisses along the line of her jaw, the hollow of her ear and down her throat. He crouched lower, nipping at her collarbone and placing a searing kiss between her breasts. He tasted each nipple, then continued down her soft belly until he was on his knees in front of her.

He placed a searing kiss at her hipbone, then the soft skin just above the cropped dark curls of her sex. Natalie gripped Colin's shoulders for support as his fingers slid between her thighs. She gasped softly as he stroked the wet heat that ached for him.

With his mouth still trailing across her thigh, Colin gently parted her with his fingers. His tongue immediately sought out her sensitive core, wrenching a desperate cry from Natalie's throat. He braced her hips with his hands as her knees threatened to give out beneath her.

She wasn't sure how much of this she could take. Standing up added a level of tension she hadn't expected. "Colin," she gasped, amazed by how her cries were growing more desperate with every second that passed.

She was on the edge, and it was clear that he intended to push her over it. Gripping her hip with one hand, he used the other to dip a finger inside her. The combination was explosive and Natalie couldn't hold back any longer. She threw her head back and cried out, her body thrashing against him with the power of her orgasm.

When it was over, Natalie slid to her knees in front of him. She lay her head on his shoulder, gasping and clinging to his biceps with both hands. She was so out of it, it took her a moment to realize Colin had picked her up. He helped her stand, then carried her to the bed only a few feet away.

"That," she panted as reason came back to her, "was one hell of a kiss."

"And that wasn't even the winning kiss," Colin said as he covered her body with his own.

"I can't even imagine it, then. It seems odd that your prize would be more a reward for me than for you."

He slipped inside her, making her overstimulated nerves spark with new sensation. "I assure you I enjoyed every second of it now, and I'll enjoy every second of it when I've won."

For that, Natalie had no response. She could only lift her hips to meet his forward advance. Clinging to him, she buried her face in his neck. His movements were slow, but forceful, a slow burn that would eventually consume everything it touched. She didn't resist the fire; she gave in to it.

She was tired of fighting. She had spent her whole life trying to protect herself from the pain and disappointment of love. She'd fought her urges for companionship, suppressed her jealousy as each of her friends found a great love she was certain she would never have.

And yet, here she was. Despite all the fighting and worrying, she had simply been overpowered. Gretchen was right. Natalie was in love.

"Oh Natalie," Colin groaned in her ear.

She loved that sound. She wanted to hear it again and again. Her name on his lips was better than a symphony orchestra.

Placing her hand against his cheek, she guided his mouth back to hers. That connection seemed to light a fire in him. Their lips still touching, he moved harder and faster than before, sweeping them both up in a massive wave of pleasure. Natalie didn't fight the currents, she just held on to the man in her arms, knowing she was safe there.

She never wanted to let go. But could she dare to hold on?

Ten

"I can't believe we're almost done with the house," Natalie said. "You've worked wonders on it."

Colin smiled. "I'm pretty pleased with the results."

"Seems a shame you can't keep it after all the work you've put in. You don't appear to care much for your own house. This place suits you more."

That was probably true, but he didn't need this place. "I can always buy another house. I'd like to see Lily and Frankie raise their family here."

"What is left for us to do?" Natalie asked as she looked around.

"I have to clean out my parents' office. I left that for last because there's so much paperwork to go through. I need to figure out what should be kept. I'm hoping we can shred most of it, but I really have no idea what they had stored away in all those drawers."

"Let's do it, then."

They walked up the stairs together and Colin opened the door to the small, dusty room he'd avoided the longest. Turning on the overhead light illuminated the big old oak desk on the far wall. It had two large file drawers, one on each side, housing any number of documents and files they'd thought were important to keep. It took up most of the space like a large man in a small dressing room.

Colin had lots of memories of his dad going over invoices at this desk long before Russell Landscaping could afford their own offices, much less their own office building in the city. This was where his mother wrote checks to pay the bills and managed correspondence. She hadn't been a big fan of email, always penning handwritten letters to friends and family.

There was also a large bookshelf on one wall with all his father's books. His dad had always been a big reader. He loved to curl up in his chair by the fireplace and read in the evenings. Volumes of books lined the shelves, and Colin dreaded going through them. As much as he felt the urge, he didn't need to keep them all, just a couple of his father's favorites.

"I'll take the shelves if you want to start on the drawers," Colin suggested. "We can throw out all the office supplies."

They each started their tasks. Natalie filled a wastebin with dried-up pens, markers and old, brittle rubber bands. After that, she started sorting through the file drawers.

Colin easily found his father's favorite book—*Treasure Island*. His father had read, and reread, that book twenty times. It was his favorite, as evidenced by the worn binding and fraying edges. He set that book aside.

It would go on Colin's shelf until he passed it on to his children. Other volumes weren't quite as important.

Colin quickly built up a stack of books to keep, then another to donate. He scooped up a handful for charity and turned, noticing Natalie sitting stone still in the office chair. The expression on her face was one of utter devastation.

"Natalie?" he asked. "What is it?"

Looking up at him, she bit at her lip. "It's…um." She stopped, shuffling through the papers. "I started going through the filing drawers. It looks like your mother actually filed for divorce."

Colin's breath caught in his lungs. He set the books down on the desk before he dropped them. "What? You must be reading it wrong."

Natalie handed over the folder. "I don't think so. It looks like your mother filed two years before their accident."

Colin flipped through the paperwork, coming to the same conclusion despite how much it pained him. His parents didn't divorce. What was this about? Leaning back onto the desk, he tried to make sense of it all.

"It looks like she started the process, but they didn't go through with it." Somehow that still didn't make him feel much better.

"I'm sorry to hear they were in a bad place," Natalie said. "I never noticed anything wrong as a kid, but in my experience, there's no perfect marriage. Everyone has problems, despite how they might look from the outside."

Colin set down the pages and frowned. "Of course there's no perfect marriage. Just because I want to marry and have a family someday doesn't mean I think it's going to be a walk in the park. You have to work at it every day because love is a choice. But it's a choice worth making. And judging by this paperwork, it's worth fighting to keep it."

"How do you get that? I always thought your parents had a good relationship. If even they filed for divorce at one point, I don't see that as a positive sign."

"What's positive is the fact that they *didn't* get a divorce. Things got ugly, but they decided not to give up. That makes me hopeful, not disappointed. If my mother could go as far as filing for divorce and they managed to put the pieces back together, that means there's hope for any marriage."

Judging by the look on Natalie's face, he could tell she wasn't convinced. She was so jaded by other people's relationship failures that she couldn't fathom two people actually loving each other enough to fight through the tough times.

That worried him. Despite what he'd overheard at Amelia's Christmas party, he didn't feel that confident that Natalie would stay in his life. She might love him, but she was still a flight risk. When this wedding was over, the two of them might be over, too. That was the thought that kept his feelings in check when they were together.

"You know what?" he said. "Let's just put all these files in a box and I'll go through them later. I think clearing the room out is time better spent."

Natalie just nodded and started unloading files from the desk drawer into the file boxes he'd bought. They worked silently together until the room was empty of personal items, and then they hauled the boxes downstairs and into his truck.

The mood for the night had been spoiled and he hated that. His parents' near-divorce was hanging over his head, opening his eyes to things he'd never considered. It seemed strange to drink some wine and go on like he didn't know the truth.

And yet, it made him feel emboldened, too. He'd gone into this whole situation with Natalie consciously holding back. It was defensive, to keep himself from getting in too deep and getting hurt, but it also occurred to him that it might be a self-fulfilling prophecy. If he didn't give all of himself to Natalie, she wouldn't ever do the same.

If he wanted to keep Natalie in his life, he had to fight for her and be bold. His parents fought to stay together, and he was willing to do the same. But what would give her the confidence to believe in him and their relationship? She was so determined to think of marriage as a mistake that most people struggled to get out of. How could he convince her that he was in this for the long haul and she shouldn't be afraid to love him with all she had?

There was only one thing he could think of, and it was a major risk. But, as his father told him once, no risk, no reward. That philosophy had helped him build the family landscaping business into a multimillion-dollar operation across the Southeast. He had no doubt it would succeed. If he could pull it off, there was no way Natalie could turn her nose up at it.

Just like his Christmas bet, he intended to get everything that he wanted and make it into something Natalie wanted, too. He knew exactly what he needed to do. The timing couldn't be more perfect.

"What are you doing Wednesday night?" he asked.

* * *

Natalie looked out the window at the twinkling Christmas lights up ahead and knew exactly where they were. "Are you taking me to the Opryland Hotel?" Natalie asked.

"Actually, no, we're going someplace else."

Sitting back in her seat, she watched as Colin slowed and pulled into the parking area for the Grand Ole Opry. At that moment, she perked up, her mind spinning as she tried to figure out what day it was. It was the sixteenth. Blake Wright's concert was here tonight. But it was sold out…

"Colin?" she asked.

"Yes?"

"Did you…? Are we…?" She was so excited she couldn't even form the words. Why else would they be here if he hadn't managed to get tickets to the show?

"Yes, I did and yes, we are," he answered, pulling into a parking space.

She almost couldn't believe it. "There were no tickets left. They sold out in ten minutes. I know—I called."

Colin nodded as he turned off the car and faced her. "You're absolutely right. There were no seats left."

Natalie narrowed her gaze at him. "So, what? We're just going to lurk by the back door to see if we can get a glimpse of him?" She was willing to do that, of course, but it didn't seem like Colin's style.

"Something like that. Come on."

They got out of the car and he took her hand, leading her away from the crowd at the entrance and around the building toward the back. The door they were headed for said Private Entry in big red letters, and a very large man in a tight T-shirt stood watch. Colin didn't seem to care. He marched right up to him and pulled two tickets out of his jacket.

No, wait. Natalie looked closer. They weren't tickets. They were *backstage passes*. The security guard looked them over and checked the list on his clipboard.

"Welcome, Mr. Russell. So glad to have you joining us tonight." The mountain of a man stepped aside and let Natalie and Colin go into the sacred backstage of the famous concert hall.

She waited until the door shut before she lost her cool. "Are you kidding me? Backstage? We're going backstage at a Blake Wright concert? This is the Grand Ole Opry! Do you know how many amazing artists have walked where we are right now?"

Colin wasn't left with much time to answer her questions, so he just smiled and let her freak out. Passes in hand, they walked through the preconcert chaos until they located the stage manager.

"Looks like our special guests are here," the man said. "Welcome, folks. We've got two designated seats for you right over here." He indicated two chairs just off the curtained stage area. They were going to be watching the show from the wings, literally sitting unseen on the stage itself.

Natalie was so excited, she could barely sit down. Colin had to hold her hand to keep her from popping right up out of her seat. "Please tell me how you managed this," she said at last.

"Well, you know who does all the landscaping for Gaylord properties?"

She had no idea. "You?" she guessed.

"That is correct. Russell Landscaping has the contract to design and maintain all the outdoor spaces including the hotel and the concert venue. I called up a friend here and they set this up for me. Since there weren't any seats left, we had to get a little creative."

Natalie could hardly believe it. "This is amazing. I can't believe you did all this. I mean, you already gave me my Christmas present. What is this for?"

Colin shrugged. "Because I could. You told me how your dad used to take you and how much you liked Blake, so I thought it would be a nice gesture."

"Well, I'm glad I dressed appropriately," she said, looking over her off-the-shoulder red silk top and skinny jeans with cowboy boots. "You just said we were going someplace to listen to country music. I was thinking maybe a bar downtown."

"Well, I would've given away the surprise if I'd said anything else."

Natalie could only shake her head. As the opening act brushed past them to go out onstage, she muffled her squeal of delight in Colin's coat sleeve.

When Blake and his band finally took the stage, it took everything she had not to jump up and down. She tried to play it cool, since she was here because of Colin's business connections, but it was very hard. Natalie could hold her composure during any kind of wedding crisis, but this was too much.

It was not just a great concert, but there were so many memories centered around this place. Her parents had been house poor, putting everything they had into a nice home for their family at the expense of everything else. They didn't have the latest gadgets or the coolest clothes, but she went to a good school and had everything she truly needed.

But once a year, around her birthday, her dad always

took her out for what he called a Daddy-Daughter date. She'd grown up listening to his favorite country music, and starting on her fifth birthday, he took her to a show at the Opry. It didn't matter who it was or that they had the worst seats in the house. It was more about sharing something with her father.

That tradition had fallen to the wayside after the divorce, and it had broken Natalie's heart. She hadn't stepped foot back into this concert hall since the last time her daddy brought her here.

And now, here she was, backstage. She didn't talk to her father very often, but she couldn't wait to tell him about this. He'd be amazed. Maybe it would even inspire him to take another trip here with her for old times' sake.

Glancing over at Colin, she realized he looked a little anxious and not at all like he was having a good time. He was stiff, clutching his knees and not so much as tapping his toes to the music. "You don't like country music, do you?" she asked.

"Oh no," he argued. "It's fine. I'm just tired."

Natalie didn't worry too much about it, focusing on the amazing show. About halfway through, Blake started introducing the next song.

"The song I'm going to play next was one of my biggest hits," he said. "It was my first real love song, written about my wife. I want to dedicate this song tonight to a very special lady. Natalie Sharpe, please come out onto the stage."

Natalie's heart stopped in her chest. Colin tried to pull her up out of her seat, but it took a moment for her to connect everything. "Me?" she asked, but he gave her a little shove and suddenly, she was onstage where everyone could see her.

"There she is," Blake said. "Come on out here, sugar."

Natalie walked stiffly over to where Blake was standing. Under her feet were the very boards of the original stage. The lights were shining on her, the crowd cheering. She thought she might pass out.

"Are you enjoying the show?" he asked.

"Absolutely. You're awesome," she said.

Blake laughed. "Well, thank you. Do you know who else is awesome? Colin Russell. Colin, why don't you come on out here, too?"

Natalie turned and watched Colin walk out onstage. What the heck was going on? Her life had suddenly become very surreal. It was one thing for Colin to arrange for her to get to go out onstage with her idol. Both of them onstage changed everything.

Blake slapped Colin on the back. "Now, Colin tells me he has something he wants to ask you."

The whole crowed started cheering louder. The blood rushed into Natalie's ears, drowning out everything but her heart's rapid thump. She barely had time to react, her body moving like it was caught in molasses. She looked over at Colin just in time to see him slip down onto one knee. *Oh dear, sweet Jesus*. He wasn't. He couldn't be. This was not happening.

"Natalie," Colin began, "I've known you since we were teenagers. When you came back into my life, I knew you were someone special. The more time we spend together, the more I realize that I want to spend all my time with you, for the rest of my life. I love you, Natalie Sharpe. Will you marry me?"

Now Natalie was certain she was going to pass out.

She could feel the whole concert hall start to spin. Her chest grew tight, her cheeks burned. What was he thinking? All these people were watching. Blake was watching…

Colin held up the ring. It was beautiful—a large oval diamond set in platinum with a pear-shaped diamond flanking it on each side. The cut and clarity were amazing. The stone glittered with the lights on the stage, beckoning her to reach out and take it. All she had to do was say yes, and he would slip it on her finger.

And then what? They'd get married and last a few years at best? Then they'd get divorced and spend months squabbling in court? In the end, she'd become a bitter divorcée and sell this same beautiful ring in a ranting ad on Craigslist.

Yes, she loved him, but why did they have to get married? He was ruining everything they'd built together by changing their whole relationship dynamic. Love or no, she couldn't do it. She just couldn't get the words out. All she knew was that she had to get out of here. Avoiding his gaze, Natalie shook her head. "No. I'm sorry, I can't," she said, before turning and running off the stage.

As she ran, she was only aware of an eerie silence. The entire concert hall had quieted. The crew backstage all stood around in stunned confusion. Apparently no one had expected her to reject his proposal.

"Natalie!" she heard Colin yell, but she couldn't stop. She weaved in and out of people and equipment, desperately searching for the side door where they'd come in. Just as she found it, she heard the music start playing again. Life went on for everyone else, just as her life started to unravel.

Bursting through the doors, she took in a huge gulp of cool air that she desperately needed. The security guard watched her curiously as she bent over and planted her hands on her knees for support.

Marriage? He'd proposed marriage! He'd taken a perfectly wonderful evening and ruined it with those silly romantic notions. Why did he do that?

"Natalie?" Colin said as he came out the door behind her a moment later.

She turned around to face him, not sure what to say. She felt the prickle of tears start to sting her eyes. "What were you thinking?" she asked. "You know how I feel about marriage!"

"I was thinking that you loved me and wanted to be with me," he replied, his own face reddening with emotion.

"We had an agreement, Colin. We were not going to fall in love. This was supposed to be fun and easy."

"That's how it started, but it changed. For both of us. Tell me you love me, Natalie. Don't lie about it, not now."

She took a deep breath, trying to get the words out of her mouth for the first time. "I do love you," she said. "But that doesn't change my answer. I don't want to get married. That just ruins everything that we have going so perfectly right now. I've told you before I don't believe in marriage. Proposing out of the blue makes me think you don't listen to me at all. If you did, you never would've done something like…like…"

"Something so romantic and thoughtful?" he suggested. "Something so perfect and special to commemorate the moment so you'd never forget it? Something that a woman that truly loved me could never turn down?"

"Something so public!" she shouted instead. "Did you think that you could twist my arm into accepting your proposal by having four thousand witnesses? You proposed to me onstage in front of Blake Wright! All those people watching us." She shook her head, still in disbelief that the night had taken such a drastic turn. "That whole thing is probably going to end up on the internet and go viral."

Colin's hands curled into controlled fists at his sides. She could see the ring box still in one hand. "Is that what you think I was doing with all of this? I couldn't possibly have been trying to craft the perfect moment to start our lives together. Obviously, I was just *coercing you* into marrying me, because that worked out so well for me the first time."

It was perfect. It had been perfect. And if she was any other woman, it would've been the kind of story she would've told her grandchildren about. But she couldn't pull the trigger. This was too much, too soon. She'd just come to terms with loving him; she wasn't ready to sign her life away to this man. They might have known each other since they were kids, but how much did they really know about each other?

"You hardly know me, and yet you want to change me. If you really loved me, Colin, you wouldn't force me into something I don't want to do. You would understand that I need time for a step this big, and that I might never want to make that leap."

He ran his hand through his hair in incredulity. "Yes, I'm such a horrible person for inviting you to be a part of my family and to let me love you forever. What a bastard I am!"

Natalie stopped, his beautiful, yet rage-filled words

sending a tear spilling down her cheek. There was no stopping the tears now, and she hated that. She hated to cry more than anything else. How had this perfect night gone so wrong? "You can do all that without a marriage."

"But why would I want to? It doesn't make any sense, Natalie. Why can't you make that commitment to me? You know, I always thought you were such a strong woman. So in control, so self-assured. But in reality, you're a damn coward."

"What?" she asked through her tears.

"You heard me. You hide behind this big philosophical cover story about love and marriage being this forced social paradigm and whatever other crap you've recited because you're afraid of getting hurt. You're afraid to give in and let someone love you, then have it not work out."

Natalie didn't know what to say to that. It was true. She'd justified her own fears in her mind with all the statistics and academic findings she could spew. But the truth was that she used it all to keep men away. She'd done a hell of a job this time. She didn't want to lose Colin entirely, though. Couldn't they just go back to before he proposed? Pretend like tonight never happened?

"I might be scared to take the leap, but what if I'm right? What if I'd said yes and we had this big wedding and four kids and one day, we wake up and hate each other?"

"And what if we don't? What if we do all of that and we're actually happy together for the rest of our lives? Did you ever consider that option while you were wringing your hands?"

Did she dare consider it? Her mom considered it over

and over just to fail. Time had turned her into a bitter woman constantly searching for something to complete her. Natalie wouldn't let herself become like that. "I'm sorry, Colin. I just can't take that chance."

Colin stuffed his hands in his pockets, his posture stiff and unyielding. "Don't be sorry. If you don't want to marry me, that's fine. It doesn't matter what your reasoning is. But I'm done with the two of us. One marriage to a reluctant bride is enough for me. Come on, I'll drive you home."

"I think I should take a cab. That would be easier on us both."

She saw the shimmer of tears in his eyes for just a moment before he turned and walked away. Natalie could only stand and watch as he got into his car and drove away.

As his taillights disappeared into the distance, Natalie felt her heart start to crumble in her chest. She'd been so afraid to love and be loved that she had driven Colin away and made her fears a reality.

With one simple *no*, Natalie had ruined everything.

Eleven

Colin avoided going to the chapel for as long as he could. He didn't want to see Natalie. He didn't want to spend most of the evening with her, pretending everything was fine for the benefit of his sister and her fiancé. Like any injured animal, he wanted to stay in his den and lick his wounds alone.

The worst part was that he knew he'd done this to himself. Natalie had been very clear on the fact that she never wanted to get married and yet, he'd proposed to her anyway. He'd thought perhaps it was some sort of defense mechanism, insisting she didn't want it so people wouldn't pity her for not having it.

Overhearing her confession to Gretchen of being in love with him had given him a false hope. Somehow, he'd believed that offering her his heart and a lifetime commitment would not only show her he was serious, but that she had nothing to fear. That hadn't panned out at all.

What was wrong with him? Why was he so attracted to women who didn't want the same things he wanted? It was like he was subconsciously setting himself up for failure. Maybe *he* was the one who was really afraid of being hurt, so he chose women he could never really have. What a mess.

Pulling his truck into the parking lot of the chapel, he parked but didn't get out. The rehearsal was supposed to start in twenty minutes. No need to rush in just because there was no sense in going all the way home first.

Glancing out the window, he looked around at the other cars. He spotted Natalie's sports car, plus a handful of other vehicles he didn't recognize. There were no motorcycles, though. And no little hatchback. Where were Lily and Frankie?

Reaching for his phone, he dialed his sister's number. "Hello?" she shouted over a dull roar of noise around her.

"Lily, where are you?"

"We're stuck in the Vegas airport. Our flight got cancelled because of bad weather in Denver. We've been changed to a new flight, but it's not leaving until tomorrow morning."

"Tomorrow morning? You're going to miss the rehearsal and the dinner." Colin knew the weather wasn't Lily's fault, but things like this always seemed to happen when she was involved. Who booked a flight that connected through Denver in the winter, anyway?

"I know, Colin!" she snapped. "We're not going to make it in time for your choreographed circus. That's why I called Natalie first and told her. She said she'd handle things tonight and go over the details with us tomorrow afternoon before the service. We're doing what we can. It isn't the end of the world."

Nothing was ever a big deal to Lily. She said Colin was wrapped too tight and needed to loosen up, but he would counter that she needed to take some things—like her wedding day—more seriously.

"Just cancel the rehearsal dinner reservations," she continued. "It was only the wedding party and Frankie's parents, anyway."

That he could do. Thank goodness they hadn't opted for the big catered dinner with out-of-town guests. "Fine. You promise you'll be back tomorrow?"

"I can't control the weather, Colin. We'll get back as soon as we can."

Colin hung up the phone, a feeling of dread pooling in his gut. He was beginning to think this entire thing was a mistake. Lily didn't want this wedding, and he'd twisted her arm. If he hadn't done that, he wouldn't have made such a calculated error with Natalie. Lily would be happily courthouse married. He wouldn't have learned the truth about his parents' marriage yet. There also wouldn't be an extremely expensive diamond engagement ring in his coat pocket.

He needed to take it back to the jeweler, but he hadn't had the heart to do it. He'd return it on Monday when all of this was over. That would close the book on this whole misguided adventure and then, maybe, he could move on.

With a sigh, he opened the door and slipped out of the truck. After talking to Lily, he knew he needed to get inside and see what needed to be done to compensate for the absence of the engaged couple.

Inside the chapel, things were hopping. The doors to the reception hall were propped open for vendors to come in and out with decorations. He could see Gretchen and the photographer, Bree, putting out place settings on the tables. A produce truck was unloading crates of fruits and vegetables into the kitchen.

Natalie was in the center of the chaos, as always. She was setting out name cards shaped like snowflakes on a table in the crossroads of the chapel entrance. A large white tree was on the table in front of her, dripping with crystals, pearls and twinkle lights. She was stringing silver ribbon through each name card and then hanging it from a branch on the tree, creating a sparkling blizzard effect.

She reached for another, hesitating as she noticed Colin standing a few feet away. "Have you spoken with your sister?" she asked, very cold and professional once again.

"Yes. Will we still have a rehearsal?"

"Yes." Natalie set down a snowflake and turned toward him. "It's not just for the benefit of the bride and groom. It helps the pastor, the musicians and the rest of the wedding party. They only have a best man and maid of honor, so it might be a short rehearsal, but it's still needed to get everyone else comfortable with the flow."

"Are the others here?"

"We're just waiting on the maid of honor."

"What about the parts for the bride and groom in the ceremony?"

"We'll have to get someone to stand in for them both. I've had to do this before—it's not a big deal. I had a bride get food poisoning, and she missed everything leading up to the ceremony. It all turned out fine."

"Okay." Her confidence made him feel better despite the anxious tension in his shoulders. "I'll stand in for Frankie, if you need me to. I'm not in the wedding party, so I don't have anything else to do."

Natalie smiled politely and reached for her paper snowflake again. "Thanks for volunteering. You can go into the chapel and wait with the others if you like. We'll begin momentarily."

Even though he was angry with her, he couldn't stand to see the blank, detached expression on her face when she looked at him. He wanted to see those dark brown eyes filled with love, or even just the light of passion or laughter. He wanted to reach out and shake her until she showed any kind of emotion. Anger, fear, he didn't care. She had been so afraid to feel anything before they met. He worried that after their blowup, she'd completely retreat into herself. He might not be the one who got to love her for the rest of her life, but someone should.

Natalie would have to let someone, however, and he had no control over that.

He wanted to say something to her. Anything. But he didn't want to start another fight here. Instead, he nodded and disappeared into the chapel to wait with the others. That was the best thing to do if they were going to get through all this without more turmoil than they already had.

The maid of honor walked in a few minutes later with Natalie on her heels. She had her headset on and her stiff, purposeful walk had returned.

"Okay, everyone, I'm going to go over this once, quickly, then we will walk through the whole ceremony so everyone gets a feel for their roles and how it will all go."

Colin stood with his arms crossed over his chest as she handed out instructions to the string quartet in the corner, the ushers and the wedding party.

"Colin is our stand-in groom today. After you escort in your parents, you and the best man are going to follow the pastor in and wait at the front of the church for the ceremony to start. Everyone ready?"

All the people in the chapel, excepting the musicians, went out into the hall. Colin and the best man, Steve, followed Pastor Greene into the chapel, taking their places on the front platform. The string quartet played a soothing melody that sounded familiar, but he didn't know the name. At the back of the room, Natalie gave a cue to the pastor before slipping into the vestibule. He asked everyone to rise. The musicians transitioned to a different song, playing louder to announce the coming of the bridal party.

The doors opened and the maid of honor made her way down the aisle. She moved to the opposite side of the landing and waited for the doors to open a final time. The music built a sense of anticipation that made Colin anxious to see what was about to happen, even as a stand-in groom for a rehearsal.

The doors of the chapel swung open, and standing there holding a bouquet of silk flowers, was Natalie. His chest tightened as she walked down the aisle toward him. She was wearing a burgundy silk blouse and a black pencil skirt instead of a white gown, but it didn't matter. The moment was all too real to Colin.

But with every step she took, reality sunk in even more. This wasn't their rehearsal and they weren't getting married. She had turned him down, flat, in front of a couple thousand people and a country music star.

The sentimental feelings quickly dissipated, the muscles in his neck and shoulders tightening with irritation and anger.

Natalie avoided his gaze as she approached the platform. She looked only at the pastor. Her full lips were thin and pressed hard into a line of displeasure. Neither of them seemed very happy to have to go through all this so soon after their blowup.

This was going to be an interesting rehearsal.

Natalie wished there was someone else to fill in for Lily, but there just wasn't. Everyone else was preparing for tomorrow and Bree was capturing everything—including her awkward moments with Colin—on camera. All she could do was man up, grab the dummy bouquet and march down the aisle so they could get through this.

"Frankie will take Lily's hand and help her up onto the platform," the pastor explained. "Lily will pass her bouquet to the maid of honor to hold, then I will read the welcome passages about marriage."

Natalie took Colin's hand, ignoring the thrill that ran up her arm as they touched. She clenched her teeth as she handed off the bouquet and listened to the pastor go through his spiel. They had opted for the traditional, nondenominational Christian service, passing on any long biblical passages. Colin had insisted that Lily didn't want to stand up here for a drawn-out religious service. She wanted to get married and then cue the party.

"When I finish, Frankie and Lily will turn to face each other and hold hands while they recite the vows."

This was the part Natalie was dreading. Turning to Colin, she took the other hand he offered. It was awkward to stare at his chest, so she forced her chin up to meet his eyes. The initial contact was like a punch to her stomach. There wasn't a hint of warmth in those golden eyes. He hated her, and she understood that. She had thrown his love in his face. She didn't know what else to do. Say yes? Dive headfirst into the fantasy of marriage like everyone else? She could see now how easy it was to get swept up into it. The current was strong.

Even now, as they stood on the altar together, she felt her body start to relax and her resistance fade. Colin repeated Frankie's vows, the words of love and trust making Natalie's chest ache. His expression softened as he spoke, slipping a pretend ring onto her finger.

When it was her turn to recite Lily's vows, the anxiety was gone. She felt a sense of peace standing here with Colin, as though that was where they were truly meant to be. She loved him. She was scared, but she loved him and had loved him since she was fifteen years old. She'd never felt this way for anyone else because of that. Her heart was already taken, so why would she have any desire to love or marry another man?

She wanted to marry Colin. There was no question of it now. Why did she have to have this revelation two days too late?

She felt her hands start to tremble in his as her voice began to shake as well. Colin narrowed his gaze at her, squeezing her hands tighter to calm the tremble. She was glad to have an imaginary ring, because she was certain she would've dropped any real jewelry trying to put it on his finger.

Natalie felt tears form in her eyes as the pastor talked about their holy vows. She wanted to interrupt the rehearsal, to blurt out right then and there that she was wrong. She was sorry for letting her fears get in the way. And most important, that she very desperately wanted to marry him.

"I'll pronounce them man and wife, then instruct Frankie to kiss the bride," the pastor explained. "They'll kiss, holding together long enough for the photographer to get a good shot. Then Lily will get her bouquet and the couple will turn out to face the congregation. I'll announce them as Mr. and Mrs. Frank Watson, and then you'll exit the chapel."

The musicians started playing the exit song. Colin offered his arm and she took it. They stepped down the stairs and along the aisle to the back of the chapel.

When they walked through the doorway, he immediately pulled away from her. She instantly missed the warmth and nearness of his touch, but she knew the moment had passed. The Colin standing beside her now hated her once again.

She recovered by returning to her professional duties. She waited until the maid of honor and best man came out of the chapel behind them, then she returned to the doorway, clapping. "Great job everyone. Now, at this point, the bridal party will be escorted away so the guests can move into the reception hall, then we'll bring you back into the chapel to take pictures. Does anyone have any questions?"

Everyone shook their heads. It was a small wedding and not particularly complicated aside from the absence of the bride and groom. "Great. Let's make sure everyone is here at the chapel by three tomorrow. We'll do some pictures with Bree before the ceremony. If anything happens, you all have my cell phone number."

People started scattering from the room, Colin

amongst them. "Colin?" she called out to him before she lost her nerve.

He stopped and turned back to face her. "Yes?"

"Can I talk to you for a minute?"

"About what?" She'd never seen him so stiff and un-friendly. It was even worse than it had been before the rehearsal. "Everything for the wedding is set, isn't it?"

"Yes, of course."

"Then we have nothing to talk about."

His abrupt shutdown rattled her. "I, I mean, could you please just give me two minutes to talk about what happened at the concert?"

He shook his head, his jaw so tight it was like stone. "I think you said all you needed to say on that stage, don't you?"

She had said a lot, but she had said all the wrong things. "No. Please, Colin. You don't understand how much I—"

He held up his hand to silence her. "Natalie, stop. You don't want to marry me. That's fine. I'm through with trying to convince unwilling women to be my wife. But like I said that night, I'm done. I don't want to discuss it ever again. Let's just forget it ever hap-pened so we can get through this wedding without any more drama, okay?"

Before she could answer, Colin turned and disap-peared from the chapel. Natalie heard the chime as he opened the front door and headed for his truck.

With every step he took, she felt her heart sink fur-ther into her stomach. Her knees threatened to give out from under her, forcing her to sit down in one of the rear pews. She held it together long enough for the musicians to leave, but once she was alone, she completely came undone.

It had been a long time since Natalie cried—good and cried. She got teary at the occasional commercial or news article. She'd shed a tear with Amelia when she lost her first baby in the spring and a few at the concert the other night. But nothing like this. Not since… she paused in her tears to think. Not since her father left Christmas day.

She dropped her face into her hands, trying not to ugly sob so loudly that it echoed through the chapel. There were a lot of people going in and out of the building today, but she didn't want anyone to see her in such a wretched state.

"Natalie?" a voice called from behind her, as if on cue.

She straightened to attention, wiping her eyes and cheeks without smearing her mascara. "Yes?" she replied without turning around to expose her red, puffy face. "What do you need?"

Natalie sensed the presence move closer until she noticed Gretchen standing at the entrance of the pew beside her. "I need you to scoot over and tell me what the hell is going on."

She complied, knowing there was no way out of this now. Gretchen settled into the seat, politely keeping her gaze trained on the front of the chapel. She didn't say a word, waiting for Natalie to spill her guts on her own time.

"I like Christmas," Natalie confessed. "I like the lights and the food and the music. My holiday humbug days are behind me."

"What? That's why you're crying?"

"Yes. No. Yes and no. I'm crying because I've finally found my Christmas spirit and it doesn't matter. None of it matters because Colin and I are over."

Gretchen groaned in disappointment. "What happened? You seemed pretty enamored with him a few days ago."

"He…proposed. Onstage at the Blake Wright concert. In front of everyone."

"Well, I could see how a lifetime promise of love and devotion in front of thousands of witnesses could ruin a relationship."

Natalie noted her friend's flat tone. "I panicked. And I said no. And I didn't do it well. I said some pretty ugly things to him."

Gretchen put her arm around Natalie's shoulder. "Why are you fighting this so hard? What are you afraid of, Natalie?"

"I'm afraid…" She took a deep breath. "I'm afraid that I'm going to let myself fall for the fantasy and he's going to leave."

"The fantasy?" Gretchen questioned.

"Love. Marriage."

"How can you still see it as a fantasy when you know you're in love with him?"

"Because I can't be certain it's real. This could just be a biological attachment to ensure the care of my nonexistent offspring. And even if it is real, I can't be sure it will last."

"You can't be certain of anything in life, Natalie. Maybe it's biology, maybe it's not. But by pushing Colin away, you're guaranteeing that you're going to lose him. It doesn't matter if your feelings will last now."

"I know," Natalie said with a sigh. "I realized that

today when we were standing on the altar during the rehearsal. Up there, holding his hands and looking into his eyes, I realized that I want to be with Colin. I want to marry him. He's worth the risk. But it's too late. I've ruined everything. He won't even speak to me about anything but Lily's wedding."

"I think he might just need a little time. You've both got a lot on your minds with the wedding. They're so stressful. But once that's done, I say reach out to him. Put your heart on the line the way he did. Take the risk. If he says no, you haven't lost anything. But if you can get him to listen to how you feel, you can gain everything."

Natalie nodded and dried the last of her tears. Gretchen was right. How had she become a relationship expert so quickly?

She knew what she had to do now. She had to hand her heart to Colin on a silver platter and pray he didn't crush it.

Twelve

Colin was trying to keep his mind occupied. Just a few more hours and all this would be over. He could give the keys to the house to his sister, pay the bill for the wedding and walk out of this place like he'd never fallen in love with Natalie Sharpe.

Sure, it would be that easy.

He was busying himself by greeting guests as they came into the chapel. He assisted the ushers in handing out programs, hugging and kissing friends and family as they came in. A lot of folks had shown up for Lily's big day and he was pleased. They had sent out a lot of email invitations, but in the rush, he wasn't sure who had accepted until they walked in the door.

He was very surprised to see Natalie's mother and father walk into the chapel. They had big smiles on their faces as they chatted and made their way over to him.

Perhaps time and distance had healed their wounds, even if Natalie's remained fresh.

"Mr. Sharpe," Colin said, shaking the man's hand.

"How are you, son?"

"Doing well," he lied. "So glad you could make it for Lily and Frankie's big day."

He hugged Natalie's mother and the usher escorted them all down the aisle to their seats. Casually, he glanced at his watch. It was getting close to time. He'd expected to see Frankie by now, but every bearded, tattooed guy that caught his eye was just a guest of the groom.

Glancing across the foyer, he spotted Natalie and instantly knew that something was wrong. She looked decidedly flustered and he didn't expect that of her, even after everything that happened last night. She looked very put-together, as usual, in a light gray linen suit with her headset on and her crystal-encrusted tablet clutched to her chest, but there was an anxiety lining her dark eyes.

As much as he didn't want to talk to her, he made his way through the crowd of arriving wedding guests to where she was standing. "What's the matter?"

Taking him by the elbow, she led him into the hallway near her office where they were out of the guests' earshot. "They're not here yet."

"They who?"

"Your sister and her fiancé. The flight they were supposed to be on landed four hours ago, I checked, but I haven't heard a word from either of them. I've got a hair and makeup crew twiddling their thumbs. The wedding starts in thirty minutes and I've got no couple to marry."

An icy-cold fear started rushing through his veins. He'd worried about this almost from the moment he'd insisted that Lily have a formal wedding. It didn't surprise him at all. She'd given in to his request far too easily. He should've known she'd do something like this when the opportunity arose. "I'm sure they're on their way," he said, trying to soothe her nerves even as his lit up with panic. "This has to happen all the time, right?"

"No. It's *never* happened. I have had grooms bail, brides bail, but never both of them together. You've got to track her down. Now. She's not answering my calls."

"Okay. I'll try calling her right now." He stepped away from her office and went down the hall to the far corner where the sounds of the crowd wouldn't interfere. As he was about to raise the phone to his ear, it vibrated and chimed in his hand. When he looked down, it was like someone had kicked him in the stomach. The air was completely knocked out of him.

It was a photo text from his sister. She and Frankie were standing under the Chapel of Love sign, sporting wedding rings. They were wearing jeans. She had a little veil on her head and a carnation bouquet in her hand. "Guess what? We decided to stay in Vegas and elope! Sorry about the plans."

Sorry about the plans. His chest started to tighten. Sorry about the plans? There were two hundred people in the chapel, a staff in the kitchen preparing the dinner. There were *ten thousand dollars'* worth of flowers decorating the ballroom. That was just the ballroom! But the bride and groom decided to elope in Vegas. So sorry.

When he was finally able to look up from his phone, he caught Natalie's eye from across the hall. She looked the way he felt, with a distraught expression on her face. She held up her own phone to display the same picture he was looking at.

They moved quickly toward each other, meeting in the middle. "What do we do?"

Natalie took a deep breath. "Well, obviously there isn't going to be a wedding, so we can send the preacher home. The food and band are already paid for, and there's no sense in it all going to waste. So if I were you, I'd lie and tell them that Lily and Frankie got stuck in Vegas because of bad weather and decided to elope. Invite them to celebrate at the reception, have dinner, eat the cake and send everyone home."

Colin dropped his face into his hands. How had this week turned into such a disaster? His proposal to Natalie couldn't have gone worse. His sister was a no-show for her own wedding. He was feeling like he wanted to just walk out the door and lock himself in his bedroom until the New Year.

He supposed her suggestion was sensible. There was no point in wasting all that food. "I guess that's what we'll have to do, then. What a mess. I'm going to kill her when she gets home. I mean it."

"There is one other option," she said in a voice so small he almost didn't hear it.

Colin looked up to see Natalie nervously chewing at her lip. "What other option?"

She looked at him for a moment, a determined tilt to her chin that hadn't been there before. "This is going to sound crazy, but hear me out, okay?"

"At this point, I'm open to anything."

"I'm sorry, Colin. I'm sorry about the way I reacted to your proposal. I know I hurt you and I didn't intend to. But you were right, I was just scared. My whole life I've seen relationships fall apart and I told myself I'd never put myself through that. And then I fell in love with you anyway. I didn't know what to do. When you proposed, the moment was so perfect and I just panicked. I ruined it all and I can never tell you just how sorry I am. I would go back in time and change it if I could, but I can't."

Colin had certainly not been expecting this right now. With everything else going on, he wasn't entirely sure he was emotionally capable of handling her apology. "Natalie, can we talk about this later? I understand you want to get this off your chest, but we're in the middle of a crisis here."

"And I'm trying to fix it," she countered. "Do you love me, Colin?"

He looked down at her heart-shaped face, her brow furrowed in worry. The headset lined her cheek, the microphone hovering right at the corner of her full, pink lips. Of course he loved her. That was what hurt the most. They loved each other, but for some reason, everything had gone wrong and he didn't understand why. Although he didn't want to admit it, he figured it couldn't hurt at this point.

"Yes, I love you, Natalie. That's why I proposed to you. I wanted to start a life with you and I thought you wanted the same thing."

"I didn't know what I wanted, but now I do. I do want to start a life with you."

Colin barely had a chance to process Natalie's words before she dropped down onto one knee in front of him. "Natalie, what are you doing?"

"I love you, Colin. There's nothing I want more than to marry you and build a life together. I'm sorry that I ruined your grand proposal, but I have another one for you. Will you marry me?"

Colin looked around, trying to see if anyone was watching the bizarre scene in front of him. "Are you proposing to me?"

Natalie took his hand and held it tightly in her own. "Yes. I want to marry you, Colin. Right now."

He stiffened, then dropped down on his own knee, so they could discuss this eye to eye. "You want to get married right now?"

She smiled wide. "Why not? We've got a chapel full of your family just a few feet away. My parents are even here. The wedding gown fits me. Not to mention that we've got a big, beautiful reception waiting that you and I planned together. It's exactly the wedding I would choose if we were going to get married any other day. It's going to go to waste if we don't use it, so why not today?"

Colin's heart started racing in his chest. Would they really go through with this? "Natalie, are you sure? I can't bear to have another wife change her mind and walk out of my life. If we get married today, we're getting married forever. Are you okay with that?"

She reached out and cupped his face, holding his cheeks in her hands. "I am very okay with that. You're not getting rid of me, mister."

"Okay, then yes, I will marry you," he said with a grin. He leaned forward to kiss her, the mouthpiece of her headset getting in the way.

"Oops," Natalie said, lifting it up. "Just as well," she noted as she leaned back. "I think we need to save our next kiss for the one at the altar, don't you?"

It was entirely possible that Natalie had lost her mind. She wasn't just getting married, she was getting married on a whim. It was crazy. It was so unlike her.

And she'd never been more excited in her life.

She wanted this more than anything, and getting married quickly was the only thing that would keep her from sabotaging herself.

Natalie rushed toward the bridal suite, reaching out to grab Gretchen's arm and drag her down the hallway with her.

"Where are we going?" she asked. "I'm supposed to be fetching something for Bree."

She kept going. "Don't worry about Bree. I need you to help me get ready."

"Help you get ready to do what?"

"To marry Colin."

A sudden resistant weight stopped her forward progress and jerked her back. "Would you like to repeat that, please?"

Natalie sighed and turned toward her. "The bride and groom aren't coming. Colin and I are getting married instead. I need you to help me get dressed."

Gretchen's jaw dropped, but she followed her willingly to the bridal suite in a state of shock. The hair and makeup crew were loitering there, waiting for the missing bride.

"Change of plans, ladies," Natalie announced, pulling off her headset and tugging the band from her ponytail. "I'm the bride now. I need the best, fastest work you can do."

She settled down in the chair and the team quickly went to work. A soft knock came a few minutes later and Bree slipped in with her camera. "Are we ready to take some pictures of the bride getting read—?" Bree stopped short when she saw Natalie in the chair. "What's going on?"

"Natalie is getting married." Gretchen held up the cell phone picture of their wayward couple. "You're taking pictures of her and Colin instead."

Bree took a deep breath and started nervously adjusting the lens on her camera. "Well, okay then. You might want to give Amelia a heads-up in the meantime. She'll have a fit if she's in the kitchen and misses the ceremony."

Gretchen nodded and slipped out. Within about twenty minutes, Natalie was completely transformed. Her ponytail was brushed out, straightened and wrapped into a French twist. She was painted with classic cat eyes, dark lashes and rosy cheeks. They opted for a nude lip with a touch of sparkle.

By the time Gretchen returned, Natalie was ready to slip into the dress. "Colin has spoken to the pastor, so he's on board. I brought your dad out of the chapel to walk you down the aisle. He's waiting outside."

Perfect. That was an important detail she hadn't considered in her rash proposal. Thank goodness her parents were both here. She'd never hear the end of it if either of them had missed her wedding.

"Let's get you in this gown," Gretchen said.

It took a few minutes to get Natalie laced and buttoned into her wedding dress. The hairdresser positioned the veil in her hair and turned her toward the full-length mirror to look at herself.

Her heart stuttered in her chest when she saw her reflection. She made for a beautiful bride. And this time, unlike at the bridal salon, she was really going to be the bride. This was suddenly her day, and her gown. She was so happy they'd chosen this dress. Any other one just wouldn't have suited her.

"Wow, honey," Gretchen said. "You look amazing. Do you have heels?"

Natalie looked down at her sensible black flats and shook her head. That was one thing she didn't have. "I guess I'll just go barefoot," she replied, kicking out of her shoes.

Gretchen picked up the bridal bouquet that was waiting in a vase on the side table. She handed it over to Natalie with a touch of glassy tears in her eyes. "I can't believe this is happening. I'm so happy for you and Colin."

Natalie took a deep breath and nodded. "I can't believe it either, really. But let's make it happen before reality sets in and I launch into a panic attack. Go tell everyone the bride is ready and cue the musicians."

Gretchen disappeared and Natalie waited a few moments until she knew the doors to the chapel were closed. She stepped out to find her father, looking dumbfounded, on the bench outside. "Hi, Daddy."

He shot up from his seat, freezing as he saw her in her dress. "You look amazing. I'm not sure what's going on, but you look more beautiful than any bride I've ever seen in my life."

Natalie leaned in to hug him. "It's a long story, but I'm glad you're here."

The music grew louder, cueing up the bride. Natalie nearly reached for her headset before she remembered she was the bride this time. "Let's go get married, Daddy."

They walked to the doors and waited for them to swing open. The chapel was filled with people, all of them standing at the bride's arrival. It was hard for her to focus on any of them, though. Her eyes instantly went to the front of the chapel.

Colin stood there in his tuxedo, looking as handsome as ever. There wasn't a touch of nervousness on his face as he watched her walk down the aisle. There was nothing but adoration and love on his face. Looking into his eyes, she felt her own anxiety slip away. It was just like at the rehearsal. Everything faded away but the two of them.

Before she knew it, they'd walked the long aisle and were standing at the front of the chapel. Her father gave her a hug and a kiss on the cheek before passing her hand off to the waiting Colin. "Take care of my girl," he warned his future son-in-law before taking his seat.

They stepped up onto the raised platform together and waited for the pastor to start the ceremony.

"Dearly beloved, we gather here today to celebrate the blessed union of Frank and Lily."

Colin cleared his throat, interrupting the pastor as a rumble of voices traveled through the chapel. "Colin and Natalie," he corrected in a whisper.

The pastor's eyes widened in panic when he realized his mistake. Natalie had worked with this pastor before and knew that he had the names typed into his text. "Oh yes, so sorry. To celebrate the blessed union of *Colin and Natalie*."

The pastor continued on, but all Natalie could hear was the beating of her own heart. All she could feel was Colin's warm hand enveloping hers. When the pastor prompted them to turn and face each other, they did, and Natalie felt a sense of peace in Colin's gaze. He smiled at her, brushing his thumbs across the backs of her hands in a soothing motion.

"Are you okay?" he whispered.

Natalie nodded. She had never been better.

"Do you, Colin Edward Russell, take Natalie Lynn Sharpe to be your lawfully wedded wife? Will you love and respect her? Will you be honest with her? Will you stand by her through whatever may come until your days on this Earth come to an end?"

"I will."

"And do you, Natalie Lynn Sharpe, take Colin Edward Russell to be your lawfully wedded husband? Will you love and respect him? Will you be honest with him? Will you stand by him through whatever may come until your days on this Earth come to an end?"

She took a deep breath, a momentary flash of panic lighting in Colin's eyes. "I will," she said with a grin.

"Fra-*Colin*," the pastor stuttered. "What token do you give of the vows you have made?"

"A ring," Colin replied, pulling the same ring box from his coat pocket that he'd presented her with on the stage Wednesday night.

"You had the ring with you?" Natalie whispered.

"I was mad, but I hadn't given up on you yet." Colin opened the box and settled the exquisite diamond ring over the tip of her finger.

"Repeat after me. I give you this ring as a token of my vow." He paused, allowing Colin to respond. "With all that I am and all that I have, I honor you, and with this ring, I thee wed."

"…and with this ring, I thee wed," Colin repeated, slipping the ring onto her finger and squeezing her hand reassuringly.

"Natalie," the pastor asked, "what token do you give of the vows you have made?"

In an instant, Natalie's blood ran cold. She'd planned every moment, every aspect of this wedding. Everything but the rings. She had no ring. "I don't have anything," she whispered to the pastor.

The pastor hesitated, looking around the room for an answer to the problem as though there would be rings dangling from the ceiling on threads. This was probably the most stressful ceremony he'd ever done.

Even though she was the bride, Natalie was still a problem solver. She turned to the pews and the faces looking up at them. "Does anyone have a man's ring we can borrow for the ceremony?"

"I have a ring," a man said, getting up from Frankie's side of the chapel.

He was obviously a friend of Frankie's. They both shared a common love of bushy beards, tattoos and bow ties with matching suspenders. He jogged up the aisle, slipping a ring off his finger and handing it to Natalie.

"Thank you," she said. "We'll give it back as soon as we get a replacement."

"That's okay, you can keep it."

He returned to his seat and Natalie looked down at the ring in her hand. It was a heavy silver band with a skull centered on it. There were glittering red stones in the eye sockets. Natalie bit her lip to keep from laughing. A ring was a ring and that was what she needed. There was no being picky right now. She placed it on the tip of Colin's finger and repeated after the pastor.

It wasn't until the ring was firmly seated on his finger that Colin looked down. He snorted in a short burst of laughter and shook his head. Skulls must not be his thing.

The pastor didn't notice. He was probably just happy

they had rings and it was time to wrap up the ceremony. "Colin and Natalie, as you have both affirmed your love for each other and have made a promise to each other to live in this union, I challenge you both to remember to cherish each other, to respect each other's thoughts and ideas, and most important, to forgive each other. May you live each day in love, always being there to give love, comfort and refuge in the good times and the bad.

"As Colin and Natalie have now exchanged vows and rings, and pledged their love and faith for each other, it is my pleasure and honor to pronounce them Man and Wife. You may kiss the bride."

"This is the part I've been waiting for," Colin said with a wide smile. He took a step forward, cradling her cheeks in his hands and lifting her lips to his own.

"Wait," Natalie whispered just before their lips touched. "I need to tell you something."

Colin hesitated, his eyes wide with panic. She realized then that he thought she was changing her mind. "You won," she said quickly.

"Won what?" he asked.

"You won the bet," she admitted with a smile. "Merry Christmas, Mr. Russell. It's time to claim your prize."

"That I will. Merry Christmas, Mrs. Russell."

The kiss was soft and tender, holding the promise of a lifetime together and a thousand more kisses to come. It sent a thrill through her whole body, both from his touch and from the knowledge that they were now husband and wife. He had promised her a life-changing kiss and that's what he had delivered in more ways than one.

"I love you," he whispered as he pulled away, careful not to smear her lipstick before they took pictures.

She could barely hear him over the applause of the

crowd, but she would know the sound of those words coming from his lips anywhere. "I love you," she said.

"Please turn and face your family and friends," the pastor said, and they complied. "I am pleased to present for the first time, Mr. and Mrs. Colin Russell."

They stepped down the stairs together as man and wife while the crowd cheered. Hand in hand, they went down the aisle as their guests showered them with tiny bits of glittery white-and-silver confetti that looked like snow falling down on them.

They stepped through the doorway into the lobby. Waiting for them was Gretchen. She had picked up Natalie's headset, stepping in as wedding planner. "Congratulations." She held out a tray of champagne to them both and escorted them to the bridal suite to wait while the guests moved to the reception hall.

Alone in the suite, Colin wrapped one arm around her waist and pulled her tight against him. "You're all mine now," he growled into her ear.

"And you're all mine. For this Christmas and every one to follow."

Epilogue

One year later, Christmas Eve

Natalie slowly made her way through the renovated kitchen carrying the glazed Christmas ham. She intended to put it on the dining room table, but Colin was quick to intercept her and snatch the platter from her hands.

"What are you doing? You don't need to be carrying heavy things."

Natalie sighed and planted her hands on her hips. Being seven months pregnant was certainly a bigger challenge than she'd expected it to be, but she was making do. "I'm just pregnant. I'm perfectly capable of doing a lot of things."

Colin put the plate on the table and turned around. "I know you are. You're capable of amazing things, my wife." He kissed her on the lips. "I'd just much rather you enjoy yourself and your friends instead of being in the kitchen."

"Okay," she agreed, "but you come with me. All the food is out and we're ready to eat."

Hand in hand, they walked into the great room in what had once been the childhood home of Lily and Colin. When Frankie and Lily had returned from Vegas, Colin had still wanted to give them the house despite everything, but Lily hadn't wanted it. Just like the wedding, she was happy with the simple apartment and less hassle.

Instead, after they got married, Colin and Natalie took up residence there. She was all too happy to call the old house her home. He sold the supermodern mansion and she sold her townhouse. After a few renovations to update some things to their liking, they moved into the house. It was where she'd had her happiest childhood memories and once she found out she was pregnant, she wanted her child to have those kinds of memories in this home, too.

The rest of the From This Moment business partners and their spouses were loitering around the seating area, warming themselves by the fireplace. Newlyweds Bree and Ian were snuggling on the couch with glasses of wine. They'd finally tied the knot in October—oddly enough, the first of the group to get engaged and the last to wed.

Gretchen was feeding a chocolate *petit four* to Julian as they stood at the front window admiring the extensive Christmas lights display Colin had put together outside. They had married in the spring in a small chapel in Tuscany, fulfilling Gretchen's dream of seeing Italy at last.

"The food is ready," Natalie announced from the entryway.

Amelia was the first to get up from her seat by the fire. "I wish you would've let me help you with that. There's no need for you to manage the whole dinner by yourself. I know what it's like to cook at seven months pregnant."

"I'm fine. You're always doing the cooking. I wanted to do it. Besides, you've got baby Hope to worry about."

Amelia gestured over her shoulder to her husband Tyler. He was standing by the Christmas tree, letting their six-month-old look at the lights and shiny ornaments. "Not really. He's hardly put her down since the day she was born."

"Still. I'm fine. I might be out of practice when it comes to Christmas, but I can still manage cooking dinner."

"Okay, but we're doing the dishes," Amelia argued.

"Absolutely," Gretchen chimed in. "You're not lifting a single fork."

"I won't fight you on that. I hate doing the dishes."

The crowd all migrated into the dining room in a chaotic rumble of conversation and laughter. They took their places around the table, with Tyler slipping Hope into her high chair.

It was hard for Natalie to believe how much their lives had all changed in the past two years. They had all found amazing men and fallen madly in love. Each of them had married, and soon, there would be two babies playing in the new chapel nursery. It was enough to make her start tearing up at the dinner table.

Damn hormones.

"I'd like to thank everyone for joining us tonight for Christmas Eve dinner. The holidays are times to be spent with friends and family and I know how important all of you are to Natalie, and to me." Colin raised his glass to the group. "Merry Christmas, everyone."

The four couples sitting around the table each raised their glasses to toast a festive holiday season. "Merry Christmas," they all cheered.

* * * * *

MILLS & BOON®

Desire™

PASSIONATE AND DRAMATIC LOVE STORIES

'High drama and lots of laughs'
—*Fabulous* magazine

Fed up with disastrous internet dates and
conflicting advice from her friends, Ellie Rigby
decides to take matters into her own hands.
Instead of looking for a man for herself, she's
going to start a dating agency where she can
use her extensive experience in finding
Mr Wrong to help others find their Mr Right.

Well, that is until a match with one of her clients,
charming, infuriating Nick, has her questioning
everything she's ever thought about love…

MILLS & BOON®

MILLS & BOON®

Why shop at millsandboon.co.uk?

Each year, thousands of romance readers find their perfect read at millsandboon.co.uk. That's because we're passionate about bringing you the very best romantic fiction. Here are some of the advantages of shopping at www.millsandboon.co.uk:

* **Get new books first**—you'll be able to buy your favourite books one month before they hit the shops

* **Get exclusive discounts**—you'll also be able to buy our specially created monthly collections, with up to 50% off the RRP

* **Find your favourite authors**—latest news, interviews and new releases for all your favourite authors and series on our website, plus ideas for what to try next

* **Join in**—once you've bought your favourite books, don't forget to register with us to rate, review and join in the discussions

Visit **www.millsandboon.co.uk**
for all this and more today!